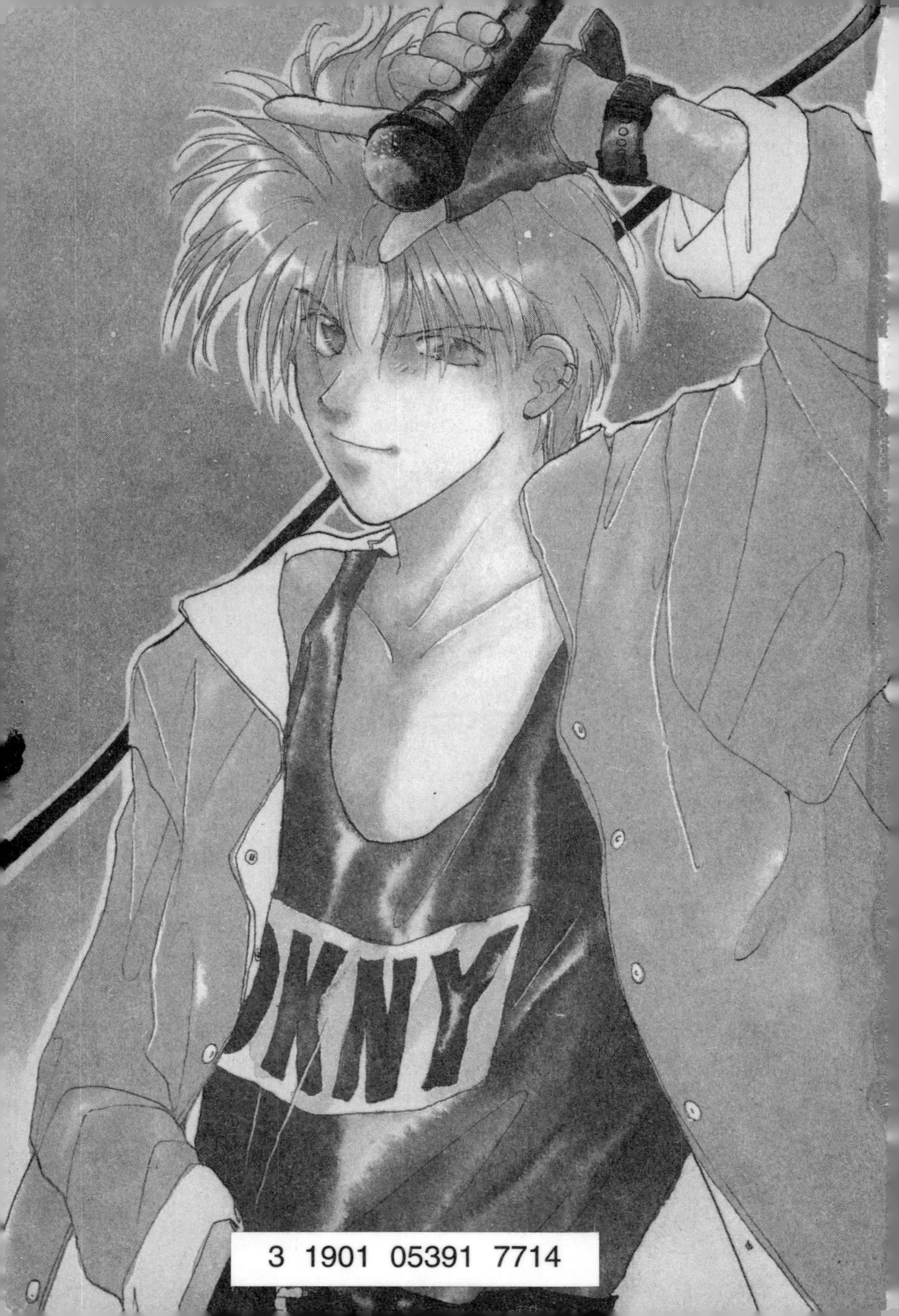
KNY

ALSO AVAILABLE FROM 🐼 **TOKYOPOP**®

MANGA

.HACK//LEGEND OF THE TWILIGHT (September 2003)
@LARGE (COMING SOON)
ANGELIC LAYER*
BABY BIRTH* (September 2003)
BATTLE ROYALE*
BRAIN POWERED*
BRIGADOON* (August 2003)
CARDCAPTOR SAKURA
CARDCAPTOR SAKURA: MASTER OF THE CLOW*
CHOBITS*
CHRONICLES OF THE CURSED SWORD
CLAMP SCHOOL DETECTIVES*
CLOVER
CONFIDENTIAL CONFESSIONS*
CORRECTOR YUI
COWBOY BEBOP*
COWBOY BEBOP: SHOOTING STAR*
DEMON DIARY
DIGIMON*
DRAGON HUNTER
DRAGON KNIGHTS*
DUKLYON: CLAMP SCHOOL DEFENDERS*
ERICA SAKURAZAWA*
FAKE*
FLCL* (September 2003)
FORBIDDEN DANCE*
GATE KEEPERS*
G GUNDAM*
GRAVITATION*
GTO*
GUNDAM WING
GUNDAM WING: BATTLEFIELD OF PACIFISTS
GUNDAM WING: ENDLESS WALTZ*
GUNDAM WING: THE LAST OUTPOST*
HAPPY MANIA*
HARLEM BEAT
I.N.V.U.
INITIAL D*
ISLAND
JING: KING OF BANDITS*
JULINE
KARE KANO*
KINDAICHI CASE FILES, THE*
KING OF HELL
KODOCHA: SANA'S STAGE*
LOVE HINA*
LUPIN III*
MAGIC KNIGHT RAYEARTH*
MAGIC KNIGHT RAYEARTH II* (COMING SOON)

MAN OF MANY FACES*
MARMALADE BOY*
MARS*
MIRACLE GIRLS
MIYUKI-CHAN IN WONDERLAND* (October 2003)
MONSTERS, INC.
PARADISE KISS*
PARASYTE
PEACH GIRL
PEACH GIRL: CHANGE OF HEART*
PET SHOP OF HORRORS*
PLANET LADDER*
PLANETES* (October 2003)
PRIEST
RAGNAROK
RAVE MASTER*
REALITY CHECK
REBIRTH
REBOUND*
RISING STARS OF MANGA
SABER MARIONETTE J*
SAILOR MOON
SAINT TAIL
SAMURAI DEEPER KYO*
SAMURAI GIRL: REAL BOUT HIGH SCHOOL*
SCRYED*
SHAOLIN SISTERS*
SHIRAHIME-SYO: SNOW GODDESS TALES* (Dec. 2003)
SHUTTERBOX (November 2003)
SORCERER HUNTERS
THE SKULL MAN*
THE VISION OF ESCAFLOWNE
TOKYO MEW MEW*
UNDER THE GLASS MOON
VAMPIRE GAME*
WILD ACT*
WISH*
WORLD OF HARTZ (COMING SOON)
X-DAY*
ZODIAC P.I. *

For more information visit www.TOKYOPOP.com

*INDICATES 100% AUTHENTIC MANGA (RIGHT-TO-LEFT FORMAT)

CINE-MANGA™

CARDCAPTORS
JACKIE CHAN ADVENTURES (COMING SOON)
JIMMY NEUTRON (September 2003)
KIM POSSIBLE
LIZZIE MCGUIRE
POWER RANGERS: NINJA STORM (August 2003)
SPONGEBOB SQUAREPANTS (September 2003)
SPY KIDS 2

NOVELS

KARMA CLUB (April 2004)
SAILOR MOON

TOKYOPOP KIDS

STRAY SHEEP (September 2003)

ART BOOKS

CARDCAPTOR SAKURA*
MAGIC KNIGHT RAYEARTH*

ANIME GUIDES

COWBOY BEBOP ANIME GUIDES
GUNDAM TECHNICAL MANUALS
SAILOR MOON SCOUT GUIDES

6-5-03

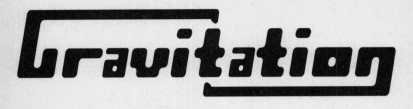

Volume 1

By
Maki Murakami

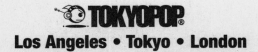

Los Angeles • Tokyo • London

Translator - Ray Yoshimoto
English Adaptation - Jamie S. Rich
Copy Editors - Tim Beedle & Paul Morrissey
Retouch and Lettering - Miyuki Ishihara
Cover Layout - Raymond Makowski

Editor -Jake Forbes
Managing Editor - Jill Freshney
Production Coordinator - Antonio DePietro
Production Manager - Jennifer Miller
Art Director - Matt Alford
Editorial Director - Jeremy Ross
VP of Production - Ron Klamert
President & C.O.O. - John Parker
Publisher & C.E.O. - Stuart Levy

Email: editor@TOKYOPOP.com
Come visit us online at www.TOKYOPOP.com

A 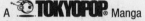 Manga

TOKYOPOP® is an imprint of Mixx Entertainment, Inc.
5900 Wilshire Blvd. Suite 2000, Los Angeles, CA 90036

ISBN: 1-59182-333-1

First TOKYOPOP® printing: August 2003

10 9 8 7
Printed in the USA

CONTENTS

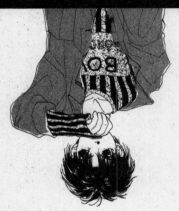

track 1 ——————————— 7

track 2 ——————————— 57

track 3 ——————————— 105

track 4 ——————————— 150

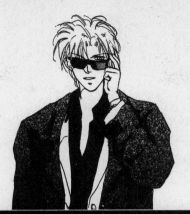

GRAVITATION

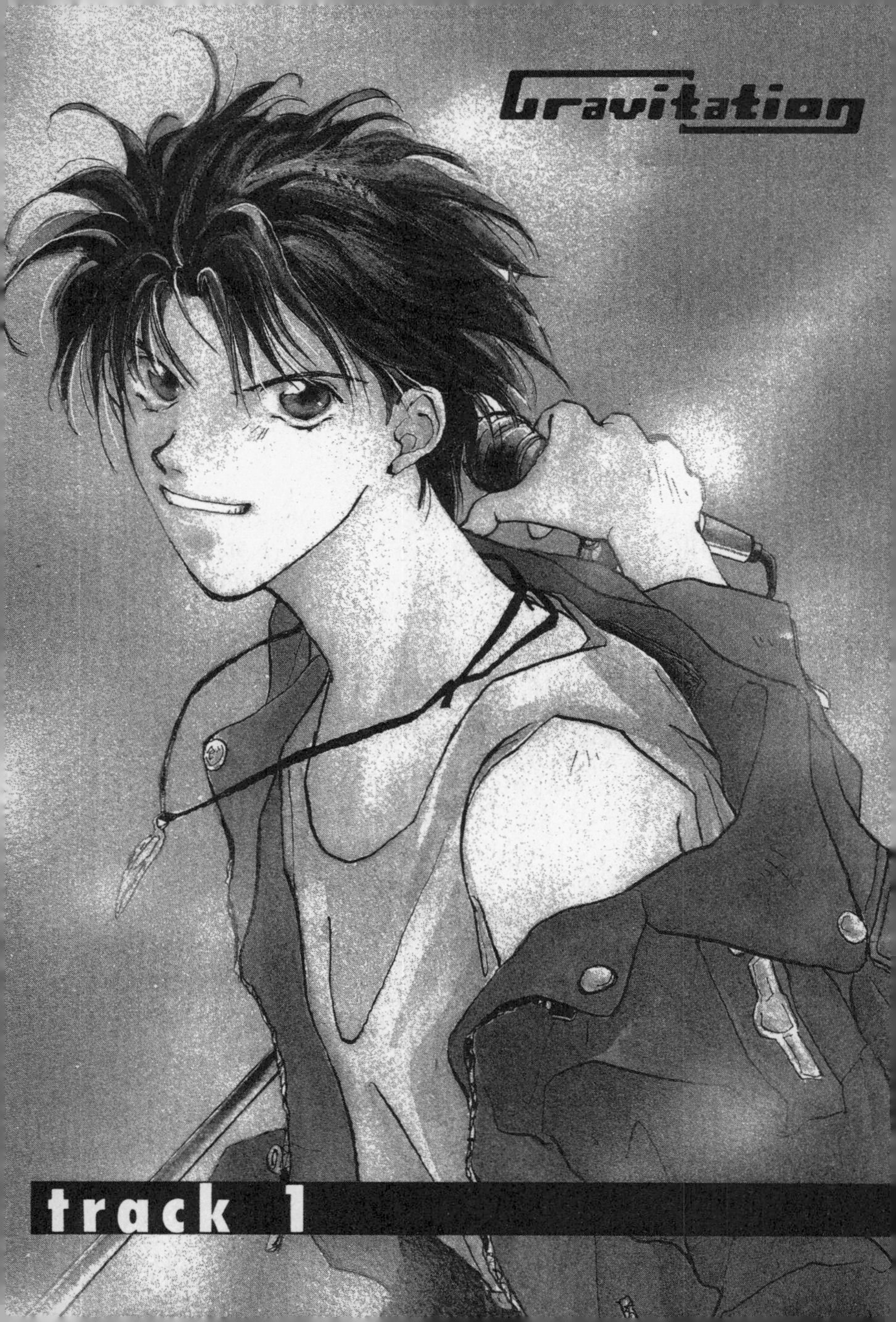
Gravitation
track 1

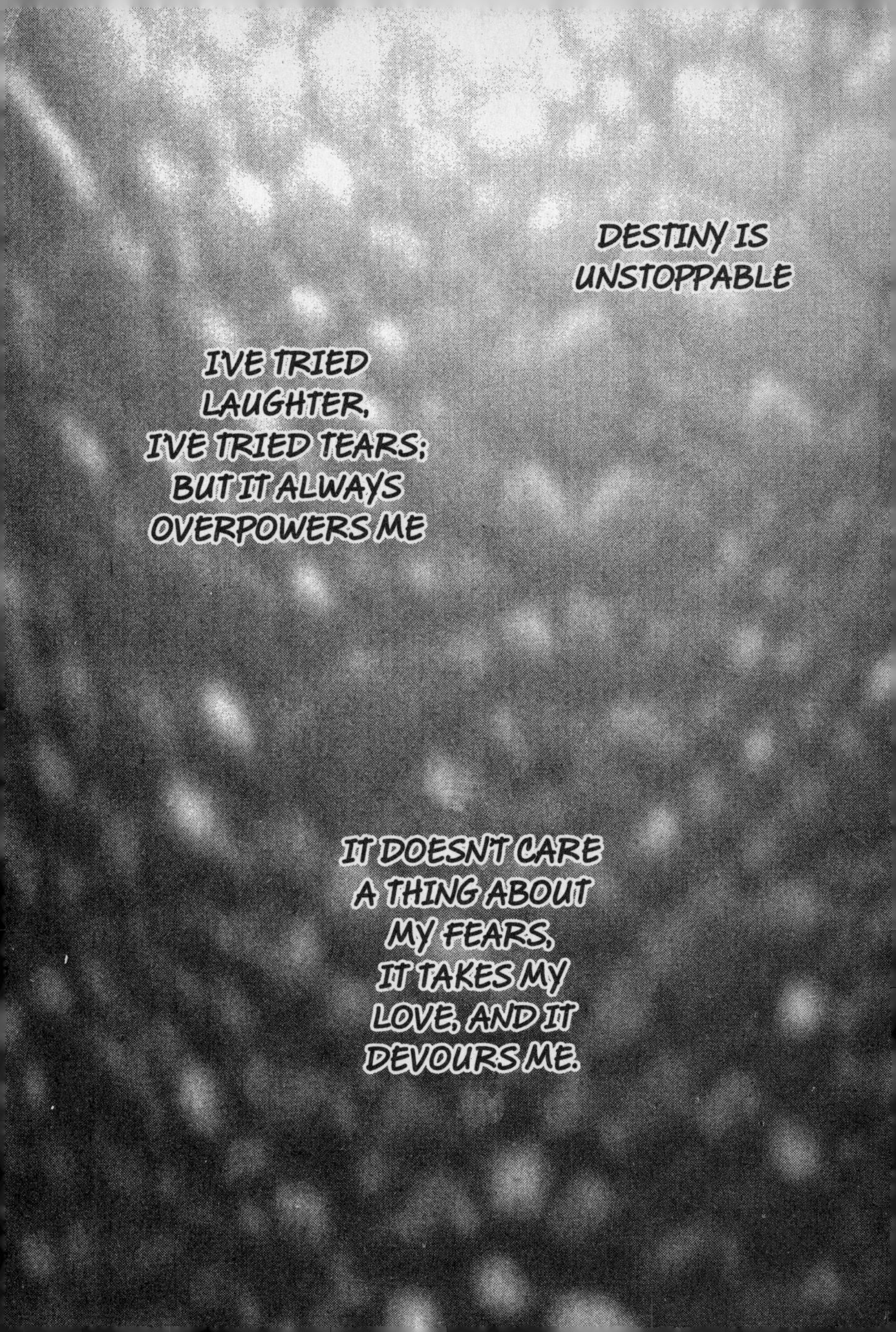
DESTINY IS UNSTOPPABLE
I'VE TRIED LAUGHTER, I'VE TRIED TEARS; BUT IT ALWAYS OVERPOWERS ME
IT DOESN'T CARE A THING ABOUT MY FEARS, IT TAKES MY LOVE, AND IT DEVOURS ME.

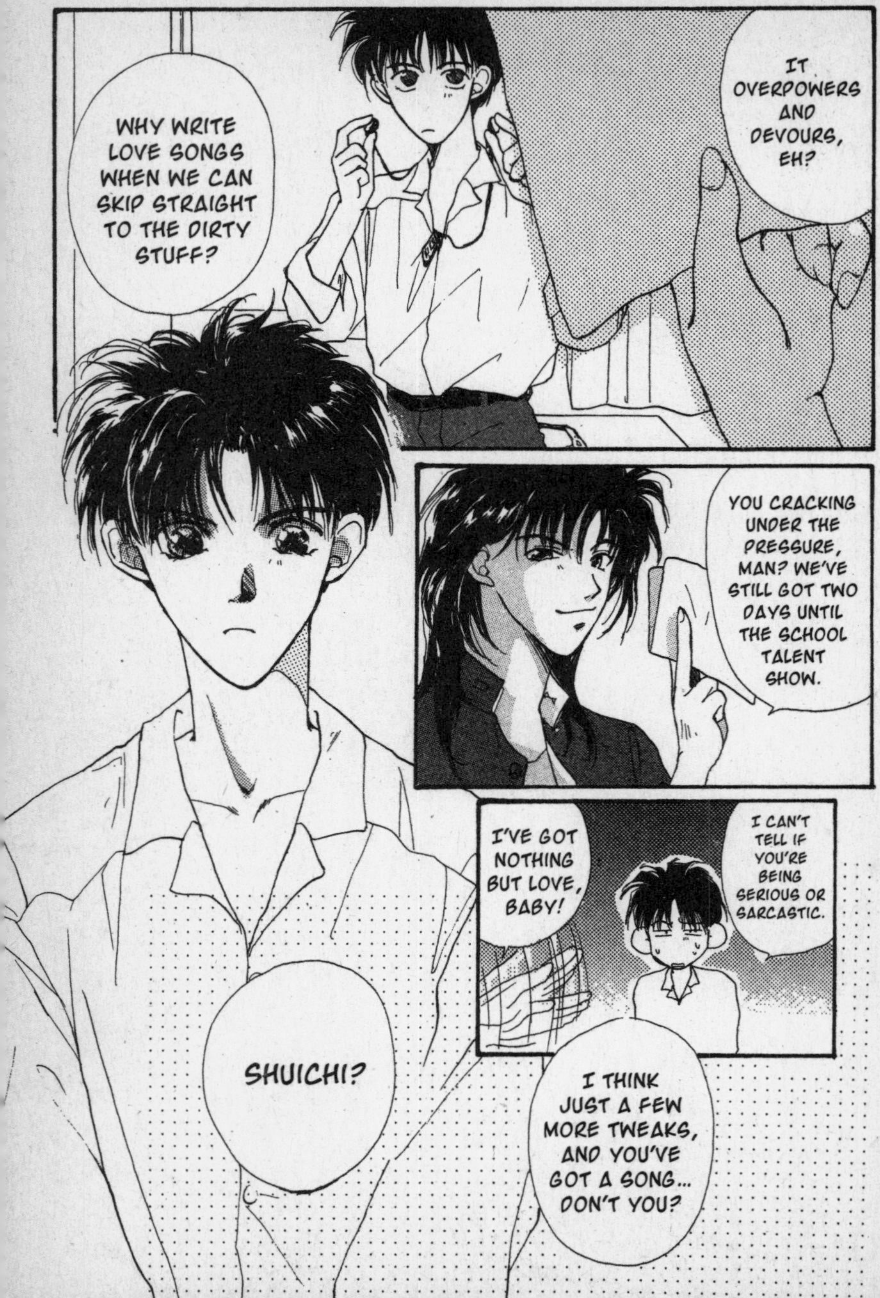
IT OVERPOWERS AND DEVOURS, EH?
WHY WRITE LOVE SONGS WHEN WE CAN SKIP STRAIGHT TO THE DIRTY STUFF?
YOU CRACKING UNDER THE PRESSURE, MAN? WE'VE STILL GOT TWO DAYS UNTIL THE SCHOOL TALENT SHOW.
I CAN'T TELL IF YOU'RE BEING SERIOUS OR SARCASTIC.
I'VE GOT NOTHING BUT LOVE, BABY!
I THINK JUST A FEW MORE TWEAKS, AND YOU'VE GOT A SONG... DON'T YOU?
SHUICHI?

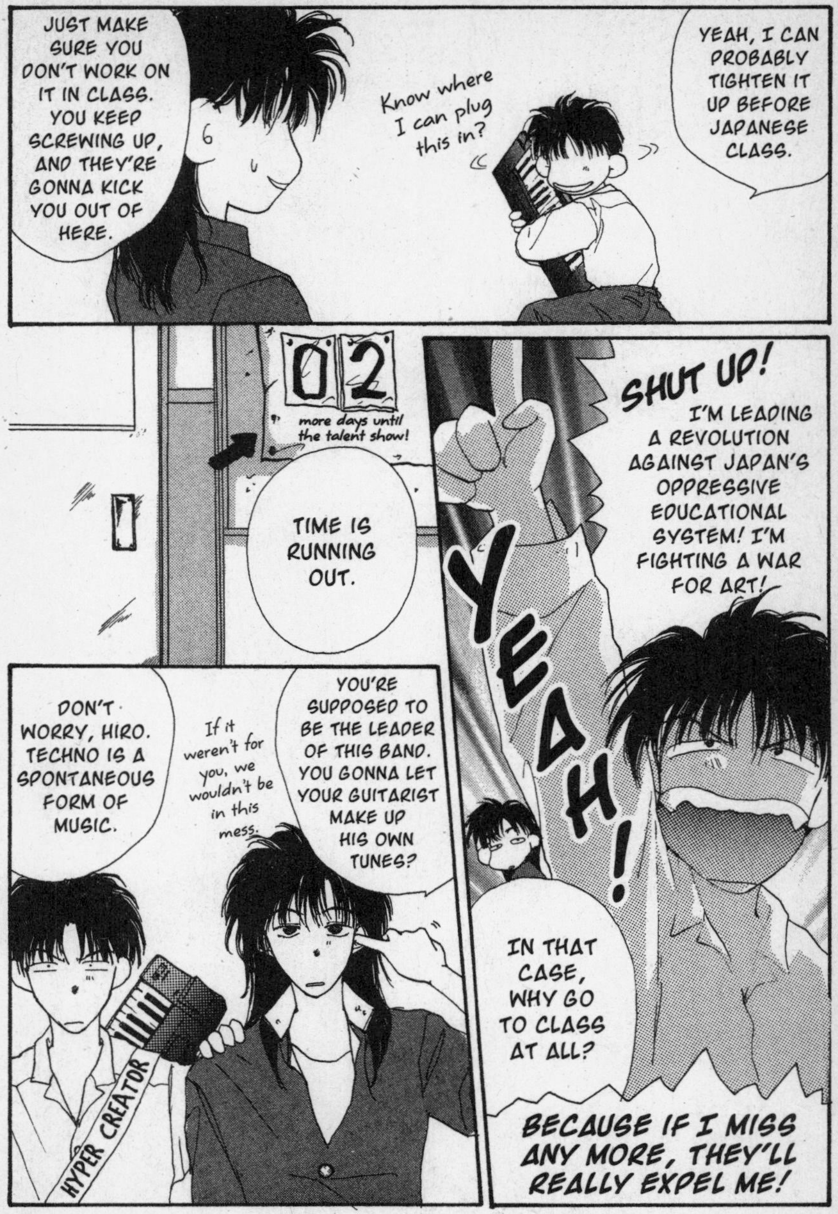
YEAH, I CAN PROBABLY TIGHTEN IT UP BEFORE JAPANESE CLASS.
Know where I can plug this in?
JUST MAKE SURE YOU DON'T WORK ON IT IN CLASS. YOU KEEP SCREWING UP, AND THEY'RE GONNA KICK YOU OUT OF HERE.
SHUT UP!
I'M LEADING A REVOLUTION AGAINST JAPAN'S OPPRESSIVE EDUCATIONAL SYSTEM! I'M FIGHTING A WAR FOR ART!
YEAH!
IN THAT CASE, WHY GO TO CLASS AT ALL?
BECAUSE IF I MISS ANY MORE, THEY'LL REALLY EXPEL ME!
02
more days until the talent show!
TIME IS RUNNING OUT.
YOU'RE SUPPOSED TO BE THE LEADER OF THIS BAND. YOU GONNA LET YOUR GUITARIST MAKE UP HIS OWN TUNES?
If it weren't for you, we wouldn't be in this mess.
DON'T WORRY, HIRO. TECHNO IS A SPONTANEOUS FORM OF MUSIC.
HYPER CREATOR

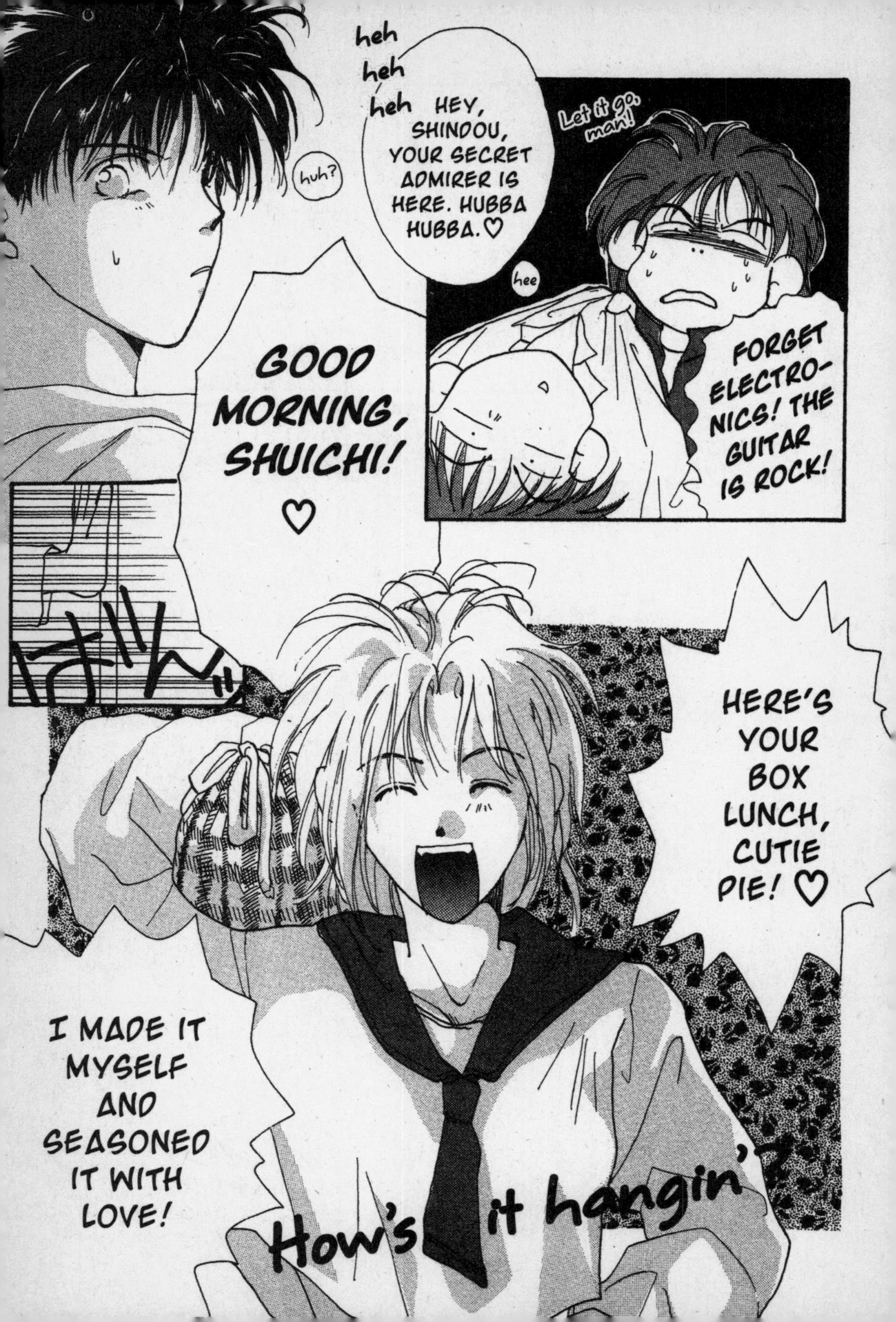
heh heh heh HEY, SHINDOU, YOUR SECRET ADMIRER IS HERE. HUBBA HUBBA. ♡
huh?
Let it go, man!
hee
FORGET ELECTRO-NICS! THE GUITAR IS ROCK!
GOOD MORNING, SHUICHI! ♡
HERE'S YOUR BOX LUNCH, CUTIE PIE! ♡
I MADE IT MYSELF AND SEASONED IT WITH LOVE!
How's it hangin'?

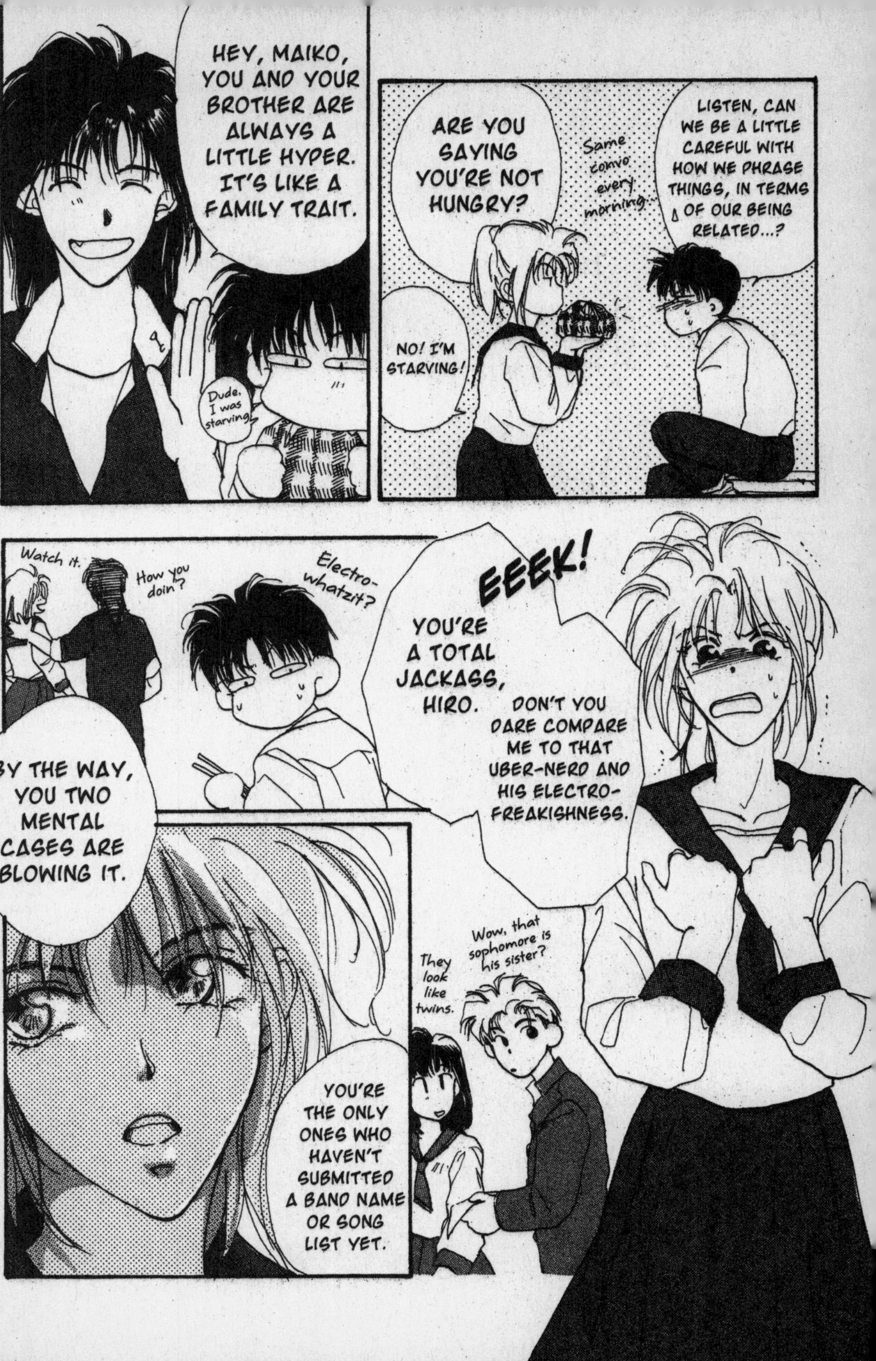
LISTEN, CAN WE BE A LITTLE CAREFUL WITH HOW WE PHRASE THINGS, IN TERMS OF OUR BEING RELATED...?
Same convo every morning...
ARE YOU SAYING YOU'RE NOT HUNGRY?
NO! I'M STARVING!
HEY, MAIKO, YOU AND YOUR BROTHER ARE ALWAYS A LITTLE HYPER. IT'S LIKE A FAMILY TRAIT.
Dude, I was starving.
EEEK!
YOU'RE A TOTAL JACKASS, HIRO.
DON'T YOU DARE COMPARE ME TO THAT UBER-NERD AND HIS ELECTRO-FREAKISHNESS.
Wow, that sophomore is his sister?
They look like twins.
Electro-whatzit?
How you doin?
Watch it.
BY THE WAY, YOU TWO MENTAL CASES ARE BLOWING IT.
YOU'RE THE ONLY ONES WHO HAVEN'T SUBMITTED A BAND NAME OR SONG LIST YET.

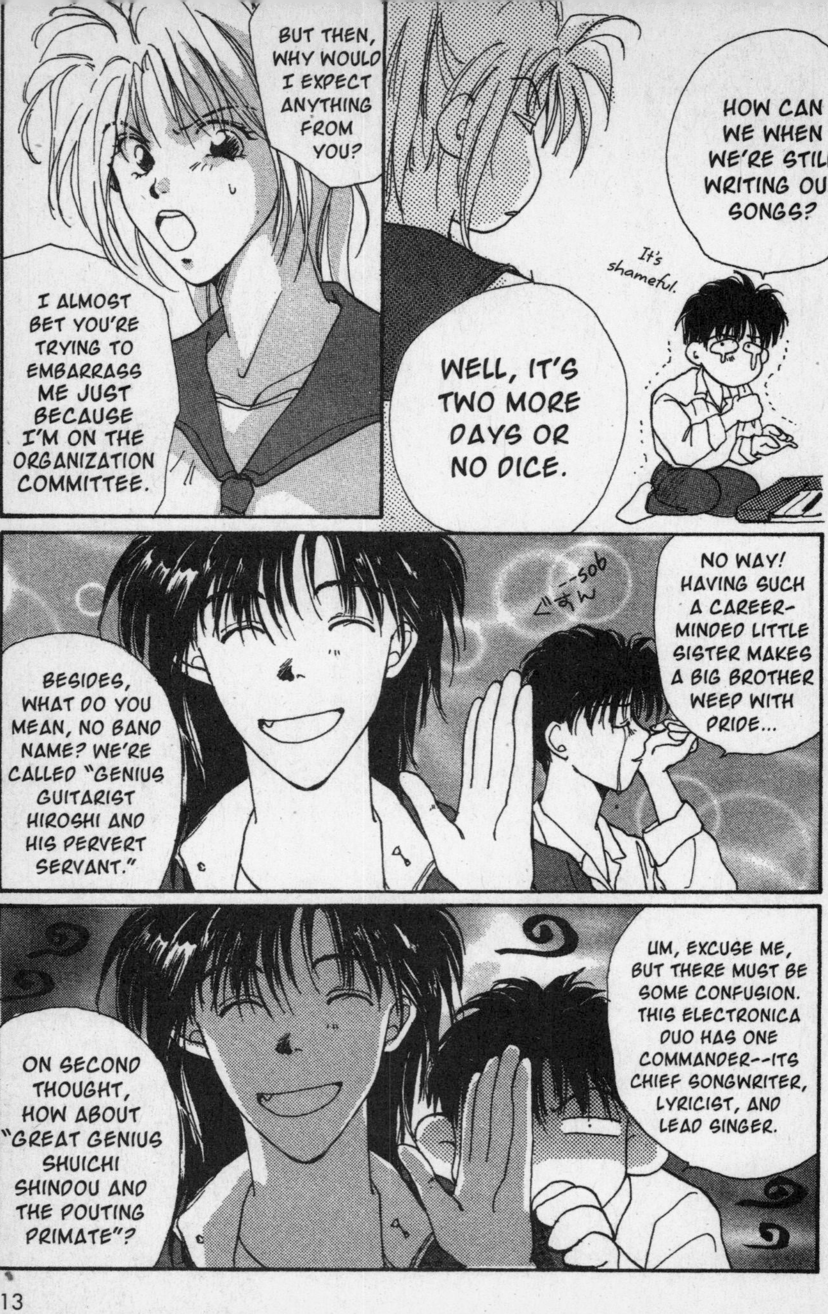
HOW CAN WE WHEN WE'RE STILL WRITING OUR SONGS?
It's shameful.
WELL, IT'S TWO MORE DAYS OR NO DICE.
BUT THEN, WHY WOULD I EXPECT ANYTHING FROM YOU?
I ALMOST BET YOU'RE TRYING TO EMBARRASS ME JUST BECAUSE I'M ON THE ORGANIZATION COMMITTEE.
NO WAY! HAVING SUCH A CAREER-MINDED LITTLE SISTER MAKES A BIG BROTHER WEEP WITH PRIDE...
--sob
BESIDES, WHAT DO YOU MEAN, NO BAND NAME? WE'RE CALLED "GENIUS GUITARIST HIROSHI AND HIS PERVERT SERVANT."
UM, EXCUSE ME, BUT THERE MUST BE SOME CONFUSION. THIS ELECTRONICA DUO HAS ONE COMMANDER--ITS CHIEF SONGWRITER, LYRICIST, AND LEAD SINGER.
ON SECOND THOUGHT, HOW ABOUT "GREAT GENIUS SHUICHI SHINDOU AND THE POUTING PRIMATE"?

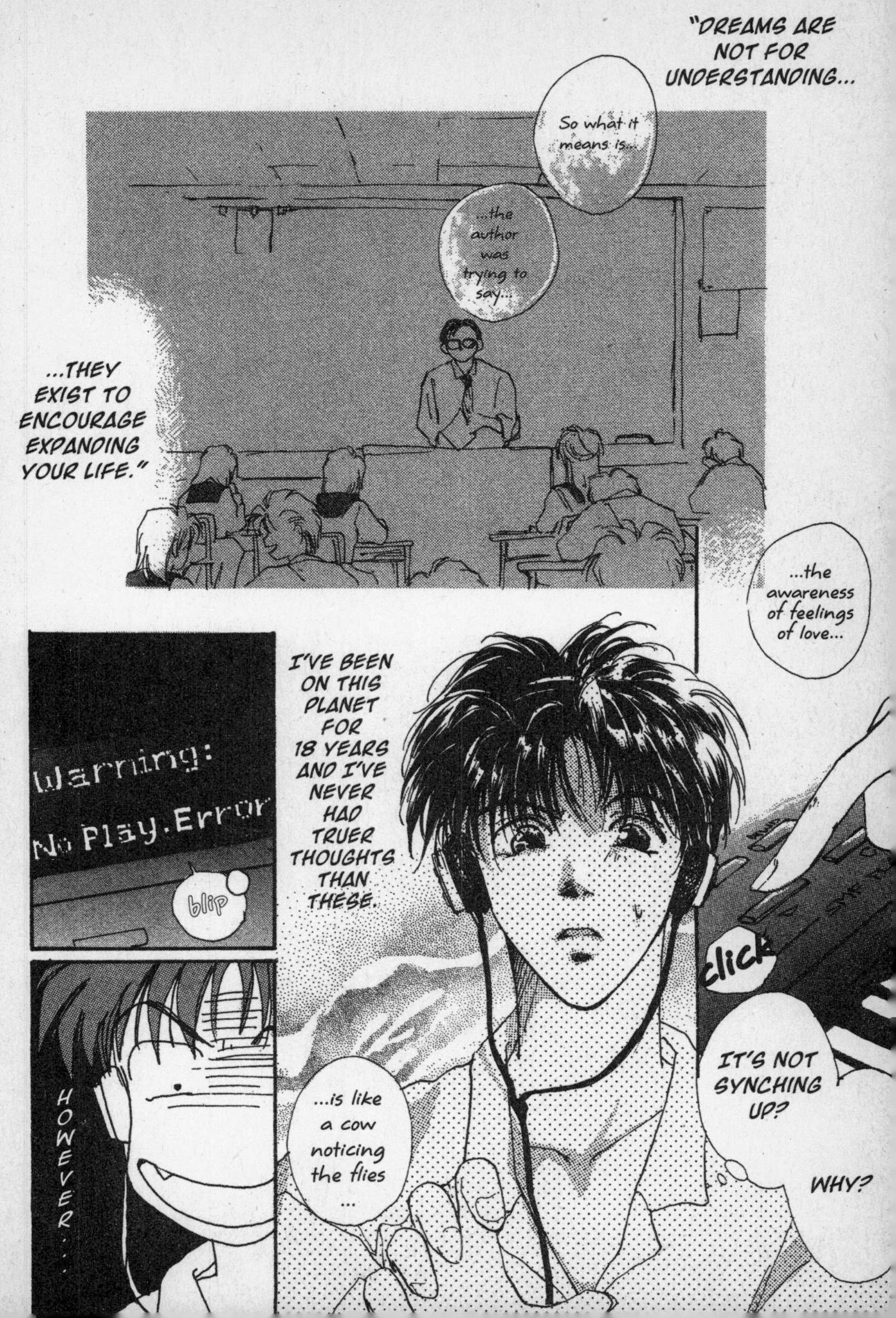
"DREAMS ARE NOT FOR UNDERSTANDING...
So what it means is...
...the author was trying to say...
...THEY EXIST TO ENCOURAGE EXPANDING YOUR LIFE."
...the awareness of feelings of love...
I'VE BEEN ON THIS PLANET FOR 18 YEARS AND I'VE NEVER HAD TRUER THOUGHTS THAN THESE.
click
IT'S NOT SYNCHING UP?
WHY?
...is like a cow noticing the flies ...
Warning:
No Play.Error
blip
HOWEVER...

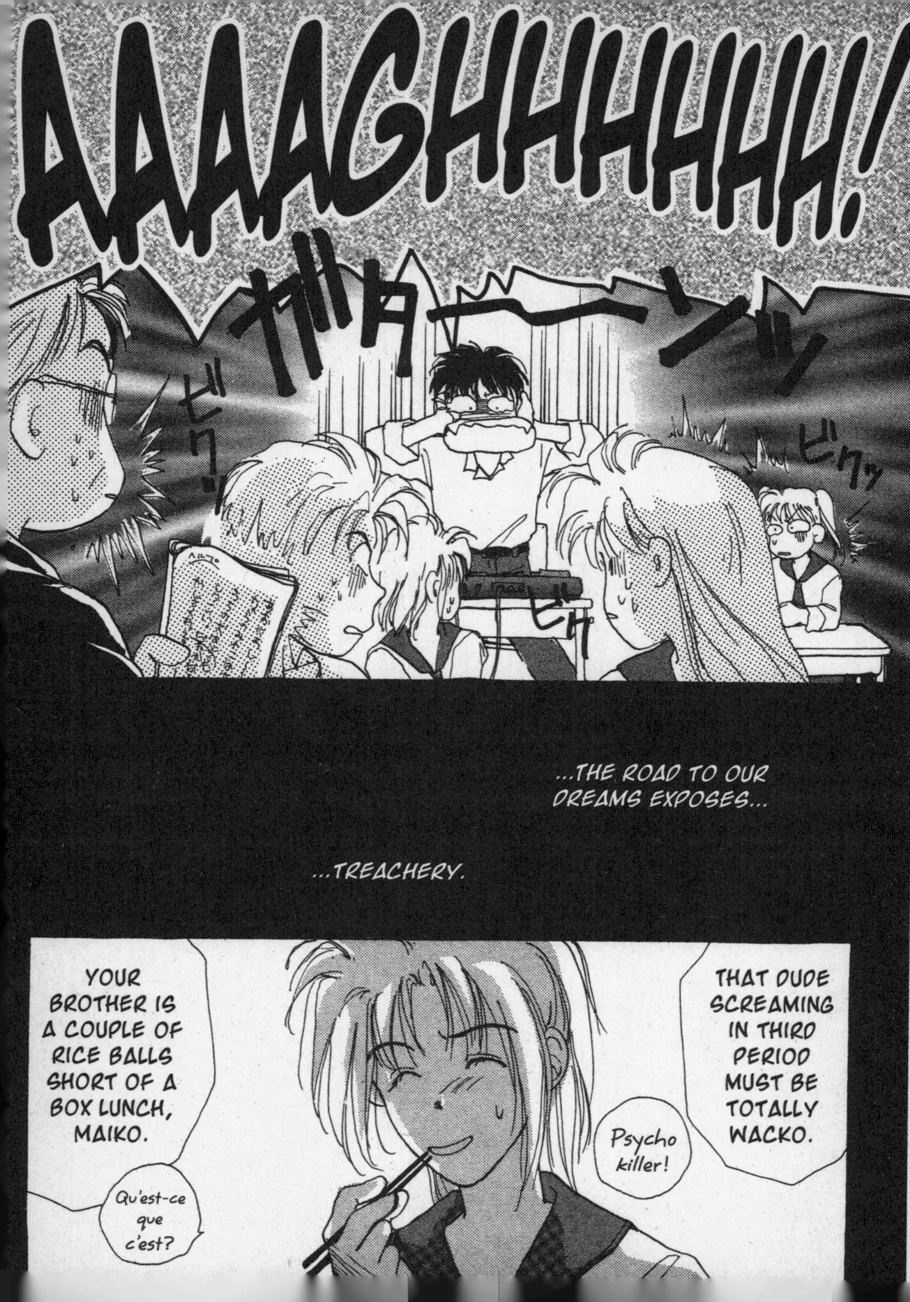
AAAGHHHHHH!
...THE ROAD TO OUR DREAMS EXPOSES...
...TREACHERY.
THAT DUDE SCREAMING IN THIRD PERIOD MUST BE TOTALLY WACKO.
Psycho killer!
YOUR BROTHER IS A COUPLE OF RICE BALLS SHORT OF A BOX LUNCH, MAIKO.
Qu'est-ce que c'est?

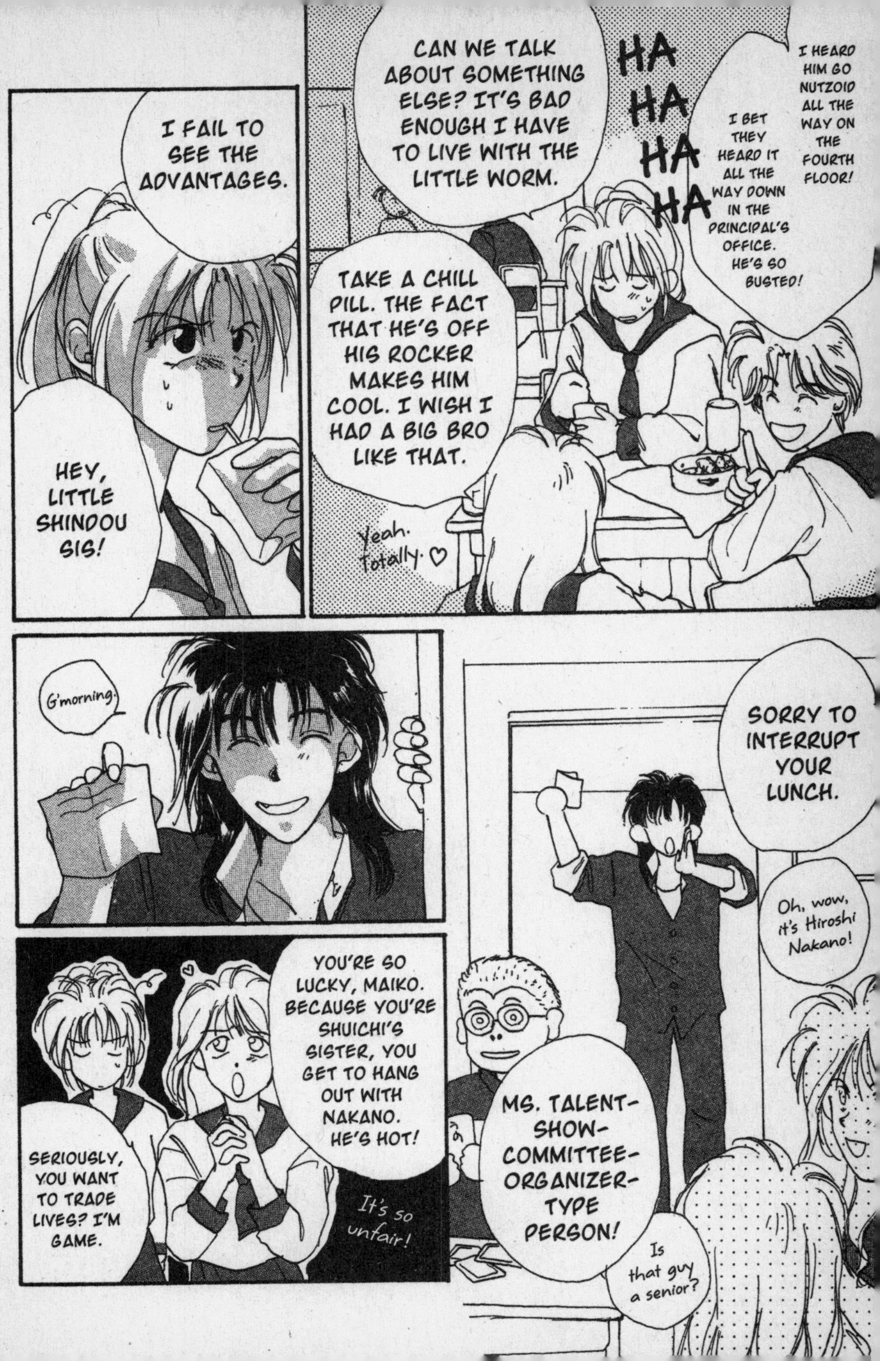
I HEARD HIM GO NUTZOID ALL THE WAY ON THE FOURTH FLOOR!
I BET THEY HEARD IT ALL THE WAY DOWN IN THE PRINCIPAL'S OFFICE. HE'S SO BUSTED!
HA HA HA HA
CAN WE TALK ABOUT SOMETHING ELSE? IT'S BAD ENOUGH I HAVE TO LIVE WITH THE LITTLE WORM.
TAKE A CHILL PILL. THE FACT THAT HE'S OFF HIS ROCKER MAKES HIM COOL. I WISH I HAD A BIG BRO LIKE THAT.
Yeah. Totally. ♡
I FAIL TO SEE THE ADVANTAGES.
HEY, LITTLE SHINDOU SIS!
SORRY TO INTERRUPT YOUR LUNCH.
Oh, wow, it's Hiroshi Nakano!
MS. TALENT-SHOW-COMMITTEE-ORGANIZER-TYPE PERSON!
Is that guy a senior?
G'morning.
YOU'RE SO LUCKY, MAIKO. BECAUSE YOU'RE SHUICHI'S SISTER, YOU GET TO HANG OUT WITH NAKANO. HE'S HOT!
It's so unfair!
SERIOUSLY, YOU WANT TO TRADE LIVES? I'M GAME.

ABOUT GRAVITATION TRACK 1

I wanted to create a story about troubled boys--that was my motive for developing GRAVITATION.

One of the difficulties of writing Track 1 was the fact that I had absolutely no time to do everything I wanted to do, like establish Shuichi's character properly. Hiro was easy, since I set him up as the always smiling, too-much-of-a-nice-guy character. In my first attempt at giving Shuichi life, he turned out to be a conservative, creepy boy. I started him off in pain and ended the story with him failing. It was really quite depressing. Good thing I trashed that first draft, don't you think? He's more fun as a lovable lunkhead... But the more I draw out his klutzy side, the more he ends up being a fool, so that ends up being a problem too.

On the other hand, he's an extremely straight and narrow guy. I'll bet his DNA strands are straight, just like his hair. I'm sure in a previous life he was a tall fir tree.

It's fun for me to draw a normal, decent guy. I'd like him to continue living his life with integrity so he can simply grow up and enjoy life. You are our sunflower. You are the straight and sure path of my life. So with those feelings, I'm gonna make him do even more stupid stuff. Yeah!

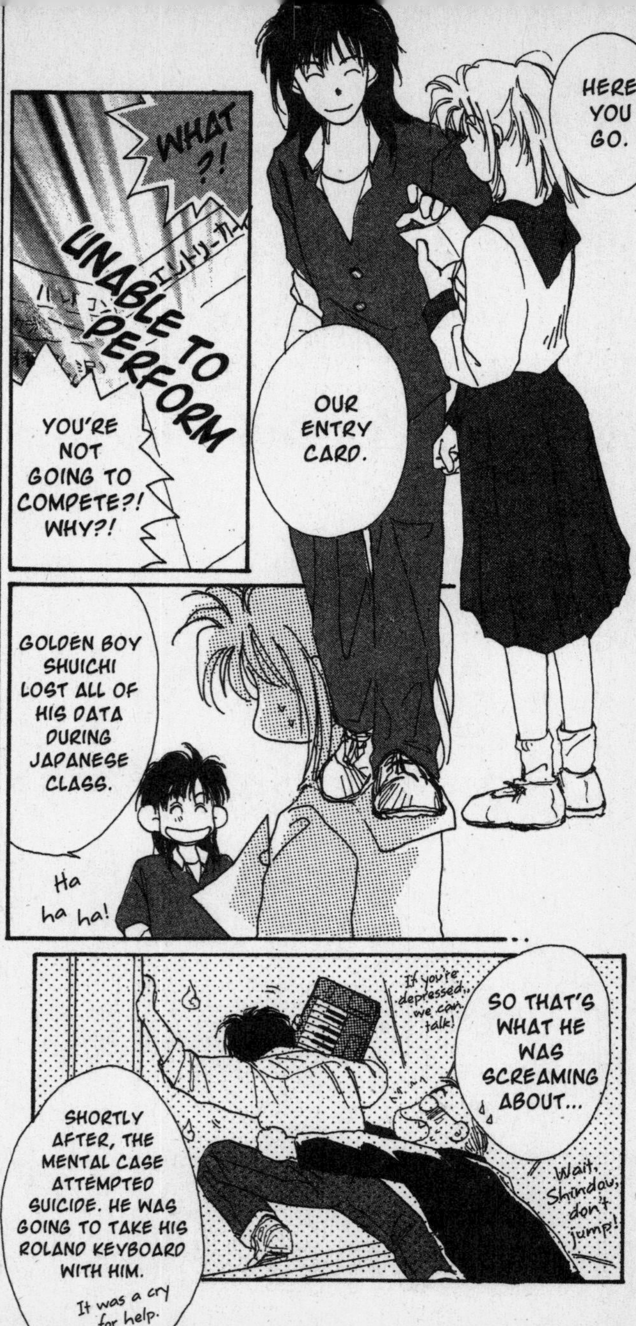
HERE YOU GO.
OUR ENTRY CARD.
WHAT?!
UNABLE TO PERFORM
YOU'RE NOT GOING TO COMPETE?! WHY?!
GOLDEN BOY SHUICHI LOST ALL OF HIS DATA DURING JAPANESE CLASS.
Ha ha ha!
SO THAT'S WHAT HE WAS SCREAMING ABOUT...
If you're depressed, we can talk!
Wait, Shindou, don't jump!
SHORTLY AFTER, THE MENTAL CASE ATTEMPTED SUICIDE. HE WAS GOING TO TAKE HIS ROLAND KEYBOARD WITH HIM.
It was a cry for help.

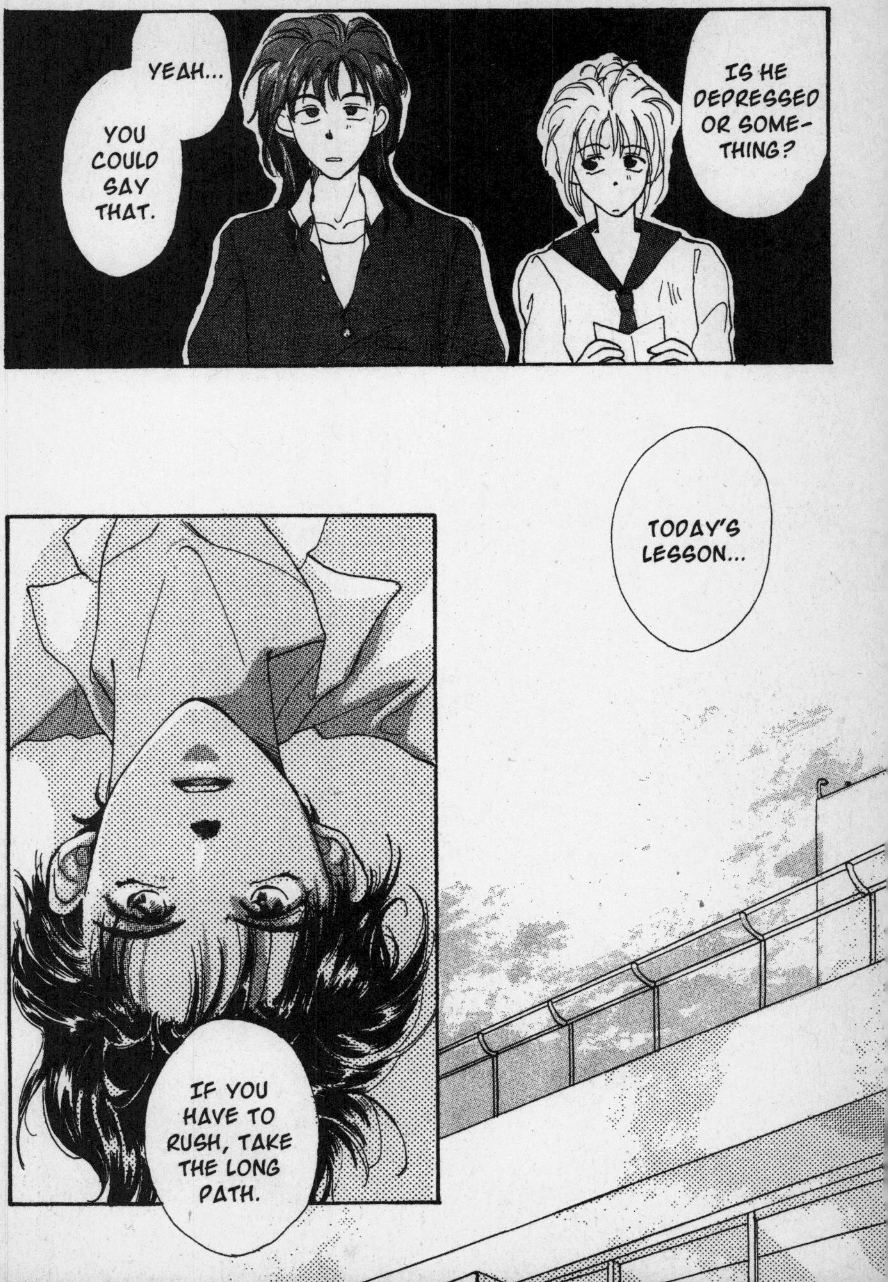
IS HE DEPRESSED OR SOME-THING?
YEAH...
YOU COULD SAY THAT.
TODAY'S LESSON...
IF YOU HAVE TO RUSH, TAKE THE LONG PATH.

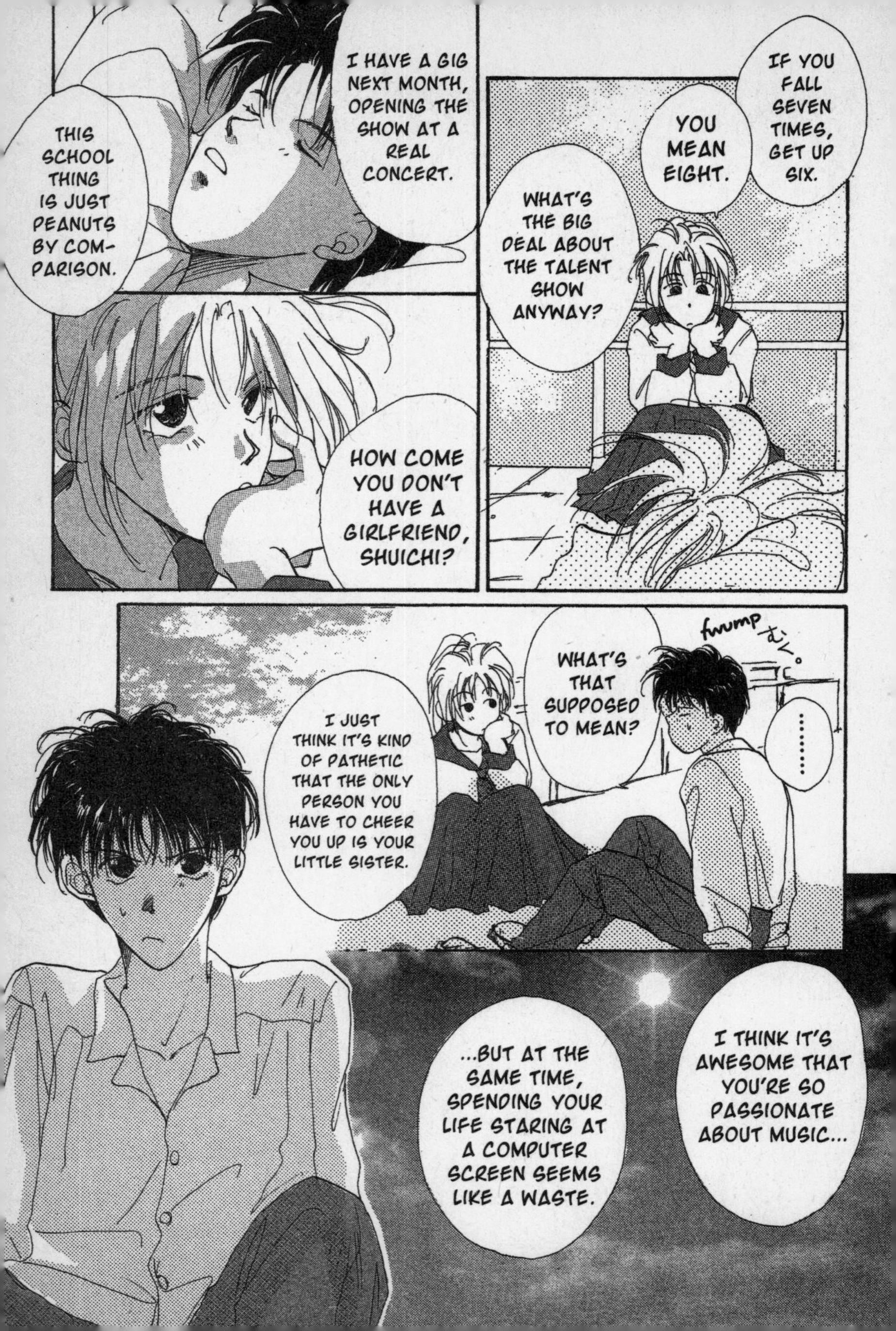
IF YOU FALL SEVEN TIMES, GET UP SIX.
YOU MEAN EIGHT.
WHAT'S THE BIG DEAL ABOUT THE TALENT SHOW ANYWAY?
I HAVE A GIG NEXT MONTH, OPENING THE SHOW AT A REAL CONCERT.
THIS SCHOOL THING IS JUST PEANUTS BY COM-PARISON.
HOW COME YOU DON'T HAVE A GIRLFRIEND, SHUICHI?
fwump
....
WHAT'S THAT SUPPOSED TO MEAN?
I JUST THINK IT'S KIND OF PATHETIC THAT THE ONLY PERSON YOU HAVE TO CHEER YOU UP IS YOUR LITTLE SISTER.
I THINK IT'S AWESOME THAT YOU'RE SO PASSIONATE ABOUT MUSIC...
...BUT AT THE SAME TIME, SPENDING YOUR LIFE STARING AT A COMPUTER SCREEN SEEMS LIKE A WASTE.

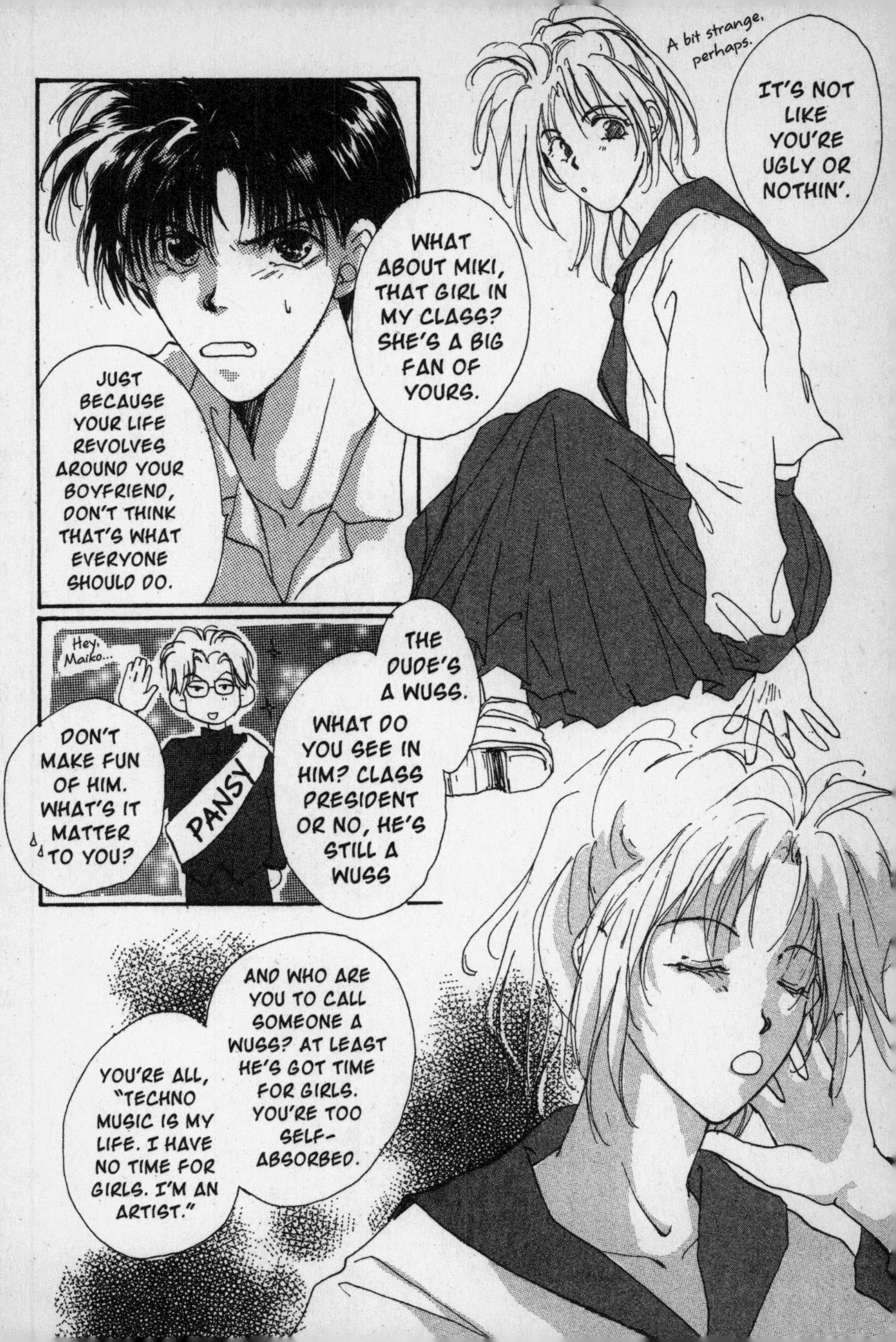
A bit strange, perhaps.
IT'S NOT LIKE YOU'RE UGLY OR NOTHIN'.
WHAT ABOUT MIKI, THAT GIRL IN MY CLASS? SHE'S A BIG FAN OF YOURS.
JUST BECAUSE YOUR LIFE REVOLVES AROUND YOUR BOYFRIEND, DON'T THINK THAT'S WHAT EVERYONE SHOULD DO.
THE DUDE'S A WUSS.
WHAT DO YOU SEE IN HIM? CLASS PRESIDENT OR NO, HE'S STILL A WUSS
Hey, Maiko...
PANSY
DON'T MAKE FUN OF HIM. WHAT'S IT MATTER TO YOU?
AND WHO ARE YOU TO CALL SOMEONE A WUSS? AT LEAST HE'S GOT TIME FOR GIRLS. YOU'RE TOO SELF-ABSORBED.
YOU'RE ALL, "TECHNO MUSIC IS MY LIFE. I HAVE NO TIME FOR GIRLS. I'M AN ARTIST."

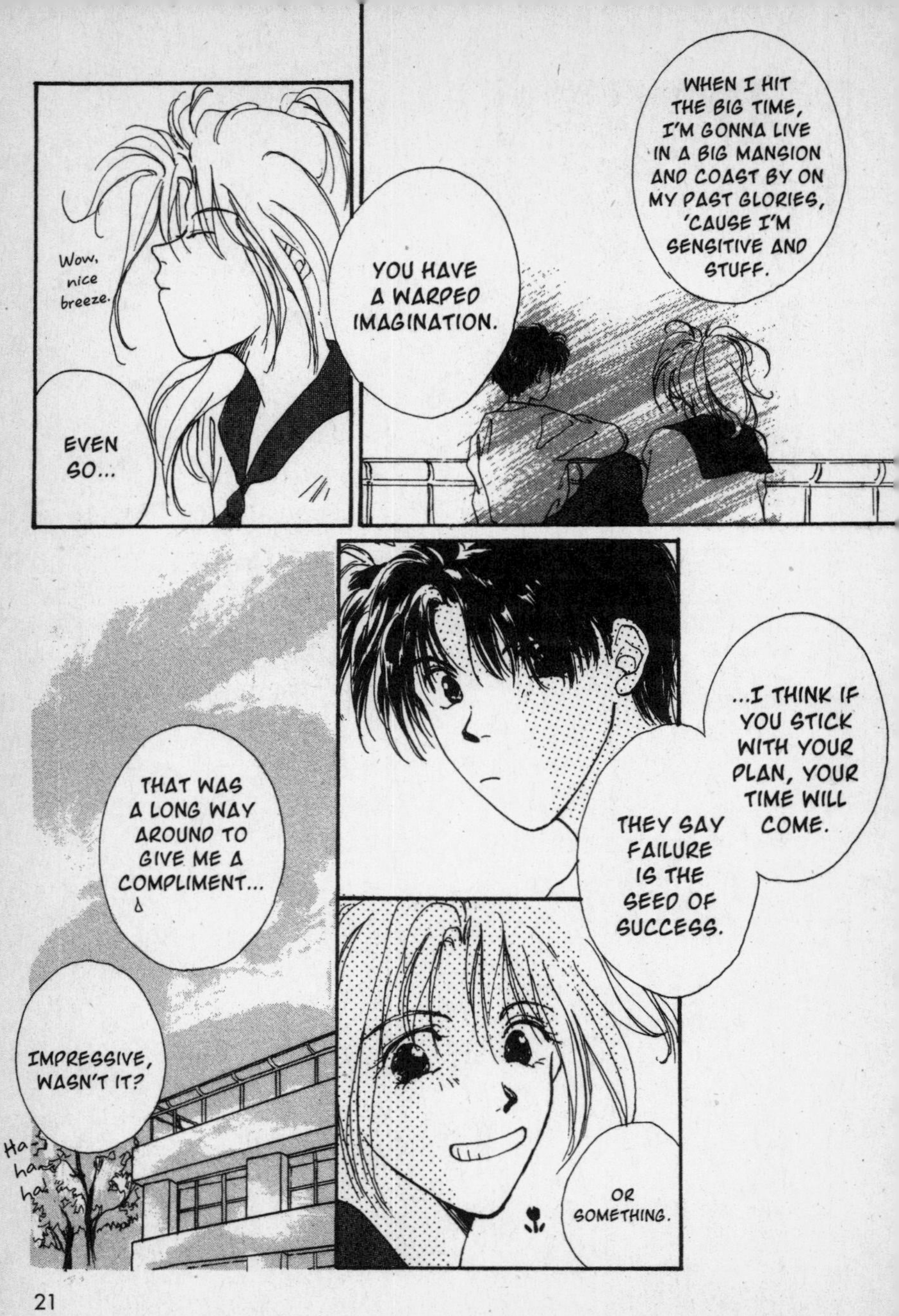
WHEN I HIT THE BIG TIME, I'M GONNA LIVE IN A BIG MANSION AND COAST BY ON MY PAST GLORIES, 'CAUSE I'M SENSITIVE AND STUFF.
YOU HAVE A WARPED IMAGINATION.
Wow, nice breeze.
EVEN SO...
...I THINK IF YOU STICK WITH YOUR PLAN, YOUR TIME WILL COME.
THEY SAY FAILURE IS THE SEED OF SUCCESS.
OR SOMETHING.
THAT WAS A LONG WAY AROUND TO GIVE ME A COMPLIMENT...
IMPRESSIVE, WASN'T IT?

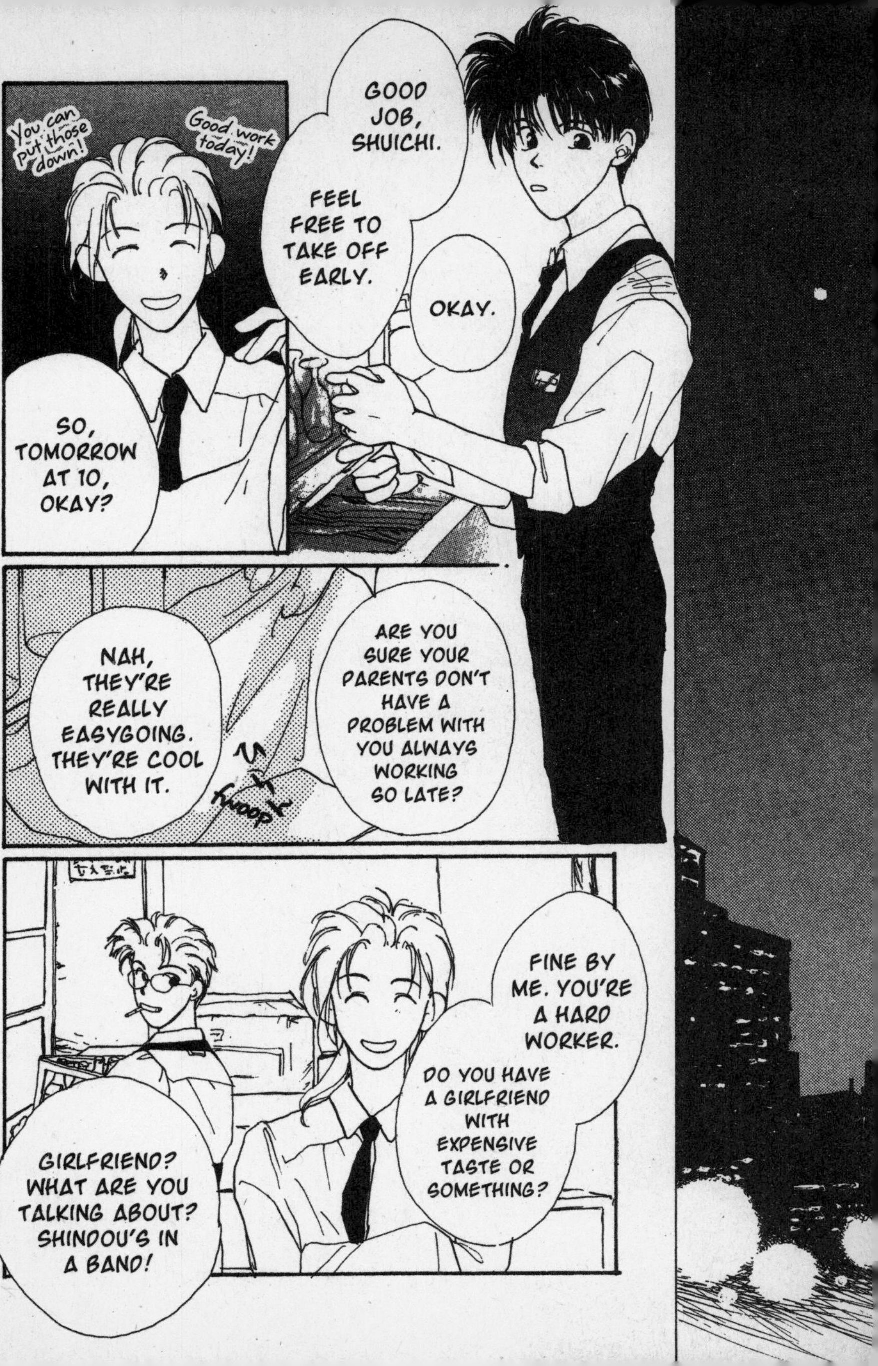
Good work today!
You can put those down!
GOOD JOB, SHUICHI.
FEEL FREE TO TAKE OFF EARLY.
OKAY.
SO, TOMORROW AT 10, OKAY?
ARE YOU SURE YOUR PARENTS DON'T HAVE A PROBLEM WITH YOU ALWAYS WORKING SO LATE?
NAH, THEY'RE REALLY EASYGOING. THEY'RE COOL WITH IT.
fwoop
FINE BY ME. YOU'RE A HARD WORKER.
DO YOU HAVE A GIRLFRIEND WITH EXPENSIVE TASTE OR SOMETHING?
GIRLFRIEND? WHAT ARE YOU TALKING ABOUT? SHINDOU'S IN A BAND!

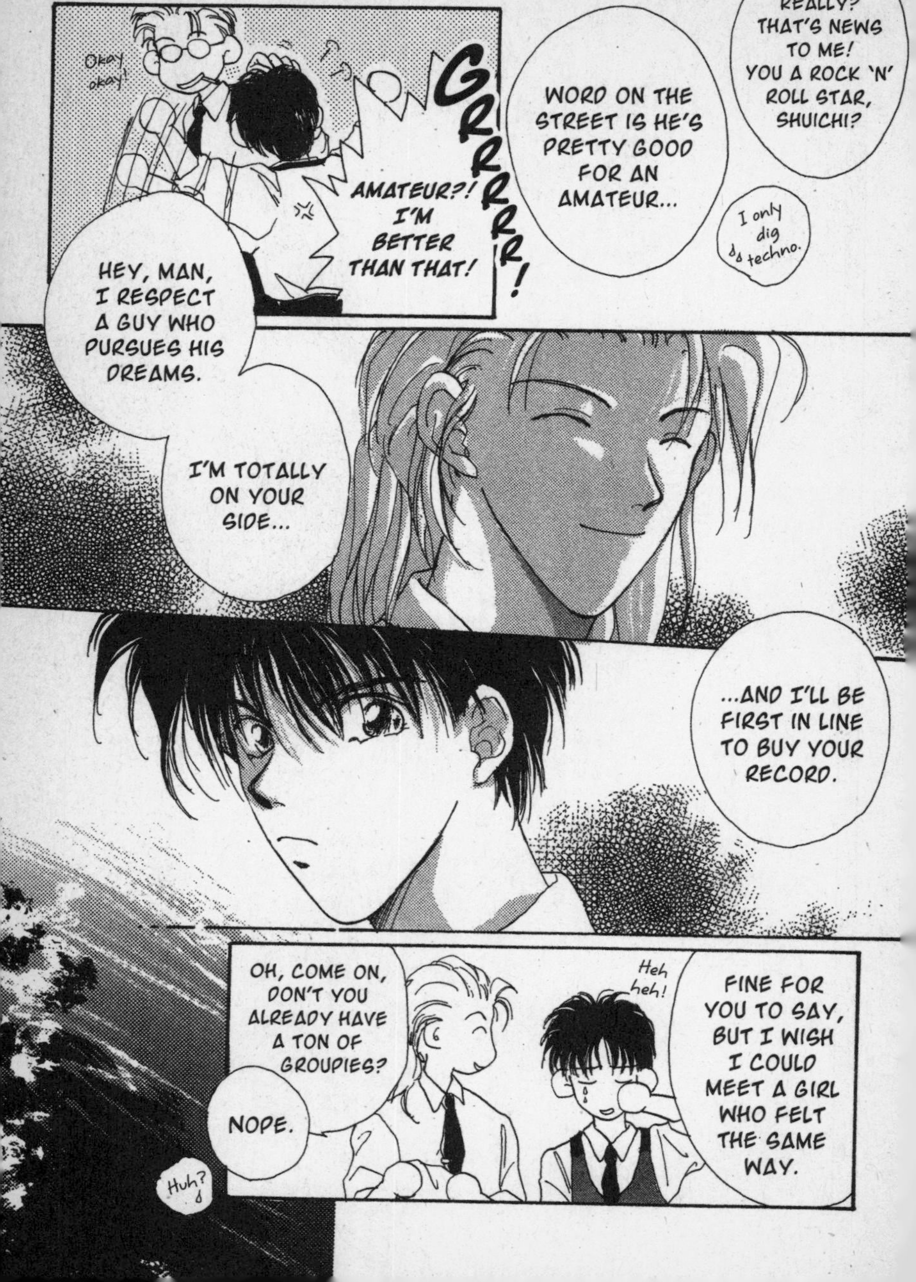
REALLY? THAT'S NEWS TO ME! YOU A ROCK 'N' ROLL STAR, SHUICHI?
I only dig techno.
WORD ON THE STREET IS HE'S PRETTY GOOD FOR AN AMATEUR...
AMATEUR?! I'M BETTER THAN THAT!
GRRRRR!
Okay okay!
HEY, MAN, I RESPECT A GUY WHO PURSUES HIS DREAMS.
I'M TOTALLY ON YOUR SIDE...
...AND I'LL BE FIRST IN LINE TO BUY YOUR RECORD.
FINE FOR YOU TO SAY, BUT I WISH I COULD MEET A GIRL WHO FELT THE SAME WAY.
Heh heh!
OH, COME ON, DON'T YOU ALREADY HAVE A TON OF GROUPIES?
NOPE.
Huh?

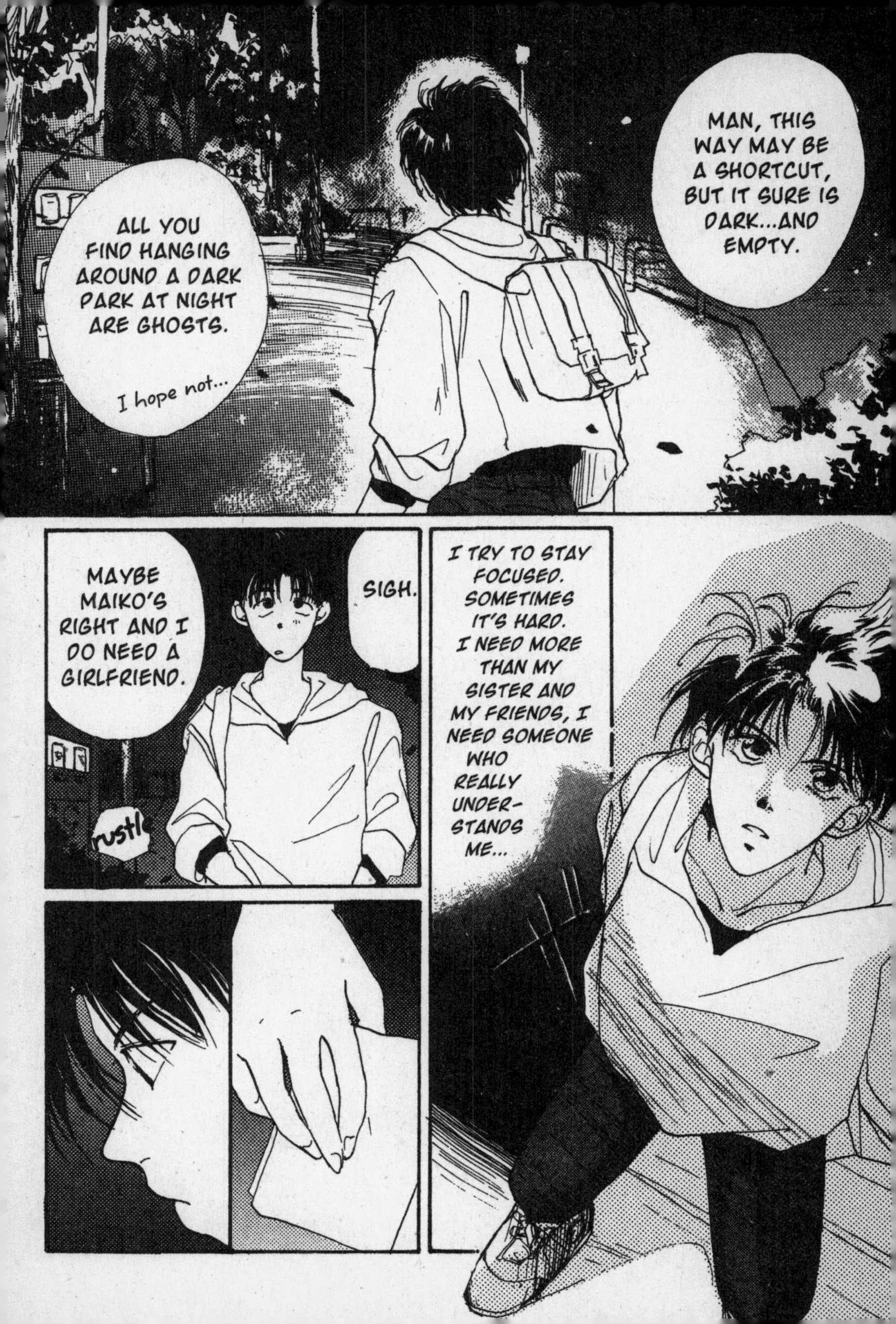
MAN, THIS WAY MAY BE A SHORTCUT, BUT IT SURE IS DARK...AND EMPTY.
ALL YOU FIND HANGING AROUND A DARK PARK AT NIGHT ARE GHOSTS.
I hope not...
I TRY TO STAY FOCUSED. SOMETIMES IT'S HARD. I NEED MORE THAN MY SISTER AND MY FRIENDS, I NEED SOMEONE WHO REALLY UNDER-STANDS ME...
SIGH.
MAYBE MAIKO'S RIGHT AND I DO NEED A GIRLFRIEND.
rustl

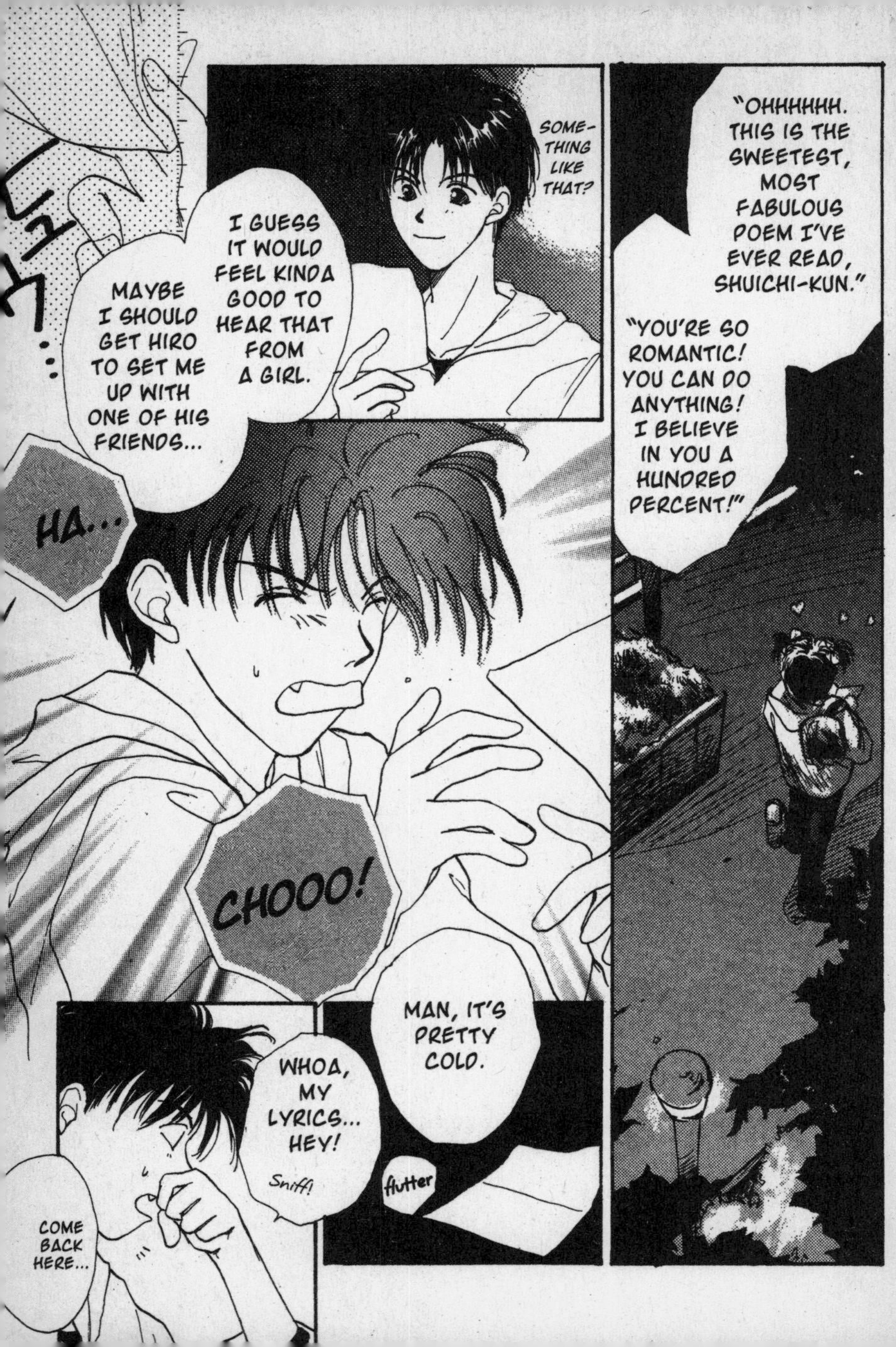
"OHHHHHH. THIS IS THE SWEETEST, MOST FABULOUS POEM I'VE EVER READ, SHUICHI-KUN."
"YOU'RE SO ROMANTIC! YOU CAN DO ANYTHING! I BELIEVE IN YOU A HUNDRED PERCENT!"
SOME-THING LIKE THAT?
I GUESS IT WOULD FEEL KINDA GOOD TO HEAR THAT FROM A GIRL.
MAYBE I SHOULD GET HIRO TO SET ME UP WITH ONE OF HIS FRIENDS...
HA...
CHOOO!
MAN, IT'S PRETTY COLD.
flutter
WHOA, MY LYRICS... HEY!
Sniff!
COME BACK HERE...

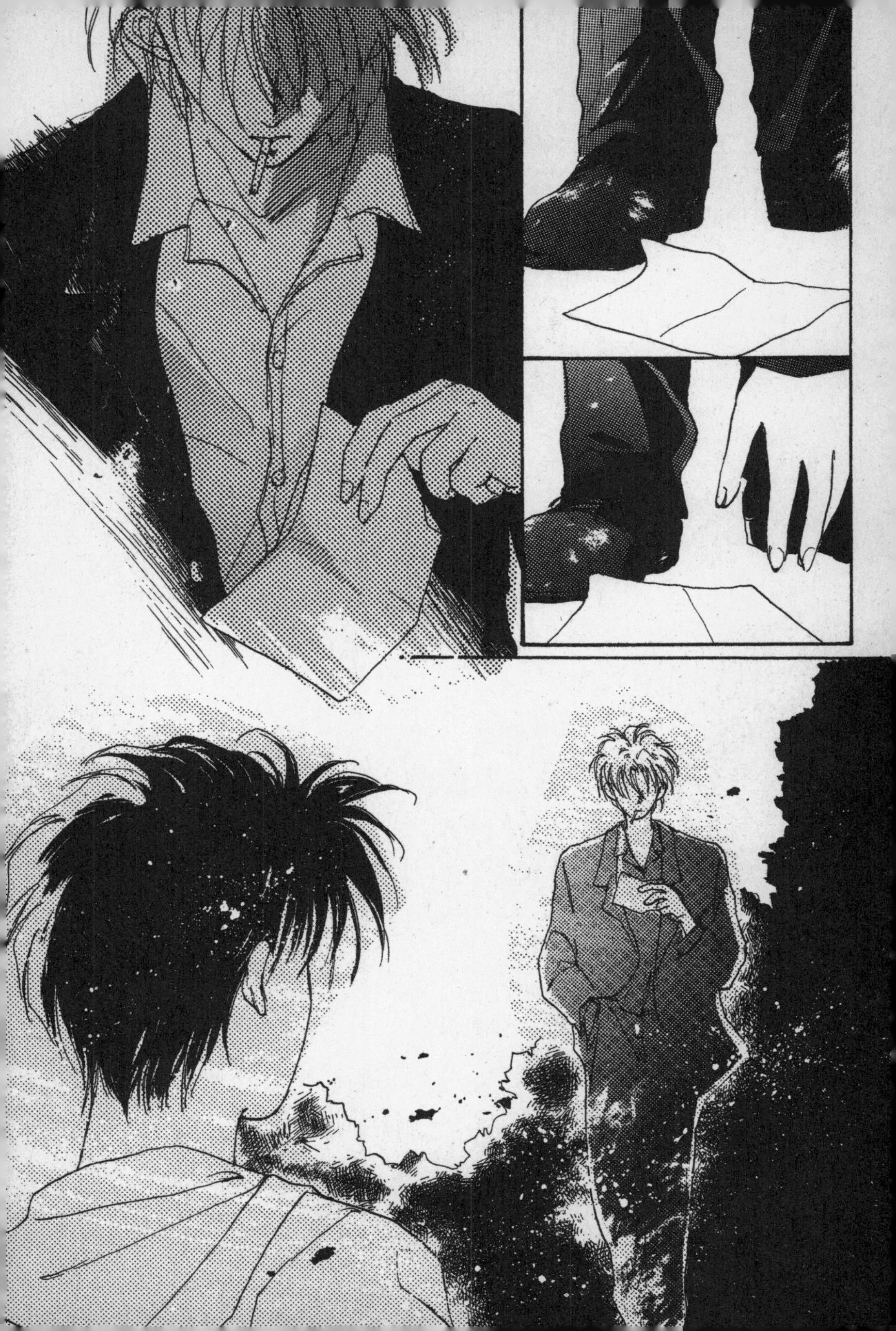

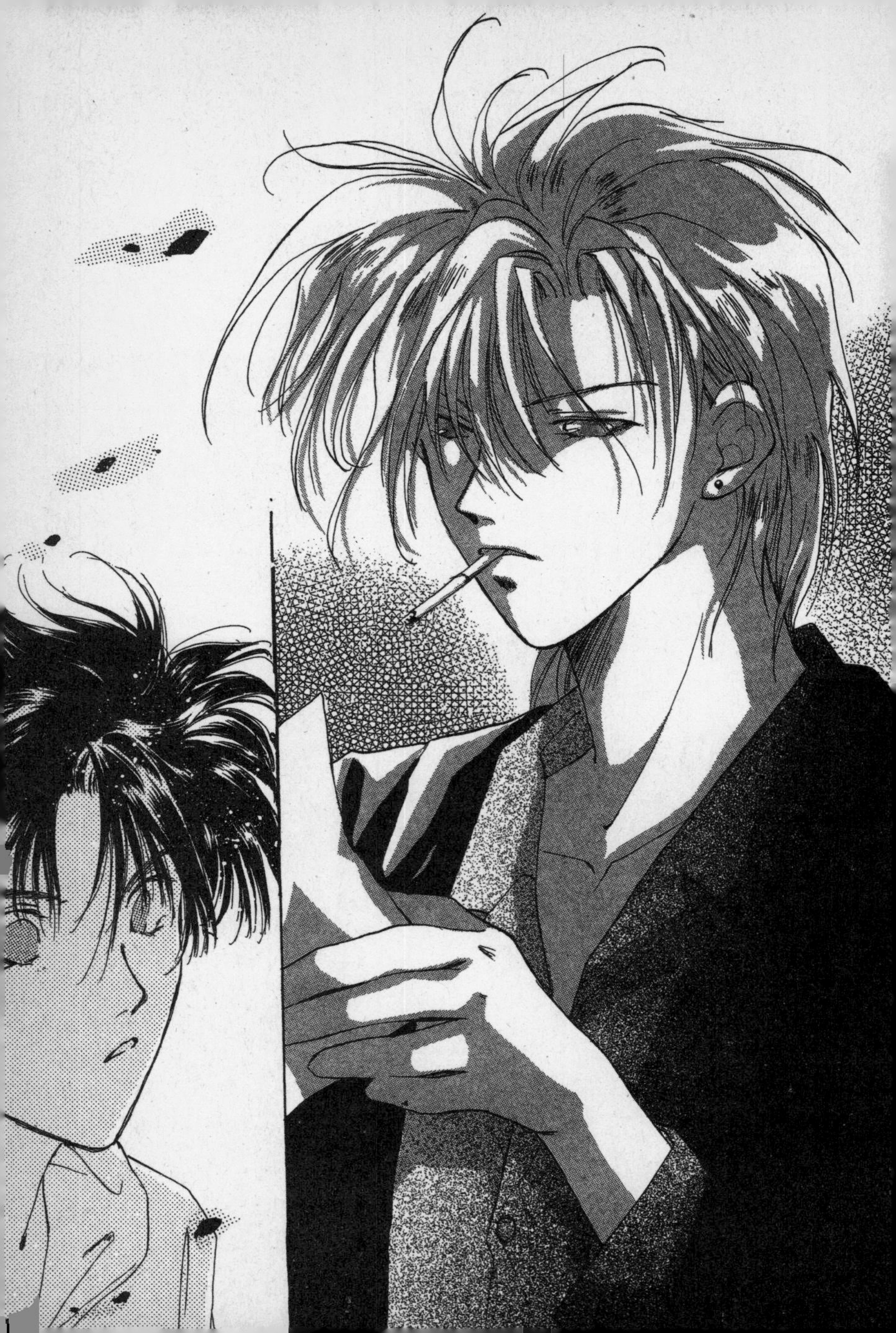

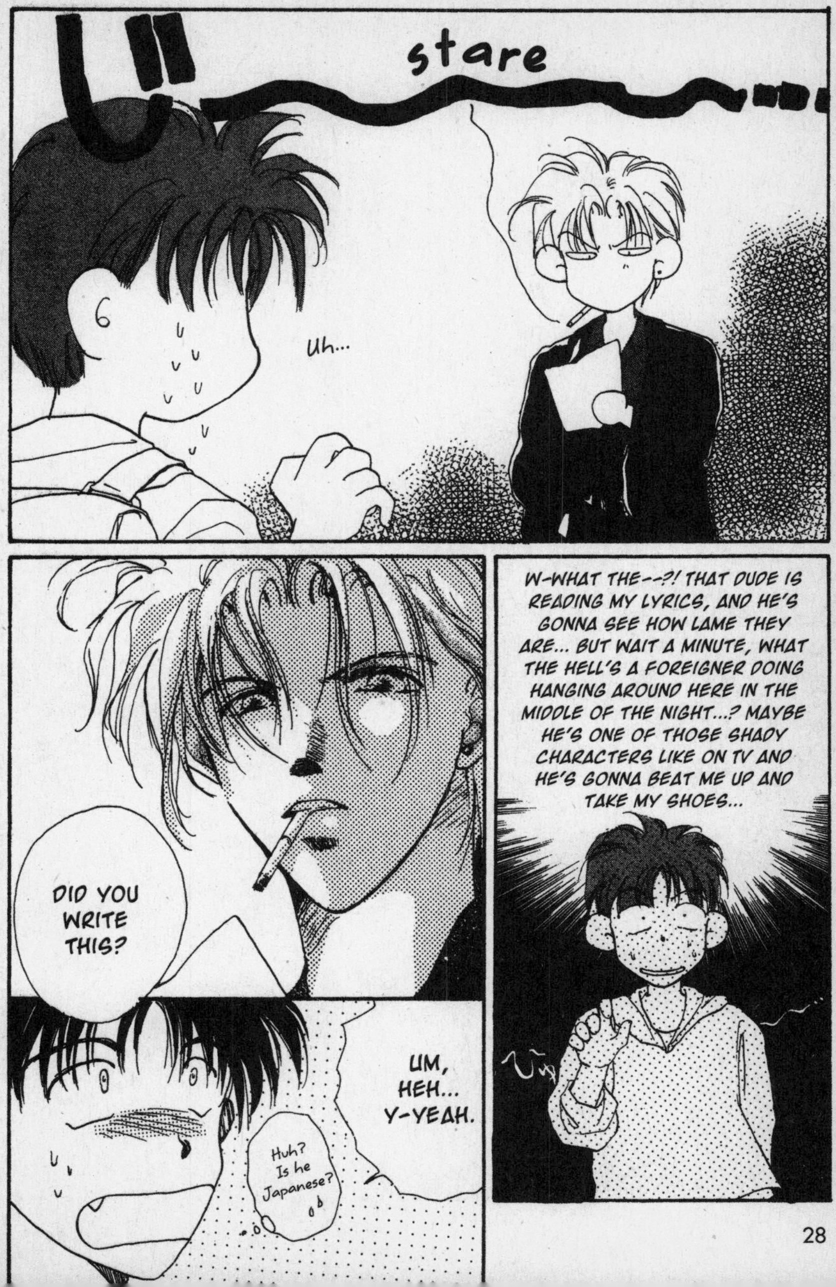
stare
Uh...
W-WHAT THE--?! THAT DUDE IS READING MY LYRICS, AND HE'S GONNA SEE HOW LAME THEY ARE... BUT WAIT A MINUTE, WHAT THE HELL'S A FOREIGNER DOING HANGING AROUND HERE IN THE MIDDLE OF THE NIGHT...? MAYBE HE'S ONE OF THOSE SHADY CHARACTERS LIKE ON TV AND HE'S GONNA BEAT ME UP AND TAKE MY SHOES...
DID YOU WRITE THIS?
UM, HEH... Y-YEAH.
Huh? Is he Japanese?

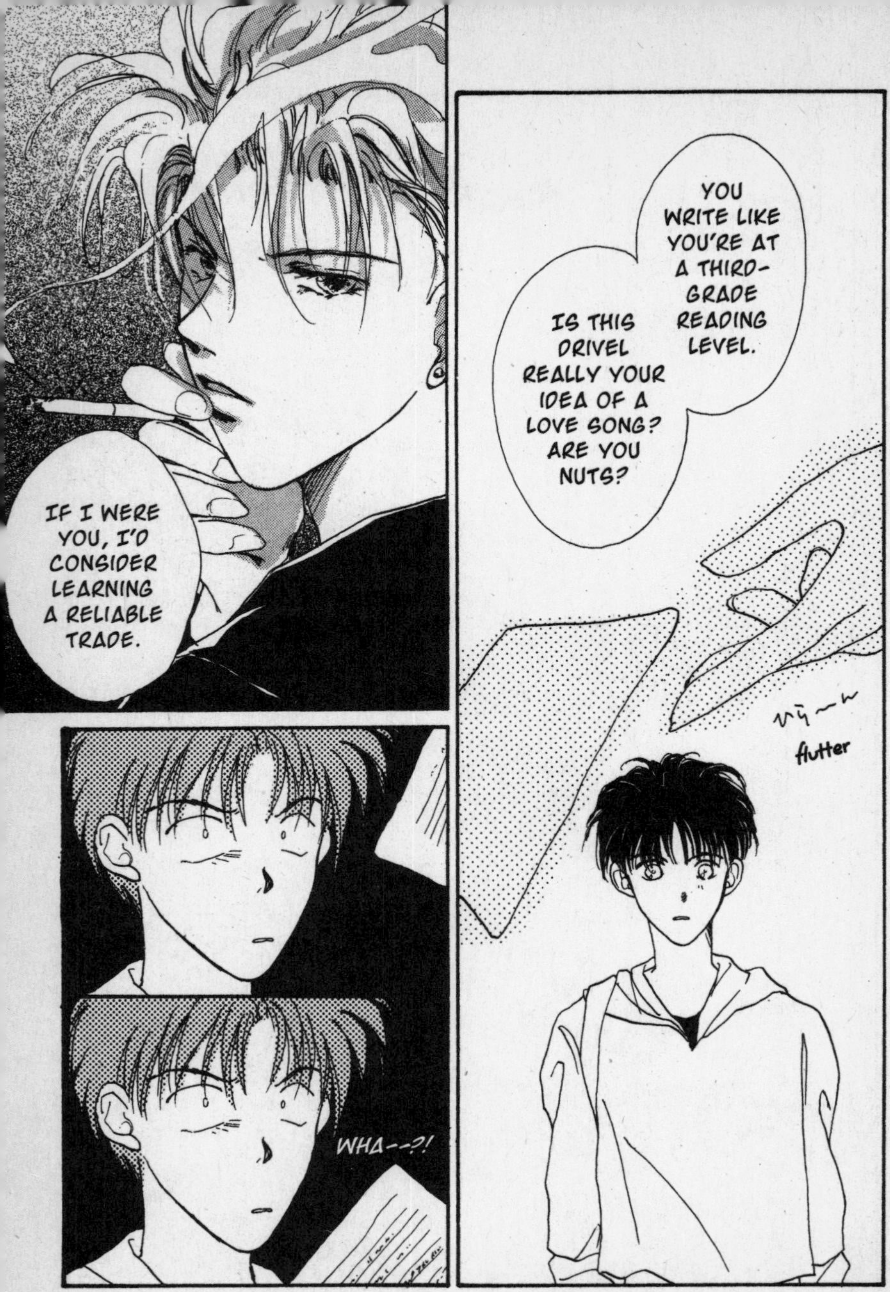
YOU WRITE LIKE YOU'RE AT A THIRD-GRADE READING LEVEL.
IS THIS DRIVEL REALLY YOUR IDEA OF A LOVE SONG? ARE YOU NUTS?
flutter
IF I WERE YOU, I'D CONSIDER LEARNING A RELIABLE TRADE.
WHA--?!

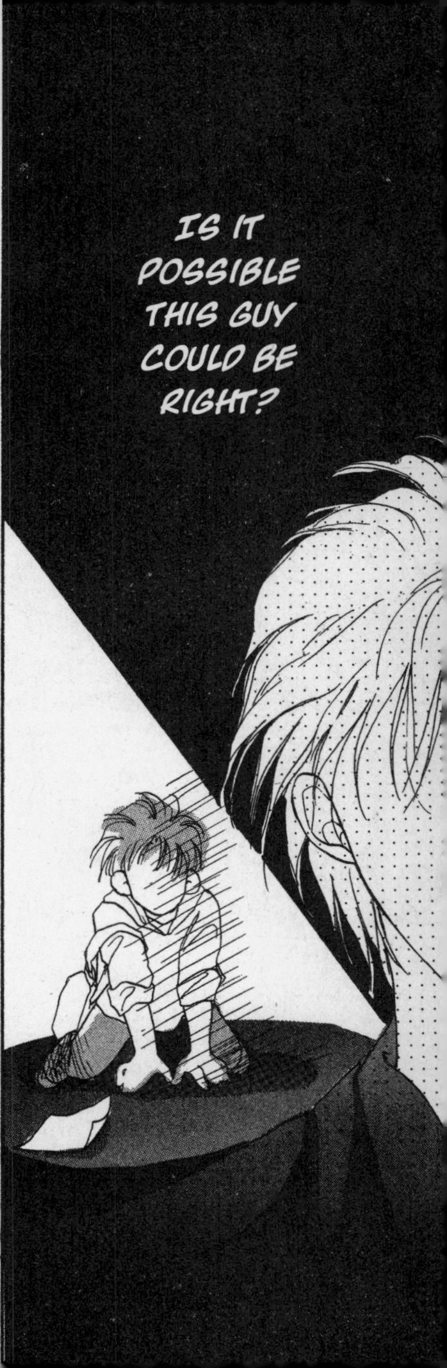
IS IT POSSIBLE THIS GUY COULD BE RIGHT?

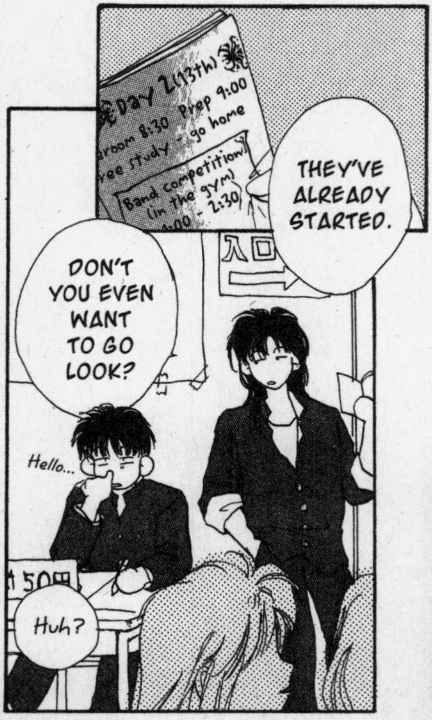
Day 2 (13th)
Prep 9:00
go home
Band competition!
(in the gym)
- 2:30
THEY'VE ALREADY STARTED.
入口
DON'T YOU EVEN WANT TO GO LOOK?
Hello...
Huh?

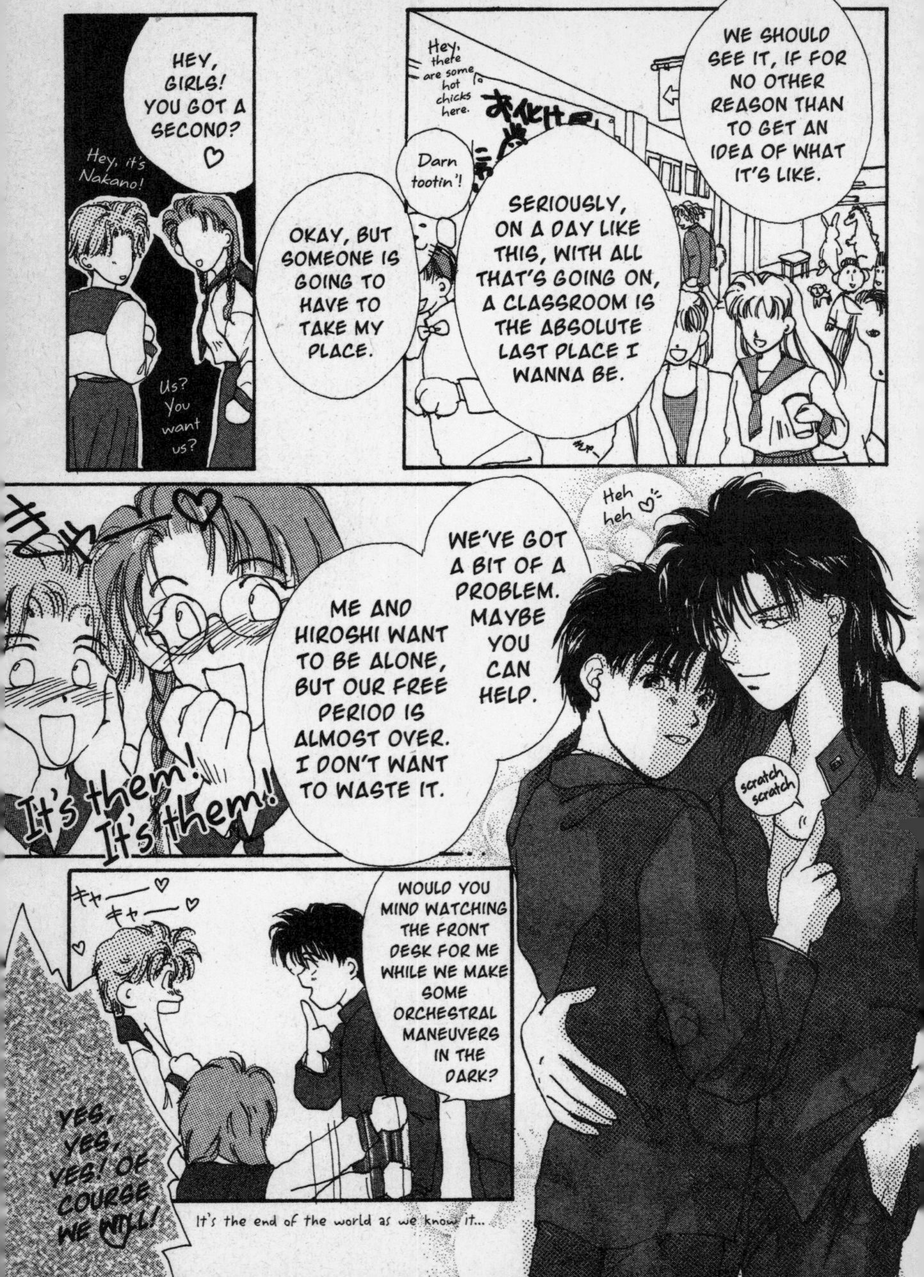
WE SHOULD SEE IT, IF FOR NO OTHER REASON THAN TO GET AN IDEA OF WHAT IT'S LIKE.
SERIOUSLY, ON A DAY LIKE THIS, WITH ALL THAT'S GOING ON, A CLASSROOM IS THE ABSOLUTE LAST PLACE I WANNA BE.
Hey, there are some hot chicks here.
Darn tootin'!
OKAY, BUT SOMEONE IS GOING TO HAVE TO TAKE MY PLACE.
HEY, GIRLS! YOU GOT A SECOND? ♡
Hey, it's Nakano!
Us? You want us?
Heh heh ♡
WE'VE GOT A BIT OF A PROBLEM. MAYBE YOU CAN HELP.
ME AND HIROSHI WANT TO BE ALONE, BUT OUR FREE PERIOD IS ALMOST OVER. I DON'T WANT TO WASTE IT.
scratch scratch
It's them! It's them!
WOULD YOU MIND WATCHING THE FRONT DESK FOR ME WHILE WE MAKE SOME ORCHESTRAL MANEUVERS IN THE DARK?
キャー ♡ キャー ♡
YES, YES, YES! OF COURSE WE WILL!
It's the end of the world as we know it...

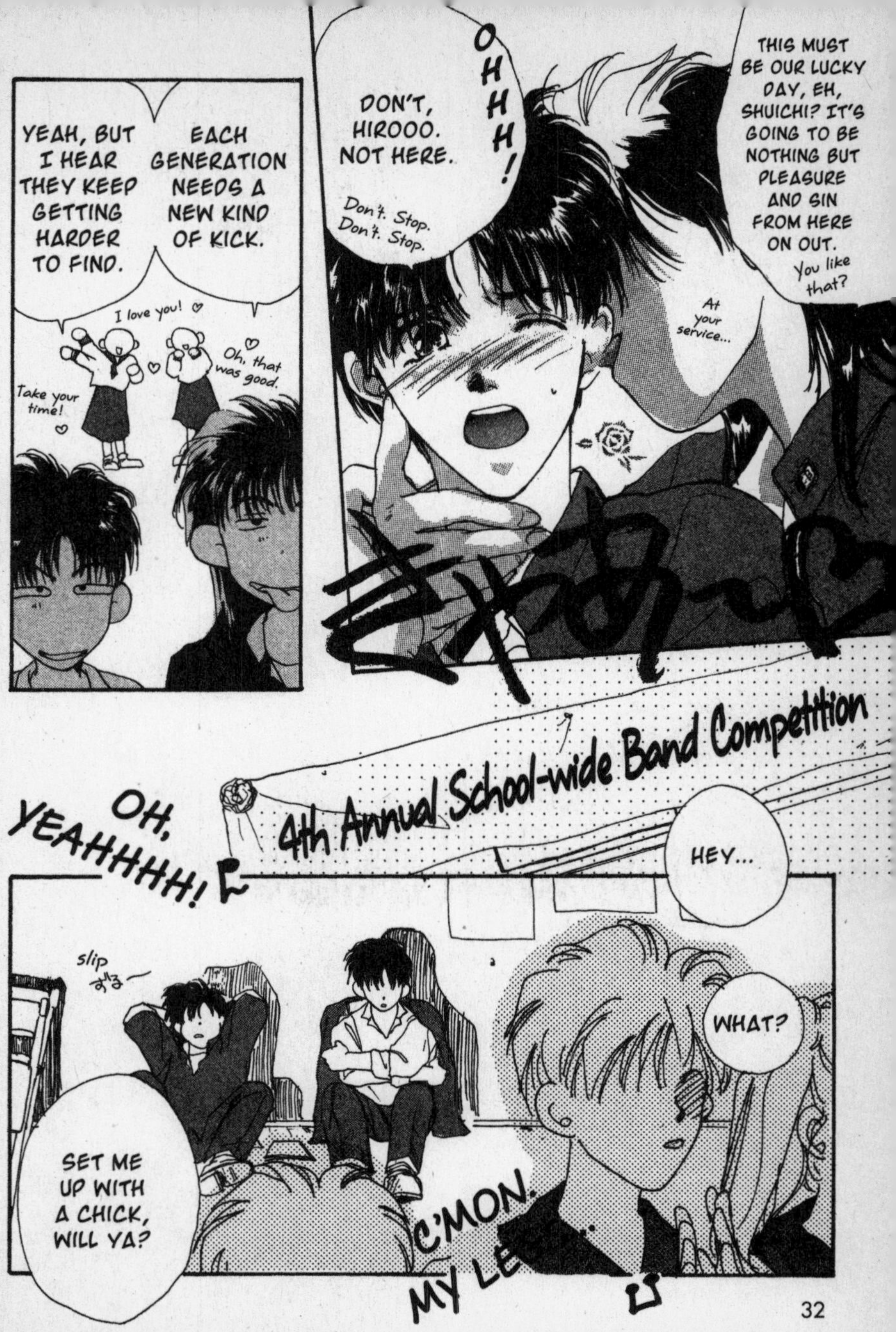
THIS MUST BE OUR LUCKY DAY, EH, SHUICHI? IT'S GOING TO BE NOTHING BUT PLEASURE AND SIN FROM HERE ON OUT.
You like that?
OHHHH!
DON'T, HIROOO. NOT HERE.
Don't. Stop. Don't. Stop.
At your service...
きゃあ〜っ
EACH GENERATION NEEDS A NEW KIND OF KICK.
YEAH, BUT I HEAR THEY KEEP GETTING HARDER TO FIND.
I love you!
Oh, that was good.
Take your time!
4th Annual School-wide Band Competition
OH, YEAHHHH!
HEY...
WHAT?
slip ずる〜
C'MON.
MY LE...
SET ME UP WITH A CHICK, WILL YA?

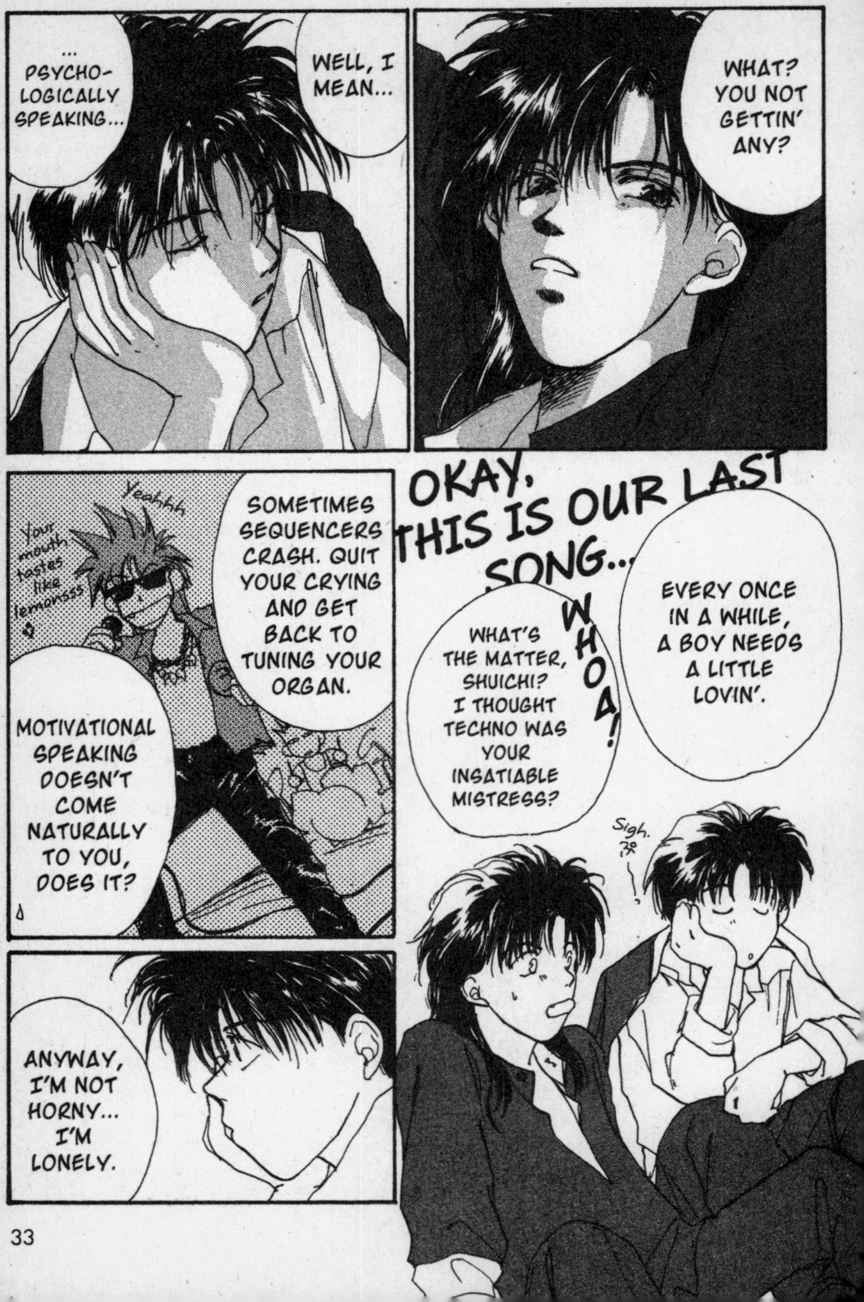
WHAT? YOU NOT GETTIN' ANY?
WELL, I MEAN...
... PSYCHO-LOGICALLY SPEAKING...
OKAY, THIS IS OUR LAST SONG...
EVERY ONCE IN A WHILE, A BOY NEEDS A LITTLE LOVIN'.
WHOA!
WHAT'S THE MATTER, SHUICHI? I THOUGHT TECHNO WAS YOUR INSATIABLE MISTRESS?
Sigh.
Yeahhh
SOMETIMES SEQUENCERS CRASH. QUIT YOUR CRYING AND GET BACK TO TUNING YOUR ORGAN.
Your mouth tastes like lemonsss
MOTIVATIONAL SPEAKING DOESN'T COME NATURALLY TO YOU, DOES IT?
ANYWAY, I'M NOT HORNY... I'M LONELY.

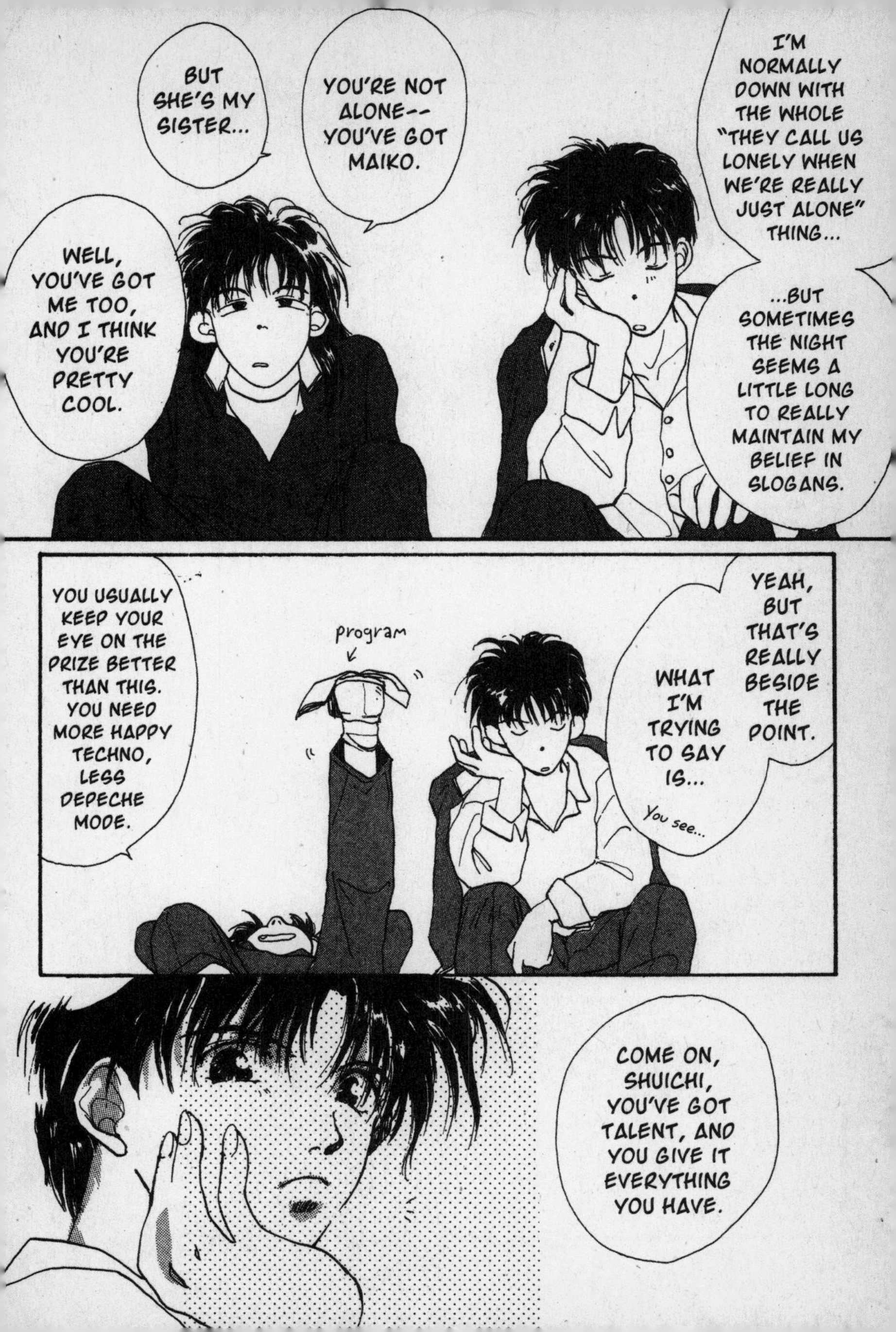
I'M NORMALLY DOWN WITH THE WHOLE "THEY CALL US LONELY WHEN WE'RE REALLY JUST ALONE" THING...
...BUT SOMETIMES THE NIGHT SEEMS A LITTLE LONG TO REALLY MAINTAIN MY BELIEF IN SLOGANS.
YOU'RE NOT ALONE-- YOU'VE GOT MAIKO.
BUT SHE'S MY SISTER...
WELL, YOU'VE GOT ME TOO, AND I THINK YOU'RE PRETTY COOL.
YEAH, BUT THAT'S REALLY BESIDE THE POINT.
WHAT I'M TRYING TO SAY IS...
You see...
program
YOU USUALLY KEEP YOUR EYE ON THE PRIZE BETTER THAN THIS. YOU NEED MORE HAPPY TECHNO, LESS DEPECHE MODE.
COME ON, SHUICHI, YOU'VE GOT TALENT, AND YOU GIVE IT EVERYTHING YOU HAVE.

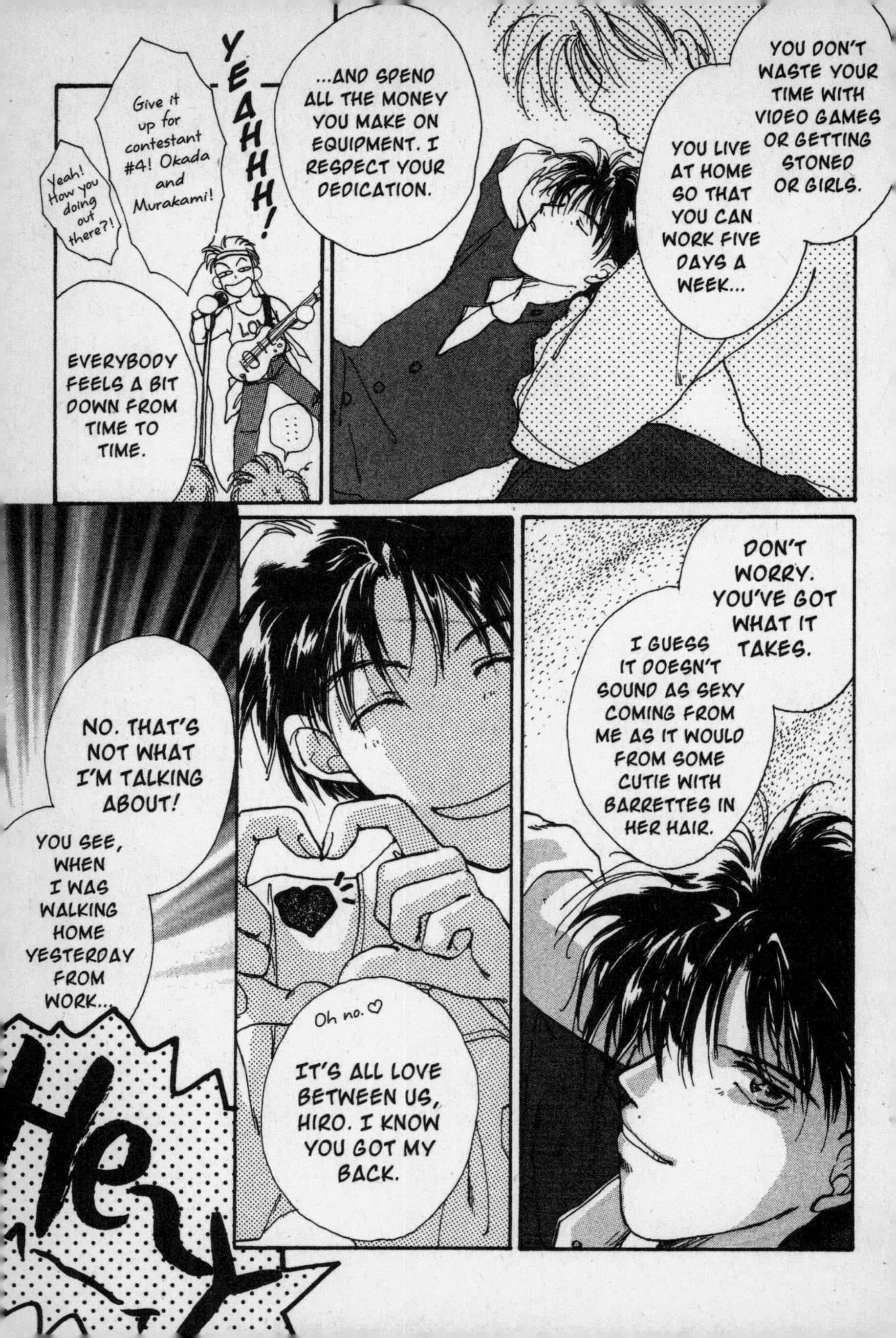
YOU DON'T WASTE YOUR TIME WITH VIDEO GAMES OR GETTING STONED OR GIRLS.
YOU LIVE AT HOME SO THAT YOU CAN WORK FIVE DAYS A WEEK...
...AND SPEND ALL THE MONEY YOU MAKE ON EQUIPMENT. I RESPECT YOUR DEDICATION.
YEAHHH!
Give it up for contestant #4! Okada and Murakami!
Yeah! How you doing out there?!
EVERYBODY FEELS A BIT DOWN FROM TIME TO TIME.
DON'T WORRY. YOU'VE GOT WHAT IT TAKES.
I GUESS IT DOESN'T SOUND AS SEXY COMING FROM ME AS IT WOULD FROM SOME CUTIE WITH BARRETTES IN HER HAIR.
Oh no. ♡
IT'S ALL LOVE BETWEEN US, HIRO. I KNOW YOU GOT MY BACK.
NO. THAT'S NOT WHAT I'M TALKING ABOUT!
YOU SEE, WHEN I WAS WALKING HOME YESTERDAY FROM WORK...
Hey

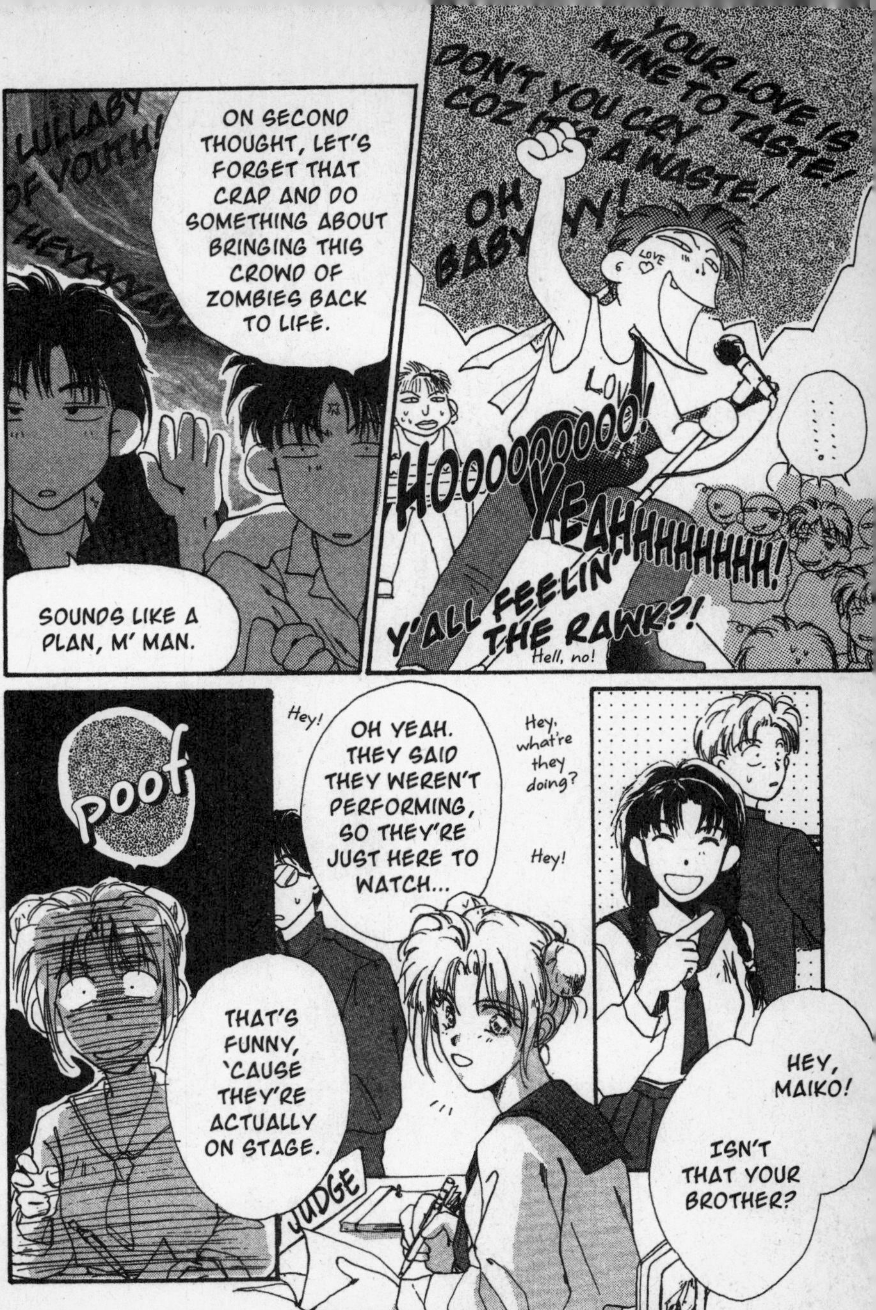
YOUR LOVE IS MINE TO TASTE!
DON'T YOU CRY COZ IT'S A WASTE!
OH BABYYYY!
HOOOOOOOOO! YEAHHHHHHHH!
Y'ALL FEELIN' THE RAWK?!
Hell, no!
LULLABY OF YOUTH!
ON SECOND THOUGHT, LET'S FORGET THAT CRAP AND DO SOMETHING ABOUT BRINGING THIS CROWD OF ZOMBIES BACK TO LIFE.
SOUNDS LIKE A PLAN, M' MAN.
HEY, MAIKO!
ISN'T THAT YOUR BROTHER?
Hey!
Hey, what're they doing?
Hey!
OH YEAH. THEY SAID THEY WEREN'T PERFORMING, SO THEY'RE JUST HERE TO WATCH...
THAT'S FUNNY, 'CAUSE THEY'RE ACTUALLY ON STAGE.
poof
JUDGE

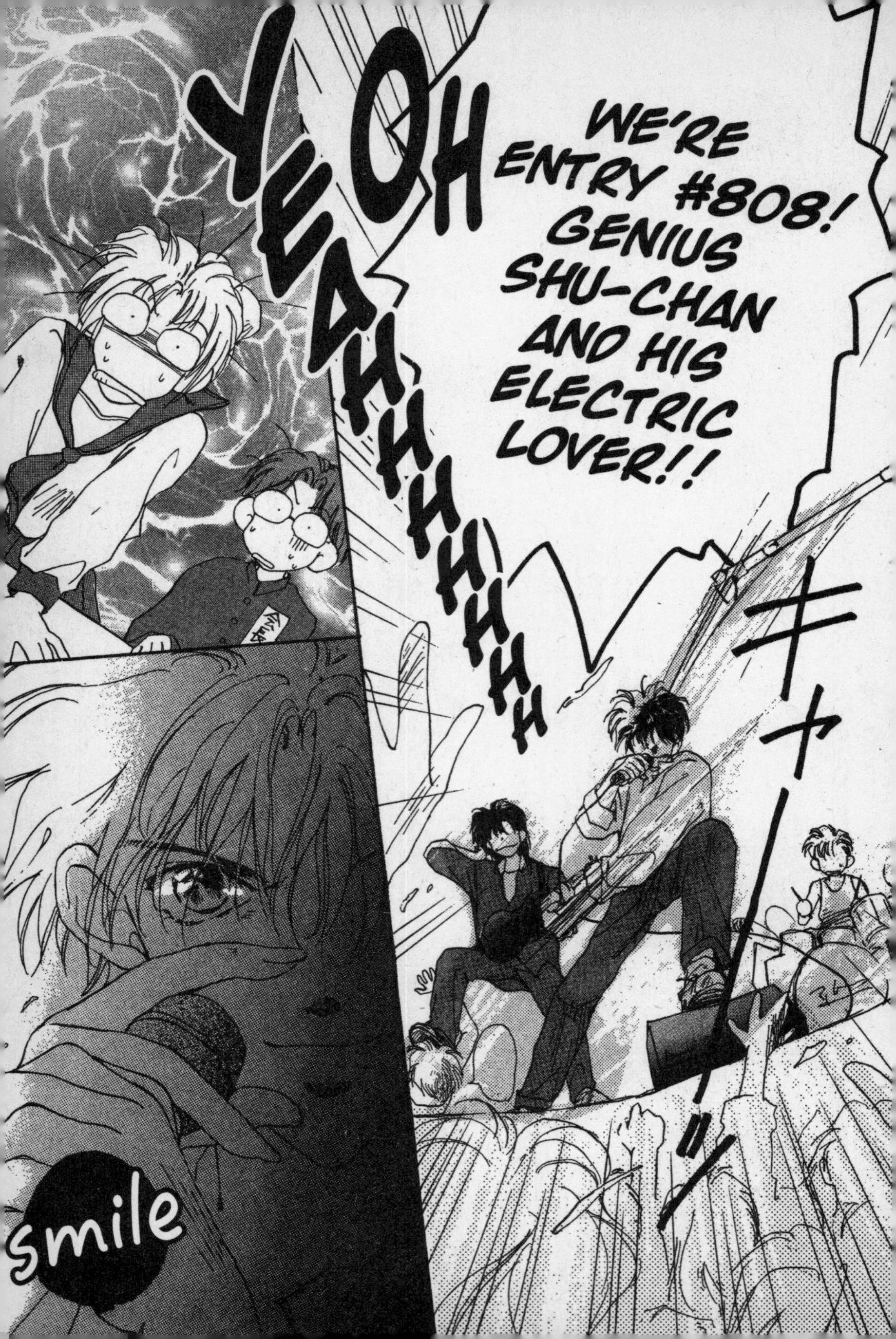
WE'RE ENTRY #808! GENIUS SHU-CHAN AND HIS ELECTRIC LOVER!!
OH YEAHHHHHHHHHHHHH
キャー!!
smile

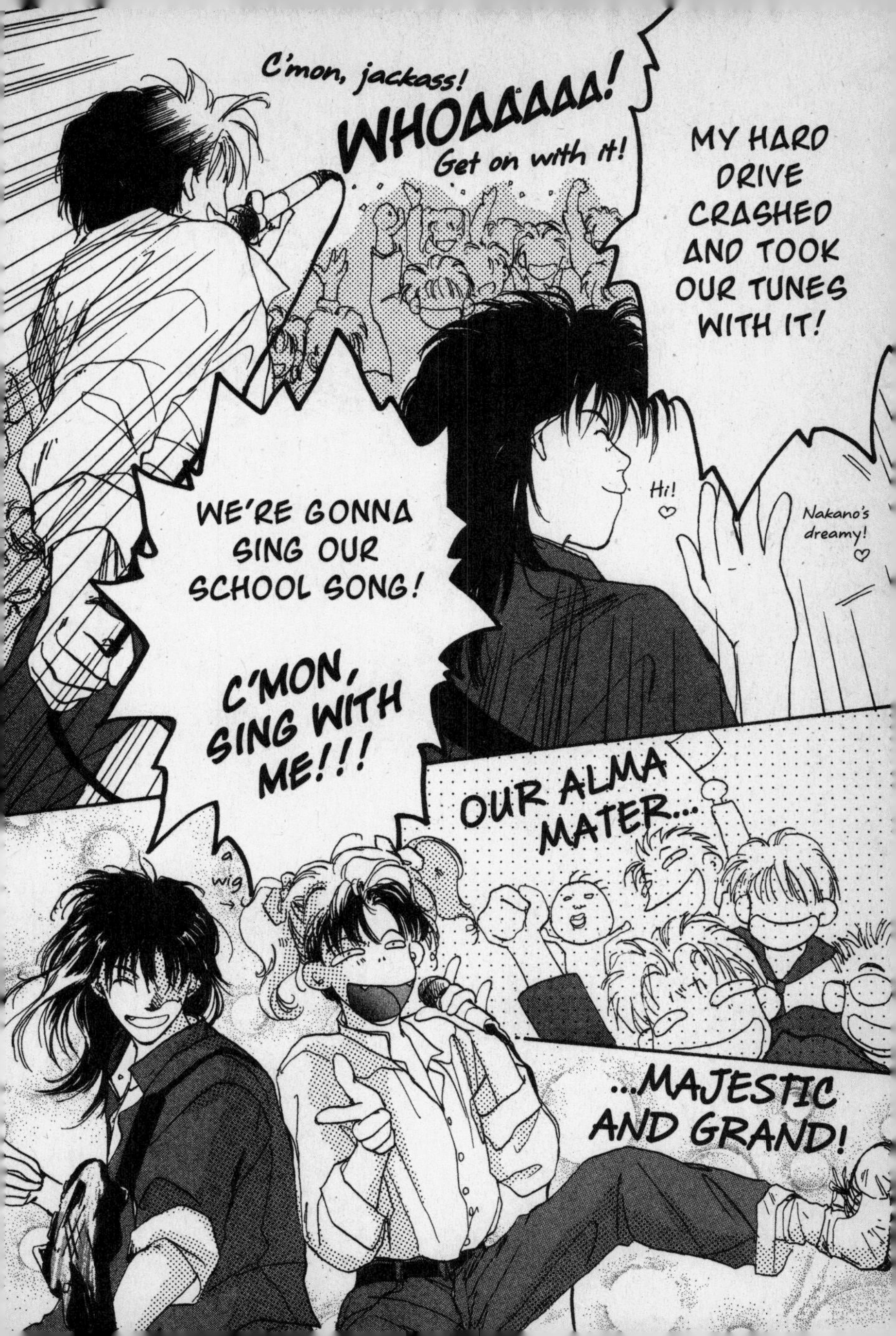
MY HARD DRIVE CRASHED AND TOOK OUR TUNES WITH IT!
C'mon, jackass!
WHOAAAAAA!
Get on with it!
Nakano's dreamy! ♡
Hi! ♡
WE'RE GONNA SING OUR SCHOOL SONG!
C'MON, SING WITH ME!!!
OUR ALMA MATER...
...MAJESTIC AND GRAND!
a wig

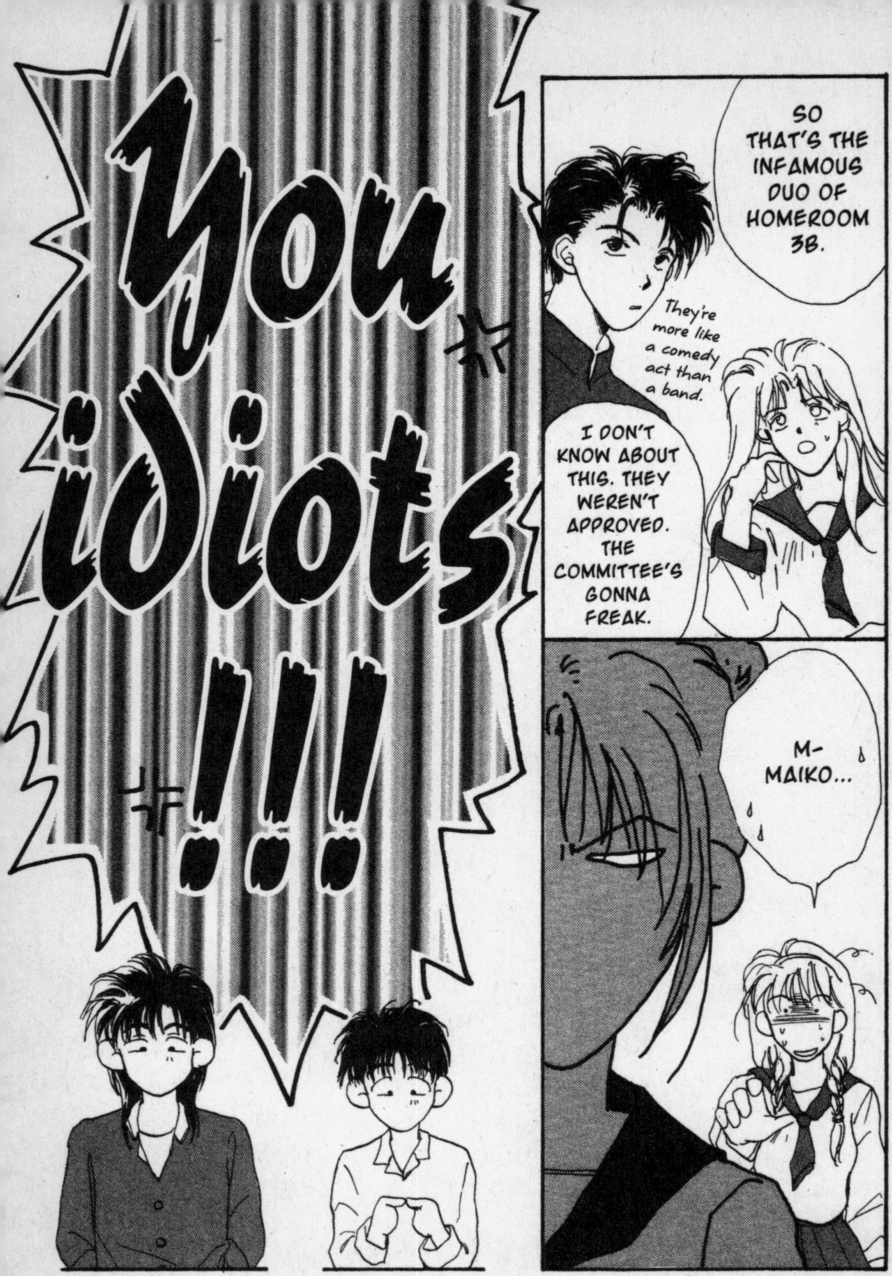
SO THAT'S THE INFAMOUS DUO OF HOMEROOM 3B.
They're more like a comedy act than a band.
I DON'T KNOW ABOUT THIS. THEY WEREN'T APPROVED. THE COMMITTEE'S GONNA FREAK.
M-MAIKO...
You idiots!!!

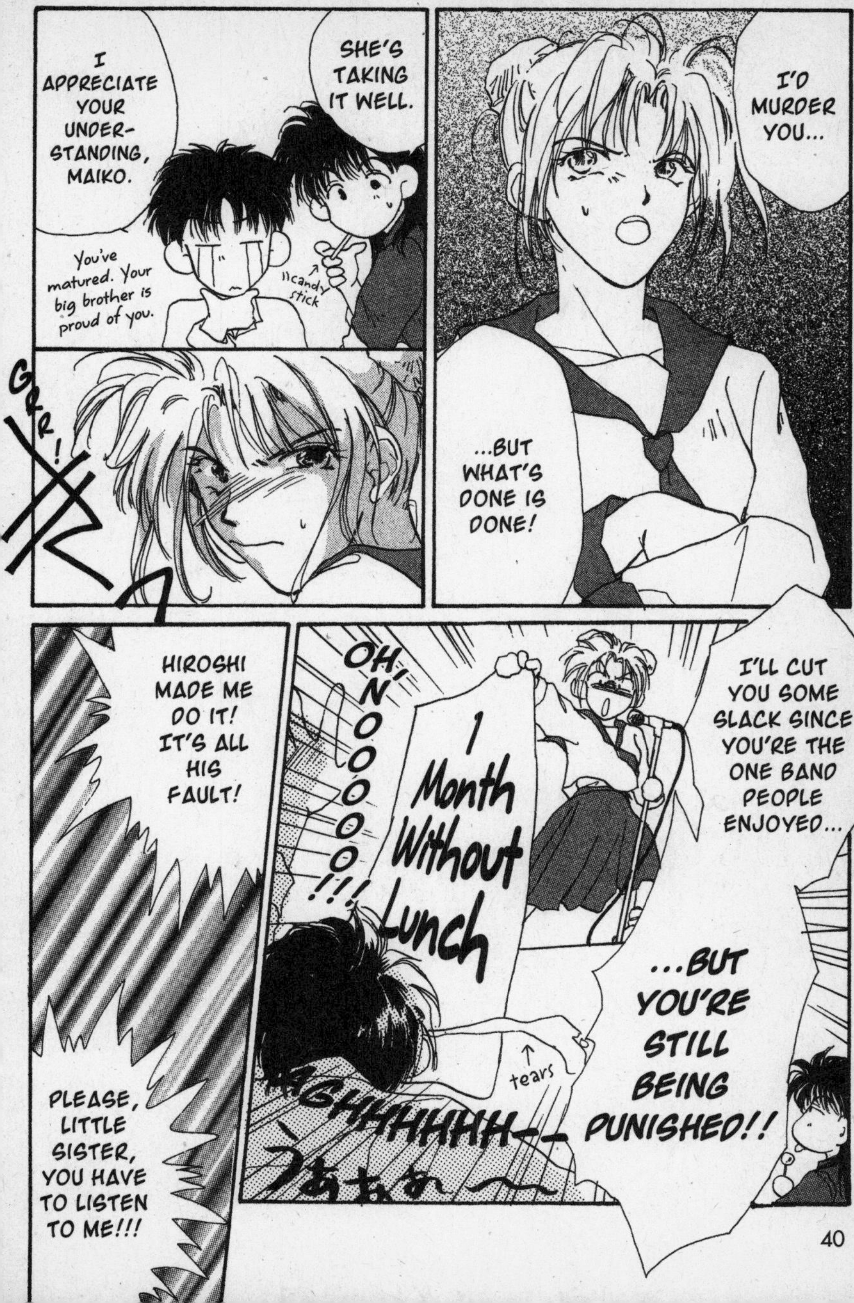
I'D MURDER YOU...
...BUT WHAT'S DONE IS DONE!
SHE'S TAKING IT WELL.
I APPRECIATE YOUR UNDER-STANDING, MAIKO.
You've matured. Your big brother is proud of you.
candy stick
GRR!
I'LL CUT YOU SOME SLACK SINCE YOU'RE THE ONE BAND PEOPLE ENJOYED...
1 Month Without Lunch
OH, NOOOOOOOOO!!!
...BUT YOU'RE STILL BEING PUNISHED!!
tears
GHHHHHH—
HIROSHI MADE ME DO IT! IT'S ALL HIS FAULT!
PLEASE, LITTLE SISTER, YOU HAVE TO LISTEN TO ME!!!

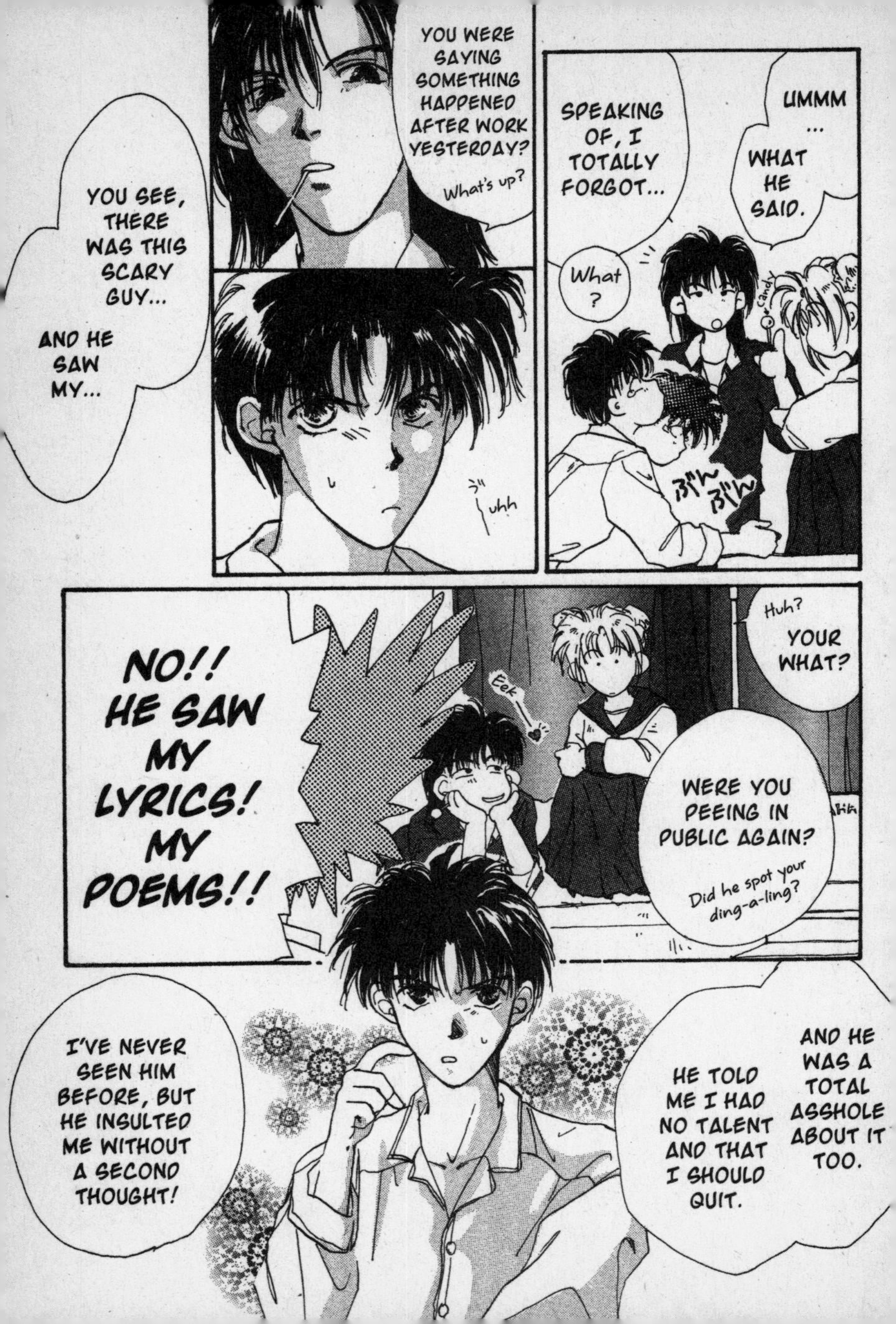
UMMM... WHAT HE SAID.
SPEAKING OF, I TOTALLY FORGOT...
What?
candy
ぶん ぶん
YOU WERE SAYING SOMETHING HAPPENED AFTER WORK YESTERDAY?
What's up?
uhh
YOU SEE, THERE WAS THIS SCARY GUY...
AND HE SAW MY...
Huh?
YOUR WHAT?
WERE YOU PEEING IN PUBLIC AGAIN?
Did he spot your ding-a-ling?
Eek
NO!! HE SAW MY LYRICS! MY POEMS!!
AND HE WAS A TOTAL ASSHOLE ABOUT IT TOO.
HE TOLD ME I HAD NO TALENT AND THAT I SHOULD QUIT.
I'VE NEVER SEEN HIM BEFORE, BUT HE INSULTED ME WITHOUT A SECOND THOUGHT!

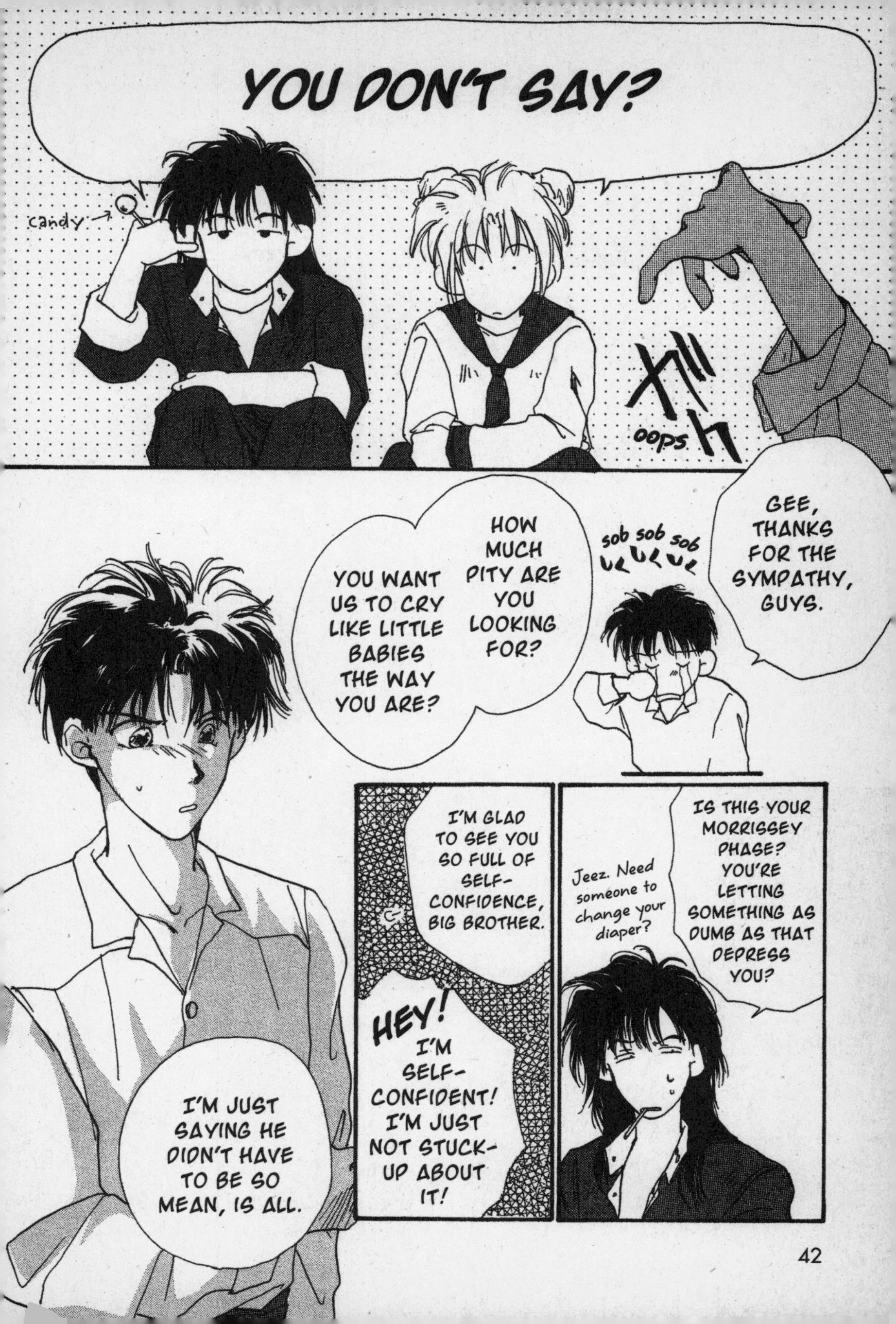
YOU DON'T SAY?
candy
oops
sob sob sob
GEE, THANKS FOR THE SYMPATHY, GUYS.
HOW MUCH PITY ARE YOU LOOKING FOR?
YOU WANT US TO CRY LIKE LITTLE BABIES THE WAY YOU ARE?
I'M JUST SAYING HE DIDN'T HAVE TO BE SO MEAN, IS ALL.
IS THIS YOUR MORRISSEY PHASE? YOU'RE LETTING SOMETHING AS DUMB AS THAT DEPRESS YOU?
Jeez. Need someone to change your diaper?
I'M GLAD TO SEE YOU SO FULL OF SELF-CONFIDENCE, BIG BROTHER.
HEY! I'M SELF-CONFIDENT! I'M JUST NOT STUCK-UP ABOUT IT!

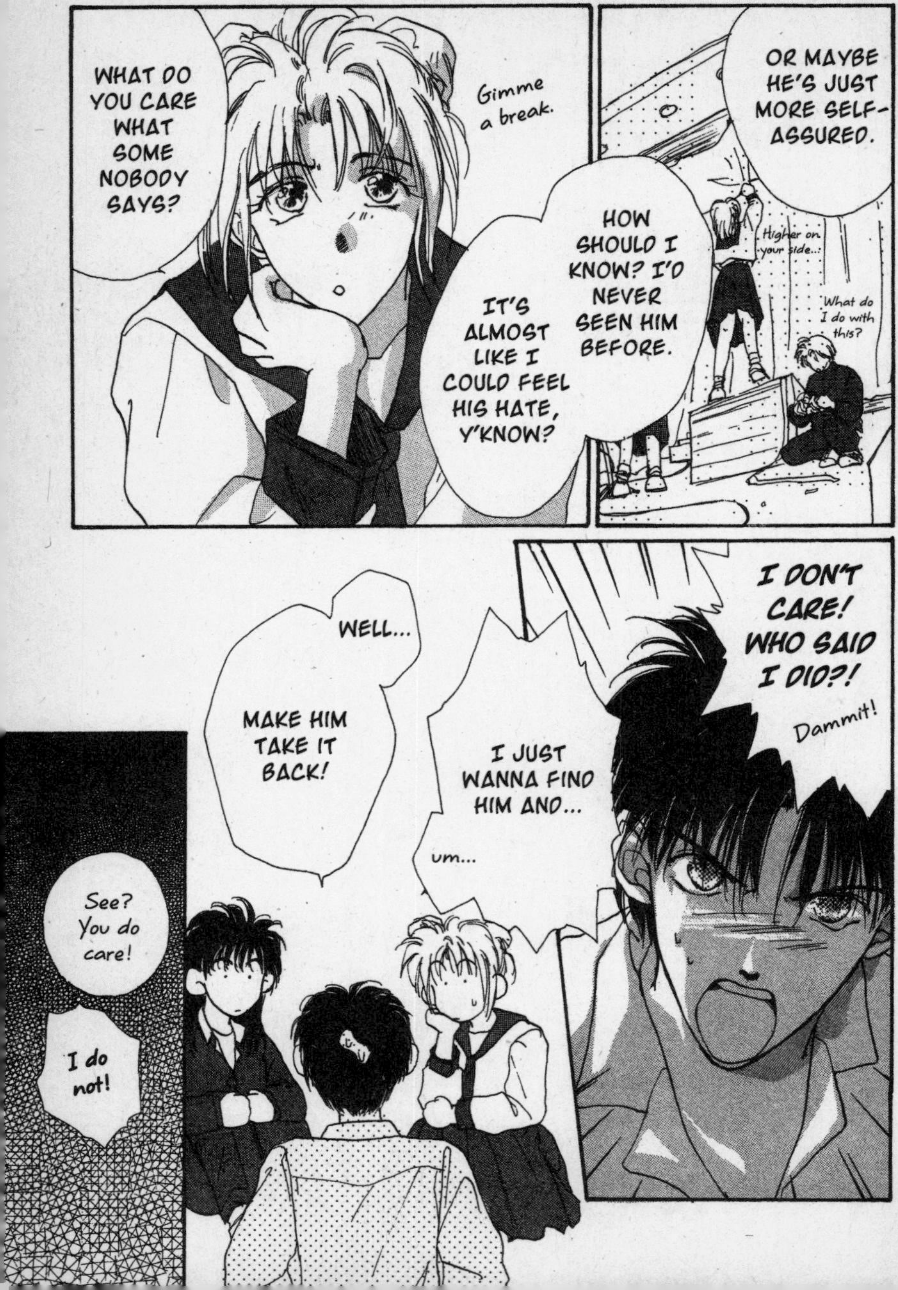
OR MAYBE HE'S JUST MORE SELF-ASSURED.
Higher on your side...
What do I do with this?
HOW SHOULD I KNOW? I'D NEVER SEEN HIM BEFORE.
IT'S ALMOST LIKE I COULD FEEL HIS HATE, Y'KNOW?
Gimme a break.
WHAT DO YOU CARE WHAT SOME NOBODY SAYS?
I DON'T CARE! WHO SAID I DID?!
Dammit!
WELL...
I JUST WANNA FIND HIM AND...
MAKE HIM TAKE IT BACK!
um...
See? You do care!
I do not!
the cleanup crew

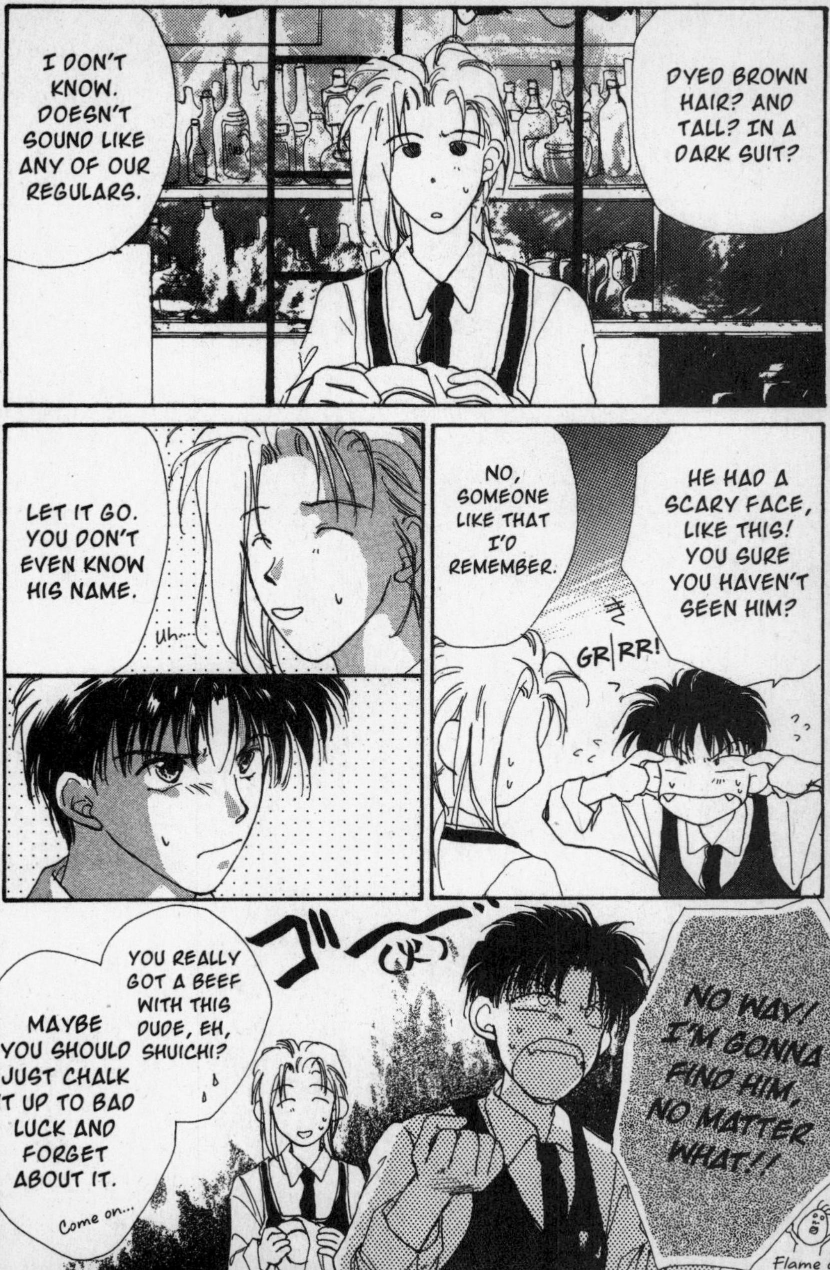
DYED BROWN HAIR? AND TALL? IN A DARK SUIT?
I DON'T KNOW. DOESN'T SOUND LIKE ANY OF OUR REGULARS.
HE HAD A SCARY FACE, LIKE THIS! YOU SURE YOU HAVEN'T SEEN HIM?
NO, SOMEONE LIKE THAT I'D REMEMBER.
GR|RR!
LET IT GO. YOU DON'T EVEN KNOW HIS NAME.
Uh...
NO WAY! I'M GONNA FIND HIM, NO MATTER WHAT!!
Flame on!
ゴー
YOU REALLY GOT A BEEF WITH THIS DUDE, EH, SHUICHI?
MAYBE YOU SHOULD JUST CHALK IT UP TO BAD LUCK AND FORGET ABOUT IT.
Come on...

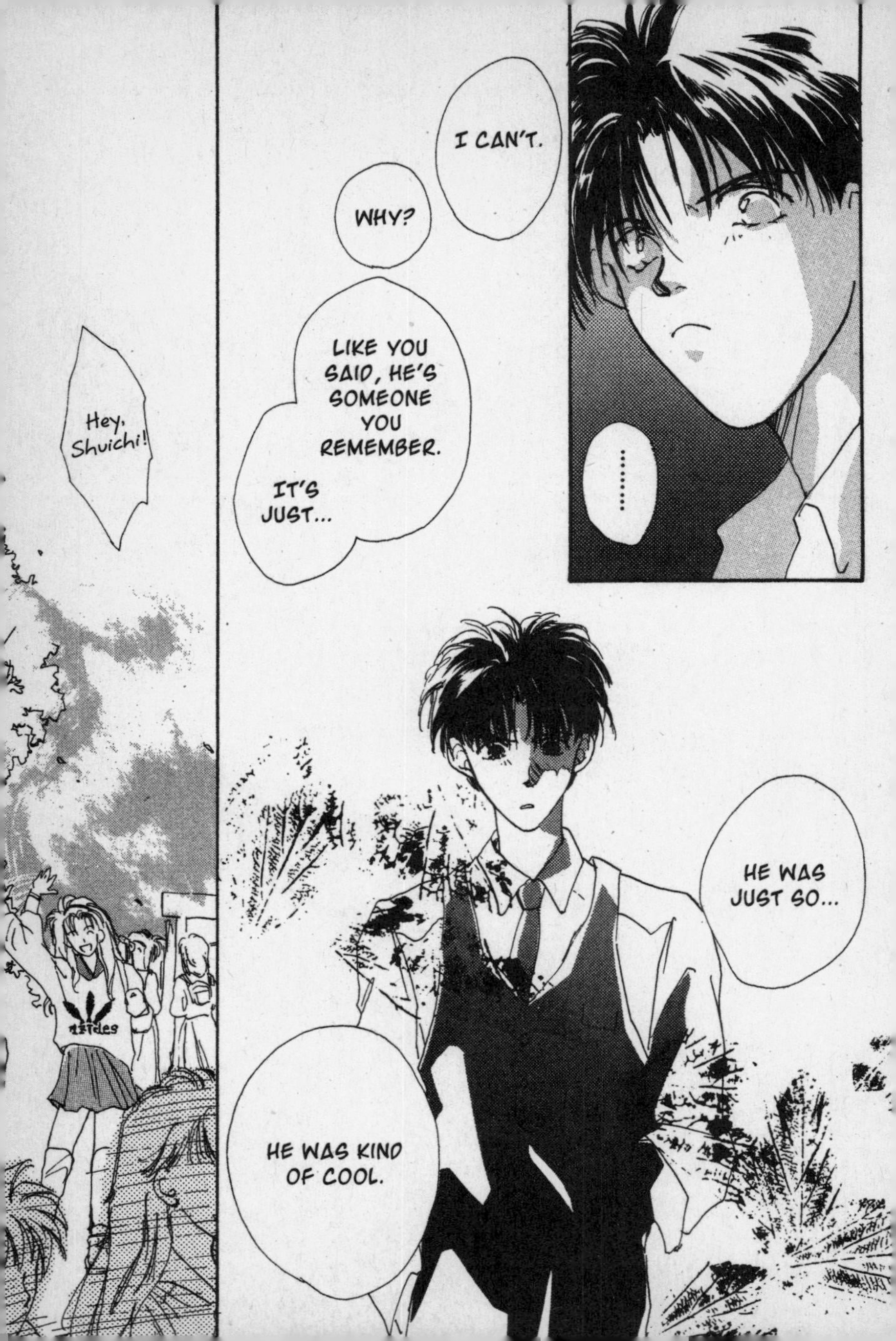
......
I CAN'T.
WHY?
LIKE YOU SAID, HE'S SOMEONE YOU REMEMBER.
IT'S JUST...
HE WAS JUST SO...
HE WAS KIND OF COOL.
Hey, Shuichi!

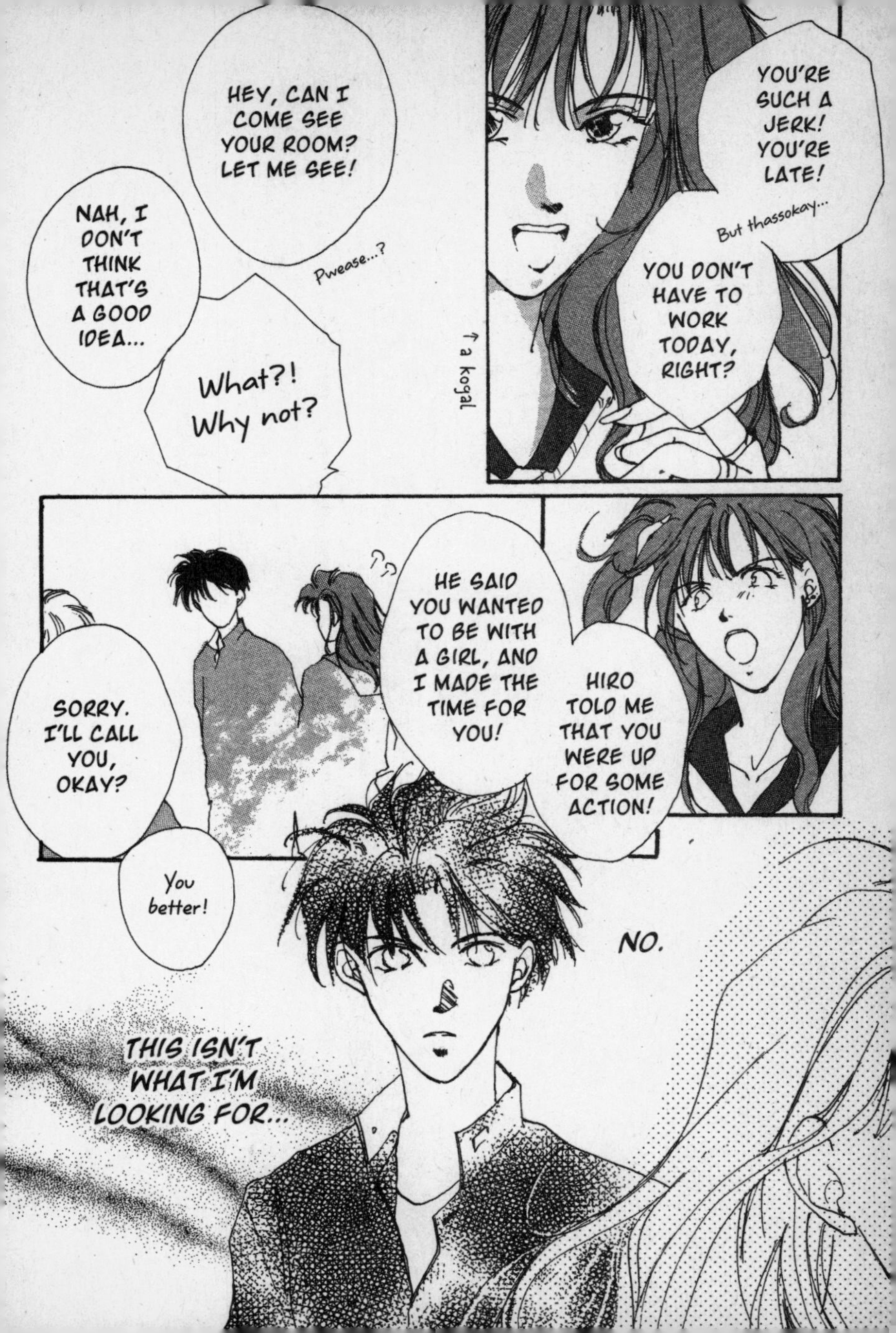
YOU'RE SUCH A JERK! YOU'RE LATE!
But thassokay...
YOU DON'T HAVE TO WORK TODAY, RIGHT?
↑ a kogal
HEY, CAN I COME SEE YOUR ROOM? LET ME SEE!
Pwease...?
NAH, I DON'T THINK THAT'S A GOOD IDEA...
What?! Why not?
HIRO TOLD ME THAT YOU WERE UP FOR SOME ACTION!
HE SAID YOU WANTED TO BE WITH A GIRL, AND I MADE THE TIME FOR YOU!
SORRY. I'LL CALL YOU, OKAY?
You better!
NO.
THIS ISN'T WHAT I'M LOOKING FOR...

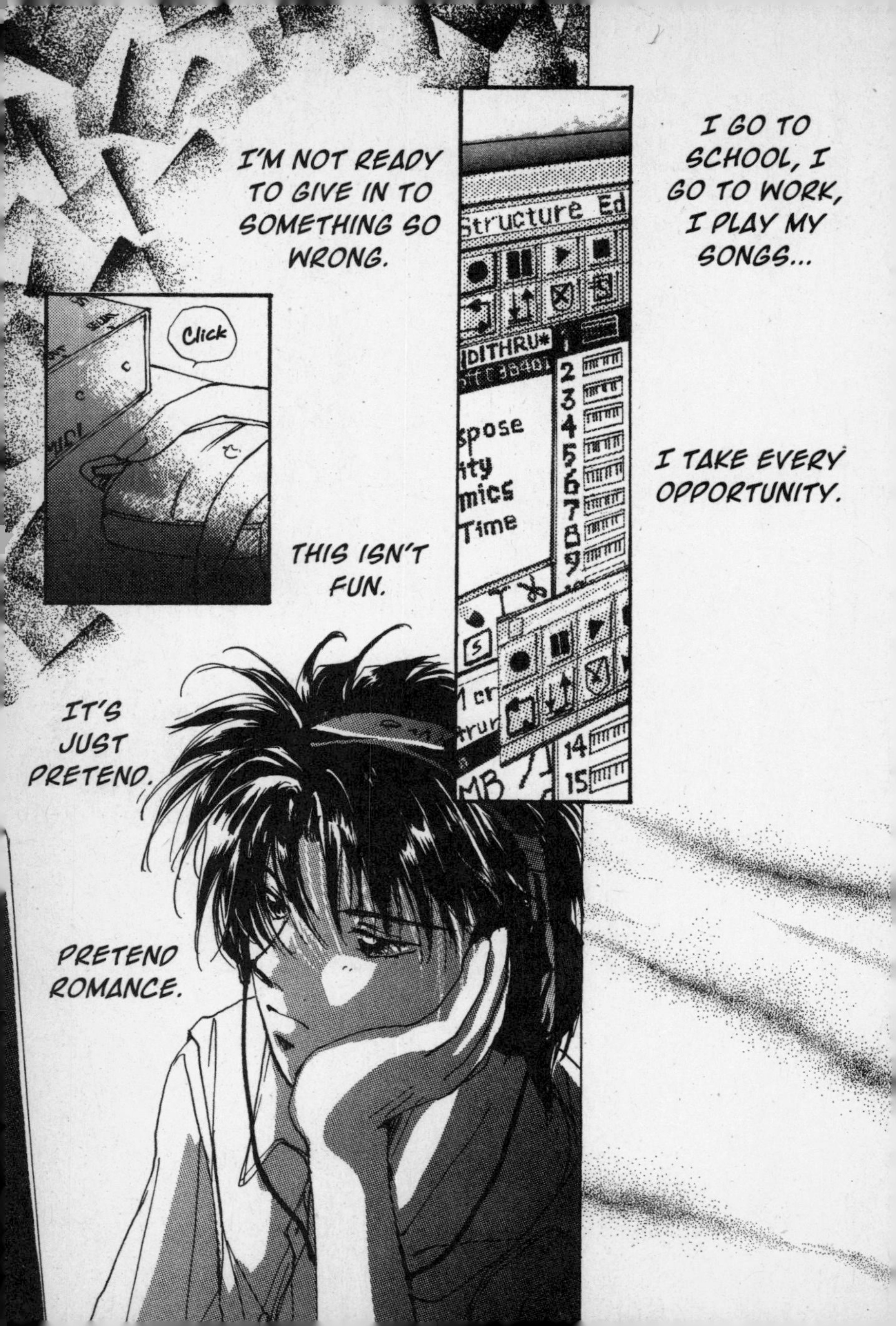
I GO TO SCHOOL, I GO TO WORK, I PLAY MY SONGS...
I TAKE EVERY OPPORTUNITY.
Structure Ed
DITHRU*
spose
ity
mics
Time
I'M NOT READY TO GIVE IN TO SOMETHING SO WRONG.
Click
THIS ISN'T FUN.
IT'S JUST PRETEND.
PRETEND ROMANCE.

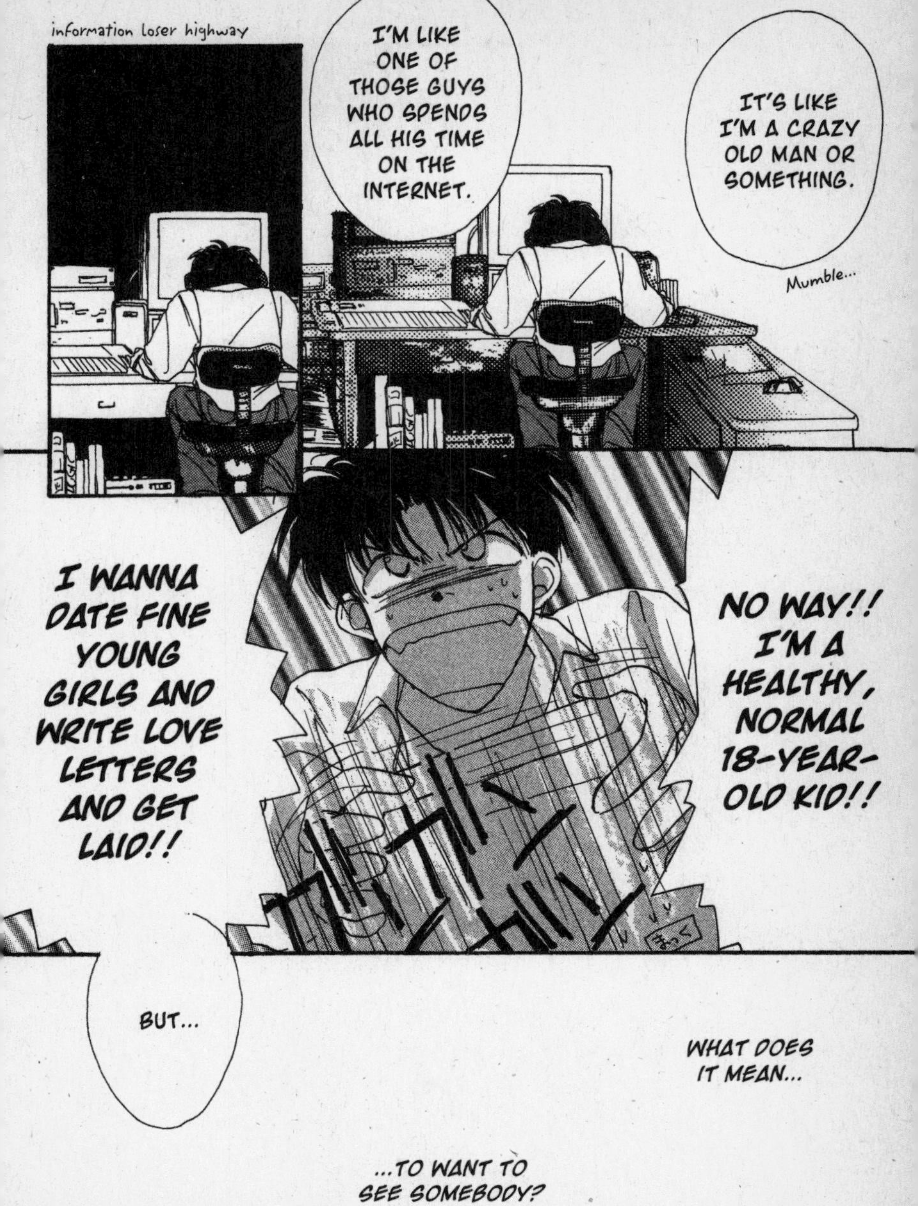
information loser highway
IT'S LIKE I'M A CRAZY OLD MAN OR SOMETHING.
Mumble...
I'M LIKE ONE OF THOSE GUYS WHO SPENDS ALL HIS TIME ON THE INTERNET.
NO WAY!! I'M A HEALTHY, NORMAL 18-YEAR-OLD KID!!
I WANNA DATE FINE YOUNG GIRLS AND WRITE LOVE LETTERS AND GET LAID!!
BUT...
WHAT DOES IT MEAN...
...TO WANT TO SEE SOMEBODY?

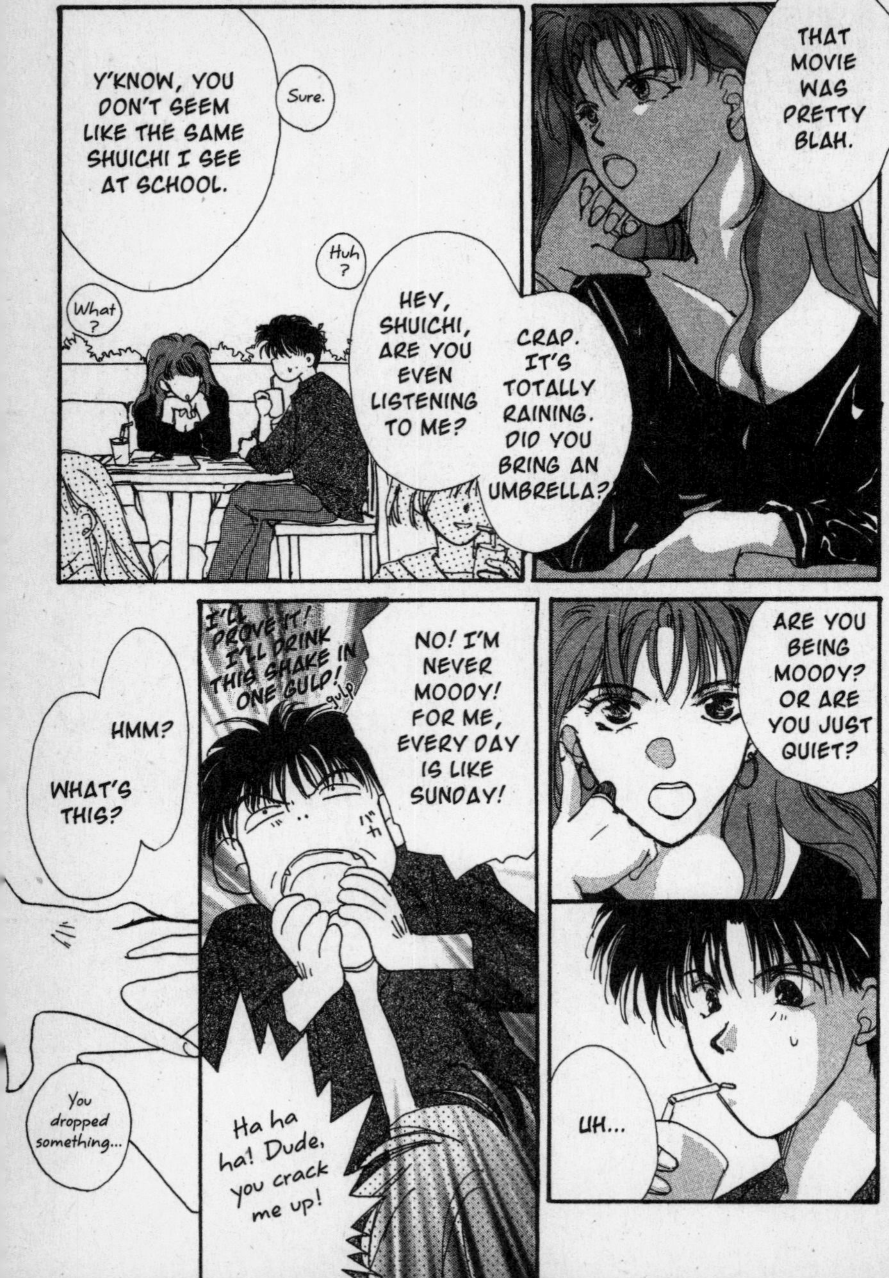
THAT MOVIE WAS PRETTY BLAH.
Y'KNOW, YOU DON'T SEEM LIKE THE SAME SHUICHI I SEE AT SCHOOL.
Sure.
CRAP. IT'S TOTALLY RAINING. DID YOU BRING AN UMBRELLA?
HEY, SHUICHI, ARE YOU EVEN LISTENING TO ME?
Huh?
What?
ARE YOU BEING MOODY? OR ARE YOU JUST QUIET?
UH...
NO! I'M NEVER MOODY! FOR ME, EVERY DAY IS LIKE SUNDAY!
I'LL PROVE IT! I'LL DRINK THIS SHAKE IN ONE GULP!
gulp
Ha ha ha! Dude, you crack me up!
HMM? WHAT'S THIS?
You dropped something...

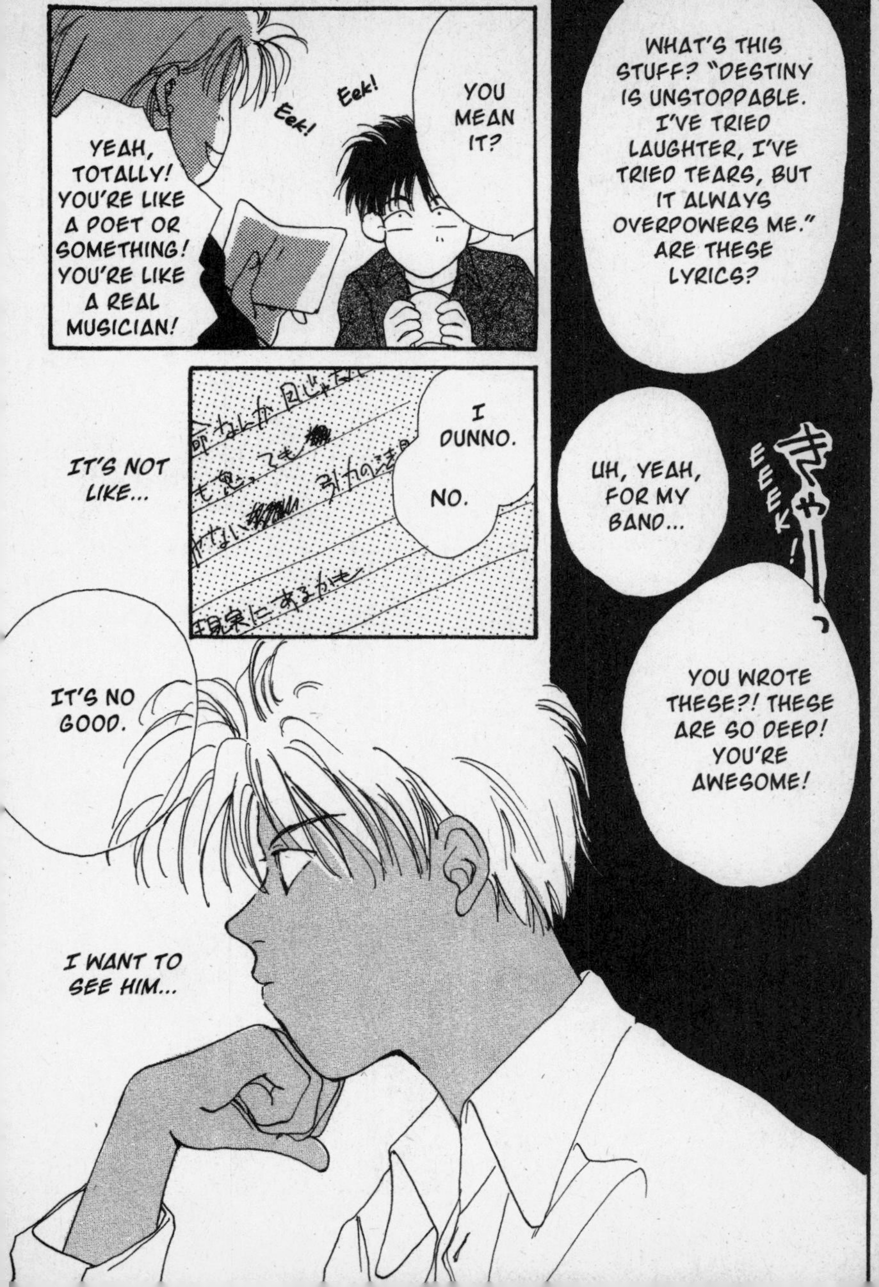
WHAT'S THIS STUFF? "DESTINY IS UNSTOPPABLE. I'VE TRIED LAUGHTER, I'VE TRIED TEARS, BUT IT ALWAYS OVERPOWERS ME." ARE THESE LYRICS?
UH, YEAH, FOR MY BAND...
EEEK!
YOU WROTE THESE?! THESE ARE SO DEEP! YOU'RE AWESOME!
YOU MEAN IT?
Eek!
Eek!
YEAH, TOTALLY! YOU'RE LIKE A POET OR SOMETHING! YOU'RE LIKE A REAL MUSICIAN!
I DUNNO.
NO.
IT'S NOT LIKE...
IT'S NO GOOD.
I WANT TO SEE HIM...

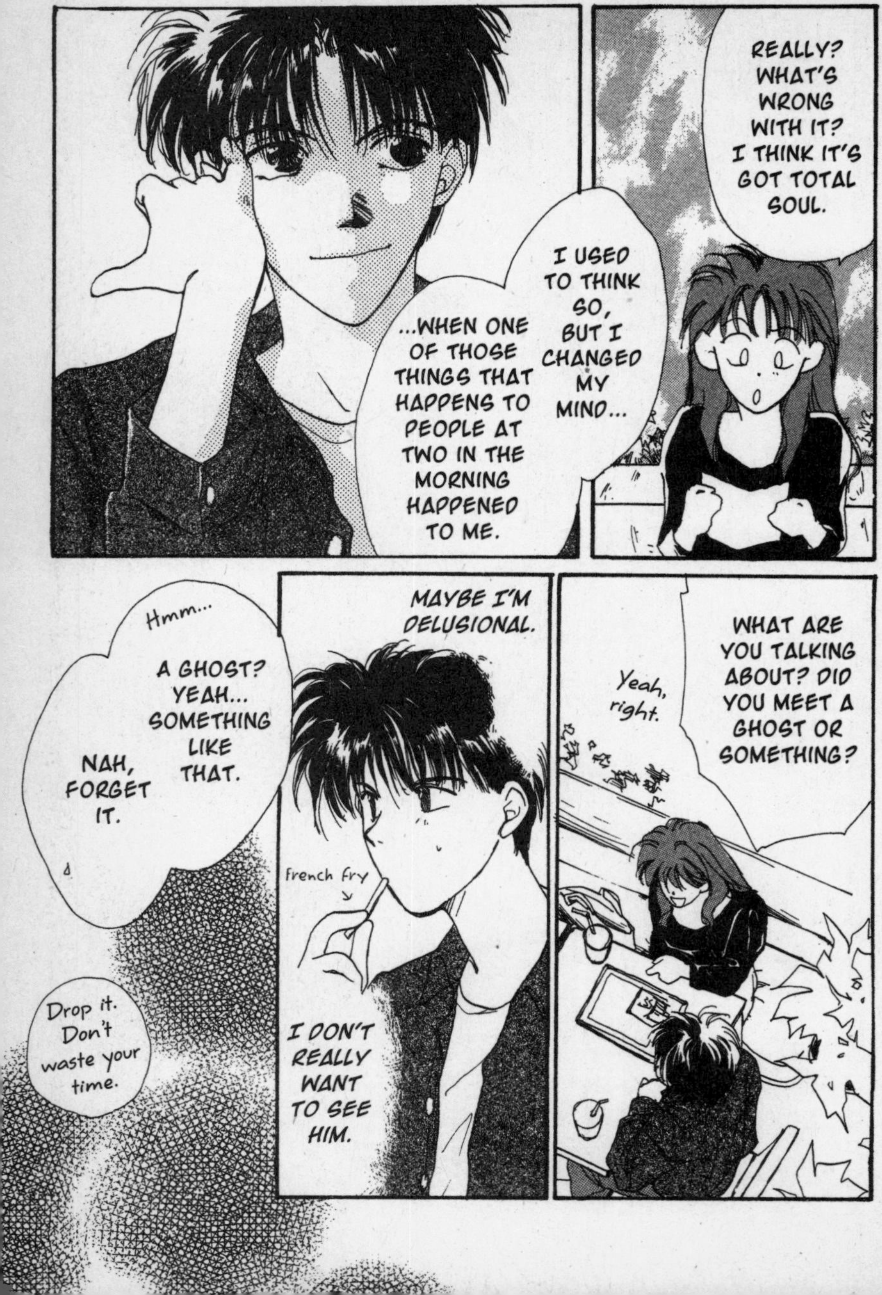
REALLY? WHAT'S WRONG WITH IT? I THINK IT'S GOT TOTAL SOUL.
I USED TO THINK SO, BUT I CHANGED MY MIND...
...WHEN ONE OF THOSE THINGS THAT HAPPENS TO PEOPLE AT TWO IN THE MORNING HAPPENED TO ME.
WHAT ARE YOU TALKING ABOUT? DID YOU MEET A GHOST OR SOMETHING?
Yeah, right.
MAYBE I'M DELUSIONAL.
French fry
I DON'T REALLY WANT TO SEE HIM.
Hmm...
A GHOST? YEAH... SOMETHING LIKE THAT.
NAH, FORGET IT.
Drop it. Don't waste your time.

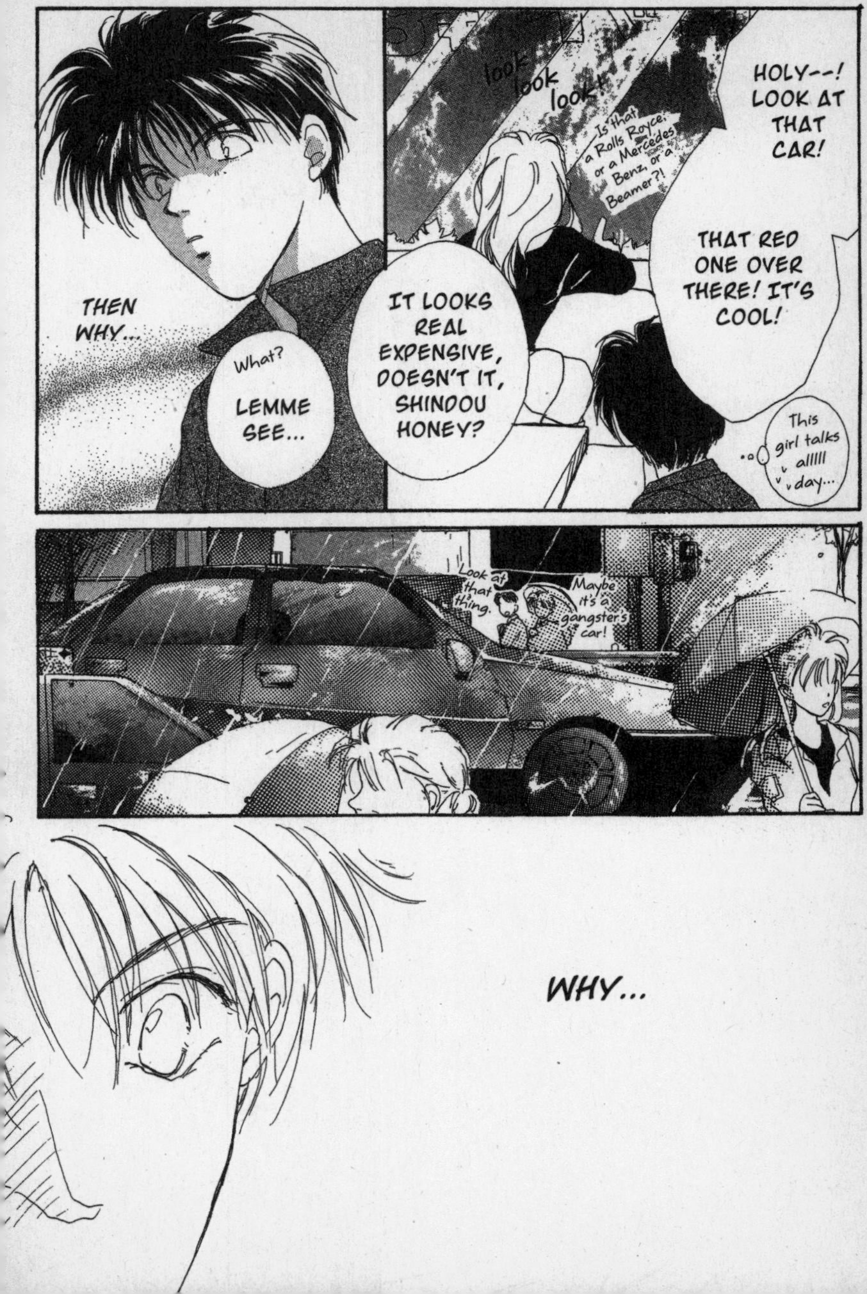

HOLY--! LOOK AT THAT CAR!
look look look!
Is that a Rolls Royce, or a Mercedes Benz, or a Beamer?!
THAT RED ONE OVER THERE! IT'S COOL!
IT LOOKS REAL EXPENSIVE, DOESN'T IT, SHINDOU HONEY?
This girl talks alllll day...
What?
LEMME SEE...
THEN WHY...
Maybe it's a gangster's car!
Look at that thing.
WHY...

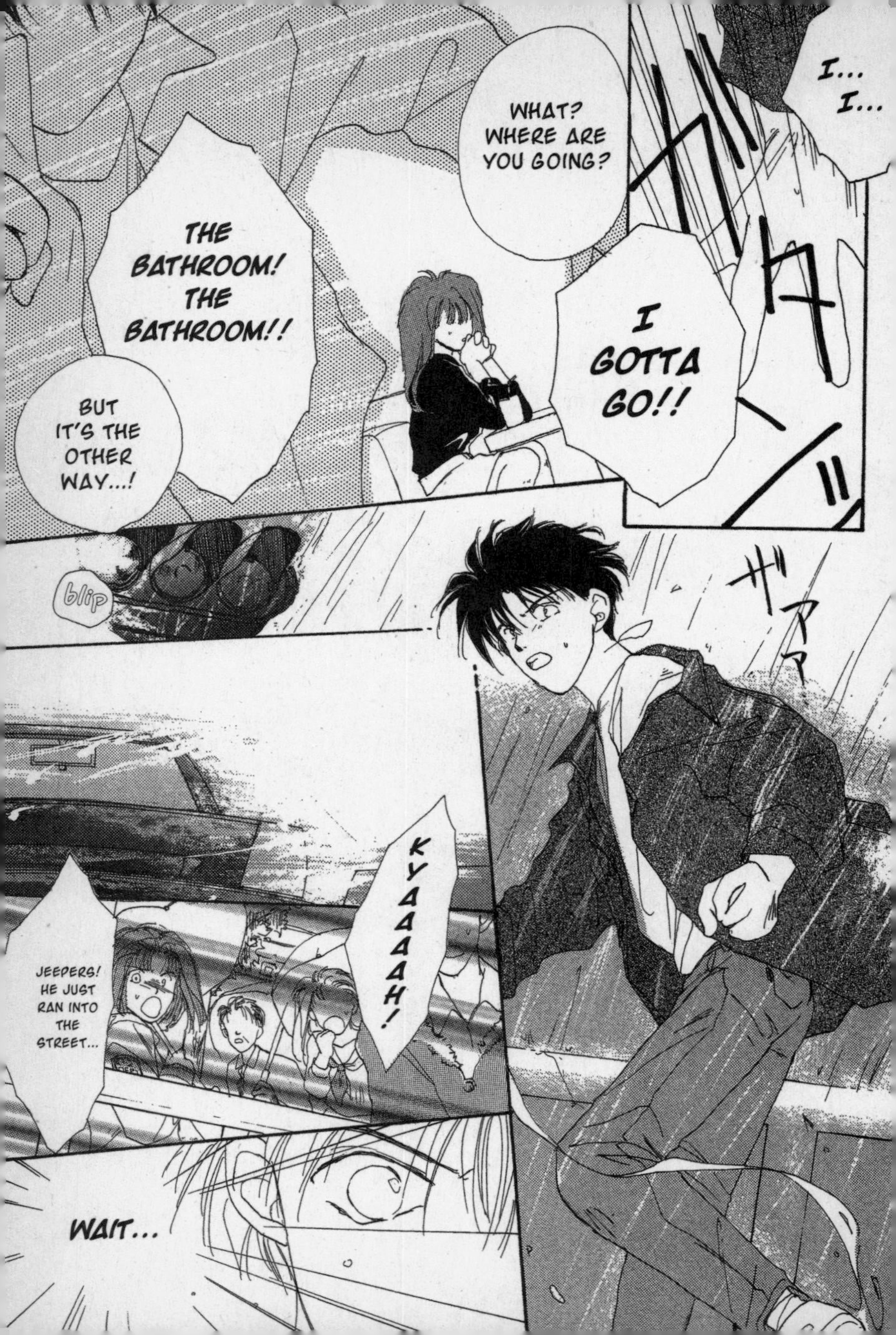
I... I...
I GOTTA GO!!
WHAT? WHERE ARE YOU GOING?
THE BATHROOM! THE BATHROOM!!
BUT IT'S THE OTHER WAY...!
blip
ザァァ
KYAAAAAH!
JEEPERS! HE JUST RAN INTO THE STREET...
WAIT...

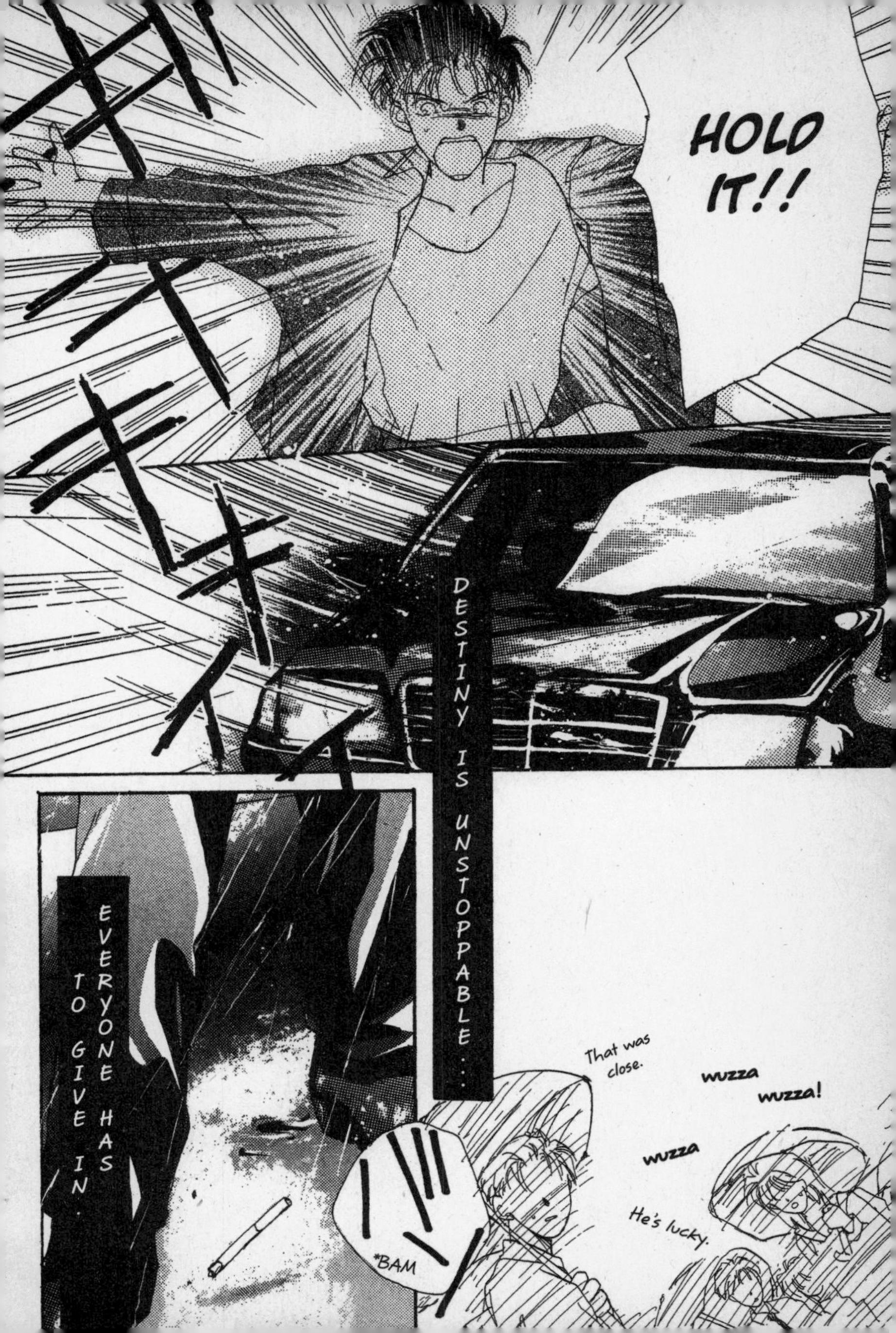
HOLD IT!!
DESTINY IS UNSTOPPABLE . . .
That was close.
wuzza wuzza!
wuzza
He's lucky.
*BAM
EVERYONE HAS TO GIVE IN.

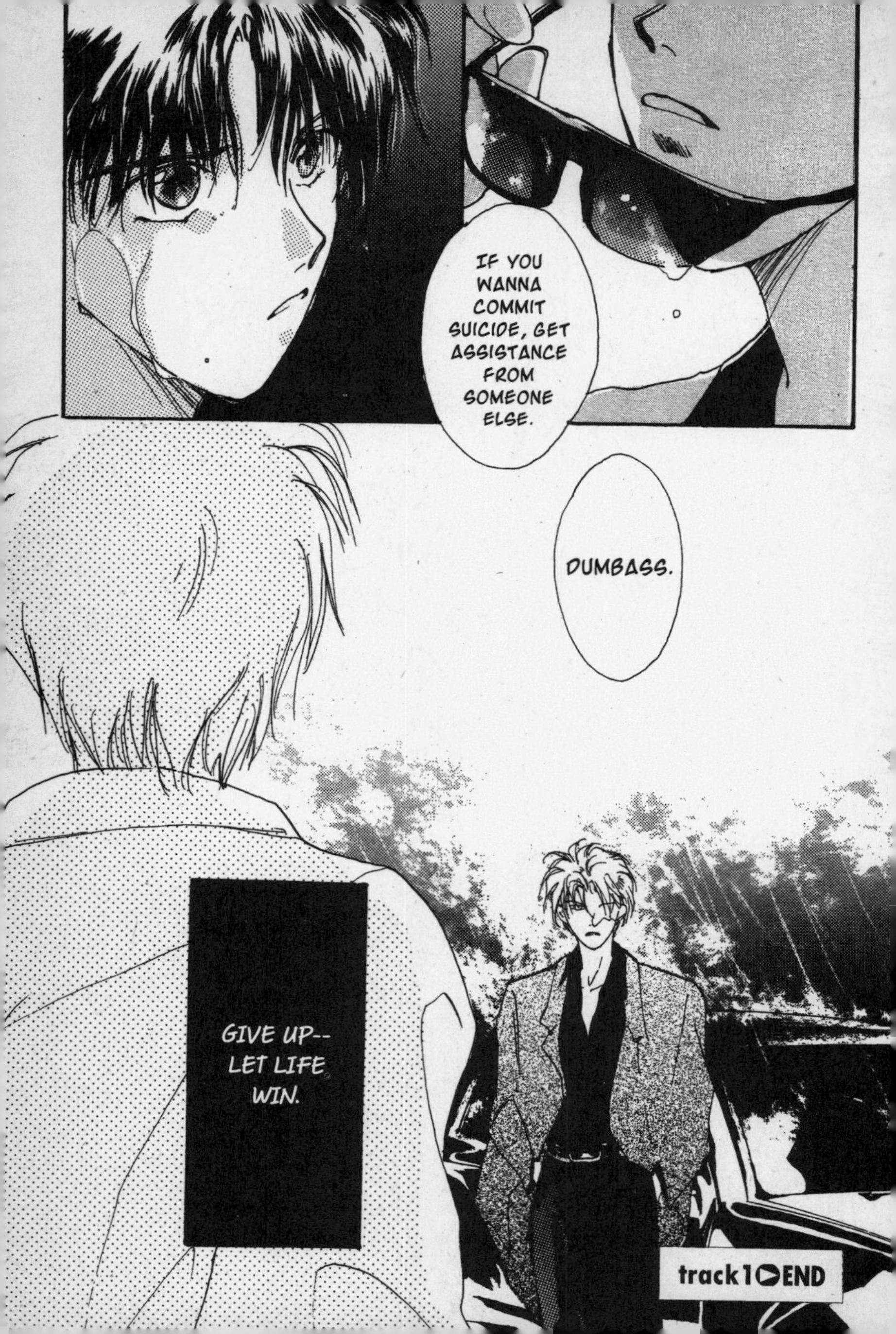
IF YOU WANNA COMMIT SUICIDE, GET ASSISTANCE FROM SOMEONE ELSE.
DUMBASS.
GIVE UP-- LET LIFE WIN.
track1 END

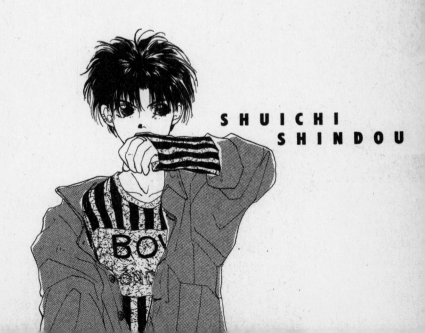

SHUICHI
SHINDOU

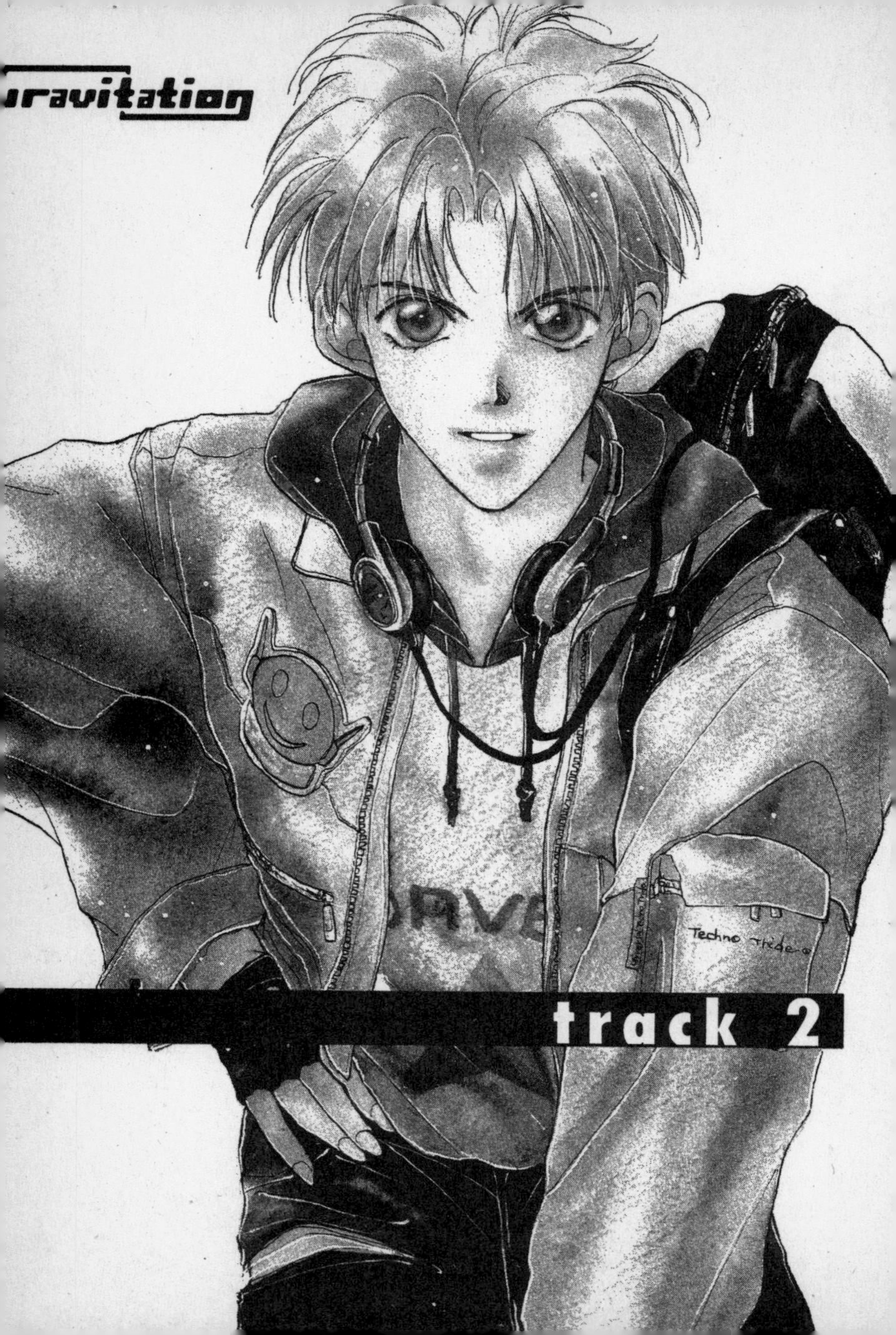
ravitation
track 2

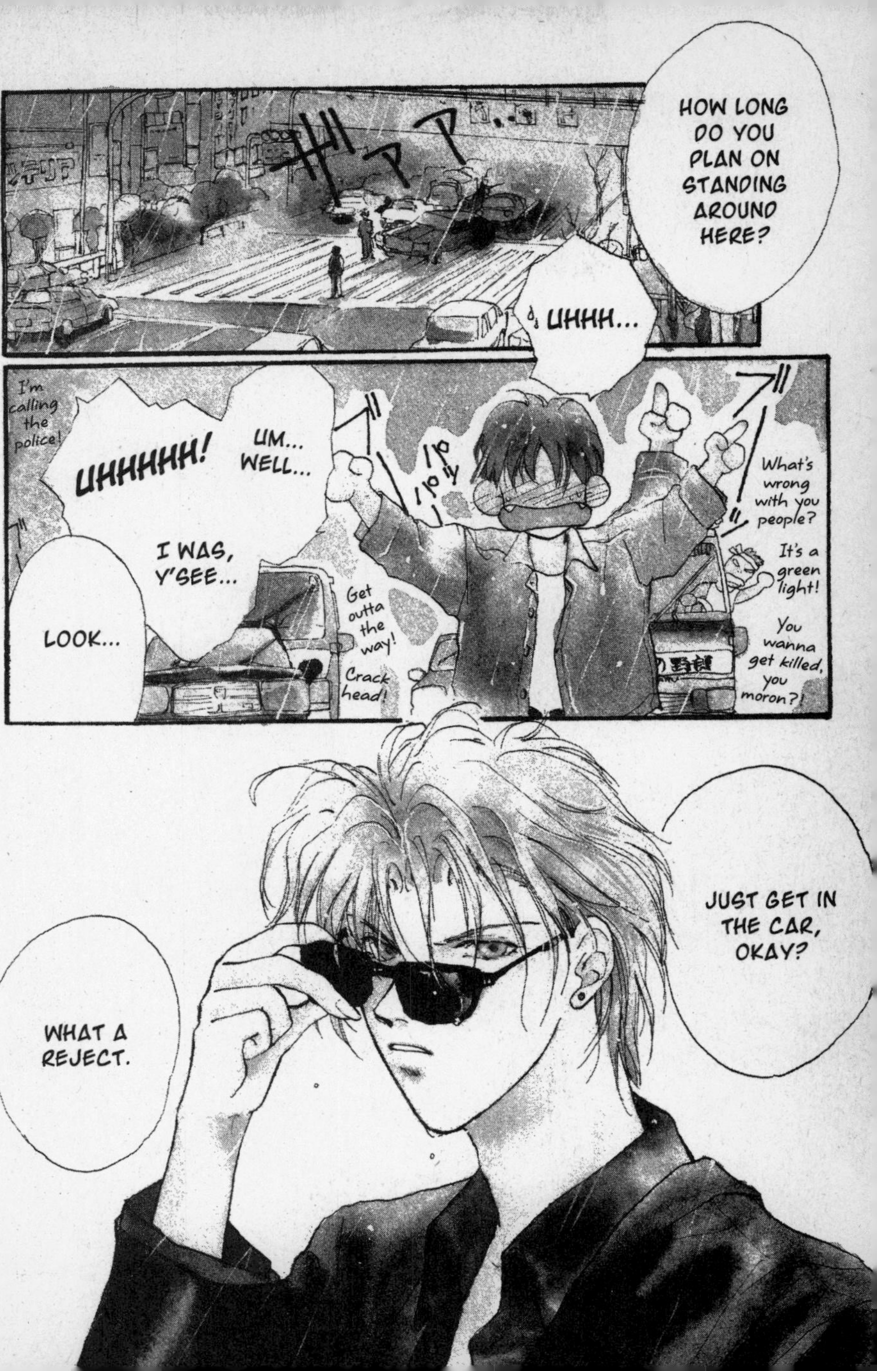
HOW LONG DO YOU PLAN ON STANDING AROUND HERE?
UHHH...
What's wrong with you people?
It's a green light!
You wanna get killed, you moron?!
Get outta the way!
Crack head!
UM... WELL...
UHHHHH!
I'm calling the police!
I WAS, Y'SEE...
LOOK...
JUST GET IN THE CAR, OKAY?
WHAT A REJECT.

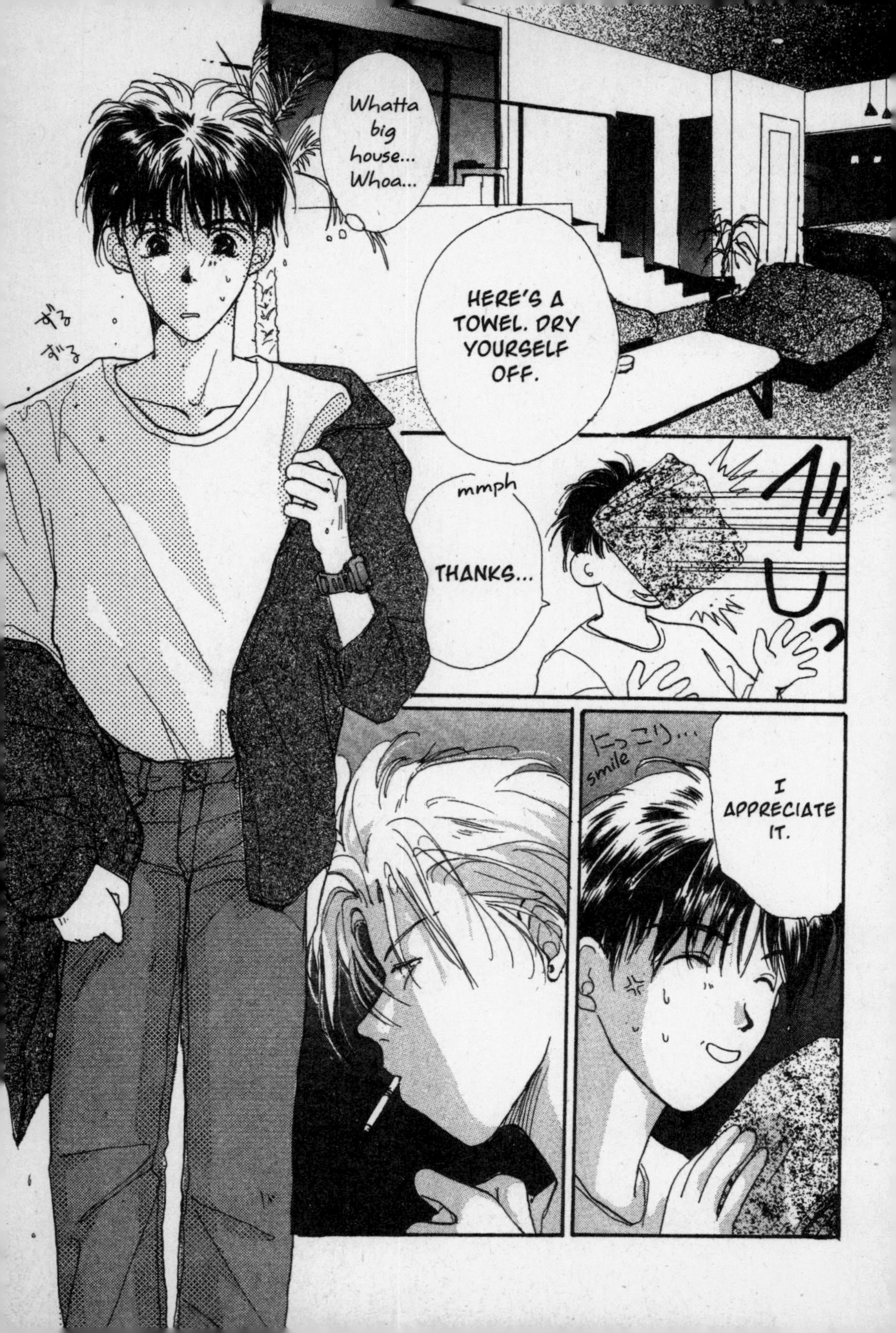
Whatta big house... Whoa...
ずる ずる
HERE'S A TOWEL. DRY YOURSELF OFF.
mmph
THANKS...
にっこり…
smile
I APPRECIATE IT.

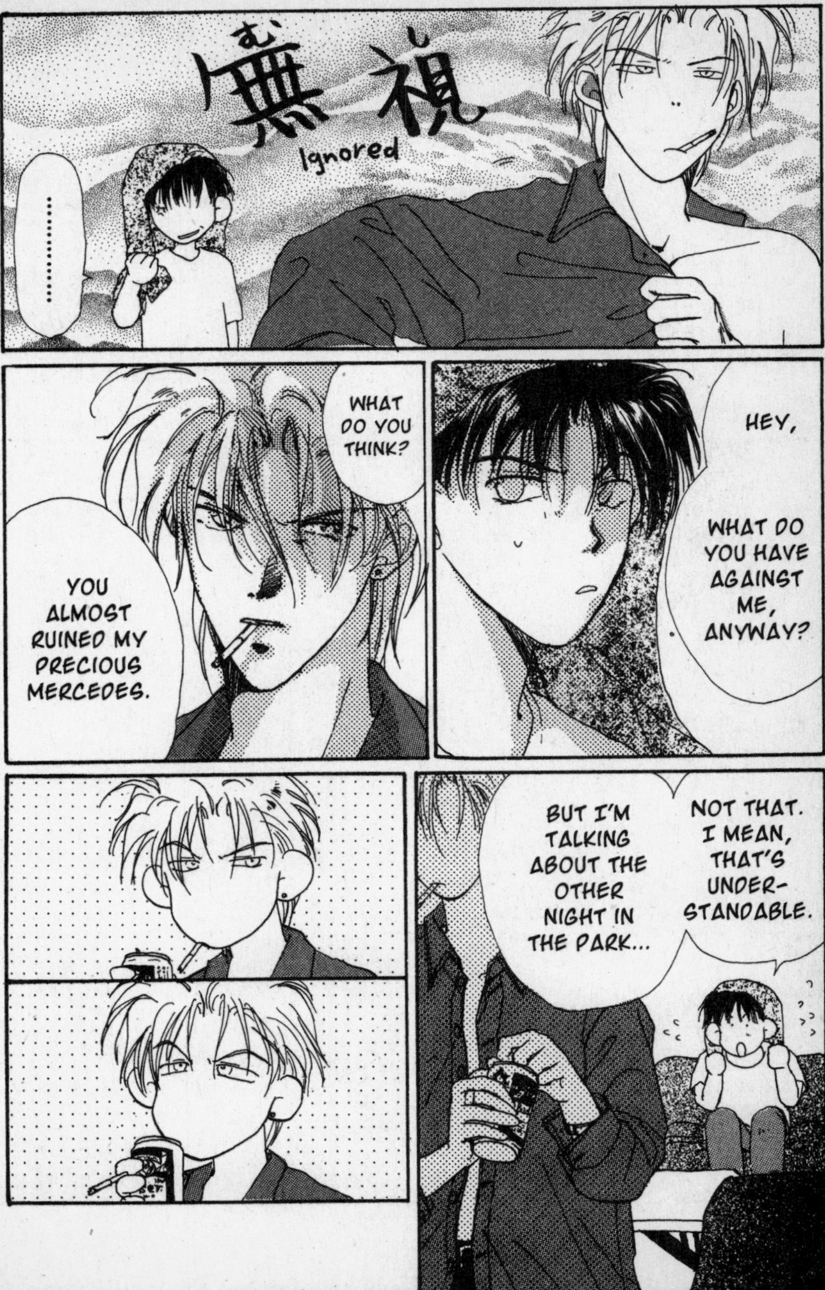
無視
むし
Ignored
......
HEY,
WHAT DO YOU HAVE AGAINST ME, ANYWAY?
WHAT DO YOU THINK?
YOU ALMOST RUINED MY PRECIOUS MERCEDES.
NOT THAT. I MEAN, THAT'S UNDER-STANDABLE.
BUT I'M TALKING ABOUT THE OTHER NIGHT IN THE PARK...

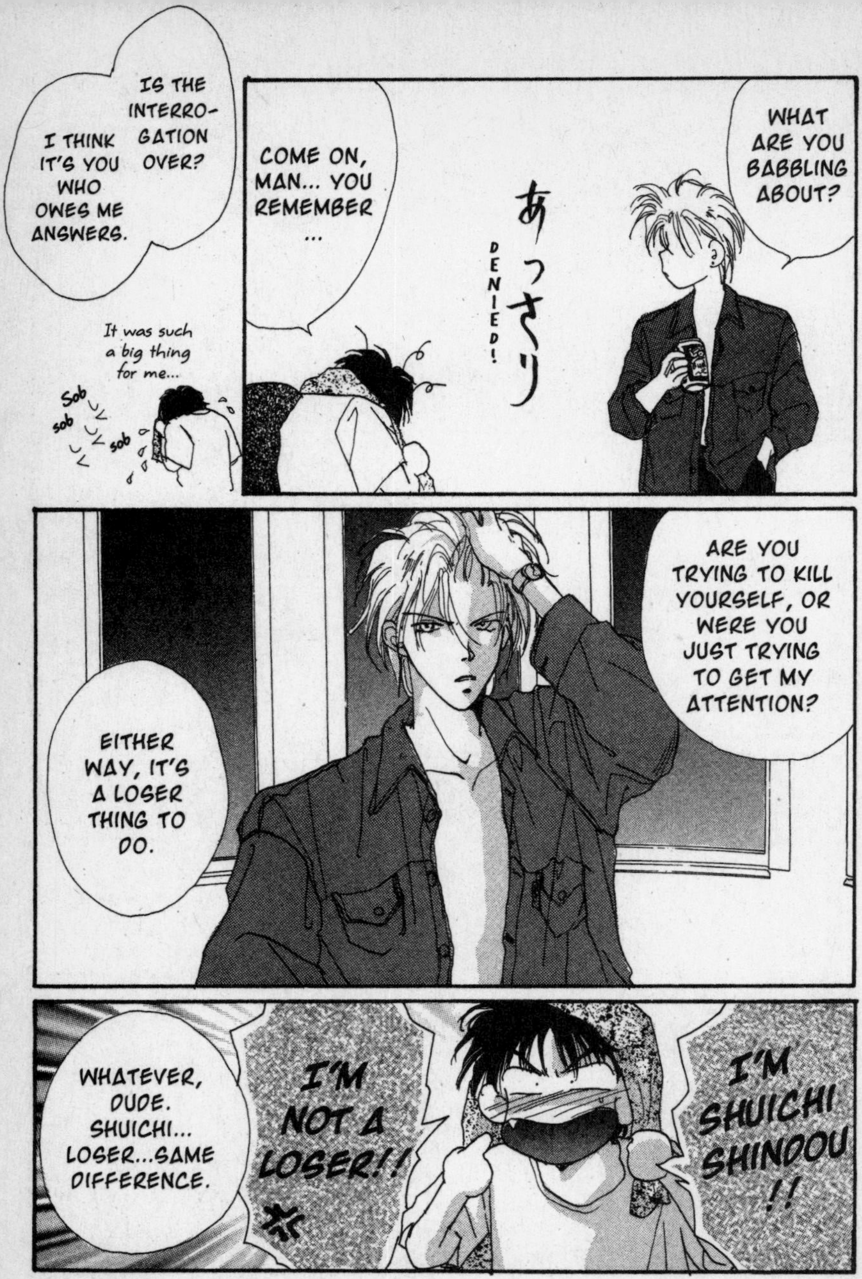
WHAT ARE YOU BABBLING ABOUT?
あっさり
DENIED!
COME ON, MAN... YOU REMEMBER ...
IS THE INTERROGATION OVER?
I THINK IT'S YOU WHO OWES ME ANSWERS.
It was such a big thing for me...
Sob sob sob
ARE YOU TRYING TO KILL YOURSELF, OR WERE YOU JUST TRYING TO GET MY ATTENTION?
EITHER WAY, IT'S A LOSER THING TO DO.
I'M SHUICHI SHINDOU!!
I'M NOT A LOSER!!
WHATEVER, DUDE. SHUICHI... LOSER...SAME DIFFERENCE.

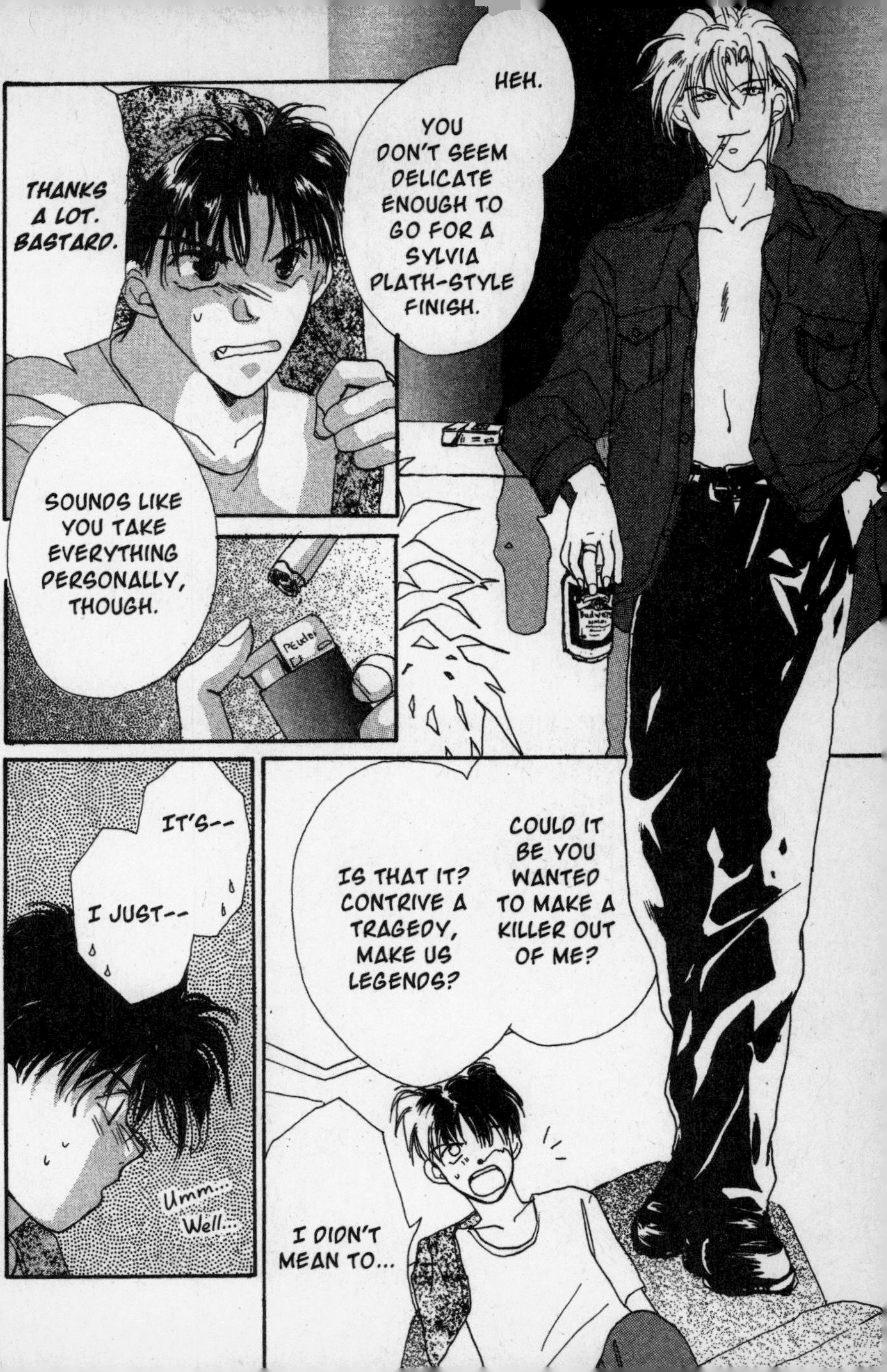
HEH.
YOU DON'T SEEM DELICATE ENOUGH TO GO FOR A SYLVIA PLATH-STYLE FINISH.
THANKS A LOT. BASTARD.
SOUNDS LIKE YOU TAKE EVERYTHING PERSONALLY, THOUGH.
COULD IT BE YOU WANTED TO MAKE A KILLER OUT OF ME?
IS THAT IT? CONTRIVE A TRAGEDY, MAKE US LEGENDS?
I DIDN'T MEAN TO...
IT'S--
I JUST--
Umm... Well...

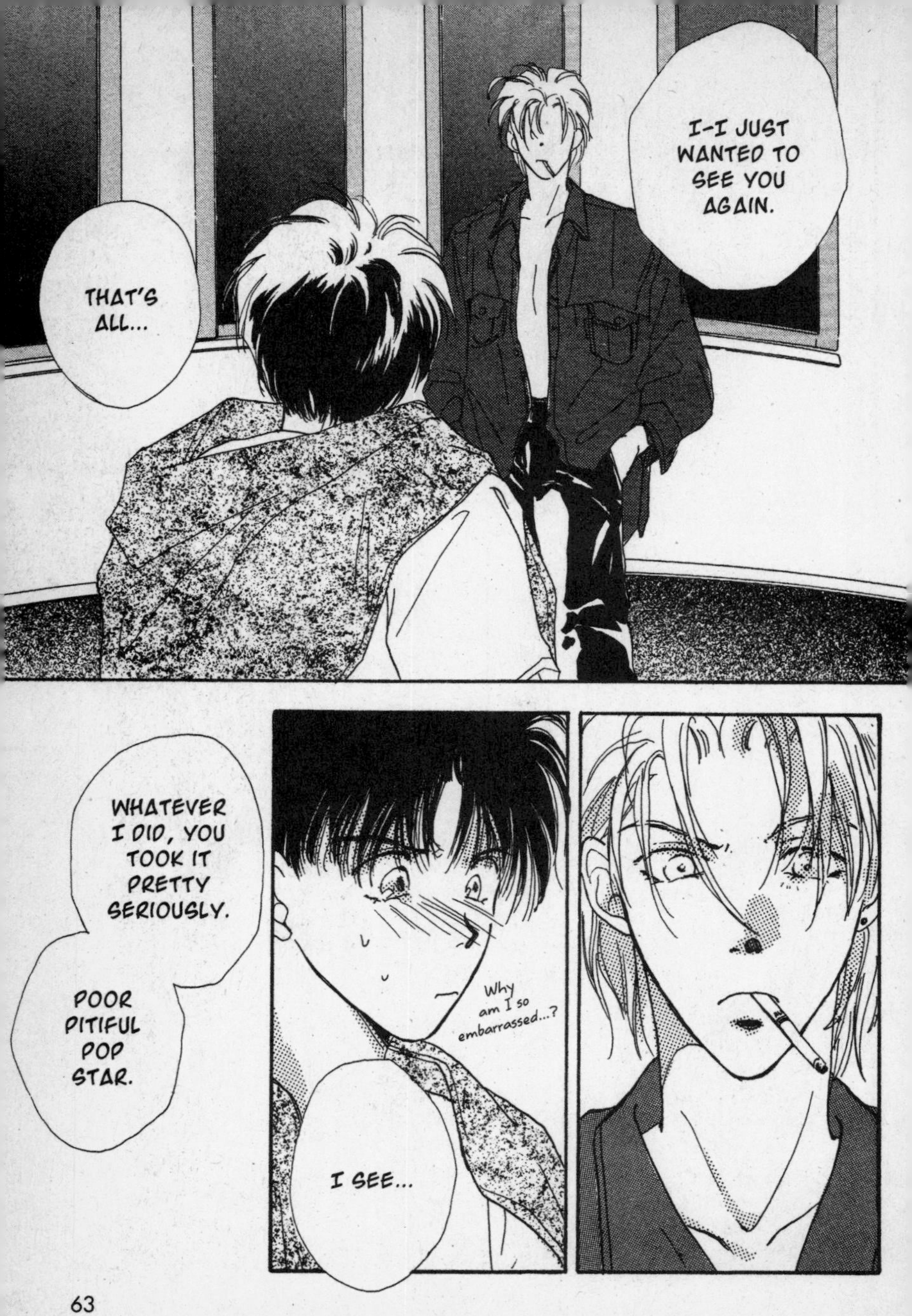

I-I JUST WANTED TO SEE YOU AGAIN.
THAT'S ALL...
Why am I so embarrassed...?
I SEE...
WHATEVER I DID, YOU TOOK IT PRETTY SERIOUSLY.
POOR PITIFUL POP STAR.

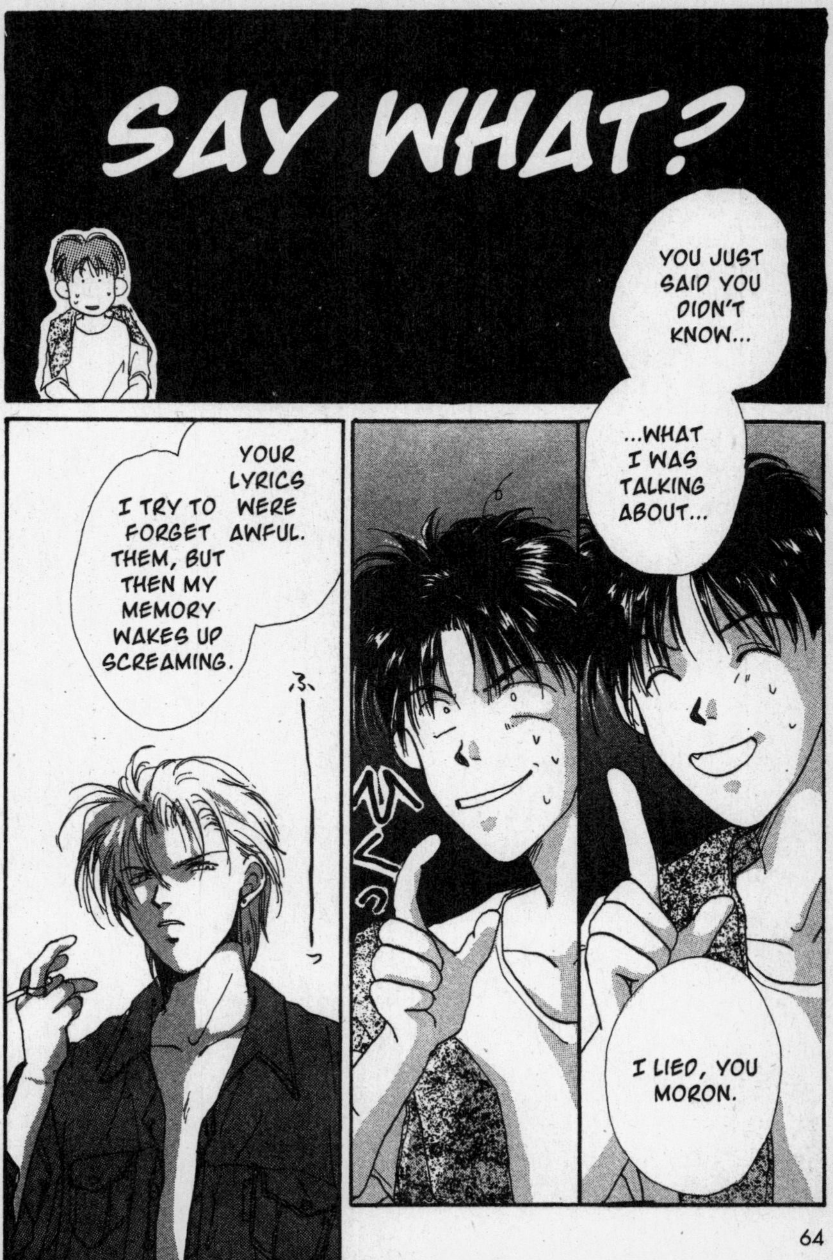
SAY WHAT?
YOU JUST SAID YOU DIDN'T KNOW...
...WHAT I WAS TALKING ABOUT...
I LIED, YOU MORON.
YOUR LYRICS WERE AWFUL.
I TRY TO FORGET THEM, BUT THEN MY MEMORY WAKES UP SCREAMING.
ふー

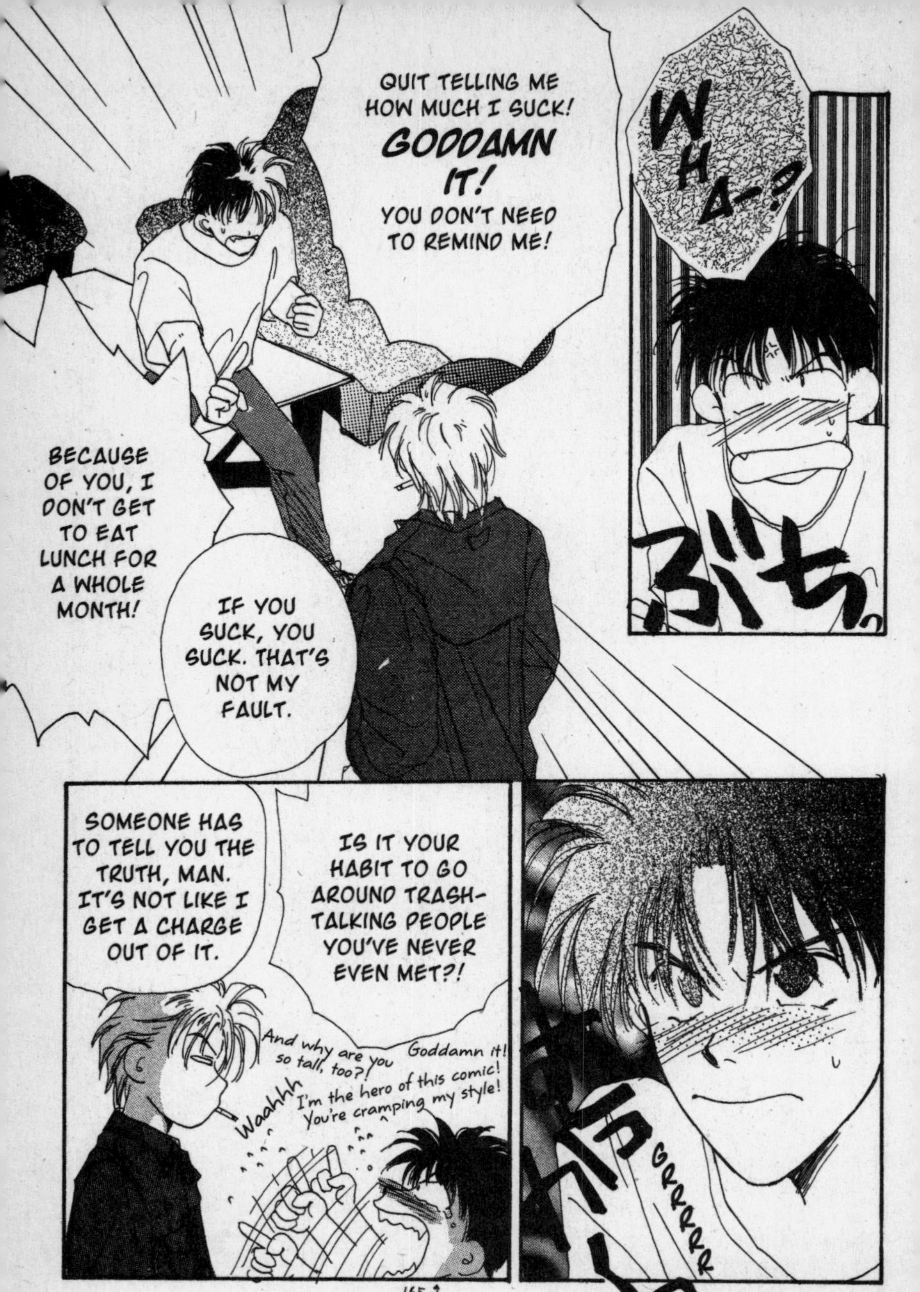
WHA-?!
ぶち
QUIT TELLING ME HOW MUCH I SUCK! GODDAMN IT! YOU DON'T NEED TO REMIND ME!
BECAUSE OF YOU, I DON'T GET TO EAT LUNCH FOR A WHOLE MONTH!
IF YOU SUCK, YOU SUCK. THAT'S NOT MY FAULT.
GRRRRRR
IS IT YOUR HABIT TO GO AROUND TRASH-TALKING PEOPLE YOU'VE NEVER EVEN MET?!
SOMEONE HAS TO TELL YOU THE TRUTH, MAN. IT'S NOT LIKE I GET A CHARGE OUT OF IT.
Goddamn it!
And why are you so tall, too?!
I'm the hero of this comic! You're cramping my style!
Waahhh

165

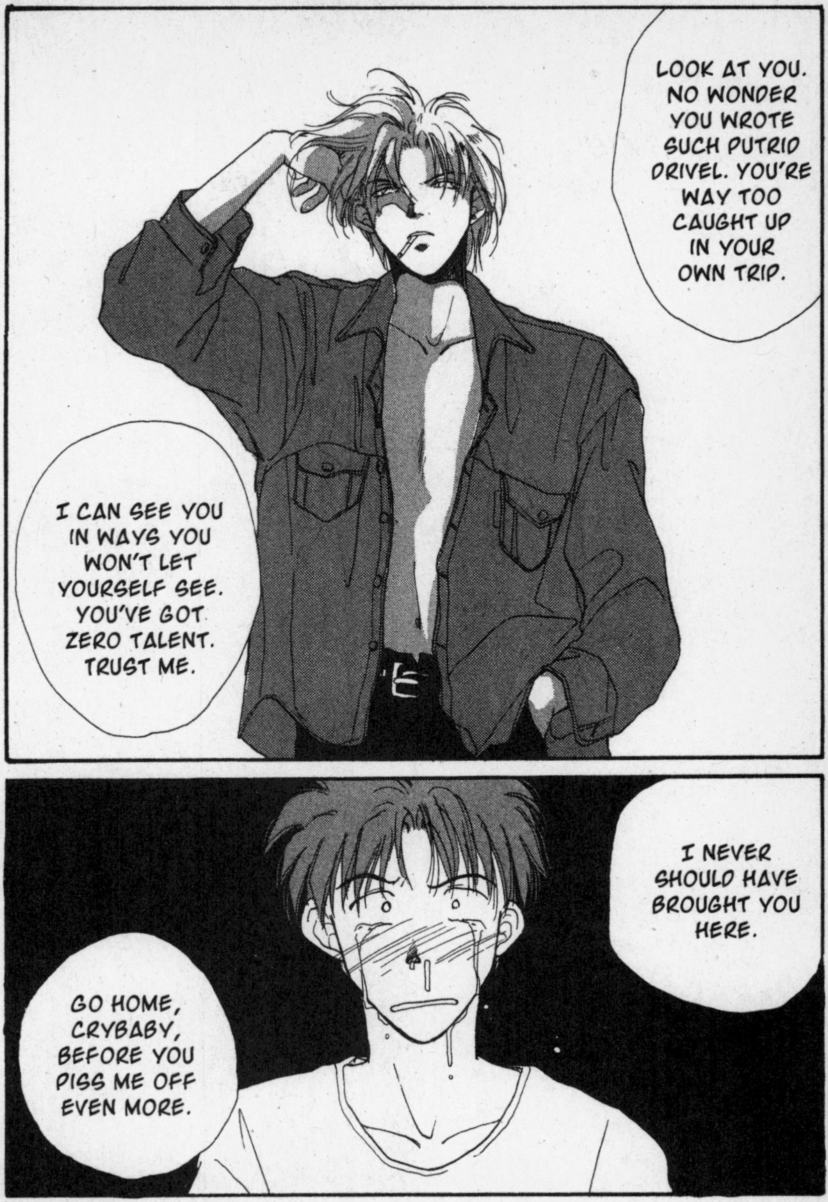
LOOK AT YOU. NO WONDER YOU WROTE SUCH PUTRID DRIVEL. YOU'RE WAY TOO CAUGHT UP IN YOUR OWN TRIP.
I CAN SEE YOU IN WAYS YOU WON'T LET YOURSELF SEE. YOU'VE GOT ZERO TALENT. TRUST ME.
I NEVER SHOULD HAVE BROUGHT YOU HERE.
GO HOME, CRYBABY, BEFORE YOU PISS ME OFF EVEN MORE.

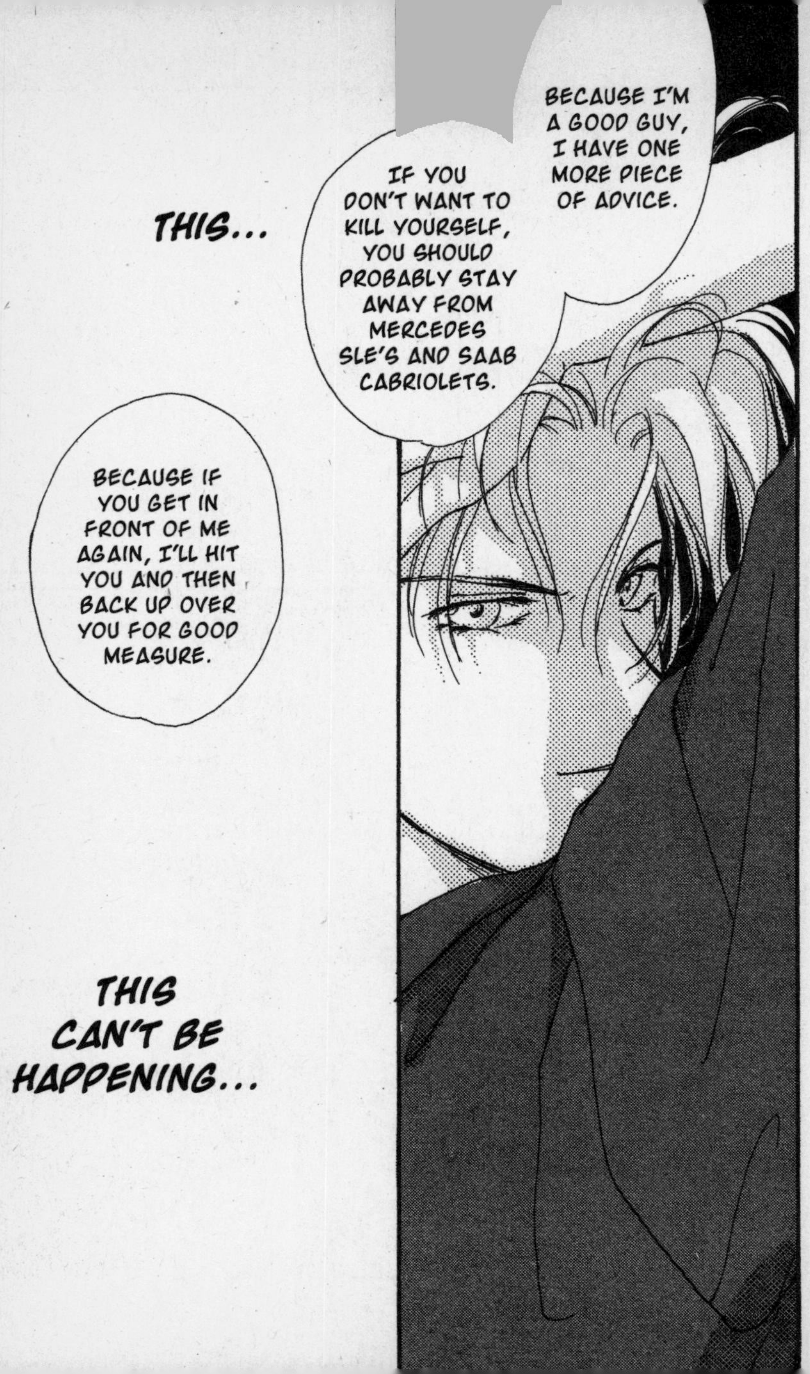
BECAUSE I'M A GOOD GUY, I HAVE ONE MORE PIECE OF ADVICE.
IF YOU DON'T WANT TO KILL YOURSELF, YOU SHOULD PROBABLY STAY AWAY FROM MERCEDES SLE'S AND SAAB CABRIOLETS.
THIS...
BECAUSE IF YOU GET IN FRONT OF ME AGAIN, I'LL HIT YOU AND THEN BACK UP OVER YOU FOR GOOD MEASURE.
THIS CAN'T BE HAPPENING...

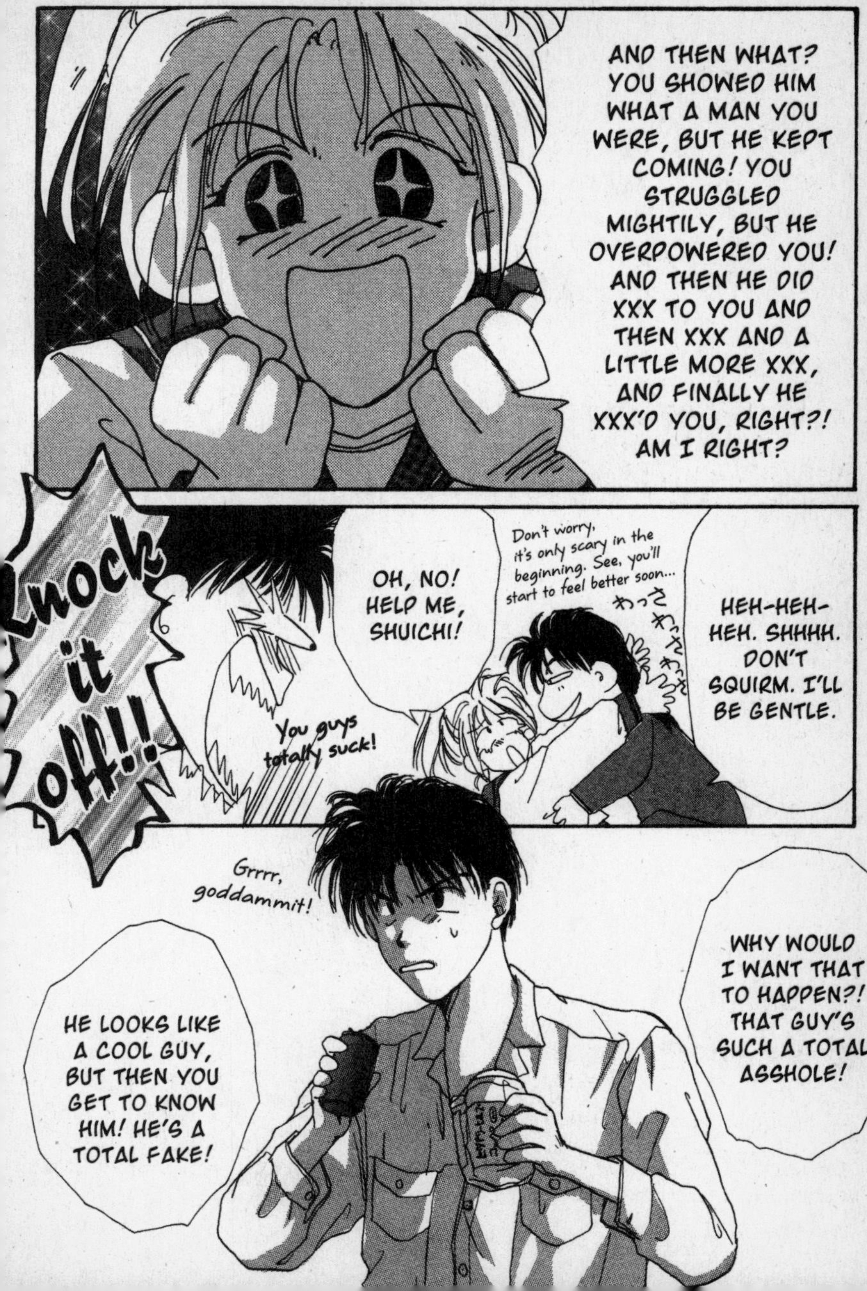
AND THEN WHAT? YOU SHOWED HIM WHAT A MAN YOU WERE, BUT HE KEPT COMING! YOU STRUGGLED MIGHTILY, BUT HE OVERPOWERED YOU! AND THEN HE DID XXX TO YOU AND THEN XXX AND A LITTLE MORE XXX, AND FINALLY HE XXX'D YOU, RIGHT?! AM I RIGHT?
HEH-HEH-HEH. SHHHH. DON'T SQUIRM. I'LL BE GENTLE.
わっさ
Don't worry, it's only scary in the beginning. See, you'll start to feel better soon...
OH, NO! HELP ME, SHUICHI!
You guys totally suck!
Knock it off!!
WHY WOULD I WANT THAT TO HAPPEN?! THAT GUY'S SUCH A TOTAL ASSHOLE!
Grrrr, goddammit!
HE LOOKS LIKE A COOL GUY, BUT THEN YOU GET TO KNOW HIM! HE'S A TOTAL FAKE!

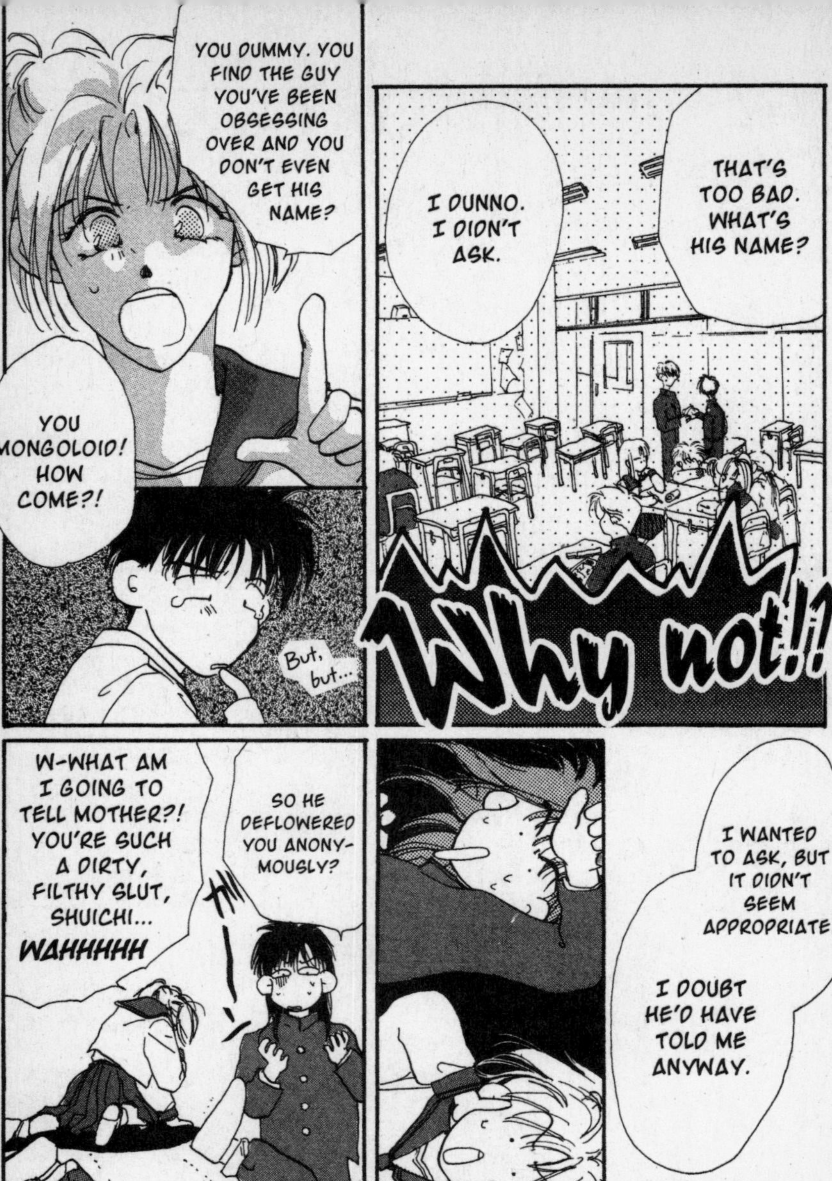
THAT'S TOO BAD. WHAT'S HIS NAME?
I DUNNO. I DIDN'T ASK.
Why not!?
YOU DUMMY. YOU FIND THE GUY YOU'VE BEEN OBSESSING OVER AND YOU DON'T EVEN GET HIS NAME?
YOU MONGOLOID! HOW COME?!
But, but...
I WANTED TO ASK, BUT IT DIDN'T SEEM APPROPRIATE.
I DOUBT HE'D HAVE TOLD ME ANYWAY.
sob
SO HE DEFLOWERED YOU ANONYMOUSLY?
W-WHAT AM I GOING TO TELL MOTHER?! YOU'RE SUCH A DIRTY, FILTHY SLUT, SHUICHI...
WAHHHHH
A BURNING QUESTION!

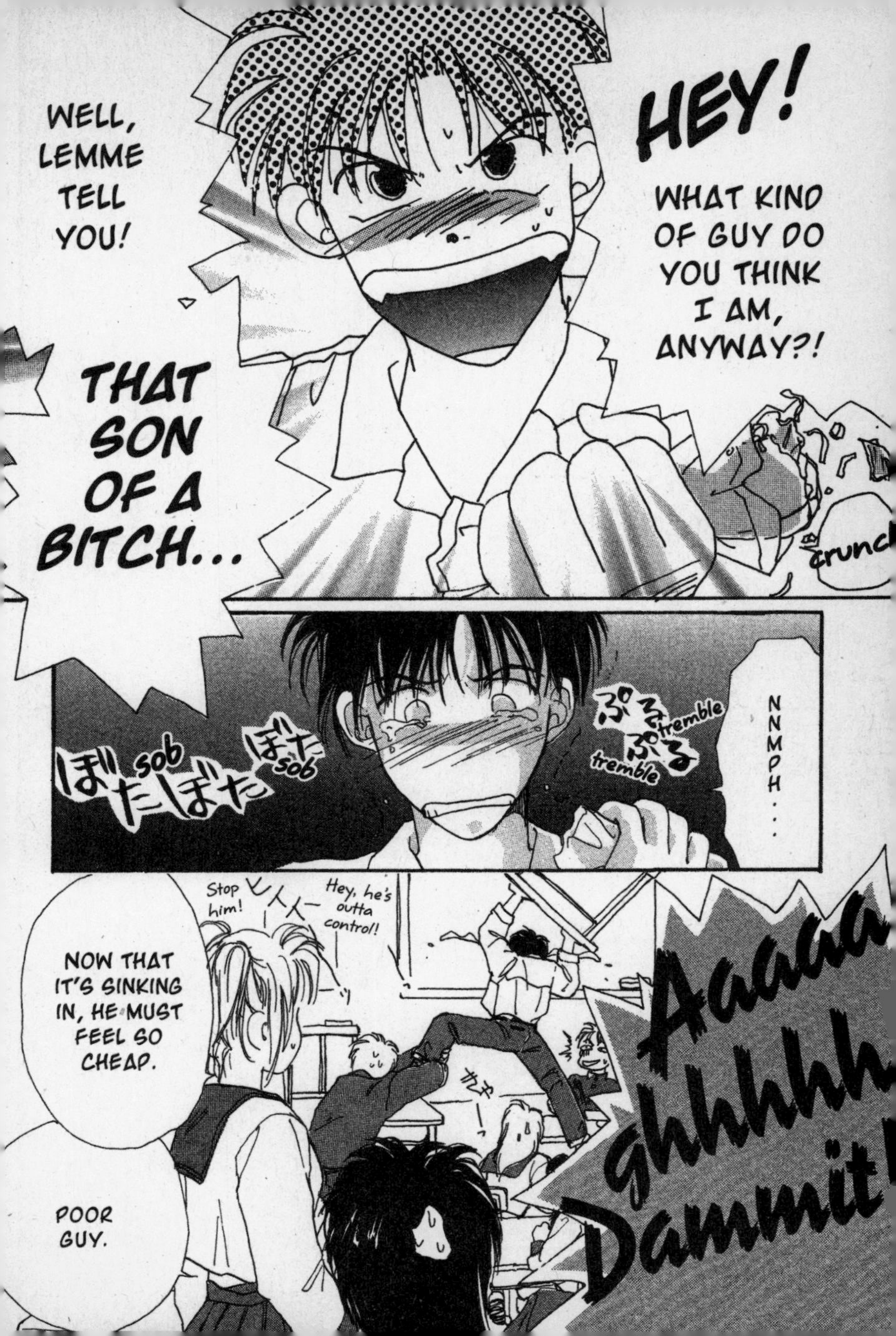
HEY!
WHAT KIND OF GUY DO YOU THINK I AM, ANYWAY?!
crunc
WELL, LEMME TELL YOU!
THAT SON OF A BITCH...
NNMPH...
ぷるぷる tremble tremble
ぼたぼた sob sob
Aaaaghhhh Dammit
Hey, he's outta control!
Stop him!
きゃー!
NOW THAT IT'S SINKING IN, HE MUST FEEL SO CHEAP.
POOR GUY.

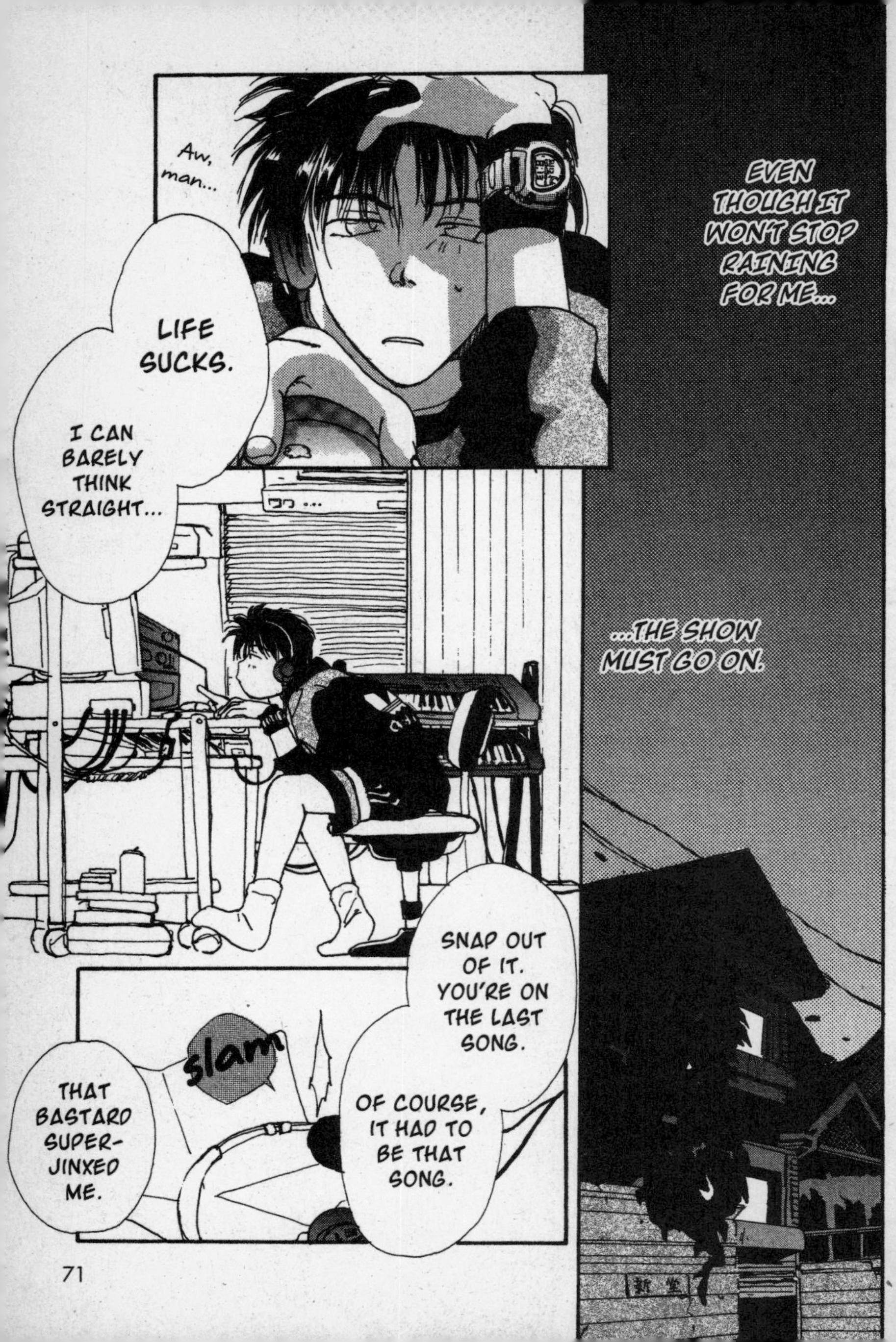
EVEN THOUGH IT WON'T STOP RAINING FOR ME...
...THE SHOW MUST GO ON.
Aw, man...
LIFE SUCKS.
I CAN BARELY THINK STRAIGHT...
SNAP OUT OF IT. YOU'RE ON THE LAST SONG.
slam
OF COURSE, IT HAD TO BE THAT SONG.
THAT BASTARD SUPER-JINXED ME.

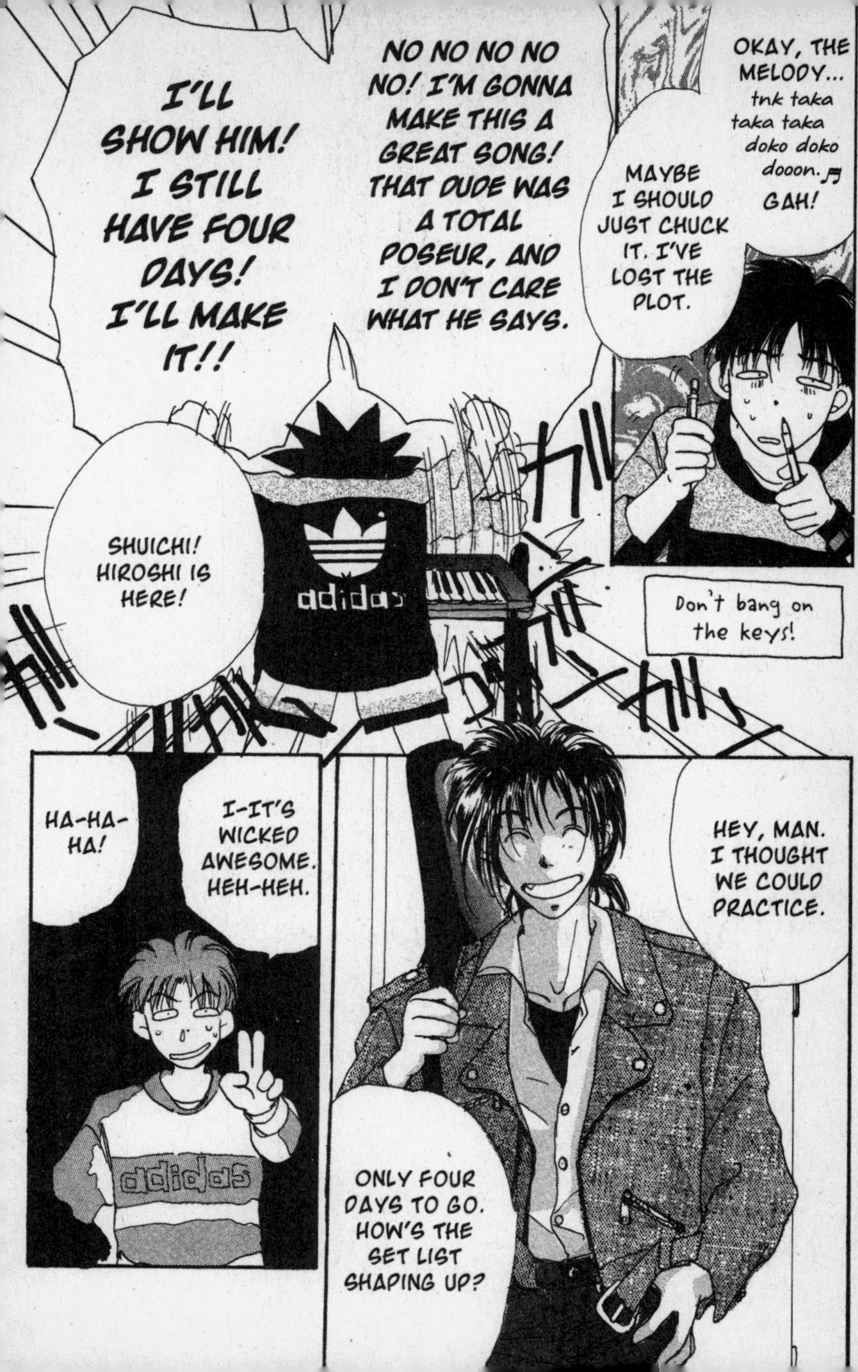
OKAY, THE MELODY... tnk taka taka taka doko doko dooon. GAH!
MAYBE I SHOULD JUST CHUCK IT. I'VE LOST THE PLOT.
NO NO NO NO NO! I'M GONNA MAKE THIS A GREAT SONG! THAT DUDE WAS A TOTAL POSEUR, AND I DON'T CARE WHAT HE SAYS.
I'LL SHOW HIM! I STILL HAVE FOUR DAYS! I'LL MAKE IT!!
Don't bang on the keys!
SHUICHI! HIROSHI IS HERE!
HEY, MAN. I THOUGHT WE COULD PRACTICE.
ONLY FOUR DAYS TO GO. HOW'S THE SET LIST SHAPING UP?
I-IT'S WICKED AWESOME. HEH-HEH.
HA-HA-HA!

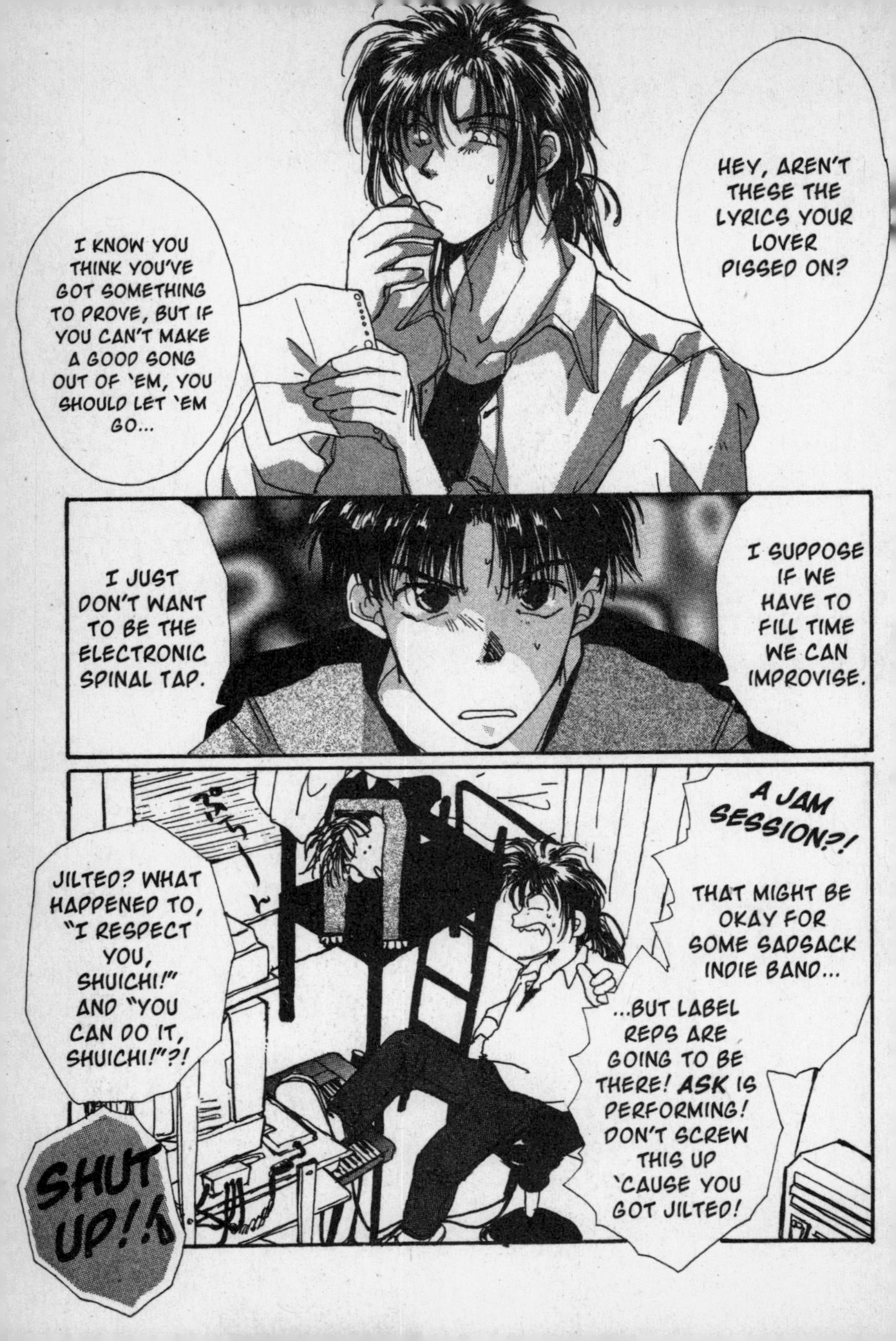
HEY, AREN'T THESE THE LYRICS YOUR LOVER PISSED ON?
I KNOW YOU THINK YOU'VE GOT SOMETHING TO PROVE, BUT IF YOU CAN'T MAKE A GOOD SONG OUT OF 'EM, YOU SHOULD LET 'EM GO...
I SUPPOSE IF WE HAVE TO FILL TIME WE CAN IMPROVISE.
I JUST DON'T WANT TO BE THE ELECTRONIC SPINAL TAP.
A JAM SESSION?!
THAT MIGHT BE OKAY FOR SOME SADSACK INDIE BAND...
...BUT LABEL REPS ARE GOING TO BE THERE! ASK IS PERFORMING! DON'T SCREW THIS UP 'CAUSE YOU GOT JILTED!
JILTED? WHAT HAPPENED TO, "I RESPECT YOU, SHUICHI!" AND "YOU CAN DO IT, SHUICHI!"?!
SHUT UP!

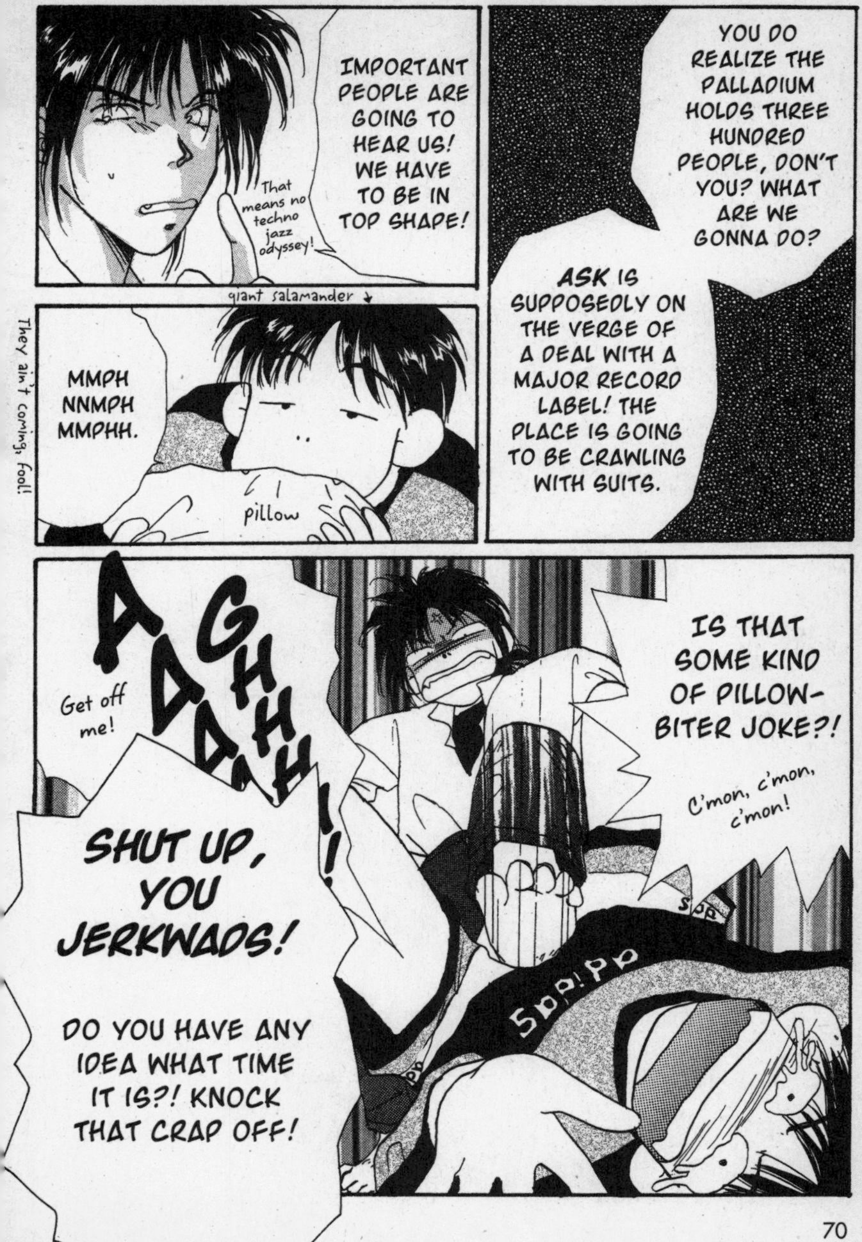
YOU DO REALIZE THE PALLADIUM HOLDS THREE HUNDRED PEOPLE, DON'T YOU? WHAT ARE WE GONNA DO?
ASK IS SUPPOSEDLY ON THE VERGE OF A DEAL WITH A MAJOR RECORD LABEL! THE PLACE IS GOING TO BE CRAWLING WITH SUITS.
IMPORTANT PEOPLE ARE GOING TO HEAR US! WE HAVE TO BE IN TOP SHAPE!
That means no techno jazz odyssey!
giant salamander
MMPH NNMPH MMPHH.
pillow
They ain't coming, fool!
IS THAT SOME KIND OF PILLOW-BITER JOKE?!
C'mon, c'mon, c'mon!
AGHHHH!
Get off me!
SHUT UP, YOU JERKWADS!
DO YOU HAVE ANY IDEA WHAT TIME IT IS?! KNOCK THAT CRAP OFF!

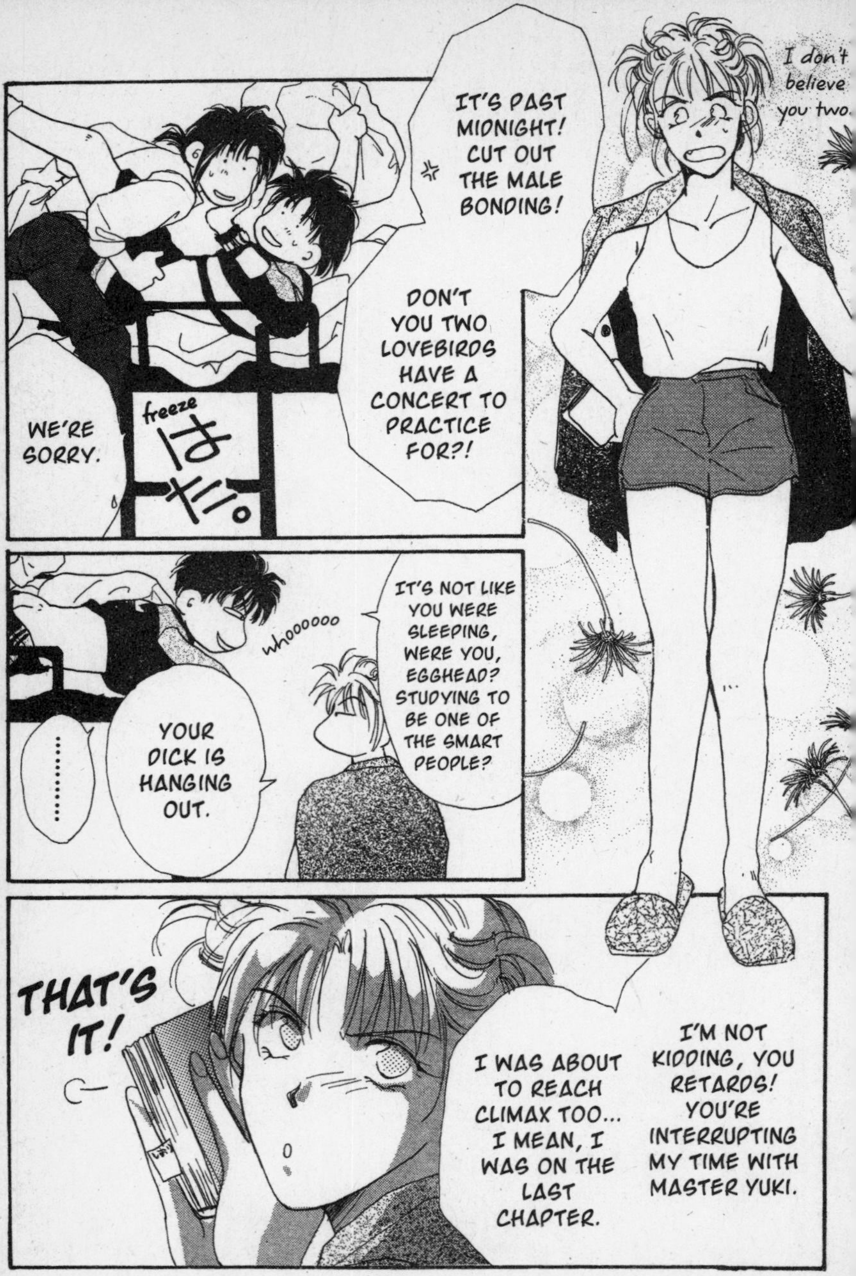
I don't believe you two.
IT'S PAST MIDNIGHT! CUT OUT THE MALE BONDING!
DON'T YOU TWO LOVEBIRDS HAVE A CONCERT TO PRACTICE FOR?!
...
freeze
はぎ。
WE'RE SORRY.
IT'S NOT LIKE YOU WERE SLEEPING, WERE YOU, EGGHEAD? STUDYING TO BE ONE OF THE SMART PEOPLE?
whoooooo
YOUR DICK IS HANGING OUT.
....
I'M NOT KIDDING, YOU RETARDS! YOU'RE INTERRUPTING MY TIME WITH MASTER YUKI.
I WAS ABOUT TO REACH CLIMAX TOO... I MEAN, I WAS ON THE LAST CHAPTER.
THAT'S IT!

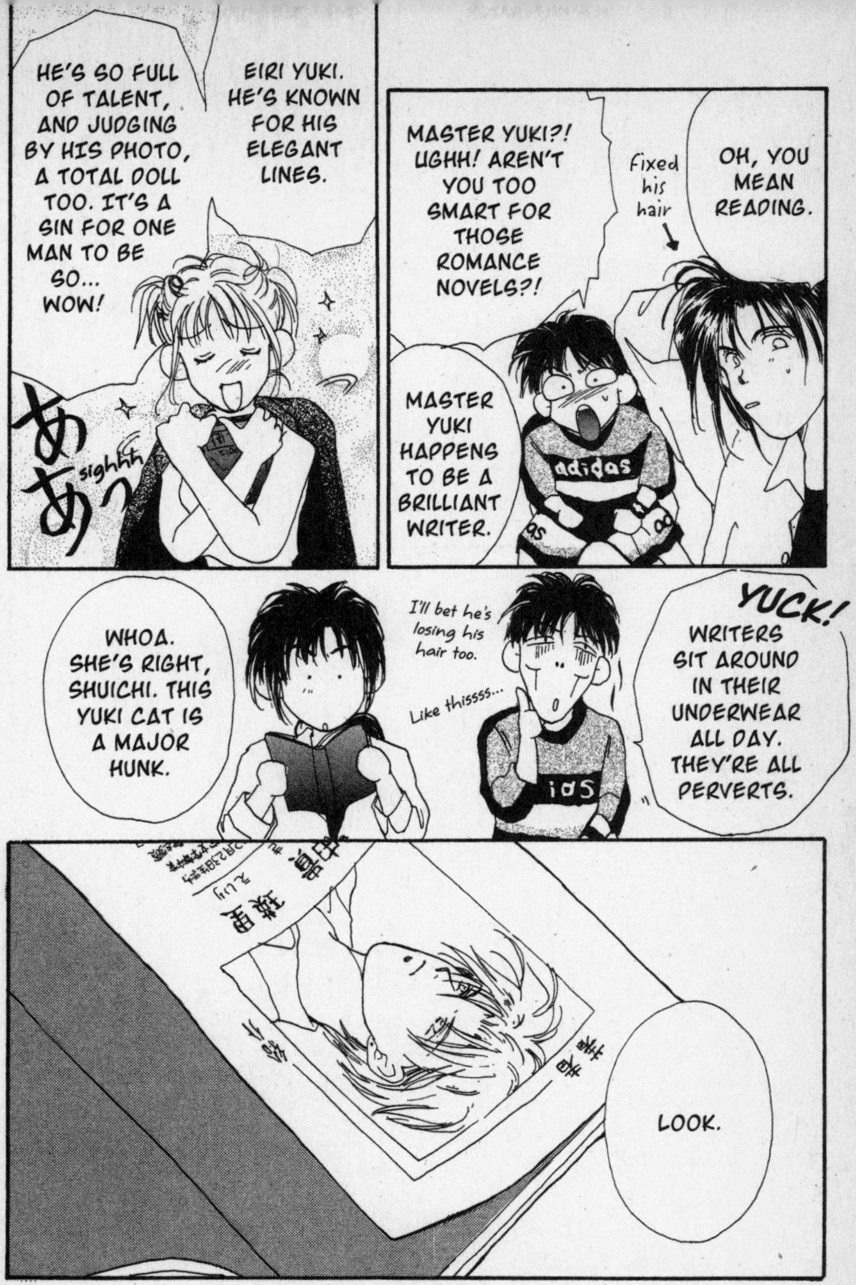
OH, YOU MEAN READING.
Fixed his hair
MASTER YUKI?! UGHH! AREN'T YOU TOO SMART FOR THOSE ROMANCE NOVELS?!
MASTER YUKI HAPPENS TO BE A BRILLIANT WRITER.
EIRI YUKI. HE'S KNOWN FOR HIS ELEGANT LINES.
HE'S SO FULL OF TALENT, AND JUDGING BY HIS PHOTO, A TOTAL DOLL TOO. IT'S A SIN FOR ONE MAN TO BE SO... WOW!
ああっ
sighhh
YUCK!
WRITERS SIT AROUND IN THEIR UNDERWEAR ALL DAY. THEY'RE ALL PERVERTS.
I'll bet he's losing his hair too.
Like thissss...
WHOA. SHE'S RIGHT, SHUICHI. THIS YUKI CAT IS A MAJOR HUNK.
LOOK.

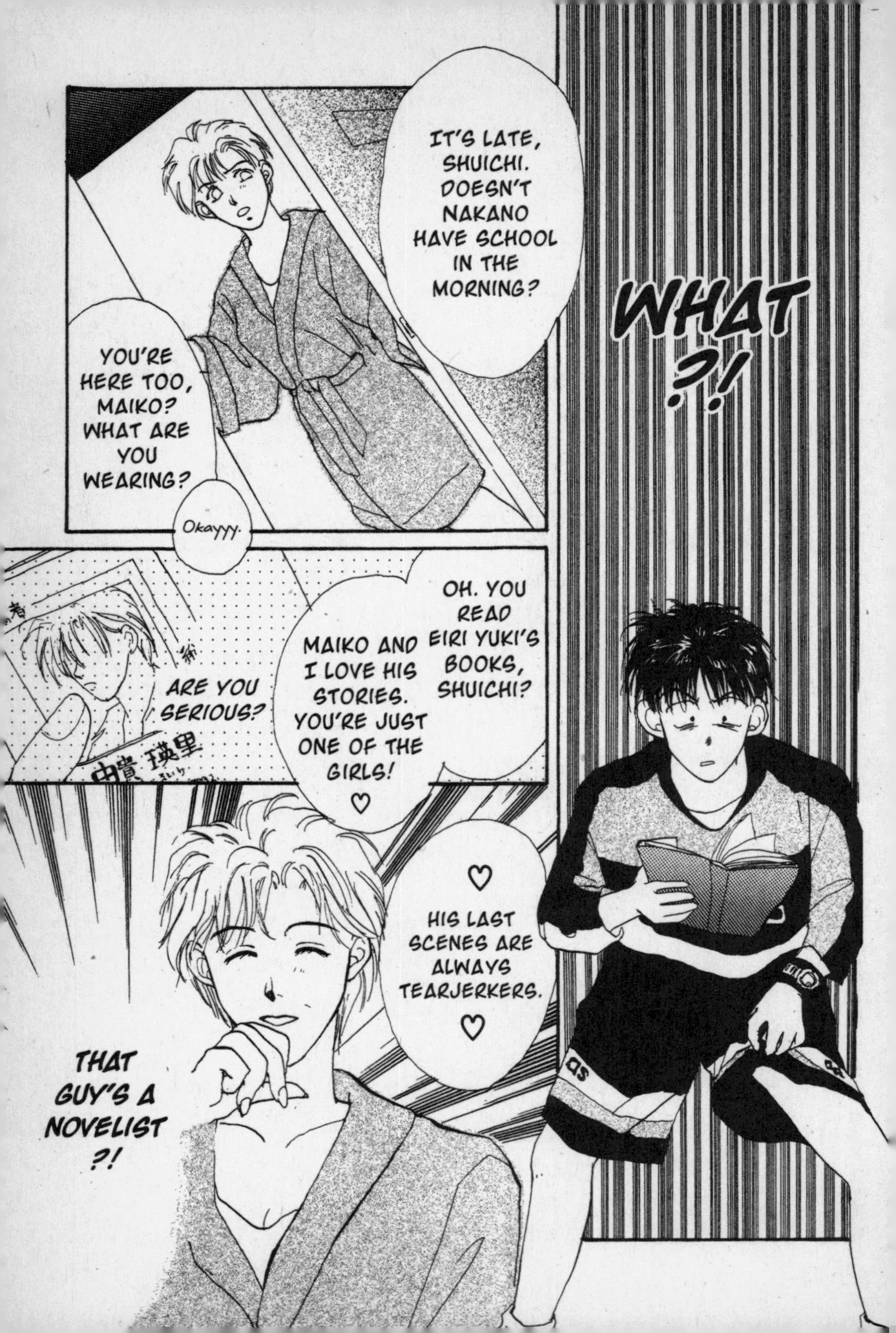
IT'S LATE, SHUICHI. DOESN'T NAKANO HAVE SCHOOL IN THE MORNING?
YOU'RE HERE TOO, MAIKO? WHAT ARE YOU WEARING?
Okayyy.
OH. YOU READ EIRI YUKI'S BOOKS, SHUICHI?
MAIKO AND I LOVE HIS STORIES. YOU'RE JUST ONE OF THE GIRLS! ♡
ARE YOU SERIOUS?
♡ HIS LAST SCENES ARE ALWAYS TEARJERKERS. ♡
WHAT ?!
THAT GUY'S A NOVELIST ?!

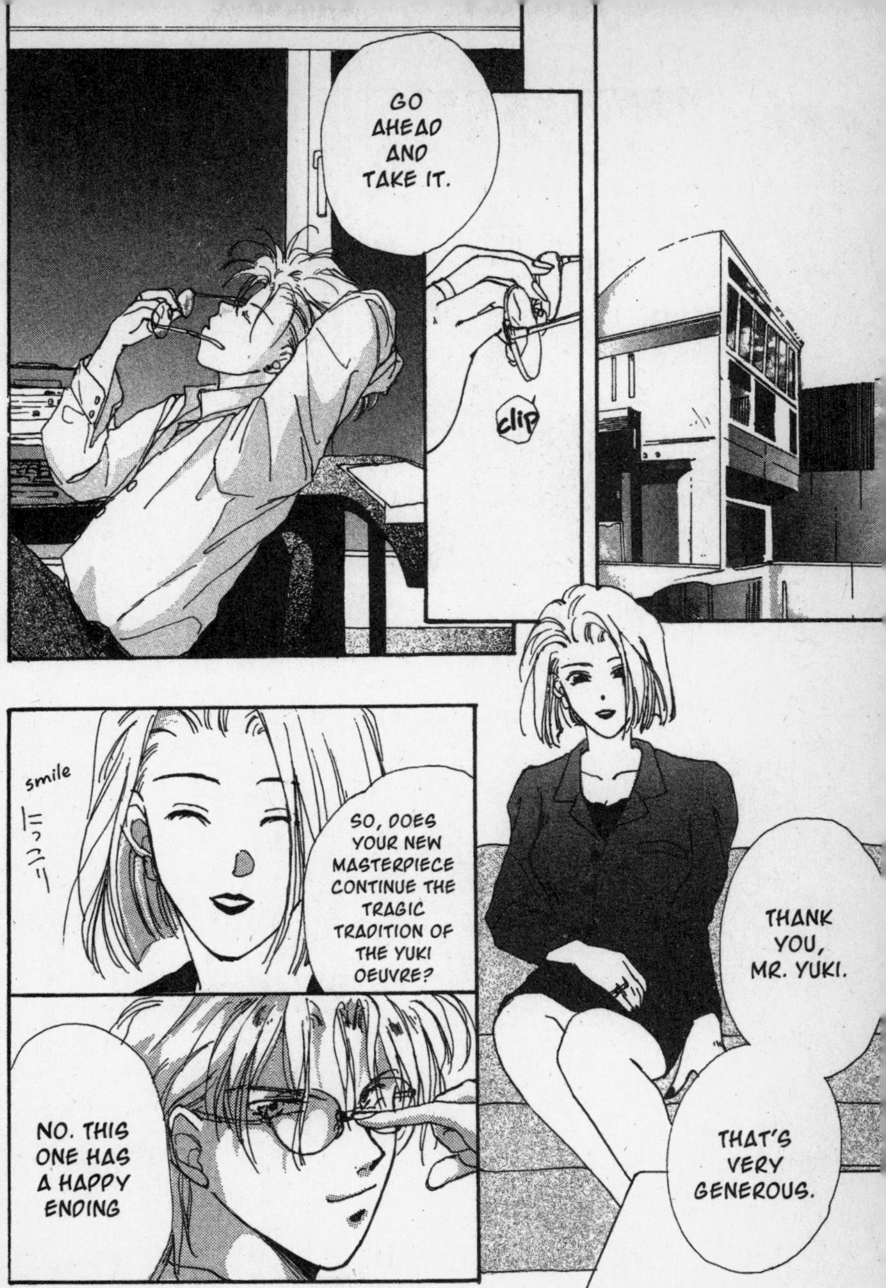
GO AHEAD AND TAKE IT.
clip
THANK YOU, MR. YUKI.
THAT'S VERY GENEROUS.
smile
SO, DOES YOUR NEW MASTERPIECE CONTINUE THE TRAGIC TRADITION OF THE YUKI OEUVRE?
NO. THIS ONE HAS A HAPPY ENDING

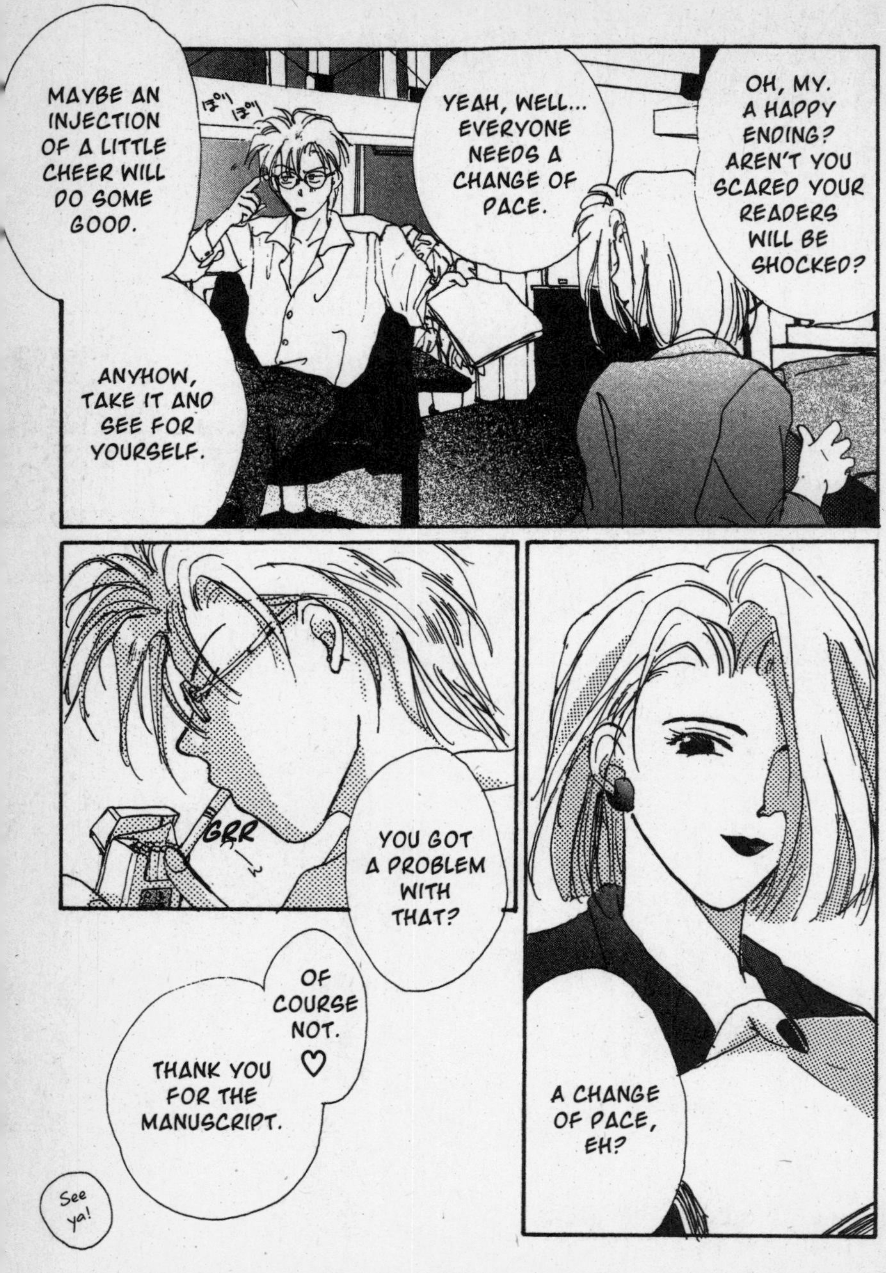
OH, MY. A HAPPY ENDING? AREN'T YOU SCARED YOUR READERS WILL BE SHOCKED?
YEAH, WELL... EVERYONE NEEDS A CHANGE OF PACE.
ぽりぽり
MAYBE AN INJECTION OF A LITTLE CHEER WILL DO SOME GOOD.
ANYHOW, TAKE IT AND SEE FOR YOURSELF.
A CHANGE OF PACE, EH?
GRR
YOU GOT A PROBLEM WITH THAT?
OF COURSE NOT. ♡
THANK YOU FOR THE MANUSCRIPT.
See ya!

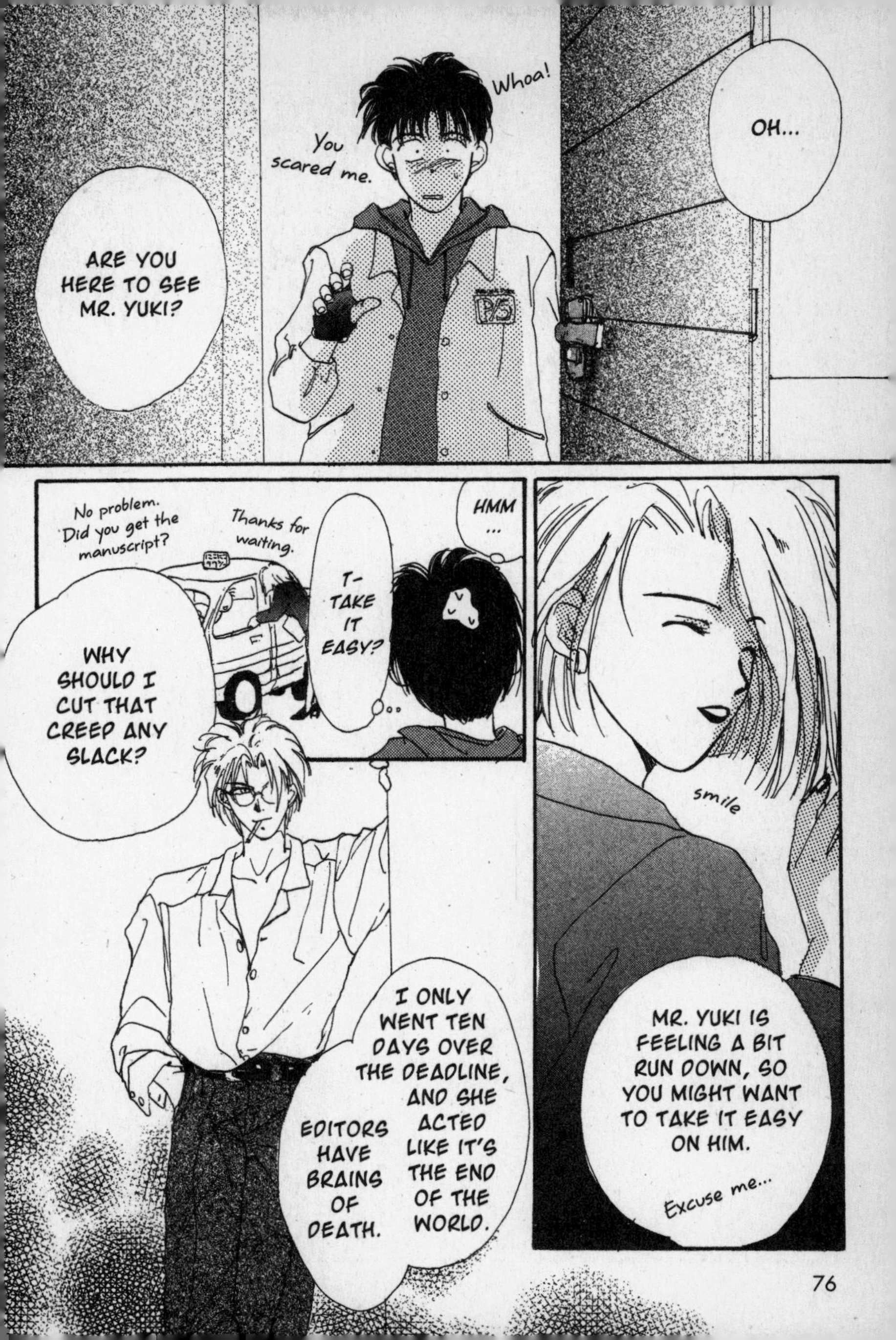
OH...
Whoa!
You scared me.
ARE YOU HERE TO SEE MR. YUKI?
smile
MR. YUKI IS FEELING A BIT RUN DOWN, SO YOU MIGHT WANT TO TAKE IT EASY ON HIM.
Excuse me...
HMM ...
T- TAKE IT EASY?
Thanks for waiting.
No problem. Did you get the manuscript?
WHY SHOULD I CUT THAT CREEP ANY SLACK?
I ONLY WENT TEN DAYS OVER THE DEADLINE, AND SHE ACTED LIKE IT'S THE END OF THE WORLD.
EDITORS HAVE BRAINS OF DEATH.

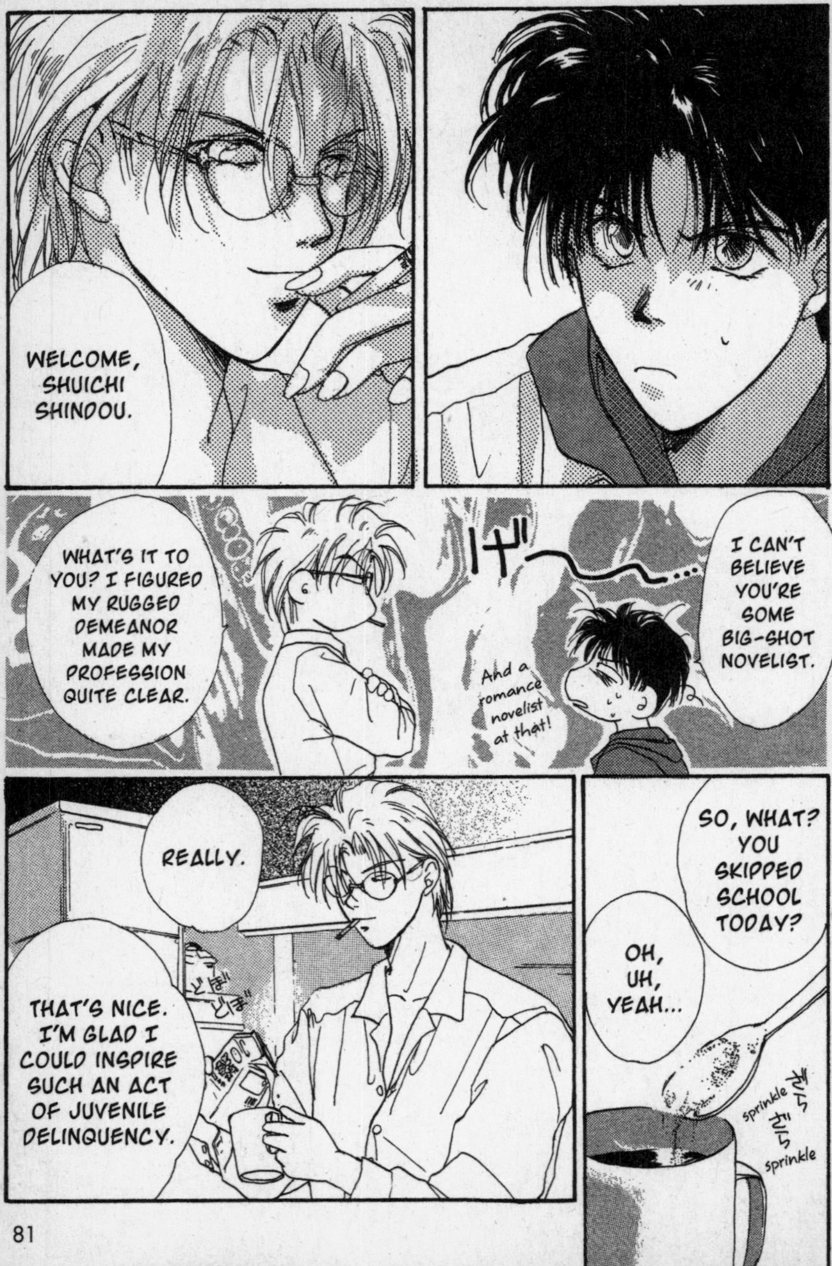
WELCOME, SHUICHI SHINDOU.
I CAN'T BELIEVE YOU'RE SOME BIG-SHOT NOVELIST.
And a romance novelist at that!
WHAT'S IT TO YOU? I FIGURED MY RUGGED DEMEANOR MADE MY PROFESSION QUITE CLEAR.
SO, WHAT? YOU SKIPPED SCHOOL TODAY?
OH, UH, YEAH...
sprinkle
sprinkle
REALLY.
THAT'S NICE. I'M GLAD I COULD INSPIRE SUCH AN ACT OF JUVENILE DELINQUENCY.

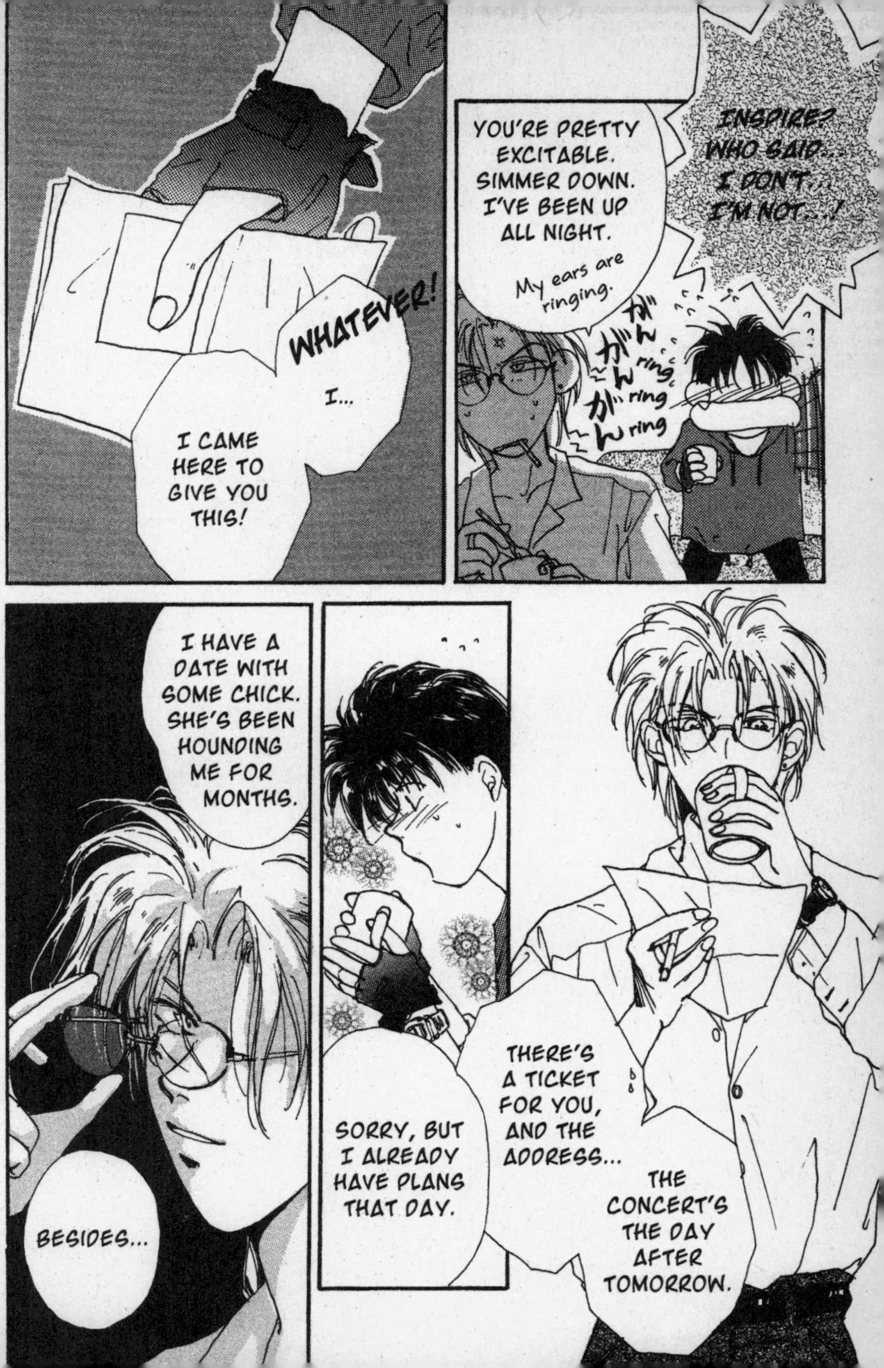

INSPIRE? WHO SAID... I DON'T... I'M NOT...!
YOU'RE PRETTY EXCITABLE. SIMMER DOWN. I'VE BEEN UP ALL NIGHT.
My ears are ringing.
がん ring
がん ring
がん ring
WHATEVER!
I...
I CAME HERE TO GIVE YOU THIS!
THERE'S A TICKET FOR YOU, AND THE ADDRESS...
THE CONCERT'S THE DAY AFTER TOMORROW.
SORRY, BUT I ALREADY HAVE PLANS THAT DAY.
I HAVE A DATE WITH SOME CHICK. SHE'S BEEN HOUNDING ME FOR MONTHS.
BESIDES...

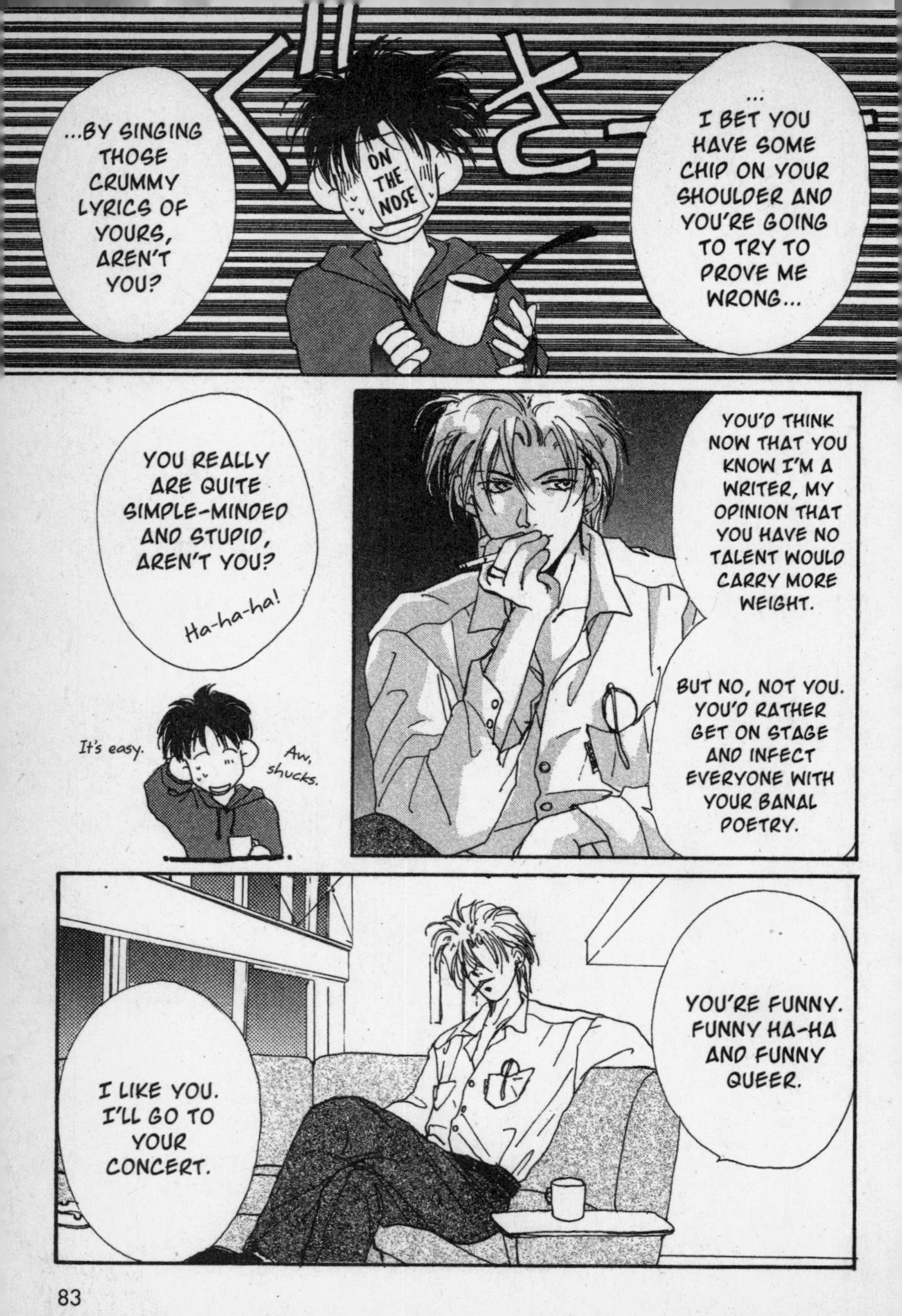
... I BET YOU HAVE SOME CHIP ON YOUR SHOULDER AND YOU'RE GOING TO TRY TO PROVE ME WRONG...
ON THE NOSE
...BY SINGING THOSE CRUMMY LYRICS OF YOURS, AREN'T YOU?
YOU'D THINK NOW THAT YOU KNOW I'M A WRITER, MY OPINION THAT YOU HAVE NO TALENT WOULD CARRY MORE WEIGHT.
BUT NO, NOT YOU. YOU'D RATHER GET ON STAGE AND INFECT EVERYONE WITH YOUR BANAL POETRY.
YOU REALLY ARE QUITE SIMPLE-MINDED AND STUPID, AREN'T YOU?
Ha-ha-ha!
Aw, shucks.
It's easy.
YOU'RE FUNNY. FUNNY HA-HA AND FUNNY QUEER.
I LIKE YOU. I'LL GO TO YOUR CONCERT.

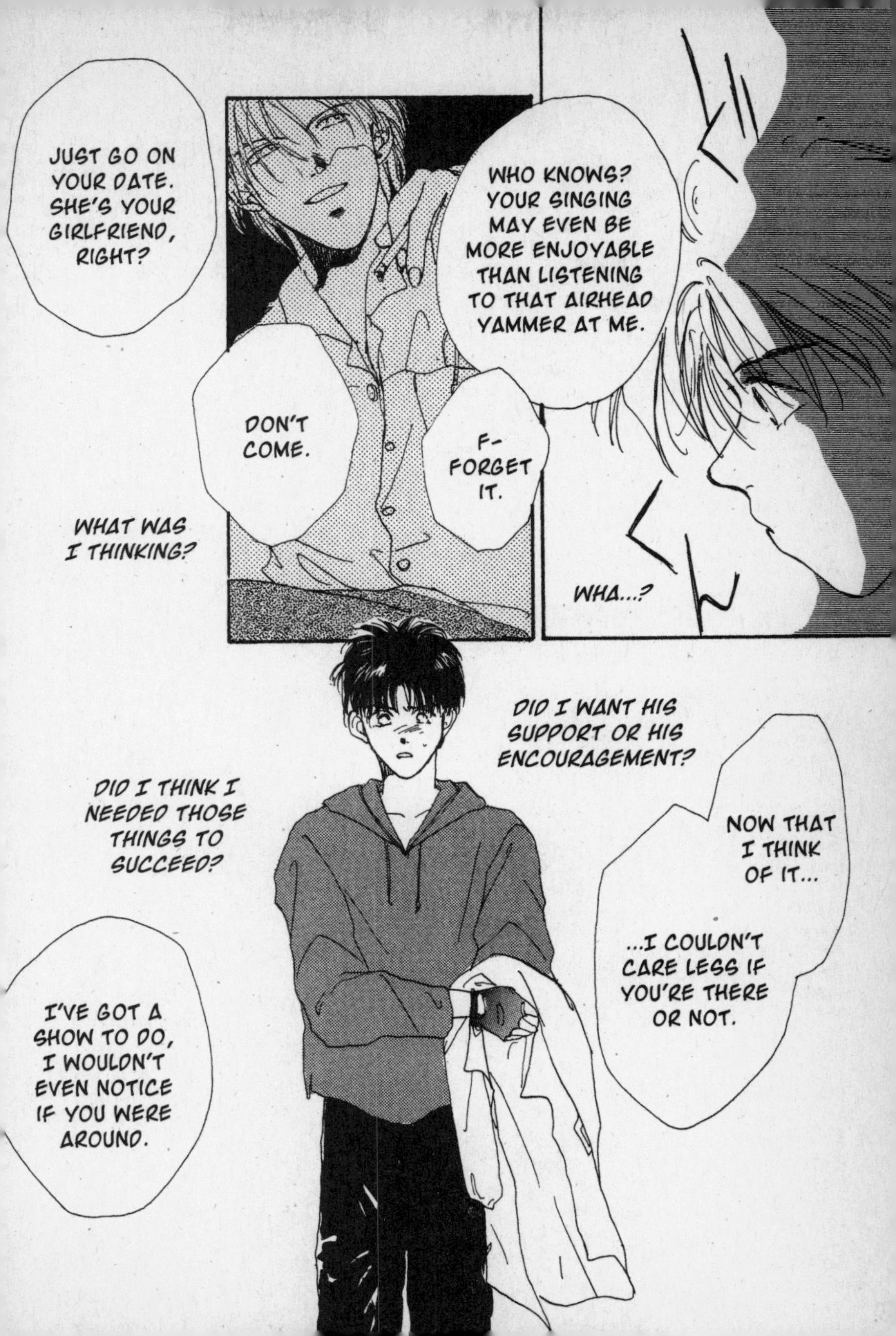
WHO KNOWS? YOUR SINGING MAY EVEN BE MORE ENJOYABLE THAN LISTENING TO THAT AIRHEAD YAMMER AT ME.
WHA...?
F-FORGET IT.
DON'T COME.
JUST GO ON YOUR DATE. SHE'S YOUR GIRLFRIEND, RIGHT?
WHAT WAS I THINKING?
DID I WANT HIS SUPPORT OR HIS ENCOURAGEMENT?
NOW THAT I THINK OF IT...
...I COULDN'T CARE LESS IF YOU'RE THERE OR NOT.
DID I THINK I NEEDED THOSE THINGS TO SUCCEED?
I'VE GOT A SHOW TO DO, I WOULDN'T EVEN NOTICE IF YOU WERE AROUND.

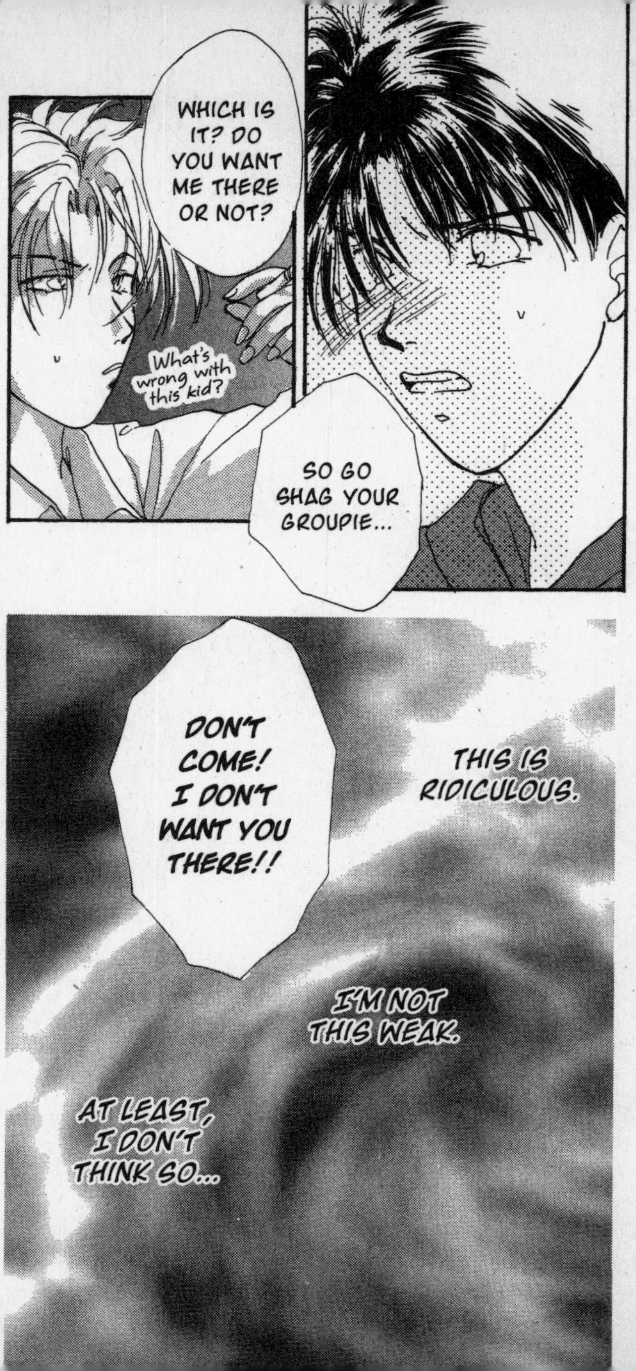
WHICH IS IT? DO YOU WANT ME THERE OR NOT?
What's wrong with this kid?
SO GO SHAG YOUR GROUPIE...
DON'T COME! I DON'T WANT YOU THERE!!
THIS IS RIDICULOUS.
I'M NOT THIS WEAK.
AT LEAST, I DON'T THINK SO...

ABOUT GRAVITATION TRACK 2

■

Compared to Track 1, the story line for Track 2 is unfurling at a devilishly fast pace. But this is only the beginning. The real fun is just starting. I think the key to this chapter is not so much showing suffering as it was being able to draw Eiri Yuki moving around. So I'm happy about that. If I didn't put as much work into Shuichi, I'm sorry. There's a little bit of regret poured into this chapter. The character of Eiri is unfathomable to the outsider. He's a good example of someone who is "unpredictable." It's like having a blow dryer inside a freezer. A walking contradiction. A sloping gravel path. Number 1 on the list of "people who would most surprise you if they really existed." But I really like the character of Eiri. He's got a mean mouth, a bad attitude. About the only good things about him are his looks and his intelligence. Guys like him—I really want to see them suffer. Is that wrong of me? I have a thing for teasing little boys like Shuichi, but it's different because I get a thrill out of punishing guys like Eiri. I guess it's a little kinky.

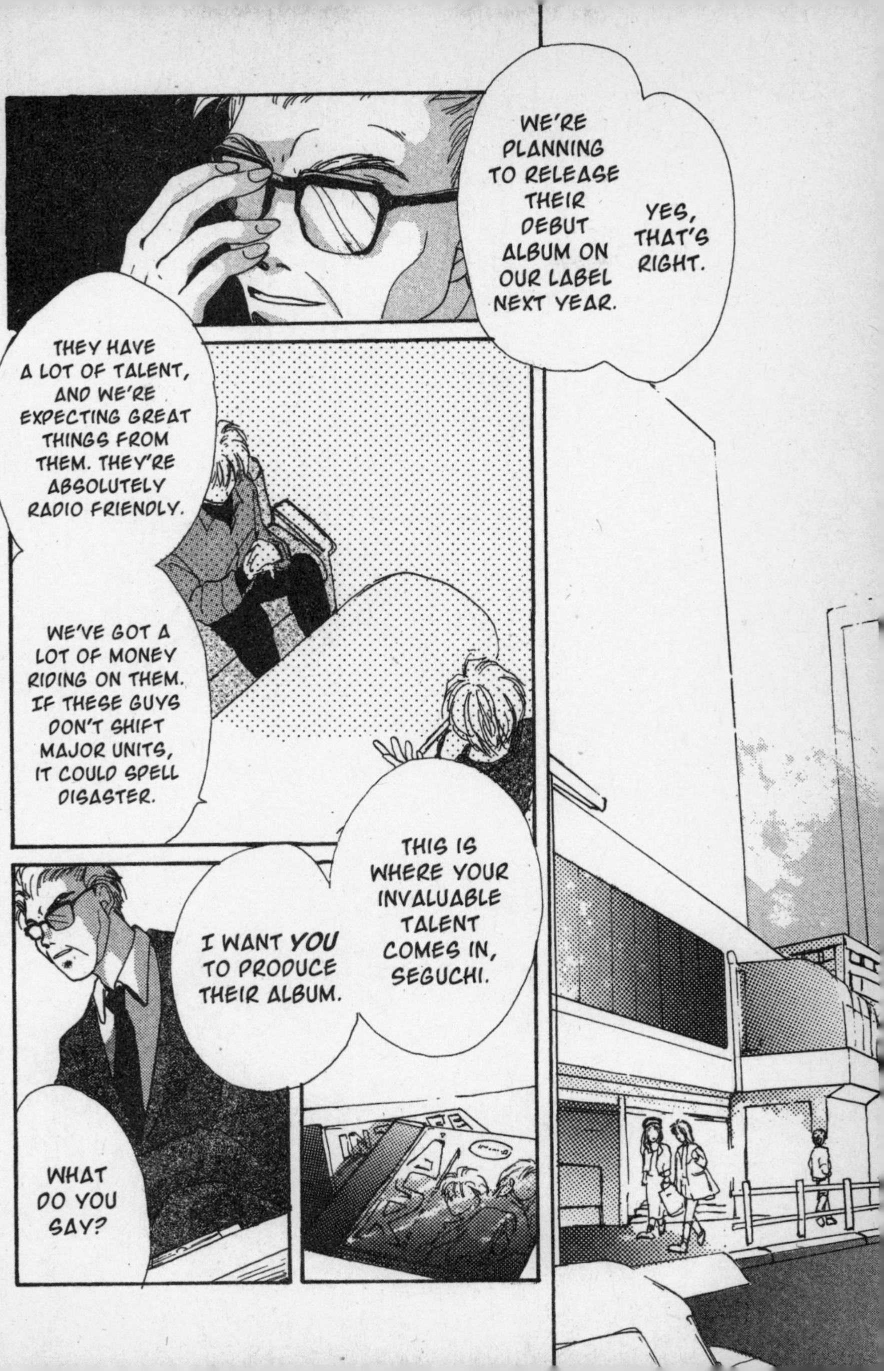
YES, THAT'S RIGHT.
WE'RE PLANNING TO RELEASE THEIR DEBUT ALBUM ON OUR LABEL NEXT YEAR.
THEY HAVE A LOT OF TALENT, AND WE'RE EXPECTING GREAT THINGS FROM THEM. THEY'RE ABSOLUTELY RADIO FRIENDLY.
WE'VE GOT A LOT OF MONEY RIDING ON THEM. IF THESE GUYS DON'T SHIFT MAJOR UNITS, IT COULD SPELL DISASTER.
THIS IS WHERE YOUR INVALUABLE TALENT COMES IN, SEGUCHI.
I WANT *YOU* TO PRODUCE THEIR ALBUM.
WHAT DO YOU SAY?

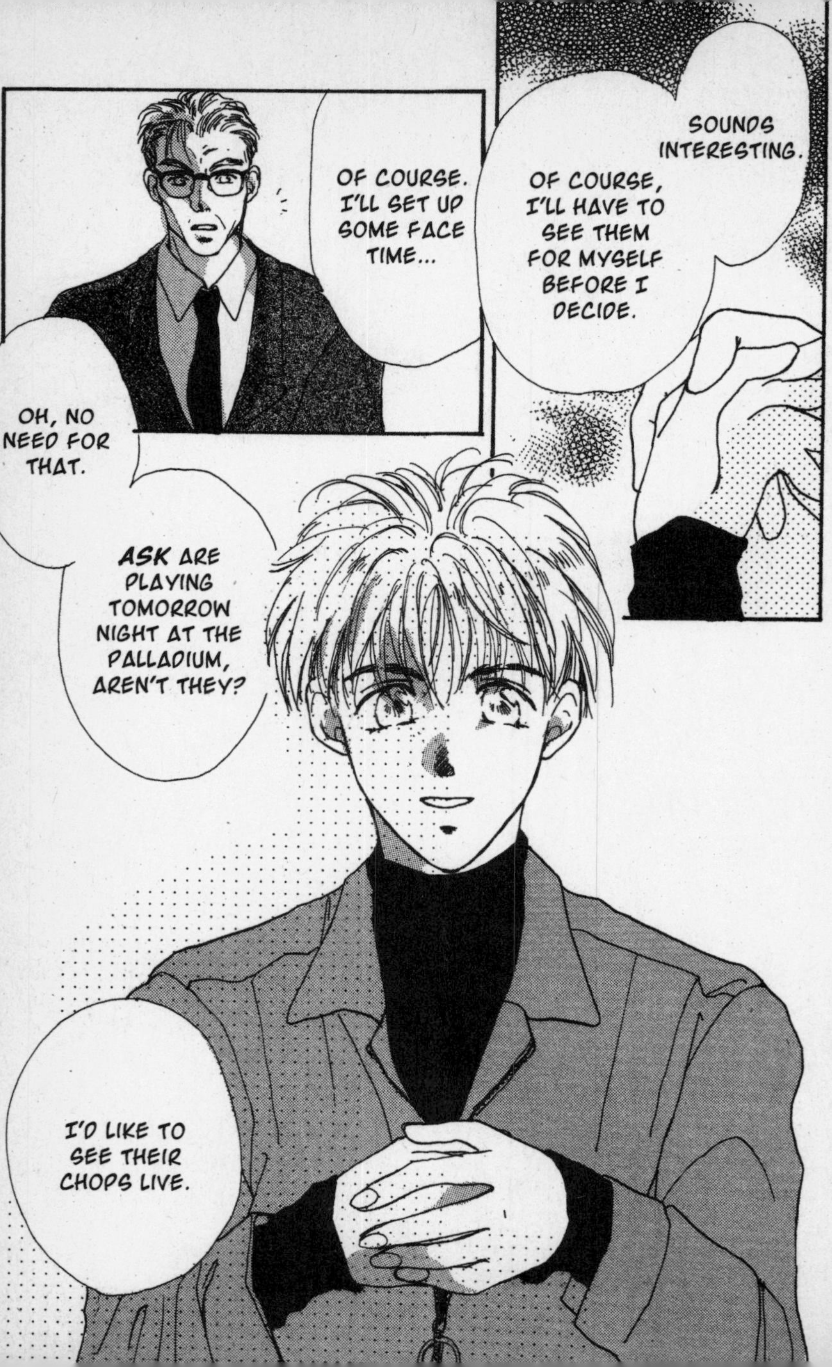
SOUNDS INTERESTING.
OF COURSE, I'LL HAVE TO SEE THEM FOR MYSELF BEFORE I DECIDE.
OF COURSE. I'LL SET UP SOME FACE TIME...
OH, NO NEED FOR THAT.
ASK ARE PLAYING TOMORROW NIGHT AT THE PALLADIUM, AREN'T THEY?
I'D LIKE TO SEE THEIR CHOPS LIVE.

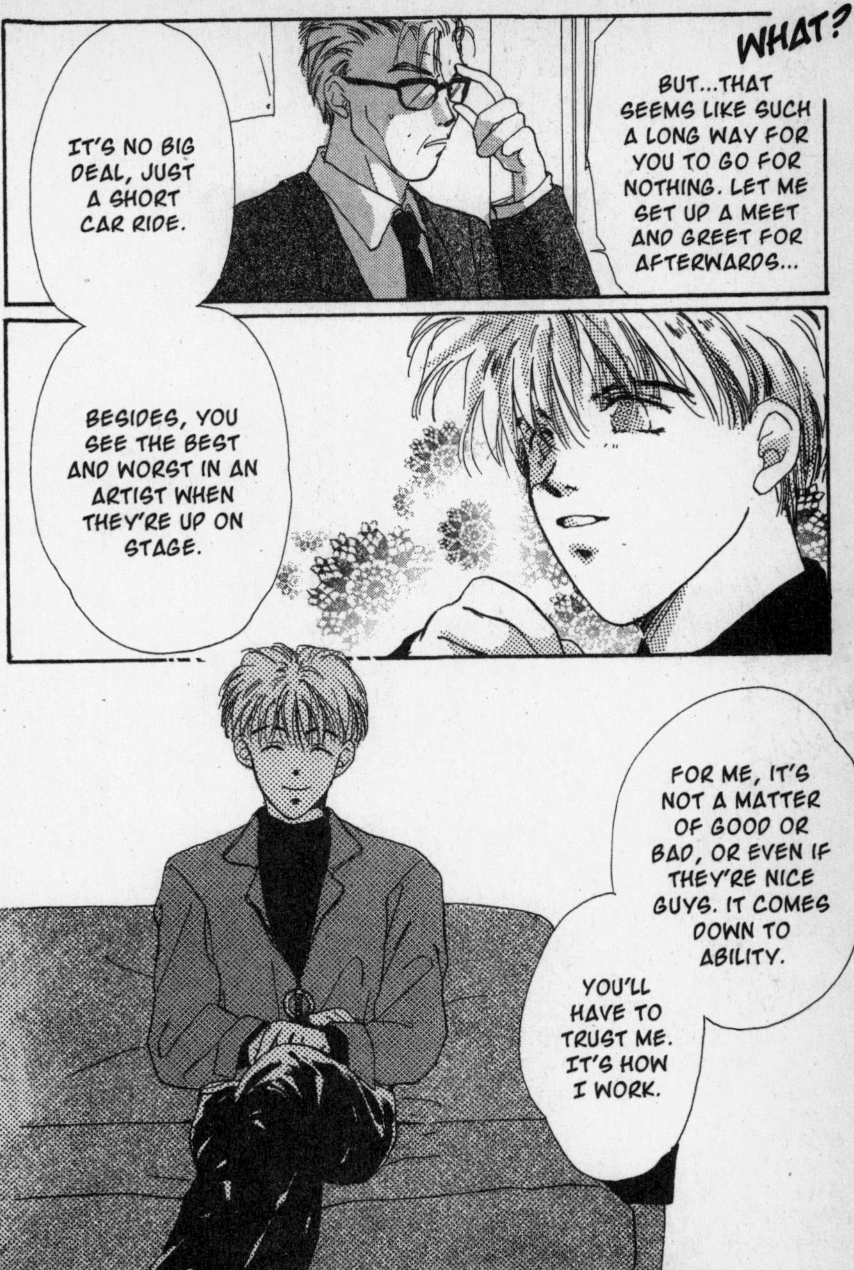
WHAT?
BUT...THAT SEEMS LIKE SUCH A LONG WAY FOR YOU TO GO FOR NOTHING. LET ME SET UP A MEET AND GREET FOR AFTERWARDS...
IT'S NO BIG DEAL, JUST A SHORT CAR RIDE.
BESIDES, YOU SEE THE BEST AND WORST IN AN ARTIST WHEN THEY'RE UP ON STAGE.
FOR ME, IT'S NOT A MATTER OF GOOD OR BAD, OR EVEN IF THEY'RE NICE GUYS. IT COMES DOWN TO ABILITY.
YOU'LL HAVE TO TRUST ME. IT'S HOW I WORK.

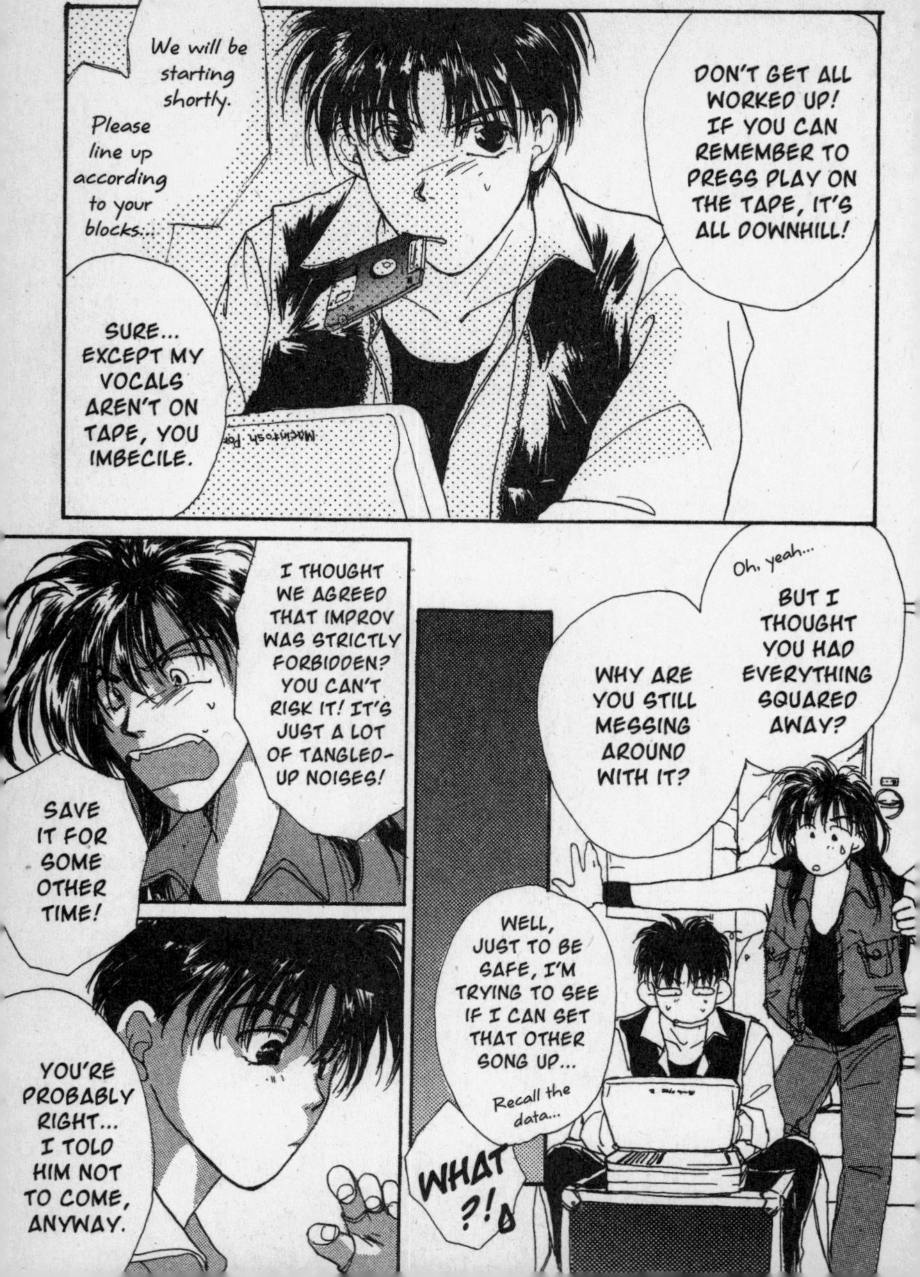
DON'T GET ALL WORKED UP! IF YOU CAN REMEMBER TO PRESS PLAY ON THE TAPE, IT'S ALL DOWNHILL!
We will be starting shortly.
Please line up according to your blocks...
SURE... EXCEPT MY VOCALS AREN'T ON TAPE, YOU IMBECILE.
Oh, yeah...
BUT I THOUGHT YOU HAD EVERYTHING SQUARED AWAY?
WHY ARE YOU STILL MESSING AROUND WITH IT?
WELL, JUST TO BE SAFE, I'M TRYING TO SEE IF I CAN SET THAT OTHER SONG UP...
Recall the data...
WHAT ?!
I THOUGHT WE AGREED THAT IMPROV WAS STRICTLY FORBIDDEN? YOU CAN'T RISK IT! IT'S JUST A LOT OF TANGLED-UP NOISES!
SAVE IT FOR SOME OTHER TIME!
YOU'RE PROBABLY RIGHT... I TOLD HIM NOT TO COME, ANYWAY.

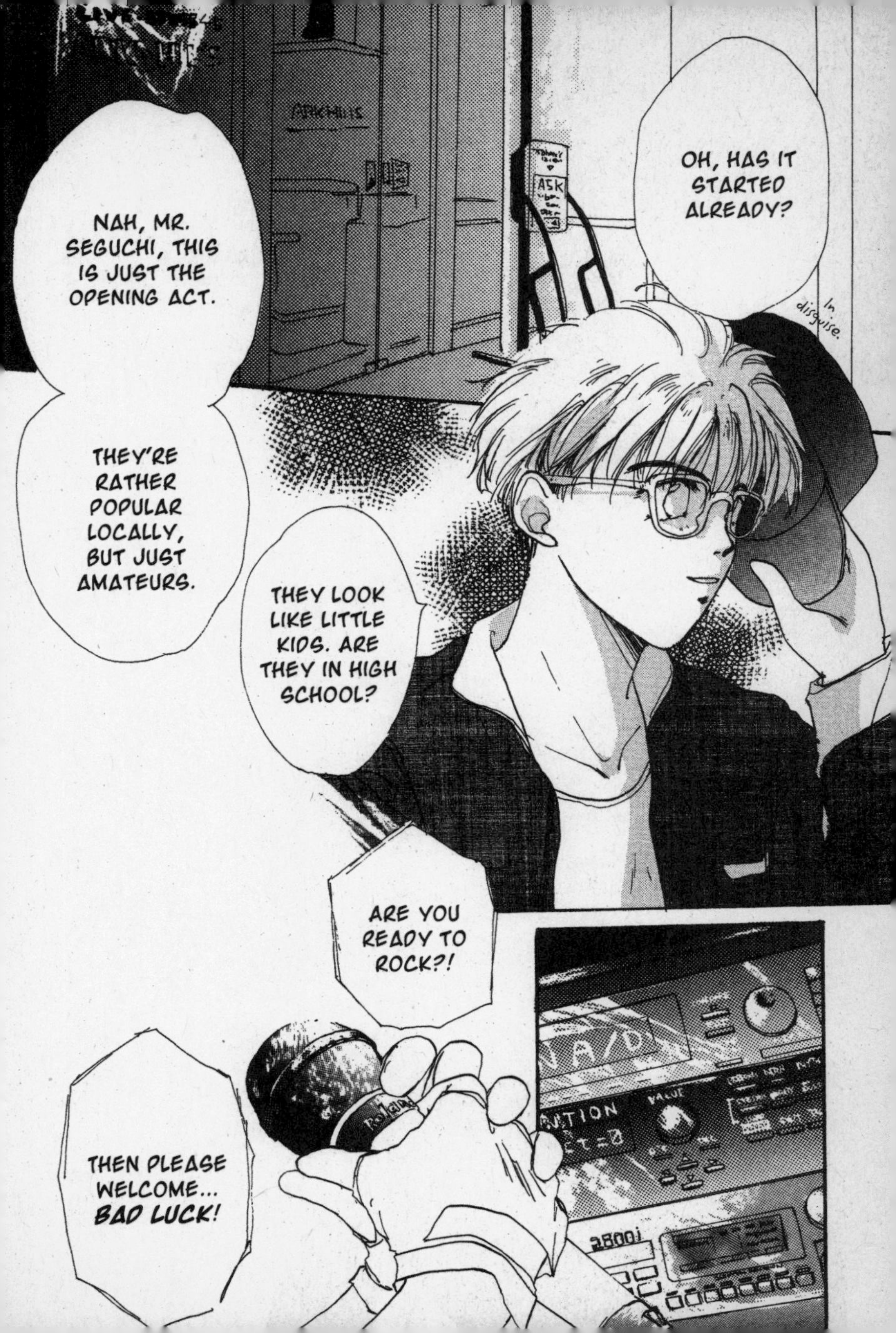
OH, HAS IT STARTED ALREADY?
In disguise.
NAH, MR. SEGUCHI, THIS IS JUST THE OPENING ACT.
THEY'RE RATHER POPULAR LOCALLY, BUT JUST AMATEURS.
THEY LOOK LIKE LITTLE KIDS. ARE THEY IN HIGH SCHOOL?
ARE YOU READY TO ROCK?!
THEN PLEASE WELCOME... *BAD LUCK!*

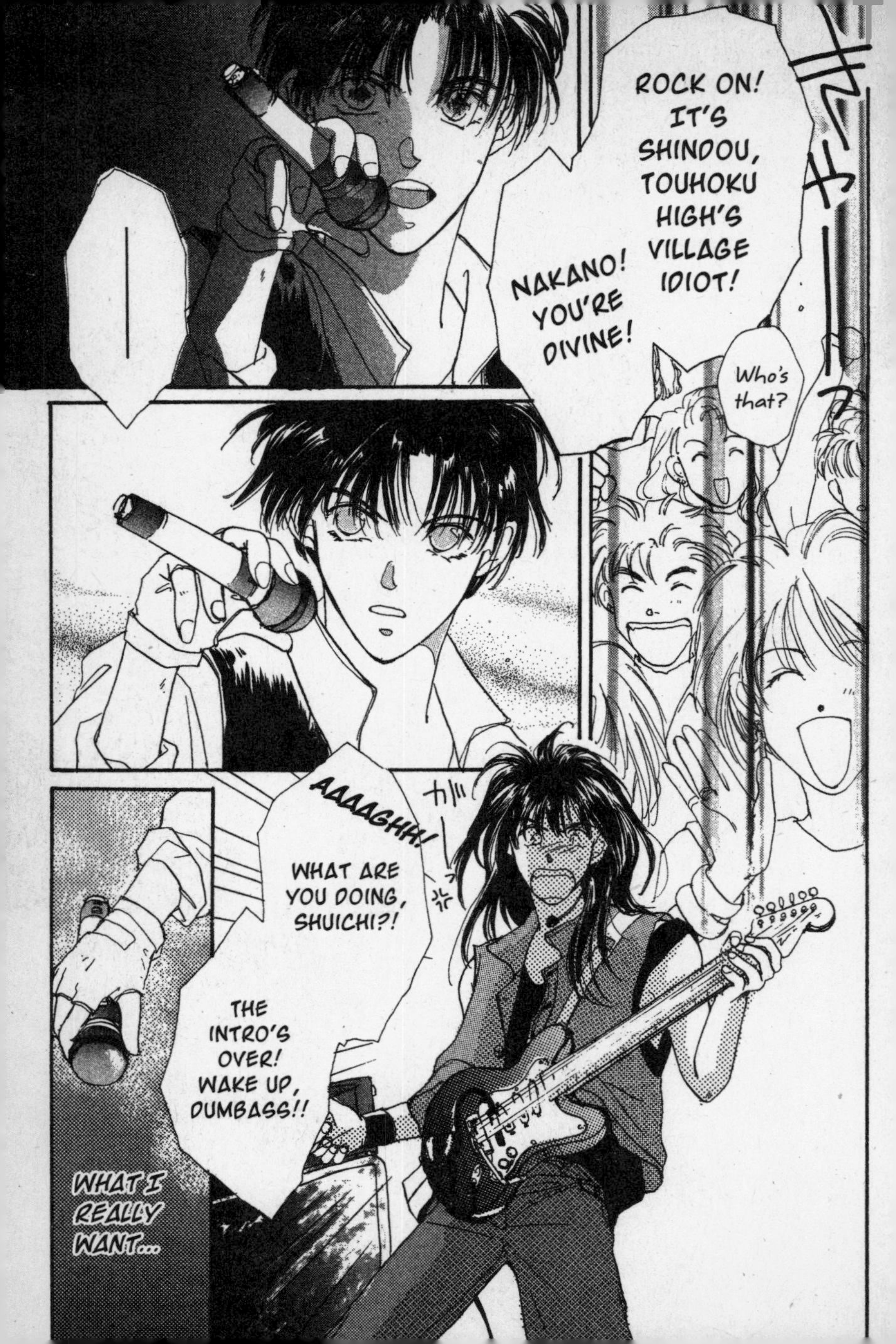
ROCK ON! IT'S SHINDOU, TOUHOKU HIGH'S VILLAGE IDIOT!
NAKANO! YOU'RE DIVINE!
Who's that?
AAAAGHH!
WHAT ARE YOU DOING, SHUICHI?!
THE INTRO'S OVER! WAKE UP, DUMBASS!!
WHAT I REALLY WANT...

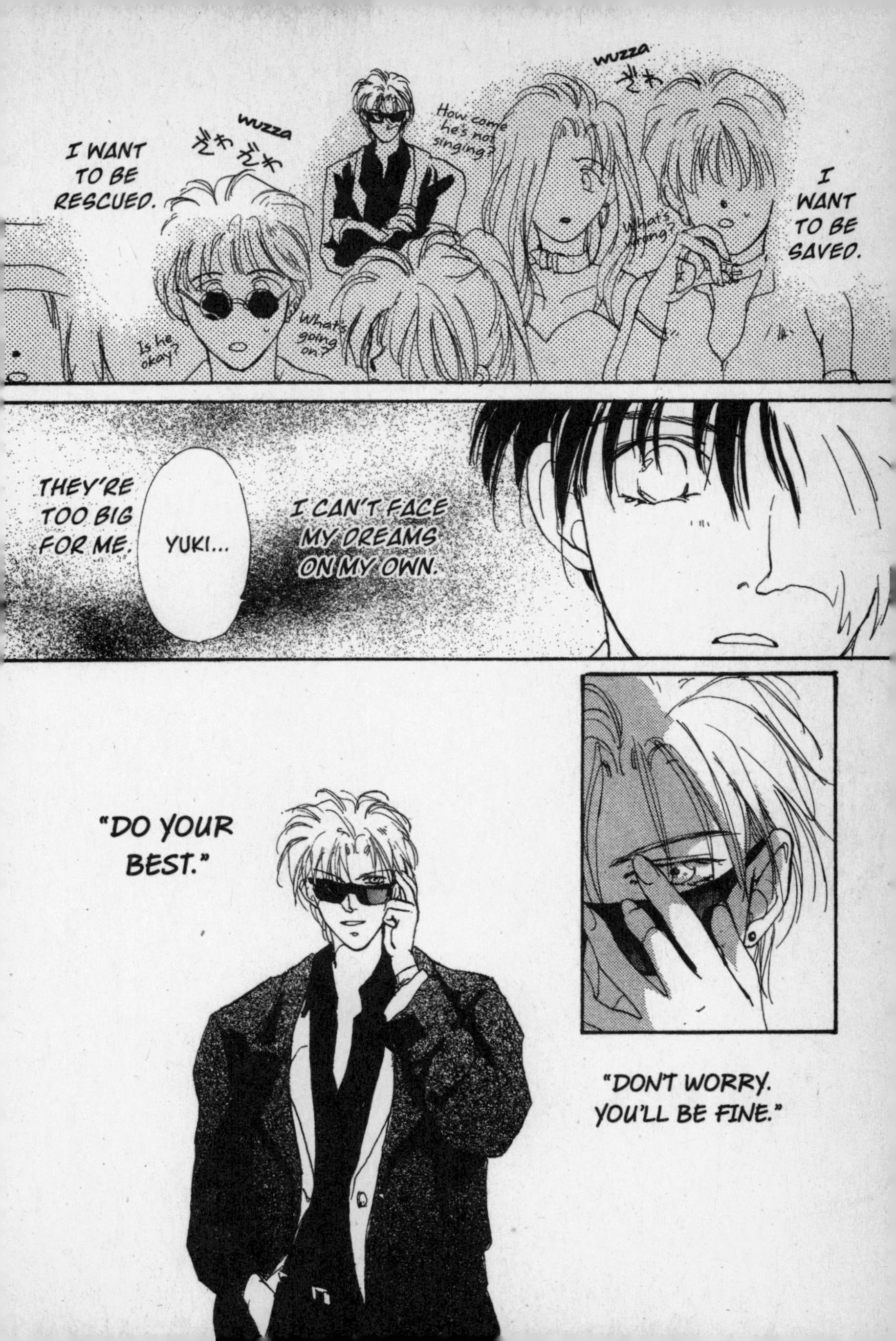
I WANT TO BE SAVED.
wuzza
What's wrong?
How come he's not singing?
wuzza
What's going on?
Is he okay?
I WANT TO BE RESCUED.
I CAN'T FACE MY DREAMS ON MY OWN.
YUKI...
THEY'RE TOO BIG FOR ME.
"DON'T WORRY. YOU'LL BE FINE."
"DO YOUR BEST."

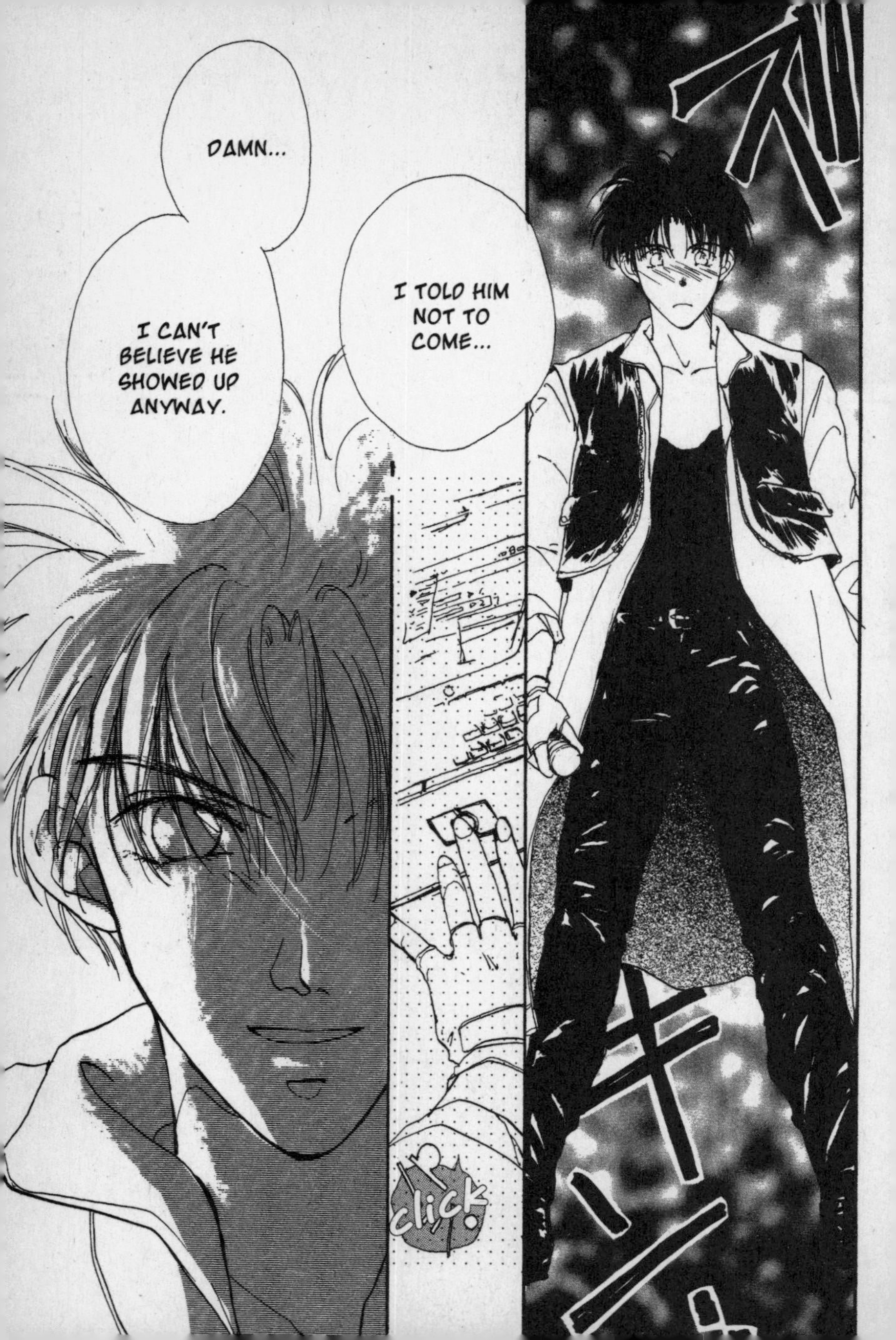
I TOLD HIM NOT TO COME...
DAMN...
I CAN'T BELIEVE HE SHOWED UP ANYWAY.
click!

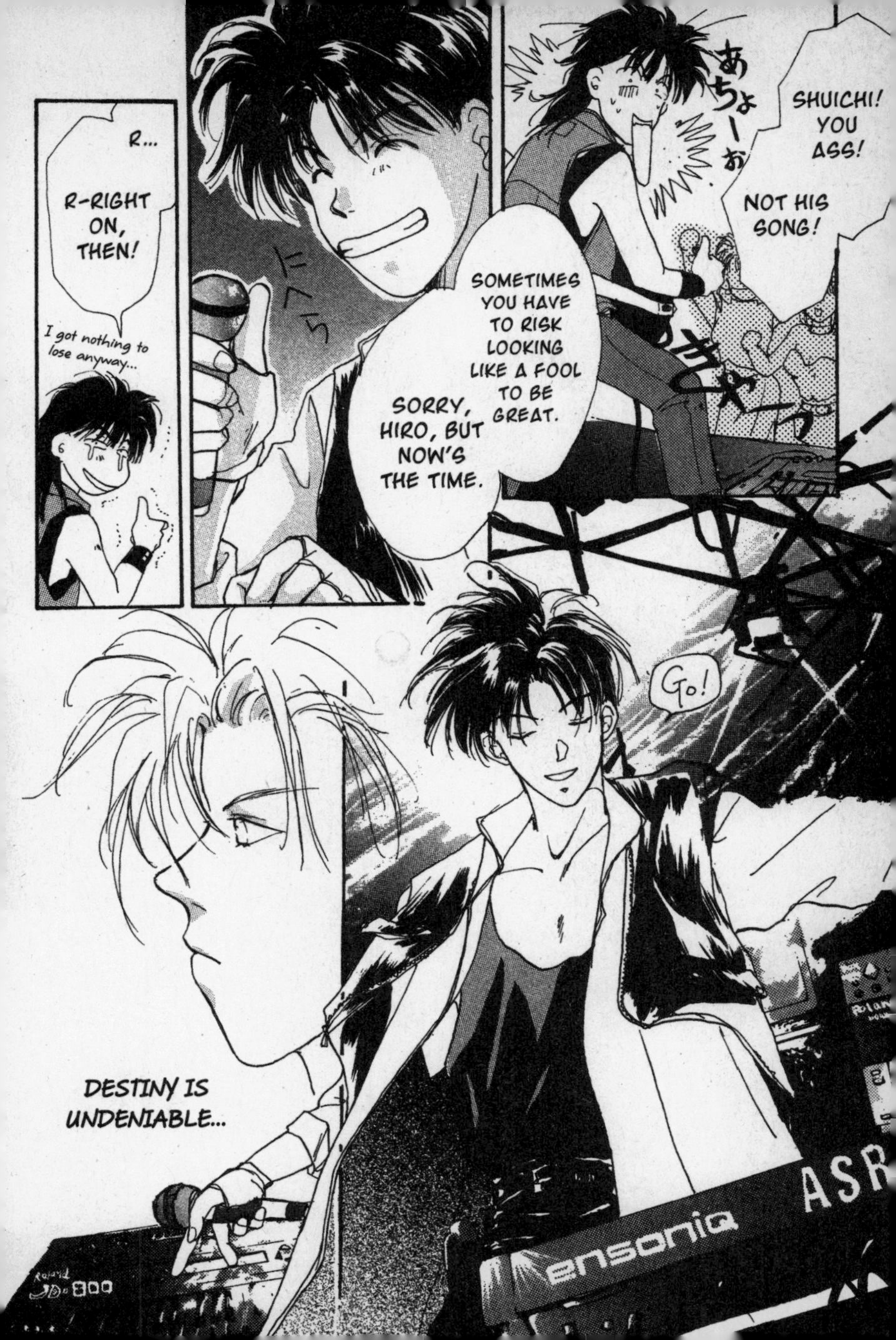
あちょーお
SHUICHI! YOU ASS!
NOT HIS SONG!
SOMETIMES YOU HAVE TO RISK LOOKING LIKE A FOOL TO BE GREAT.
SORRY, HIRO, BUT NOW'S THE TIME.
R...
R-RIGHT ON, THEN!
I got nothing to lose anyway...
Go!
DESTINY IS UNDENIABLE...
ASR
ensoniq
JD-800

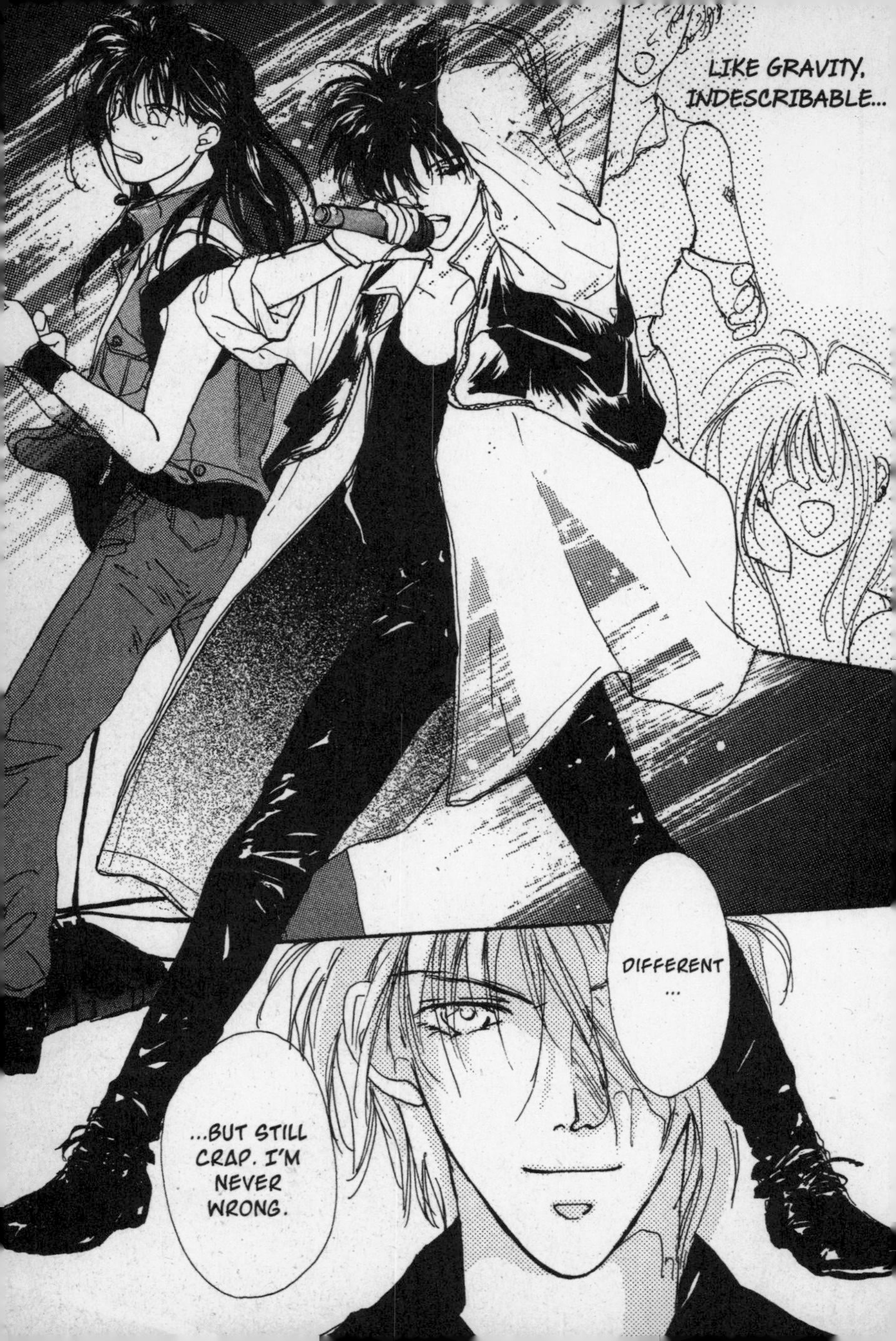
LIKE GRAVITY, INDESCRIBABLE...
DIFFERENT ...
...BUT STILL CRAP. I'M NEVER WRONG.

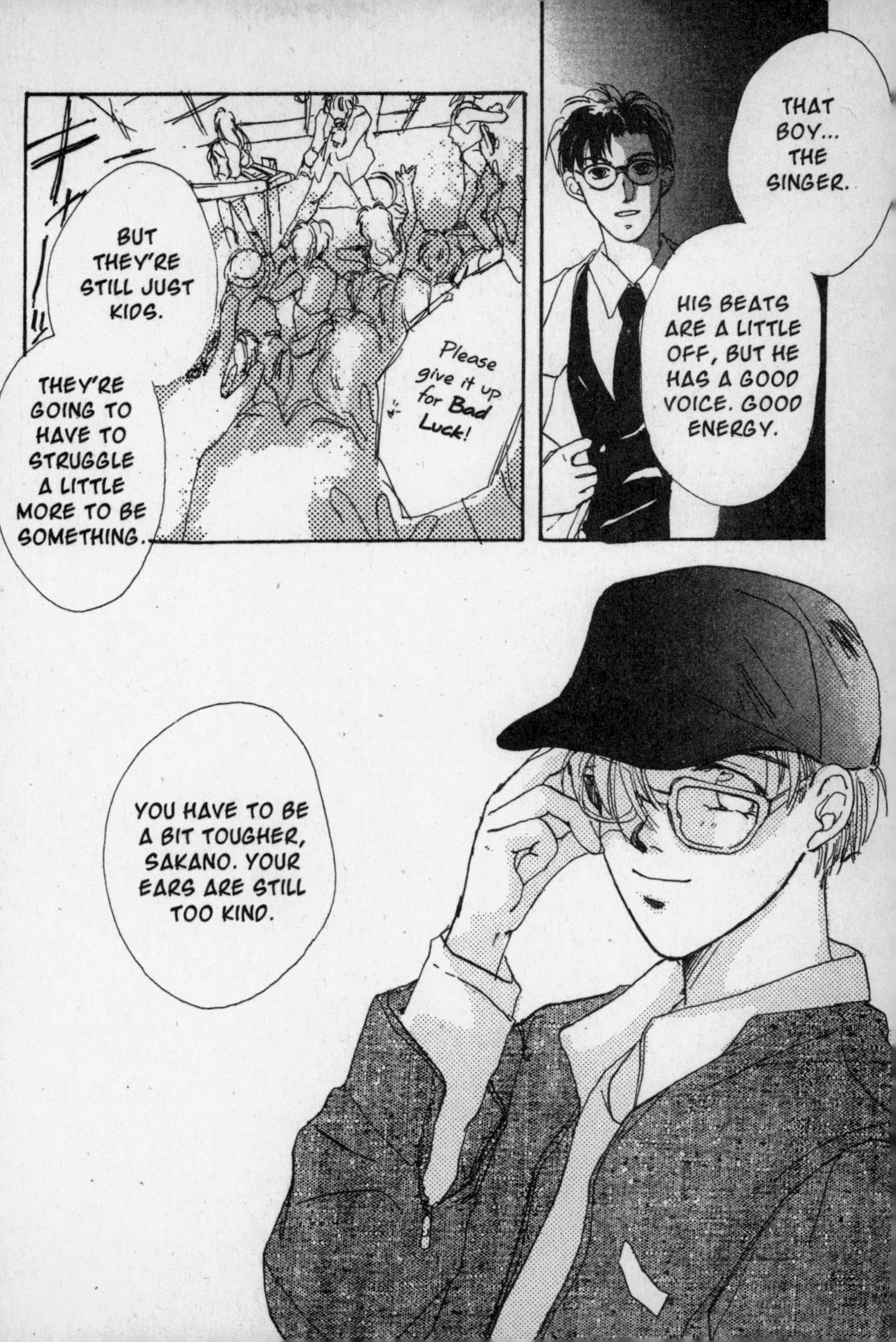
THAT BOY... THE SINGER.
HIS BEATS ARE A LITTLE OFF, BUT HE HAS A GOOD VOICE. GOOD ENERGY.
Please give it up for Bad Luck!
BUT THEY'RE STILL JUST KIDS.
THEY'RE GOING TO HAVE TO STRUGGLE A LITTLE MORE TO BE SOMETHING.
YOU HAVE TO BE A BIT TOUGHER, SAKANO. YOUR EARS ARE STILL TOO KIND.

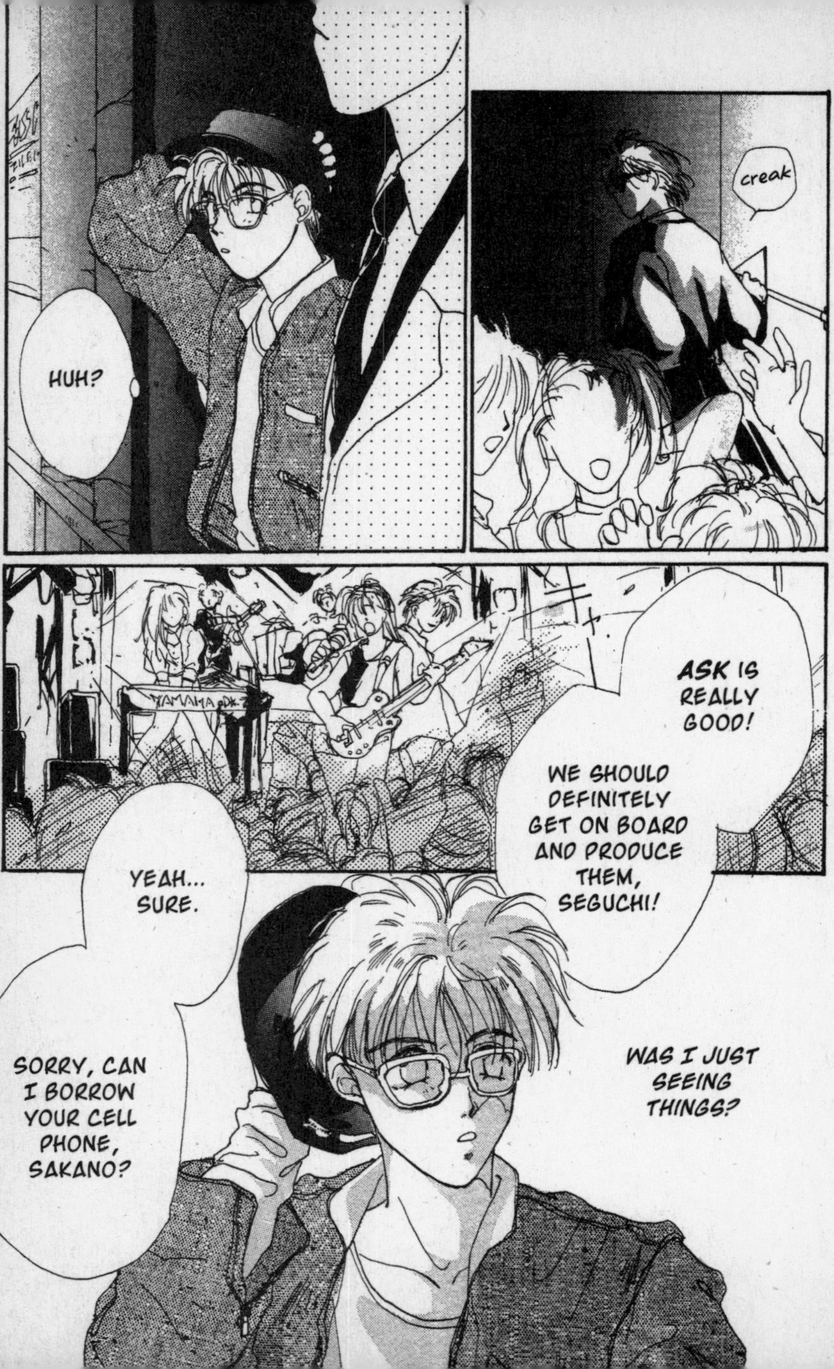
creak
HUH?
ASK IS REALLY GOOD!
WE SHOULD DEFINITELY GET ON BOARD AND PRODUCE THEM, SEGUCHI!
YEAH... SURE.
WAS I JUST SEEING THINGS?
SORRY, CAN I BORROW YOUR CELL PHONE, SAKANO?

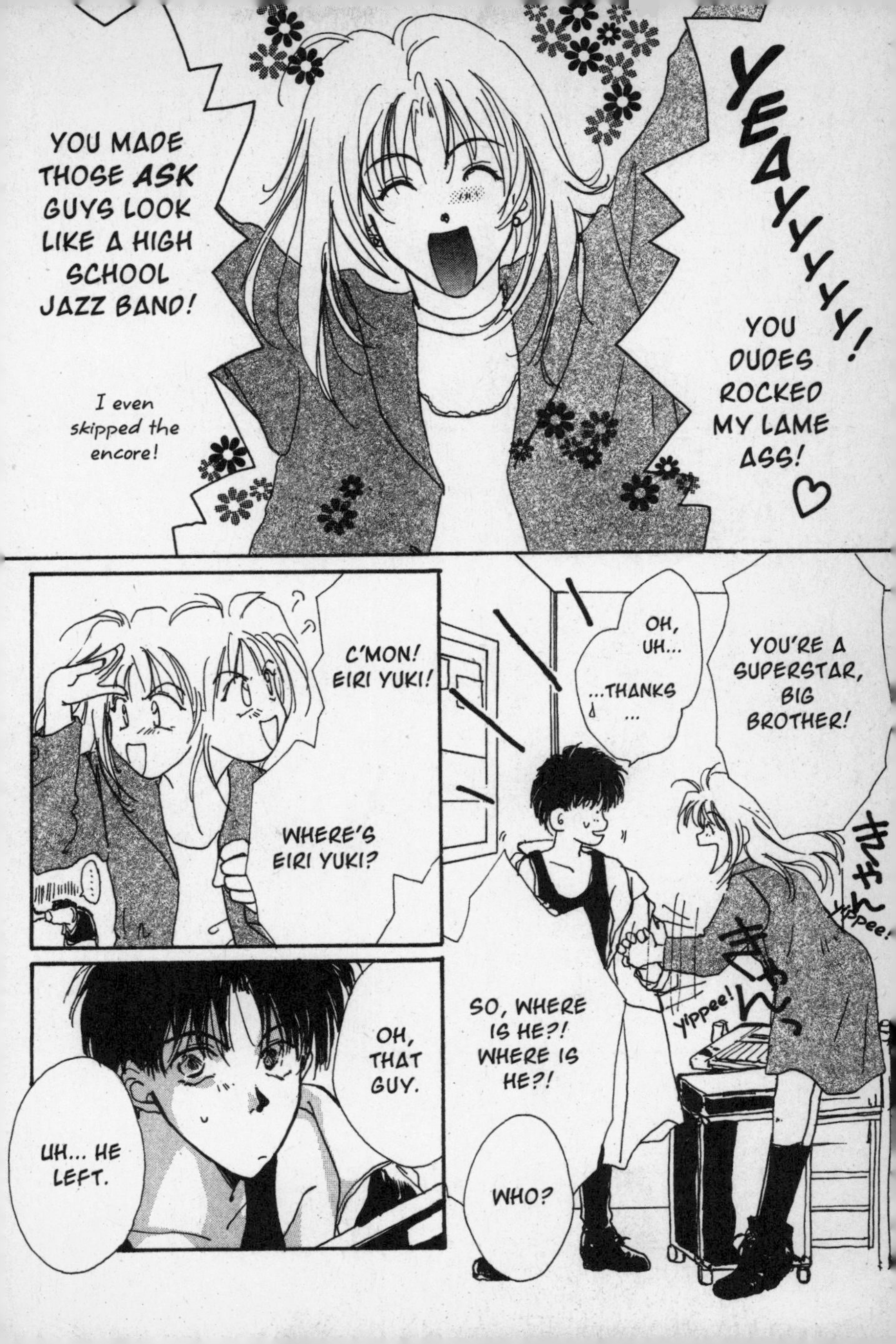
YEAYYYYYY!
YOU DUDES ROCKED MY LAME ASS! ♡
YOU MADE THOSE ASK GUYS LOOK LIKE A HIGH SCHOOL JAZZ BAND!
I even skipped the encore!
YOU'RE A SUPERSTAR, BIG BROTHER!
OH, UH... ...THANKS ...
Yippee!
Yippee!
SO, WHERE IS HE?! WHERE IS HE?!
WHO?
C'MON! EIRI YUKI!
WHERE'S EIRI YUKI?
OH, THAT GUY.
UH... HE LEFT.

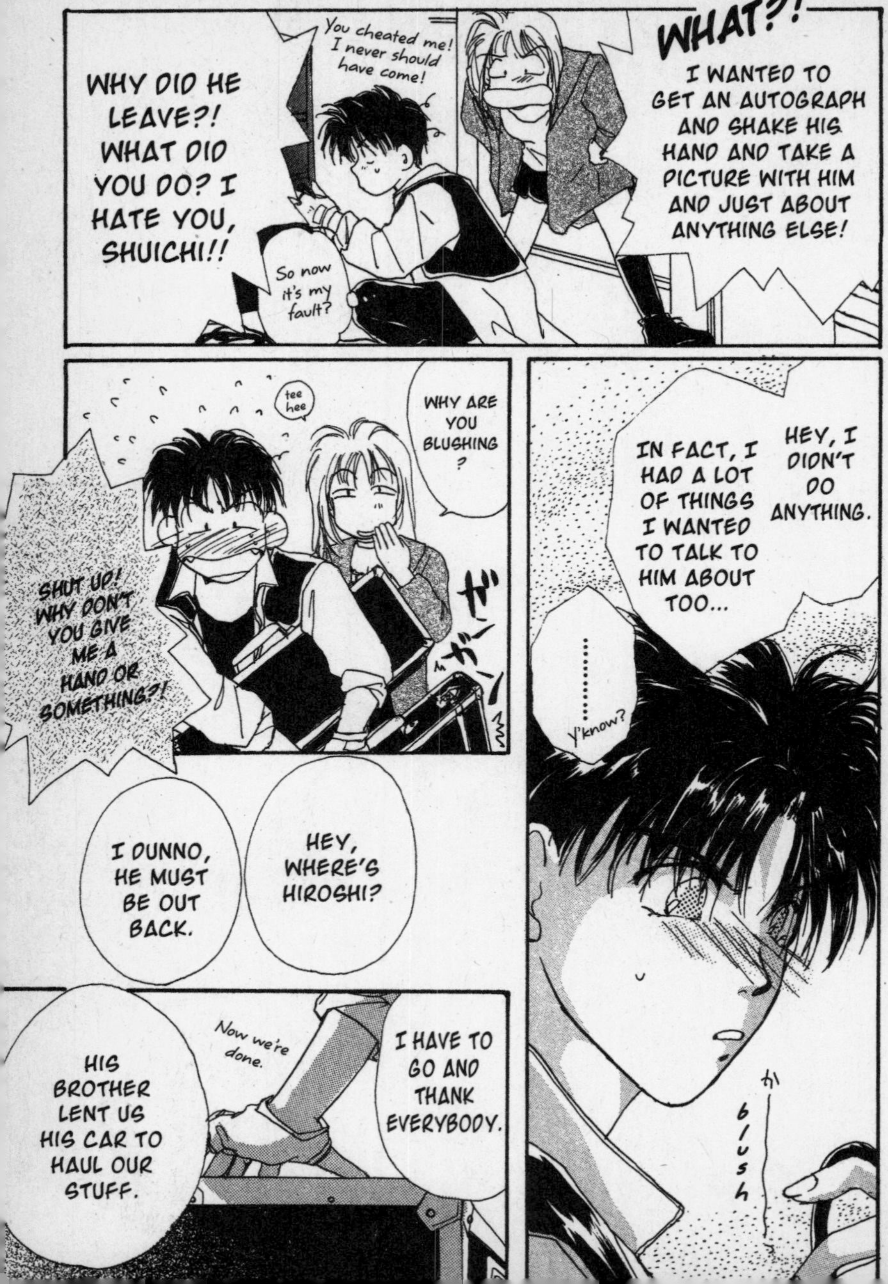

WHAT?!
I WANTED TO GET AN AUTOGRAPH AND SHAKE HIS HAND AND TAKE A PICTURE WITH HIM AND JUST ABOUT ANYTHING ELSE!
You cheated me! I never should have come!
WHY DID HE LEAVE?! WHAT DID YOU DO? I HATE YOU, SHUICHI!!
So now it's my fault?
HEY, I DIDN'T DO ANYTHING.
IN FACT, I HAD A LOT OF THINGS I WANTED TO TALK TO HIM ABOUT TOO...
......y'know?
blush
WHY ARE YOU BLUSHING?
tee hee
SHUT UP! WHY DON'T YOU GIVE ME A HAND OR SOMETHING?!
HEY, WHERE'S HIROSHI?
I DUNNO, HE MUST BE OUT BACK.
I HAVE TO GO AND THANK EVERYBODY.
Now we're done.
HIS BROTHER LENT US HIS CAR TO HAUL OUR STUFF.

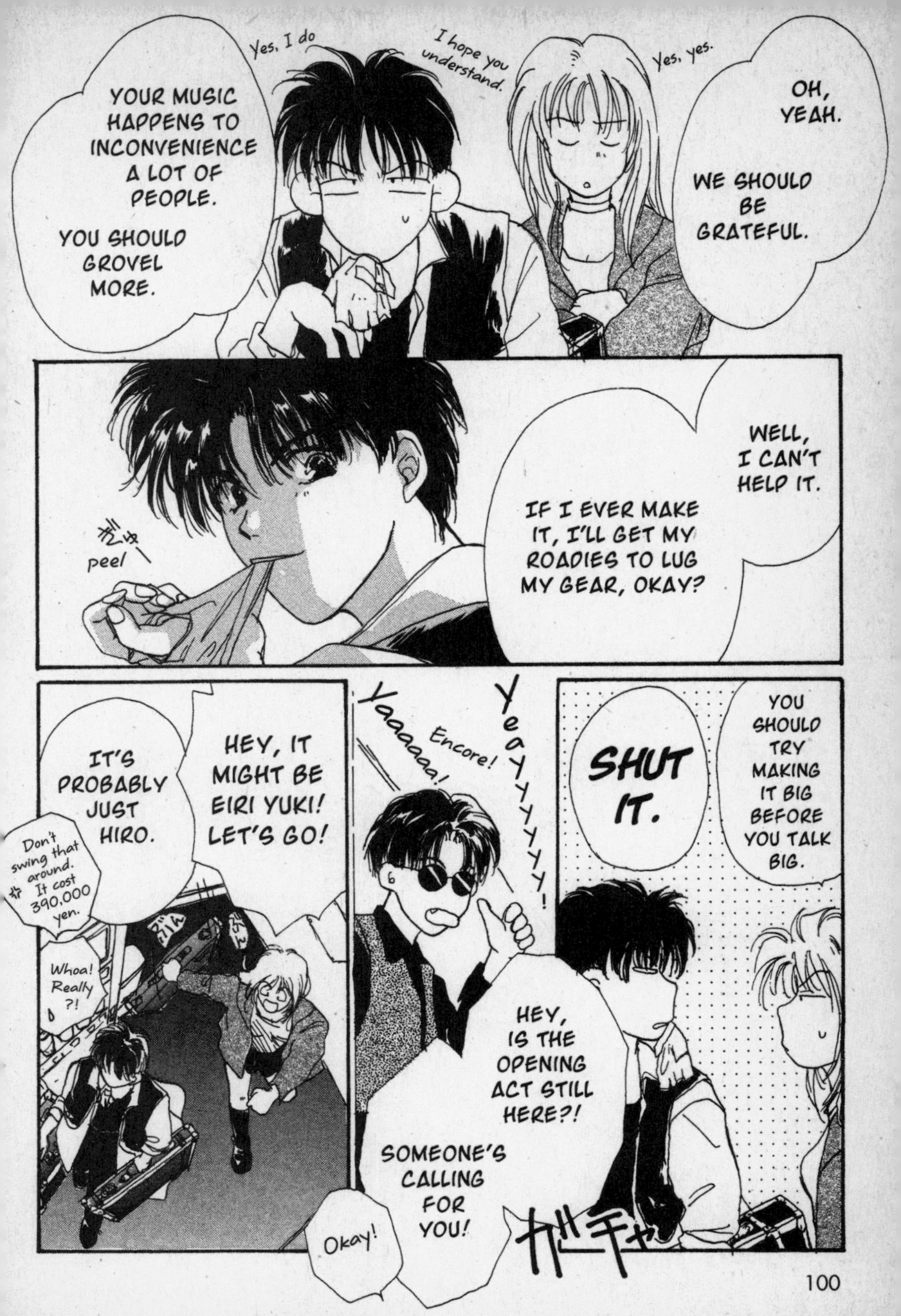
OH, YEAH.
WE SHOULD BE GRATEFUL.
Yes, yes.
I hope you understand.
Yes, I do
YOUR MUSIC HAPPENS TO INCONVENIENCE A LOT OF PEOPLE.
YOU SHOULD GROVEL MORE.
WELL, I CAN'T HELP IT.
IF I EVER MAKE IT, I'LL GET MY ROADIES TO LUG MY GEAR, OKAY?
peel
YOU SHOULD TRY MAKING IT BIG BEFORE YOU TALK BIG.
SHUT IT.
Yea———!
Encore!
Yaaaaaa!
HEY, IS THE OPENING ACT STILL HERE?!
SOMEONE'S CALLING FOR YOU!
Okay!
HEY, IT MIGHT BE EIRI YUKI! LET'S GO!
IT'S PROBABLY JUST HIRO.
Don't swing that around. It cost 390,000 yen.
Whoa! Really?!

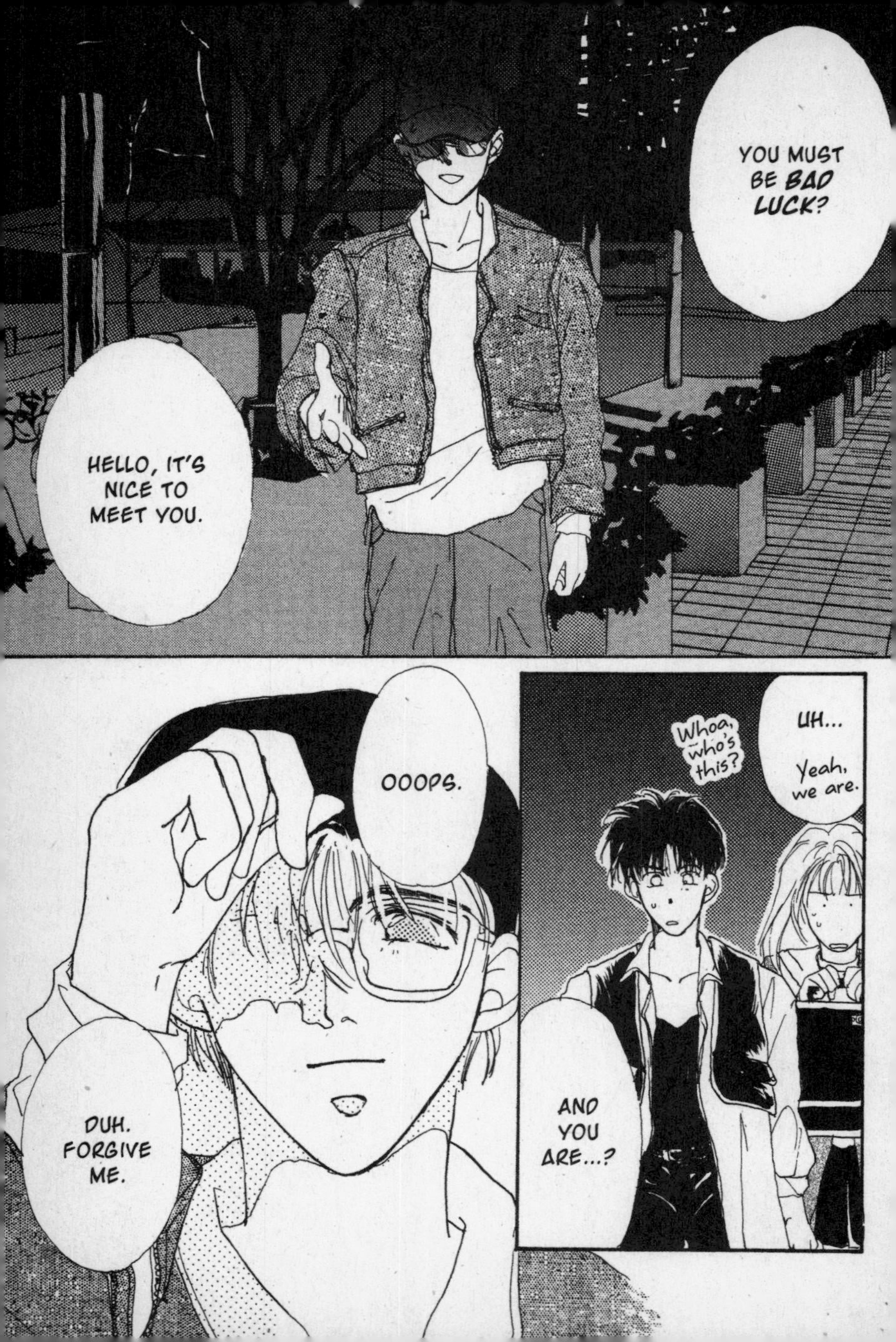
YOU MUST BE BAD LUCK?
HELLO, IT'S NICE TO MEET YOU.
UH...
Yeah, we are.
Whoa, who's this?
AND YOU ARE...?
OOOPS.
DUH. FORGIVE ME.

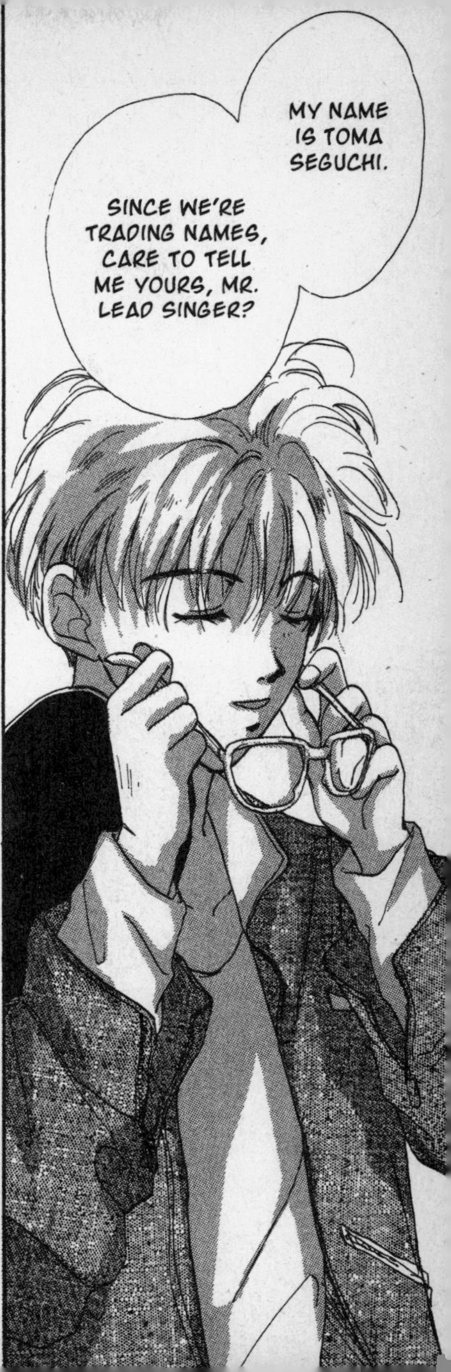
MY NAME IS TOMA SEGUCHI.
SINCE WE'RE TRADING NAMES, CARE TO TELL ME YOURS, MR. LEAD SINGER?

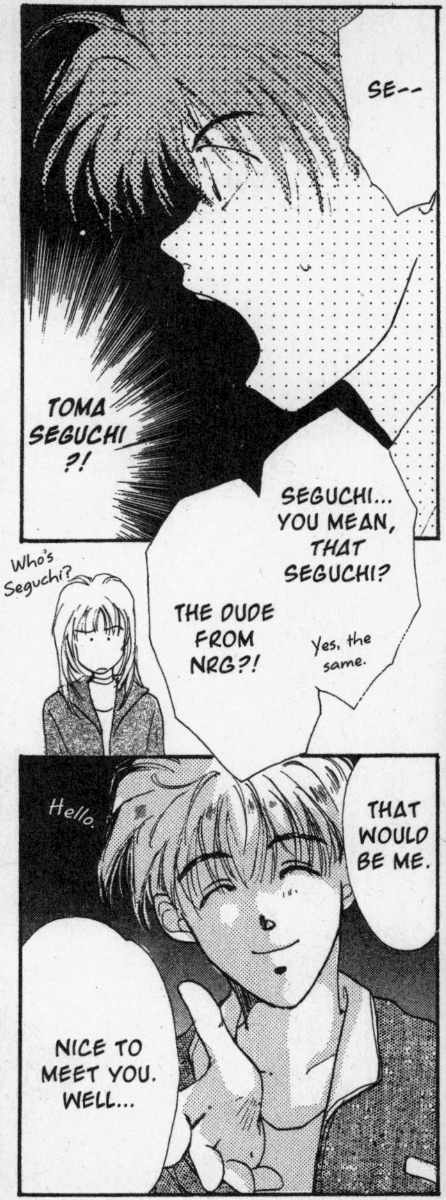
SE--
TOMA SEGUCHI ?!
SEGUCHI... YOU MEAN, THAT SEGUCHI?
THE DUDE FROM NRG?!
Yes, the same.
Who's Seguchi?
THAT WOULD BE ME.
Hello.
NICE TO MEET YOU. WELL...

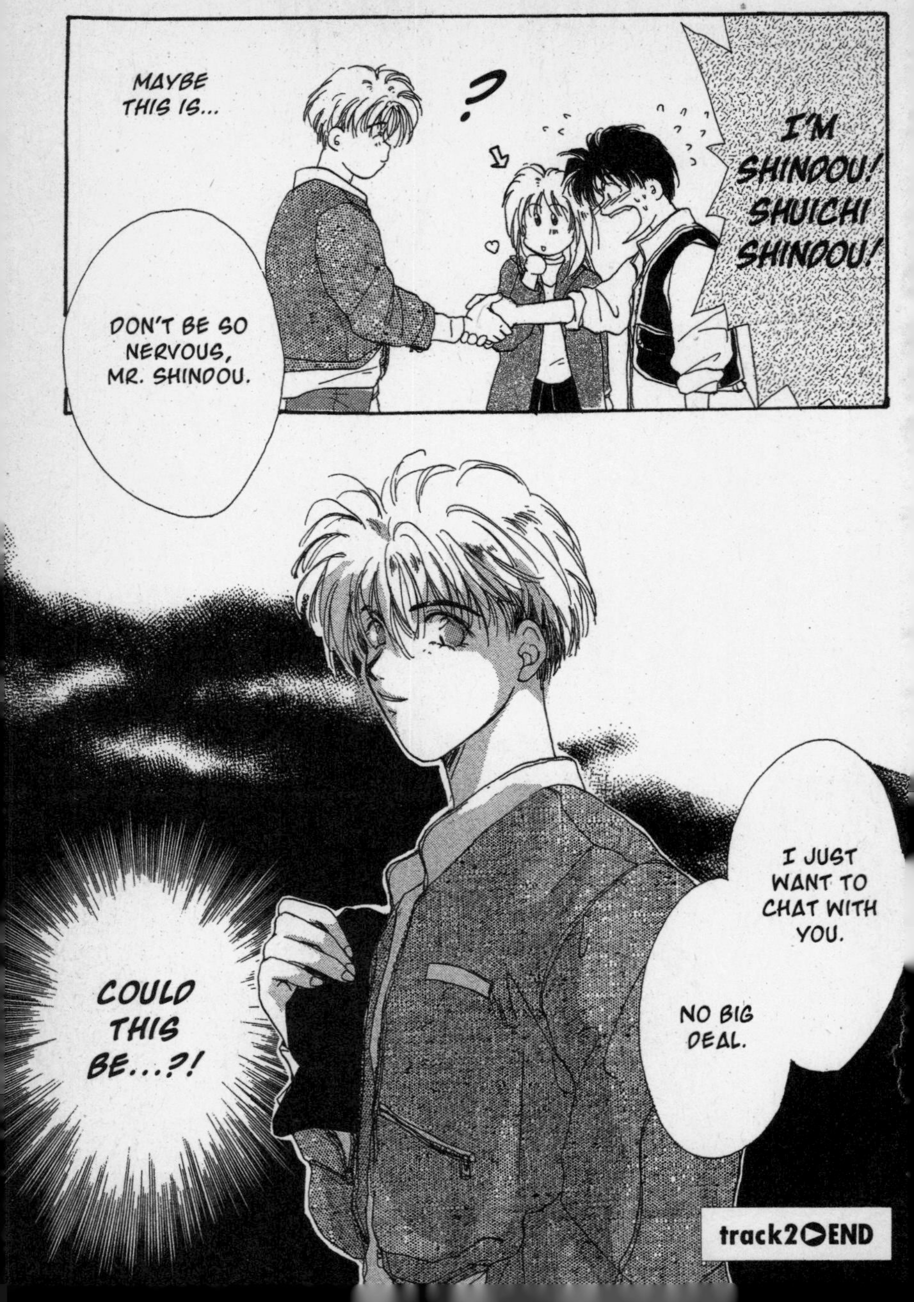
I'M SHINDOU! SHUICHI SHINDOU!
MAYBE THIS IS...
DON'T BE SO NERVOUS, MR. SHINDOU.
I JUST WANT TO CHAT WITH YOU.
NO BIG DEAL.
COULD THIS BE...?!
track2 END

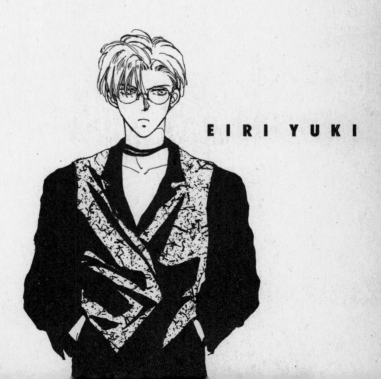

EIRI YUKI

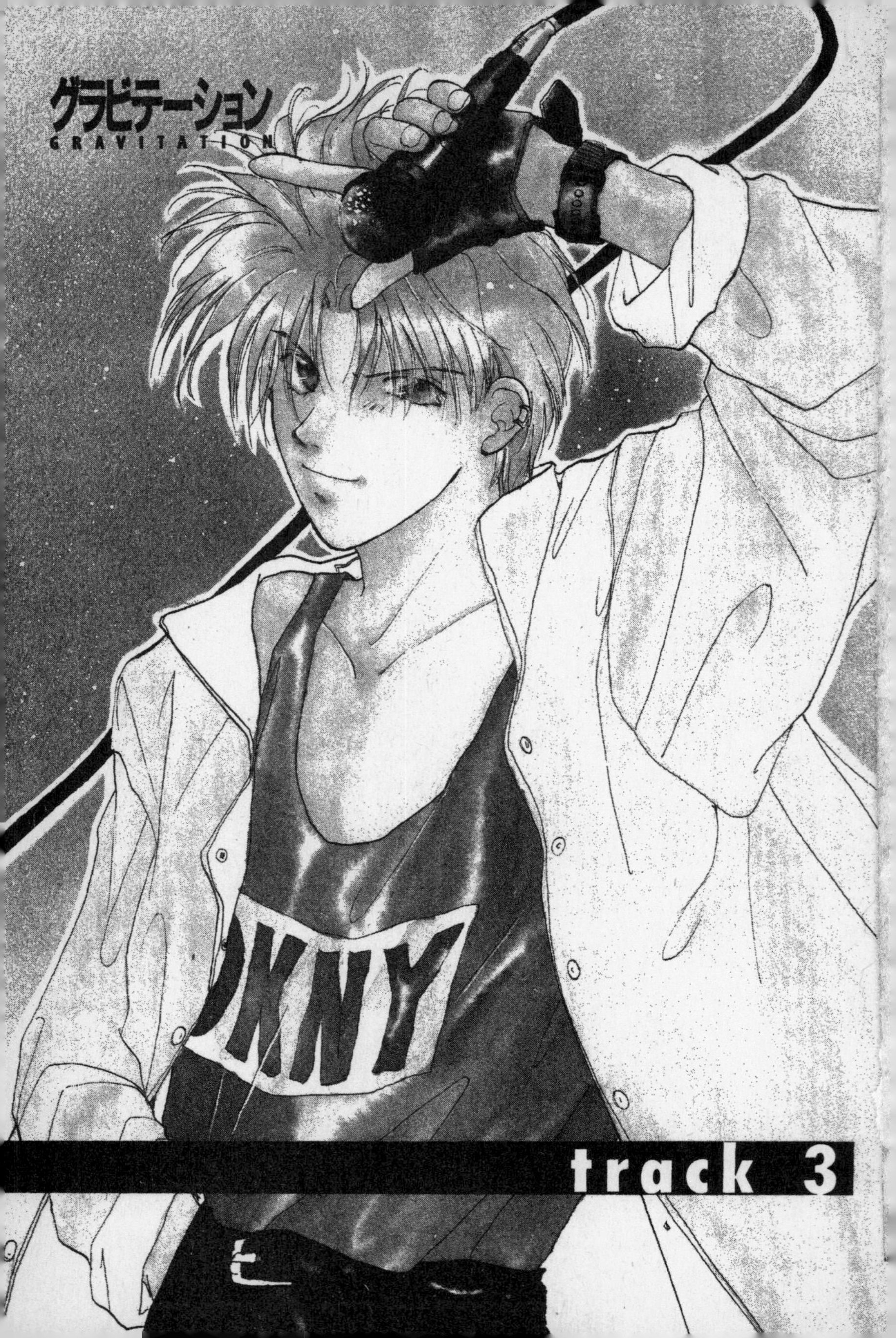
グラビテーション
GRAVITATION
track 3

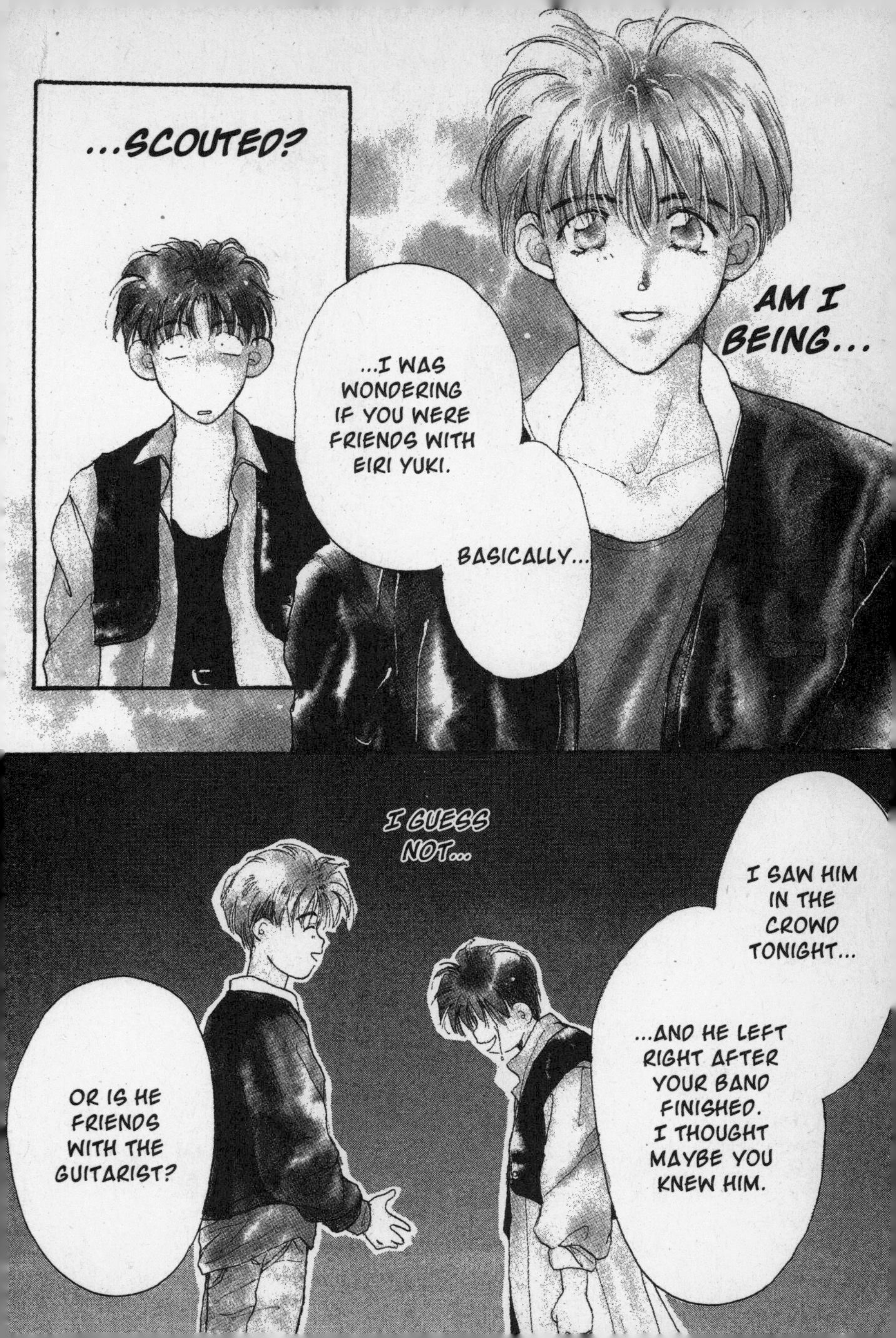
AM I BEING...
BASICALLY...
...I WAS WONDERING IF YOU WERE FRIENDS WITH EIRI YUKI.
...SCOUTED?
I SAW HIM IN THE CROWD TONIGHT...
...AND HE LEFT RIGHT AFTER YOUR BAND FINISHED. I THOUGHT MAYBE YOU KNEW HIM.
I GUESS NOT...
OR IS HE FRIENDS WITH THE GUITARIST?

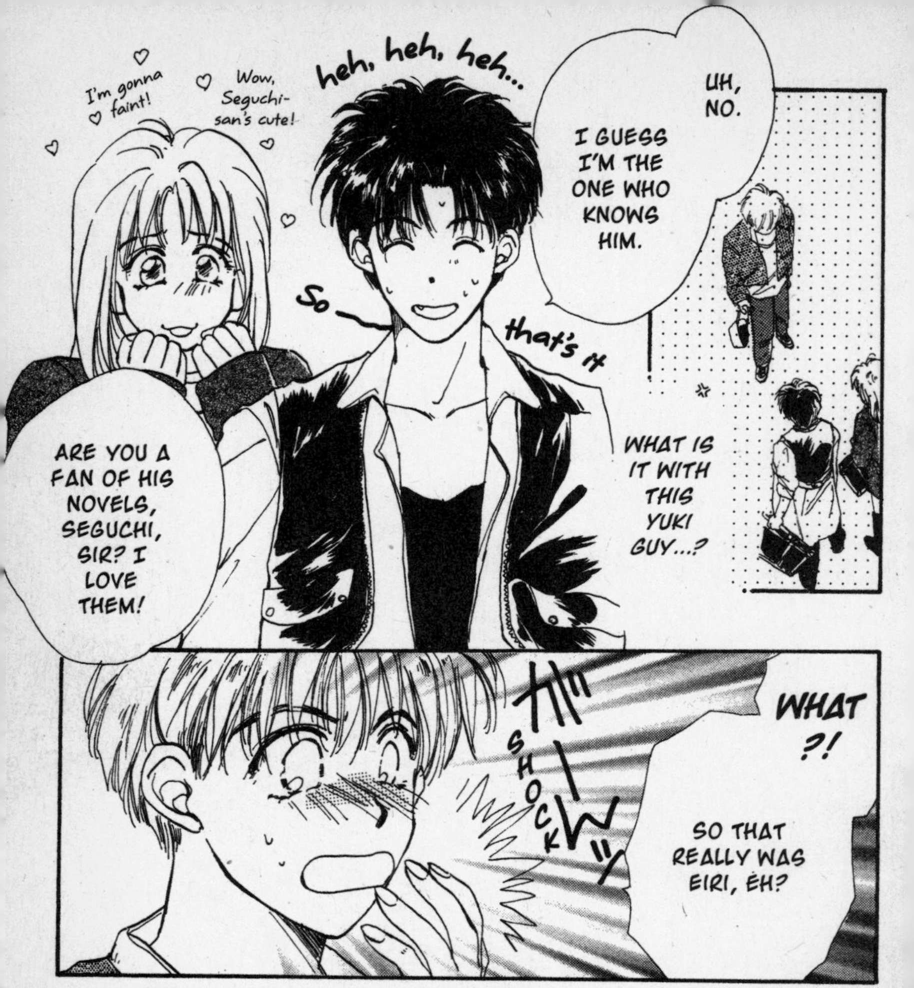
UH, NO.
I GUESS I'M THE ONE WHO KNOWS HIM.
heh, heh, heh...
So— that's it
WHAT IS IT WITH THIS YUKI GUY...?
Wow, Seguchi-san's cute!
I'm gonna faint!
ARE YOU A FAN OF HIS NOVELS, SEGUCHI, SIR? I LOVE THEM!
WHAT ?!
SO THAT REALLY WAS EIRI, EH?
SHOCK

♡ Q & A CORNER ♡

Among the many questions we get, two of the most common are "What are DTM and techno?" Techno is a music genre, the same way that rock and jazz are particular genres of music. Basically, it means music generated by computer, and has often been called "electronica." DTM is an abbreviation for desktop music, meaning created on a desktop. DTM can stand for music created on a synthesizer or computer, whether it's the actual sounds or the composition of a song.

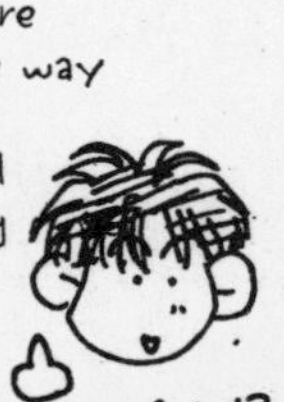
Got it?

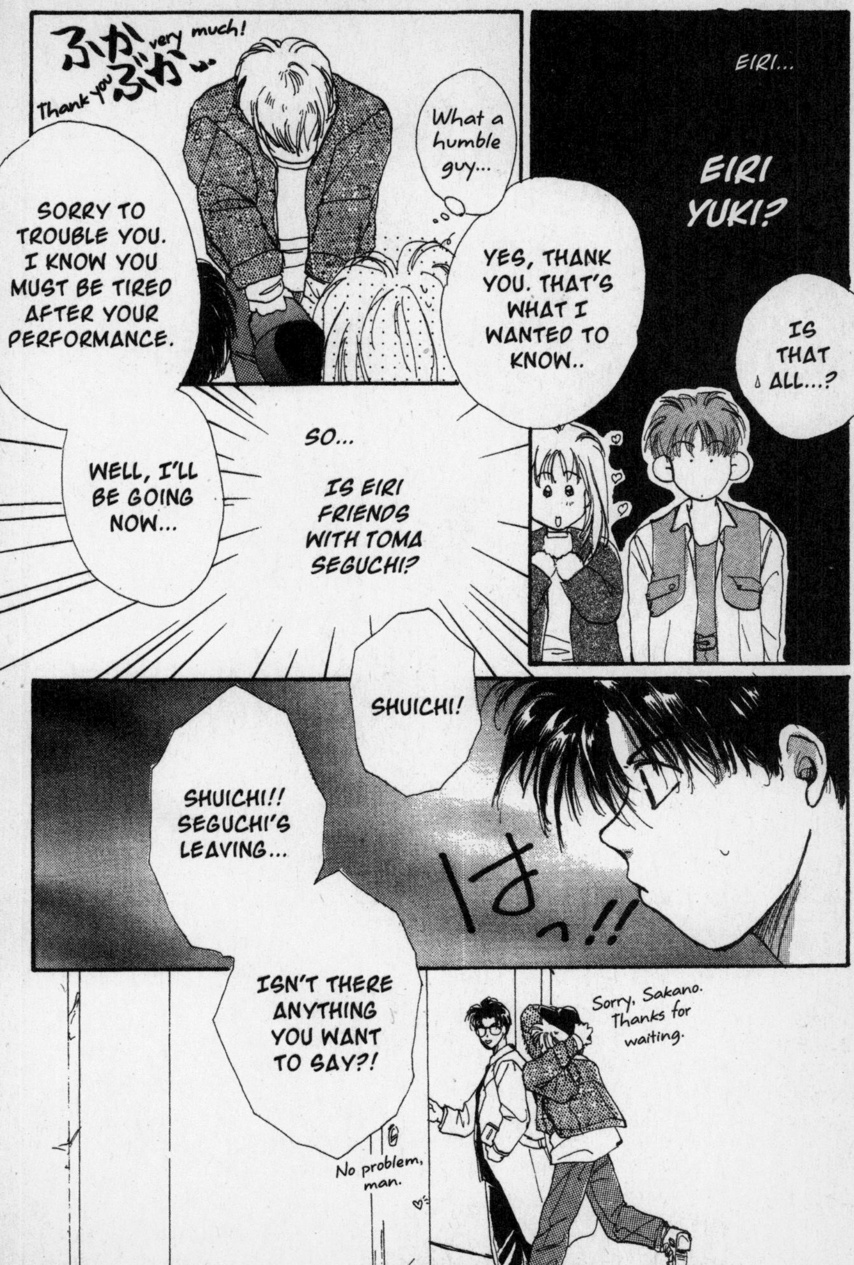
EIRI...
EIRI YUKI?
YES, THANK YOU. THAT'S WHAT I WANTED TO KNOW..
IS THAT ALL...?
What a humble guy...
ふかぶか... Thank you very much!
SORRY TO TROUBLE YOU. I KNOW YOU MUST BE TIRED AFTER YOUR PERFORMANCE.
WELL, I'LL BE GOING NOW...
SO... IS EIRI FRIENDS WITH TOMA SEGUCHI?
SHUICHI!
SHUICHI!! SEGUCHI'S LEAVING...
はっ!!
ISN'T THERE ANYTHING YOU WANT TO SAY?!
Sorry, Sakano. Thanks for waiting.
No problem, man.

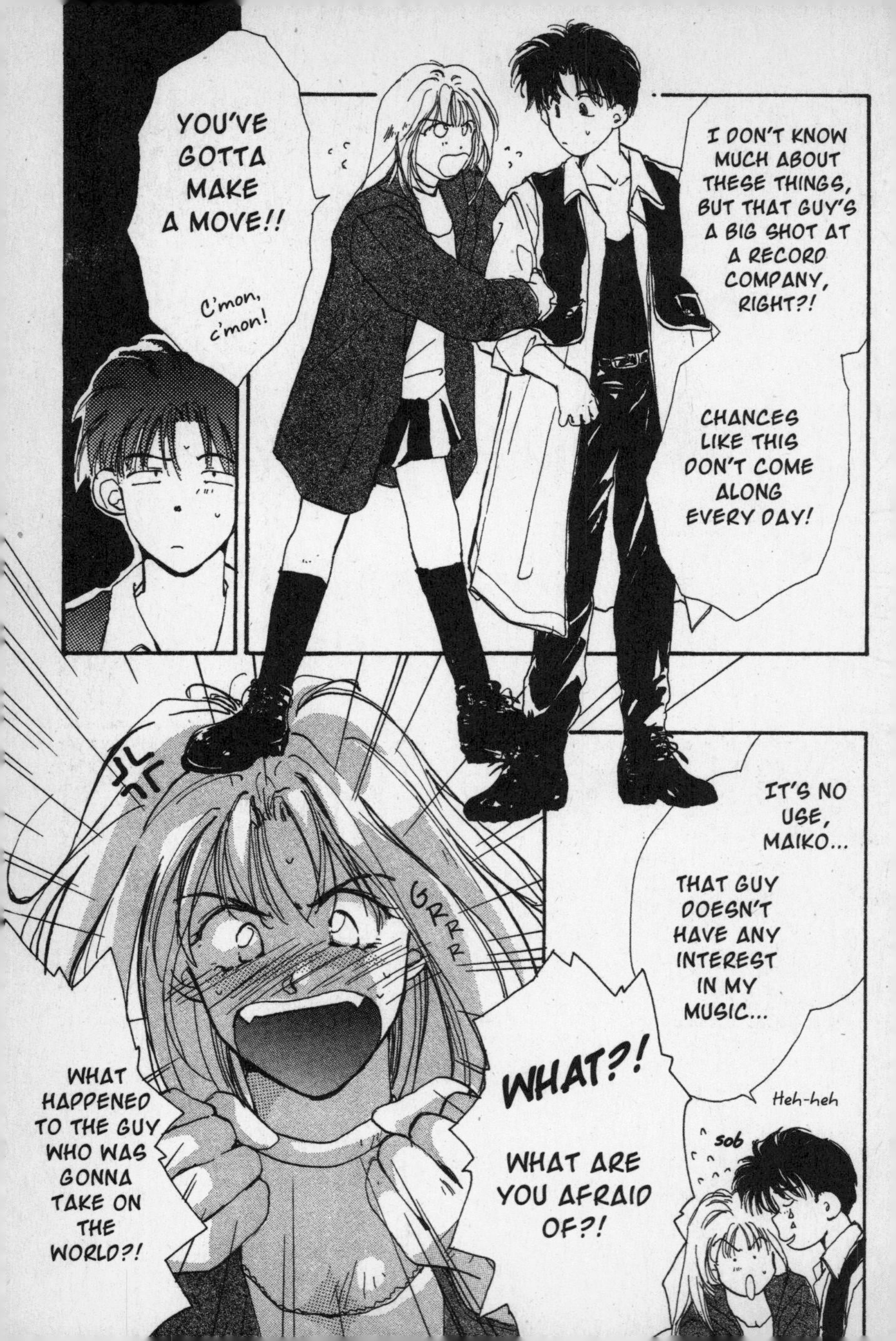

I DON'T KNOW MUCH ABOUT THESE THINGS, BUT THAT GUY'S A BIG SHOT AT A RECORD COMPANY, RIGHT?!
CHANCES LIKE THIS DON'T COME ALONG EVERY DAY!
YOU'VE GOTTA MAKE A MOVE!!
C'mon, c'mon!
IT'S NO USE, MAIKO...
THAT GUY DOESN'T HAVE ANY INTEREST IN MY MUSIC...
Heh-heh
sob
GRRR
WHAT?!
WHAT ARE YOU AFRAID OF?!
WHAT HAPPENED TO THE GUY WHO WAS GONNA TAKE ON THE WORLD?!

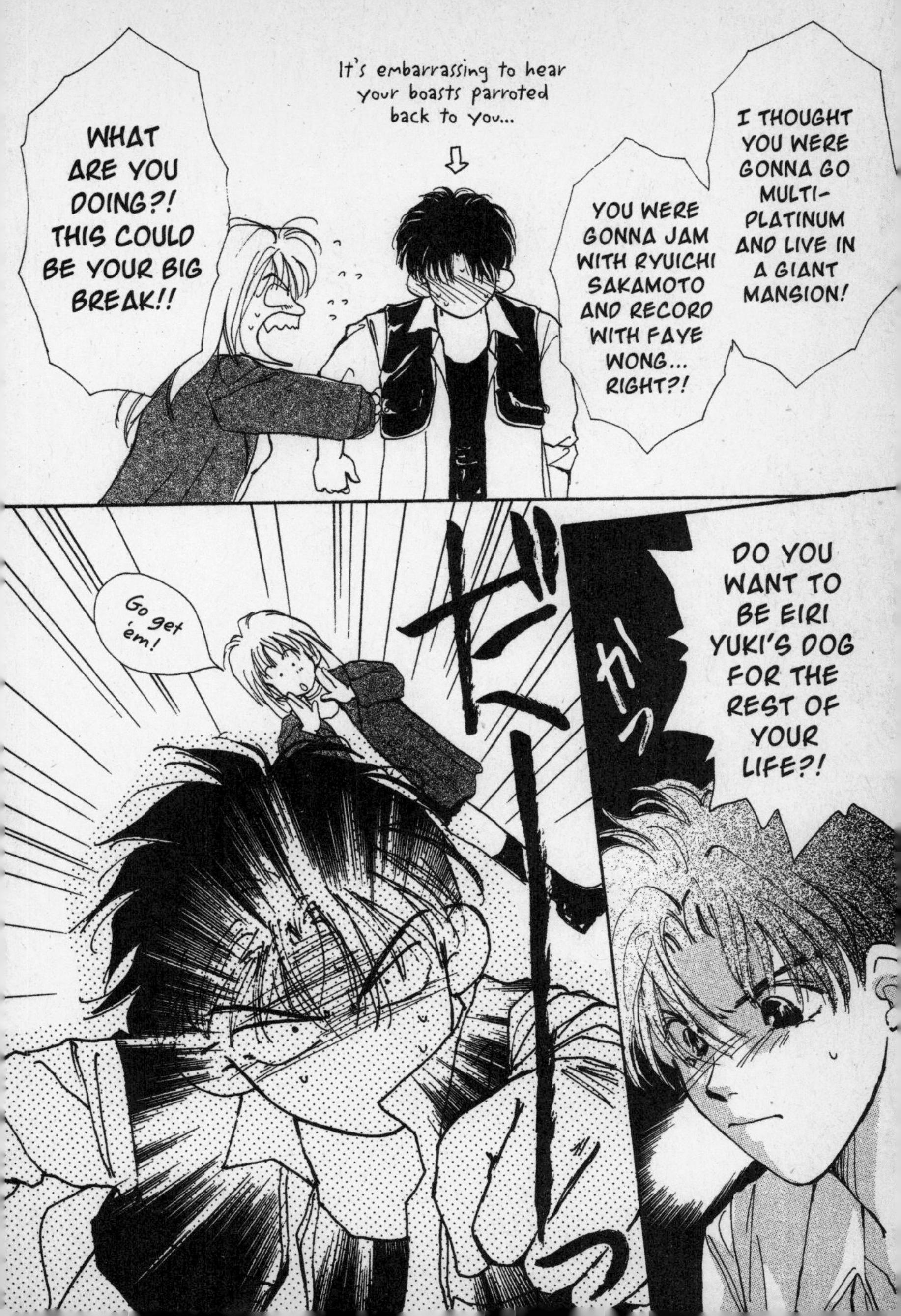
I THOUGHT YOU WERE GONNA GO MULTI-PLATINUM AND LIVE IN A GIANT MANSION!
YOU WERE GONNA JAM WITH RYUICHI SAKAMOTO AND RECORD WITH FAYE WONG... RIGHT?!
It's embarrassing to hear your boasts parroted back to you...
WHAT ARE YOU DOING?! THIS COULD BE YOUR BIG BREAK!!
DO YOU WANT TO BE EIRI YUKI'S DOG FOR THE REST OF YOUR LIFE?!
Go get 'em!

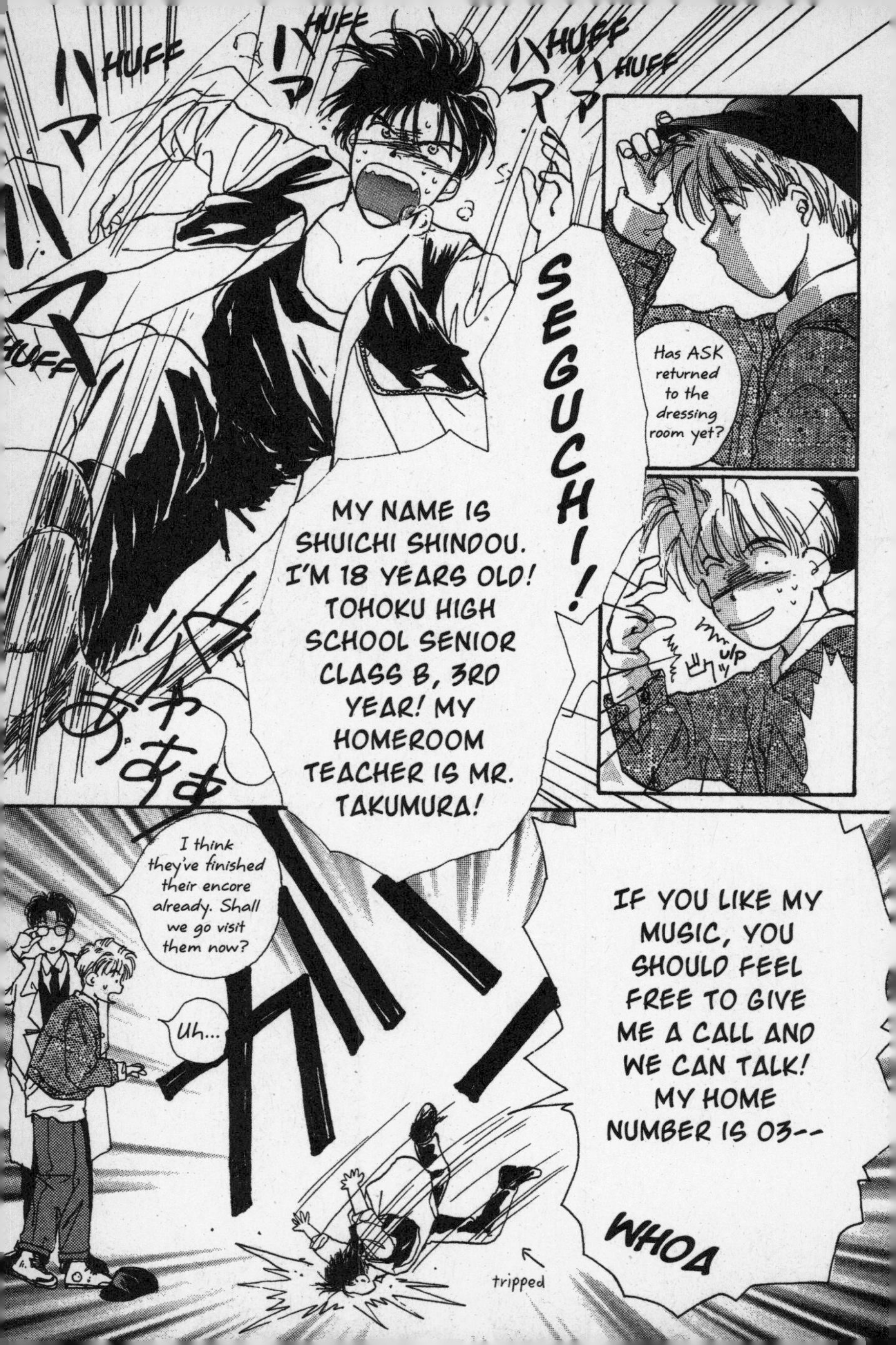
Has ASK returned to the dressing room yet?
ulp
HUFF
HUFF
HUFF
HUFF
HUFF
SEGUCHI!
MY NAME IS SHUICHI SHINDOU. I'M 18 YEARS OLD! TOHOKU HIGH SCHOOL SENIOR CLASS B, 3RD YEAR! MY HOMEROOM TEACHER IS MR. TAKUMURA!
IF YOU LIKE MY MUSIC, YOU SHOULD FEEL FREE TO GIVE ME A CALL AND WE CAN TALK! MY HOME NUMBER IS 03--
WHOA
tripped
I think they've finished their encore already. Shall we go visit them now?
Uh...

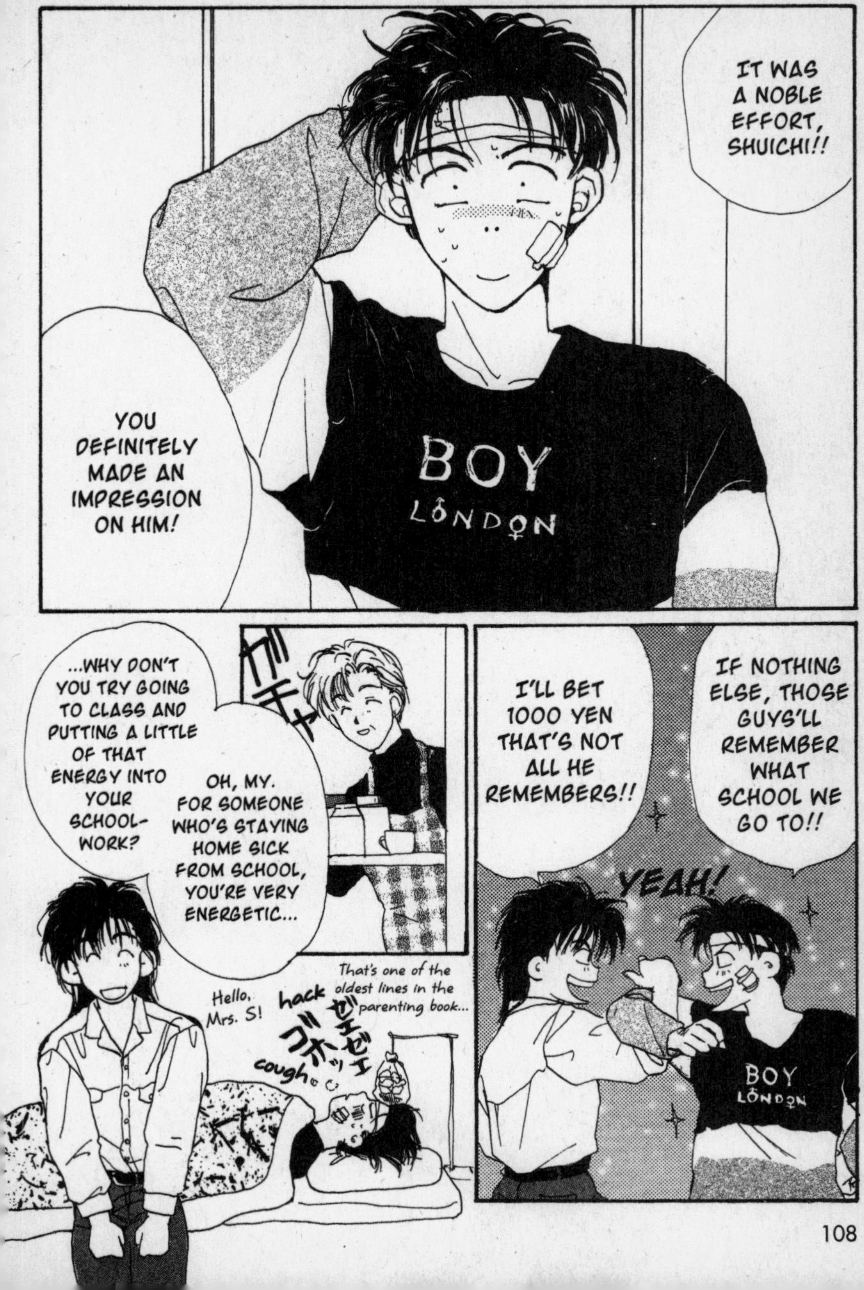
IT WAS A NOBLE EFFORT, SHUICHI!!
YOU DEFINITELY MADE AN IMPRESSION ON HIM!
BOY LONDON
IF NOTHING ELSE, THOSE GUYS'LL REMEMBER WHAT SCHOOL WE GO TO!!
I'LL BET 1000 YEN THAT'S NOT ALL HE REMEMBERS!!
YEAH!
BOY LONDON
ガチャ
OH, MY. FOR SOMEONE WHO'S STAYING HOME SICK FROM SCHOOL, YOU'RE VERY ENERGETIC...
...WHY DON'T YOU TRY GOING TO CLASS AND PUTTING A LITTLE OF THAT ENERGY INTO YOUR SCHOOL-WORK?
That's one of the oldest lines in the parenting book...
hack
ゼェゼェ
ゴホッ
cough
Hello, Mrs. S!

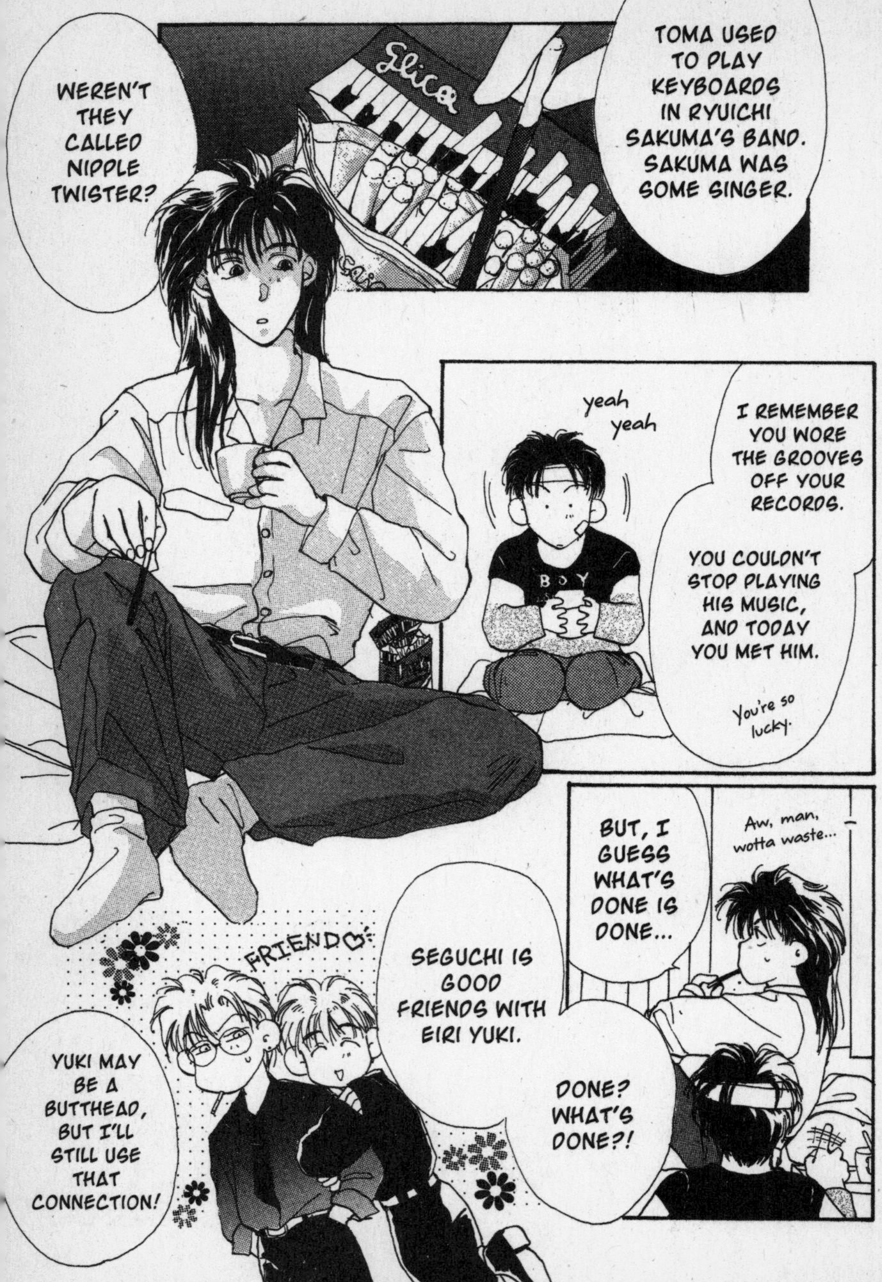
TOMA USED TO PLAY KEYBOARDS IN RYUICHI SAKUMA'S BAND. SAKUMA WAS SOME SINGER.
Glico
WEREN'T THEY CALLED NIPPLE TWISTER?
I REMEMBER YOU WORE THE GROOVES OFF YOUR RECORDS.
YOU COULDN'T STOP PLAYING HIS MUSIC, AND TODAY YOU MET HIM.
You're so lucky.
yeah yeah
Aw, man, wotta waste...
BUT, I GUESS WHAT'S DONE IS DONE...
DONE? WHAT'S DONE?!
SEGUCHI IS GOOD FRIENDS WITH EIRI YUKI.
FRIEND
YUKI MAY BE A BUTTHEAD, BUT I'LL STILL USE THAT CONNECTION!

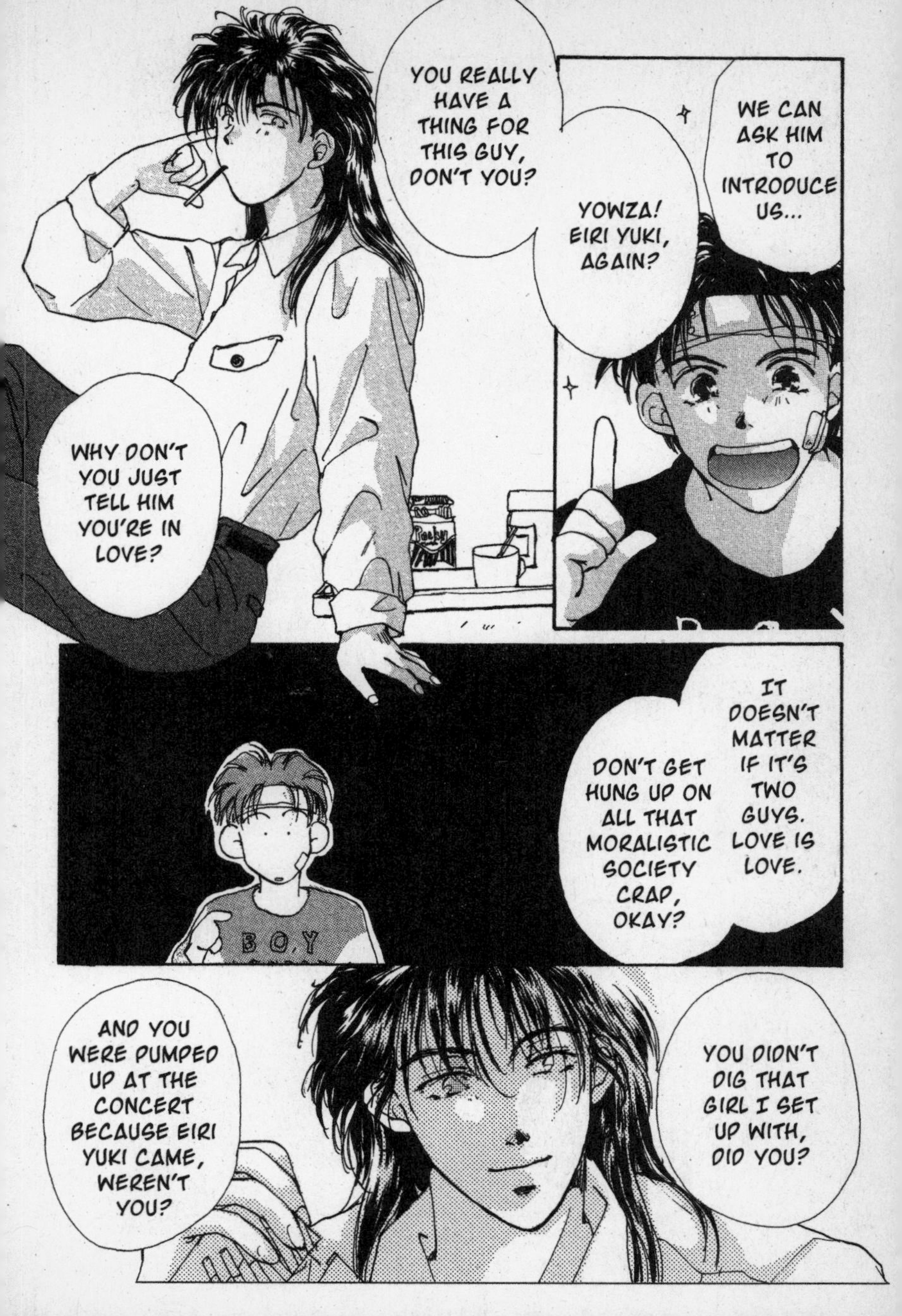
WE CAN ASK HIM TO INTRODUCE US...
YOWZA! EIRI YUKI, AGAIN?
YOU REALLY HAVE A THING FOR THIS GUY, DON'T YOU?
WHY DON'T YOU JUST TELL HIM YOU'RE IN LOVE?
IT DOESN'T MATTER IF IT'S TWO GUYS. LOVE IS LOVE.
DON'T GET HUNG UP ON ALL THAT MORALISTIC SOCIETY CRAP, OKAY?
YOU DIDN'T DIG THAT GIRL I SET UP WITH, DID YOU?
AND YOU WERE PUMPED UP AT THE CONCERT BECAUSE EIRI YUKI CAME, WEREN'T YOU?

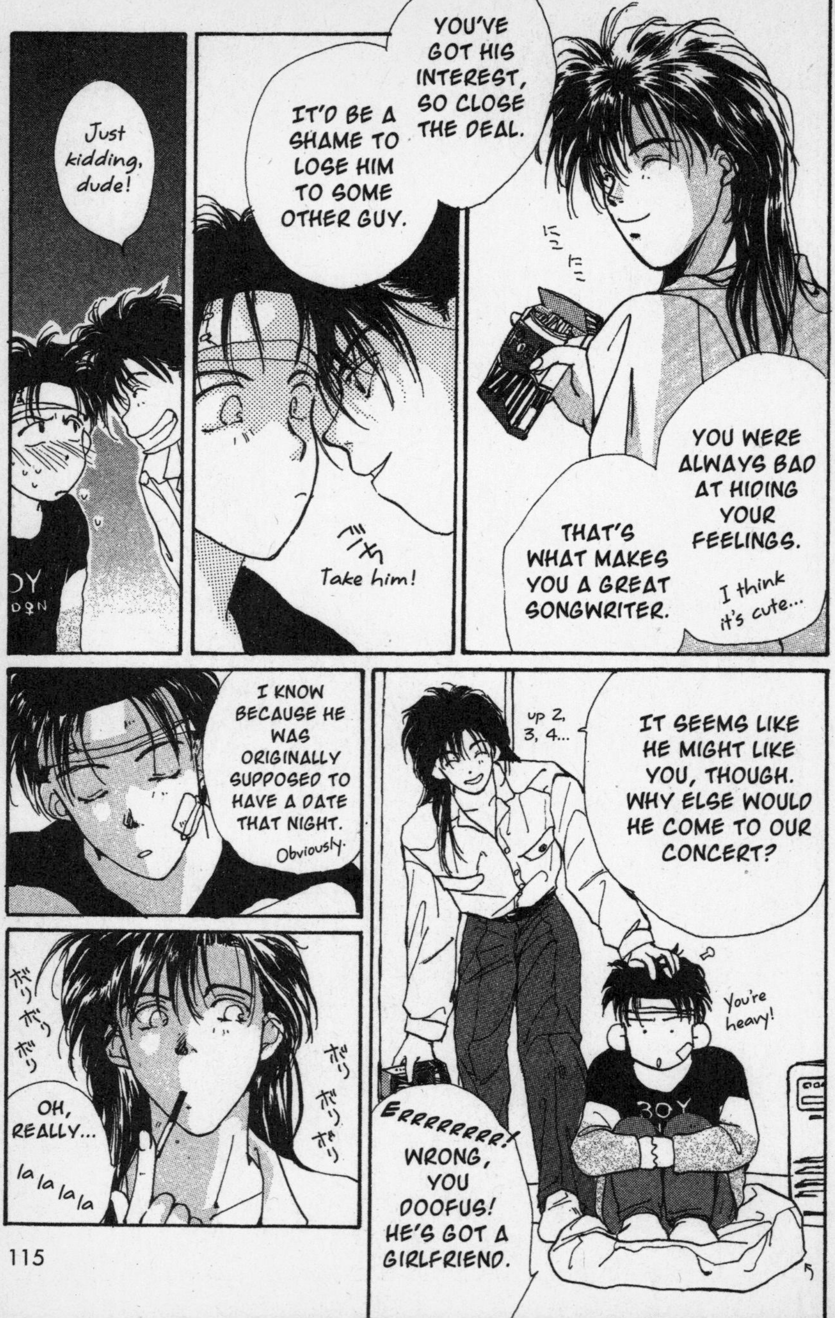
YOU'VE GOT HIS INTEREST, SO CLOSE THE DEAL.
YOU WERE ALWAYS BAD AT HIDING YOUR FEELINGS.
THAT'S WHAT MAKES YOU A GREAT SONGWRITER.
I think it's cute...
IT'D BE A SHAME TO LOSE HIM TO SOME OTHER GUY.
Take him!
Just kidding, dude!
IT SEEMS LIKE HE MIGHT LIKE YOU, THOUGH. WHY ELSE WOULD HE COME TO OUR CONCERT?
up 2, 3, 4...
You're heavy!
ERRRRRRRR! WRONG, YOU DOOFUS! HE'S GOT A GIRLFRIEND.
I KNOW BECAUSE HE WAS ORIGINALLY SUPPOSED TO HAVE A DATE THAT NIGHT.
Obviously.
OH, REALLY...
la la la la

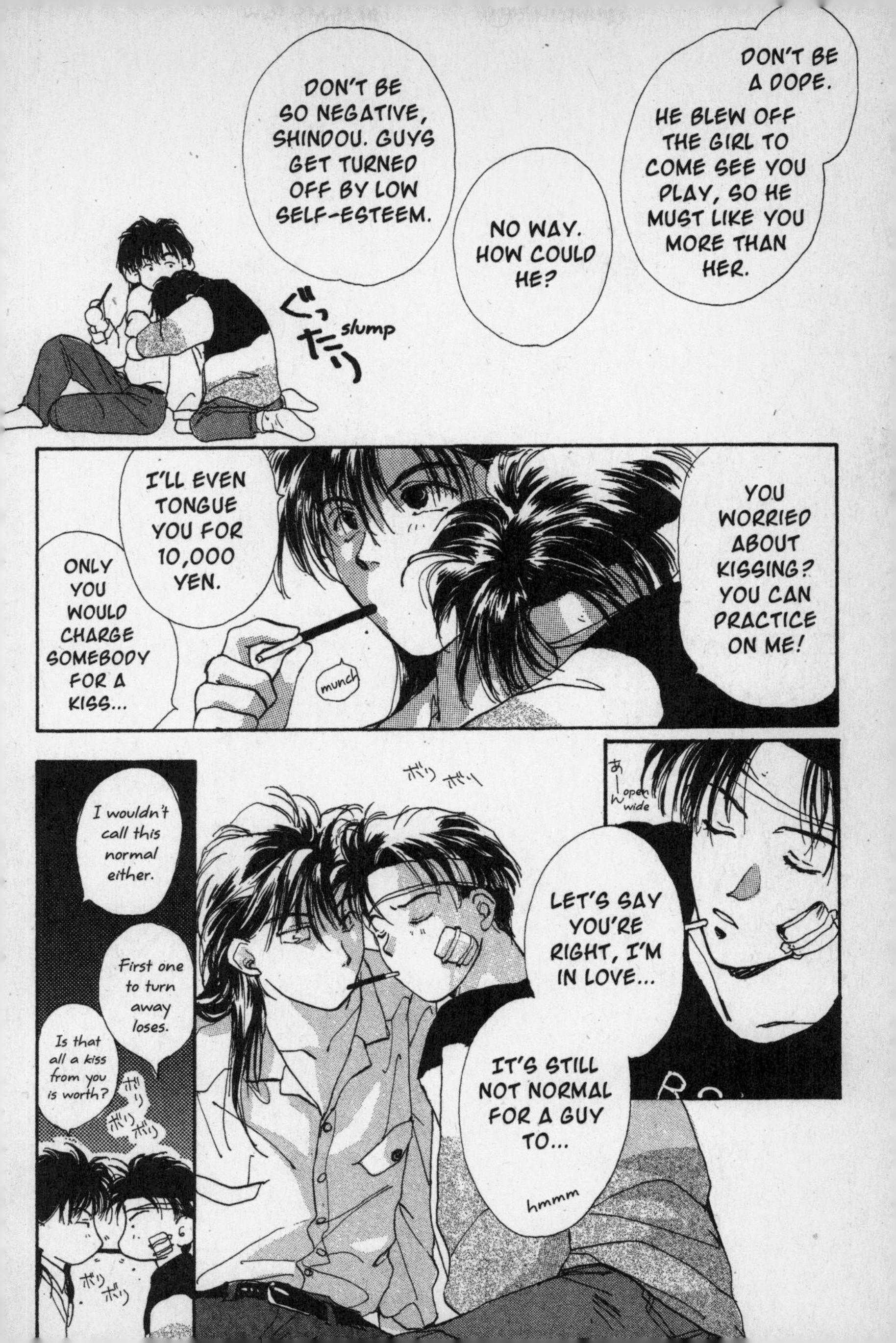
DON'T BE A DOPE.
HE BLEW OFF THE GIRL TO COME SEE YOU PLAY, SO HE MUST LIKE YOU MORE THAN HER.
NO WAY. HOW COULD HE?
DON'T BE SO NEGATIVE, SHINDOU. GUYS GET TURNED OFF BY LOW SELF-ESTEEM.
ぐったり slump
YOU WORRIED ABOUT KISSING? YOU CAN PRACTICE ON ME!
I'LL EVEN TONGUE YOU FOR 10,000 YEN.
ONLY YOU WOULD CHARGE SOMEBODY FOR A KISS...
munch
あ～ん open wide
LET'S SAY YOU'RE RIGHT, I'M IN LOVE...
IT'S STILL NOT NORMAL FOR A GUY TO...
hmmm
ボリ ボリ
I wouldn't call this normal either.
First one to turn away loses.
Is that all a kiss from you is worth?
ボリ ボリ ボリ
ボリ ボリ

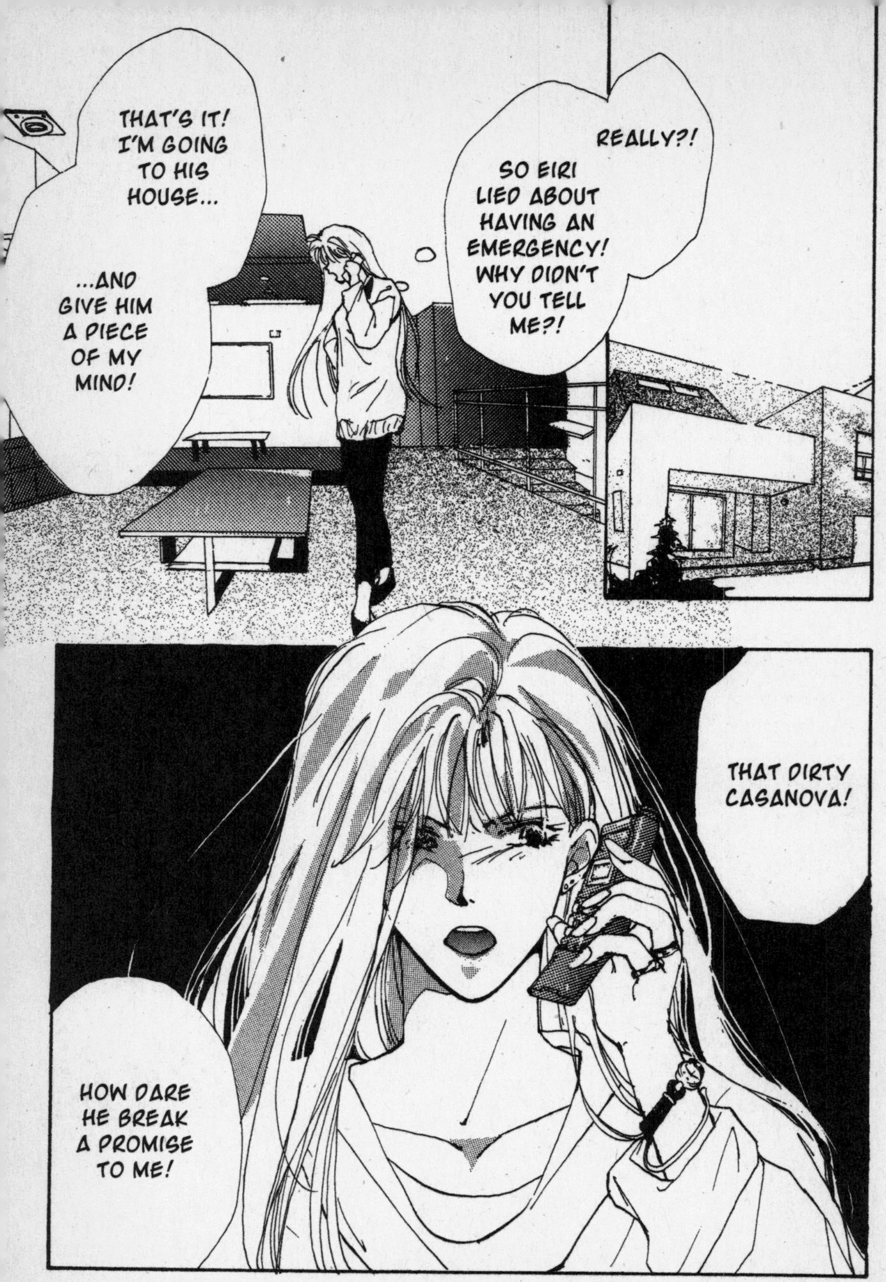
REALLY?!
SO EIRI LIED ABOUT HAVING AN EMERGENCY! WHY DIDN'T YOU TELL ME?!
THAT'S IT! I'M GOING TO HIS HOUSE...
...AND GIVE HIM A PIECE OF MY MIND!
THAT DIRTY CASANOVA!
HOW DARE HE BREAK A PROMISE TO ME!

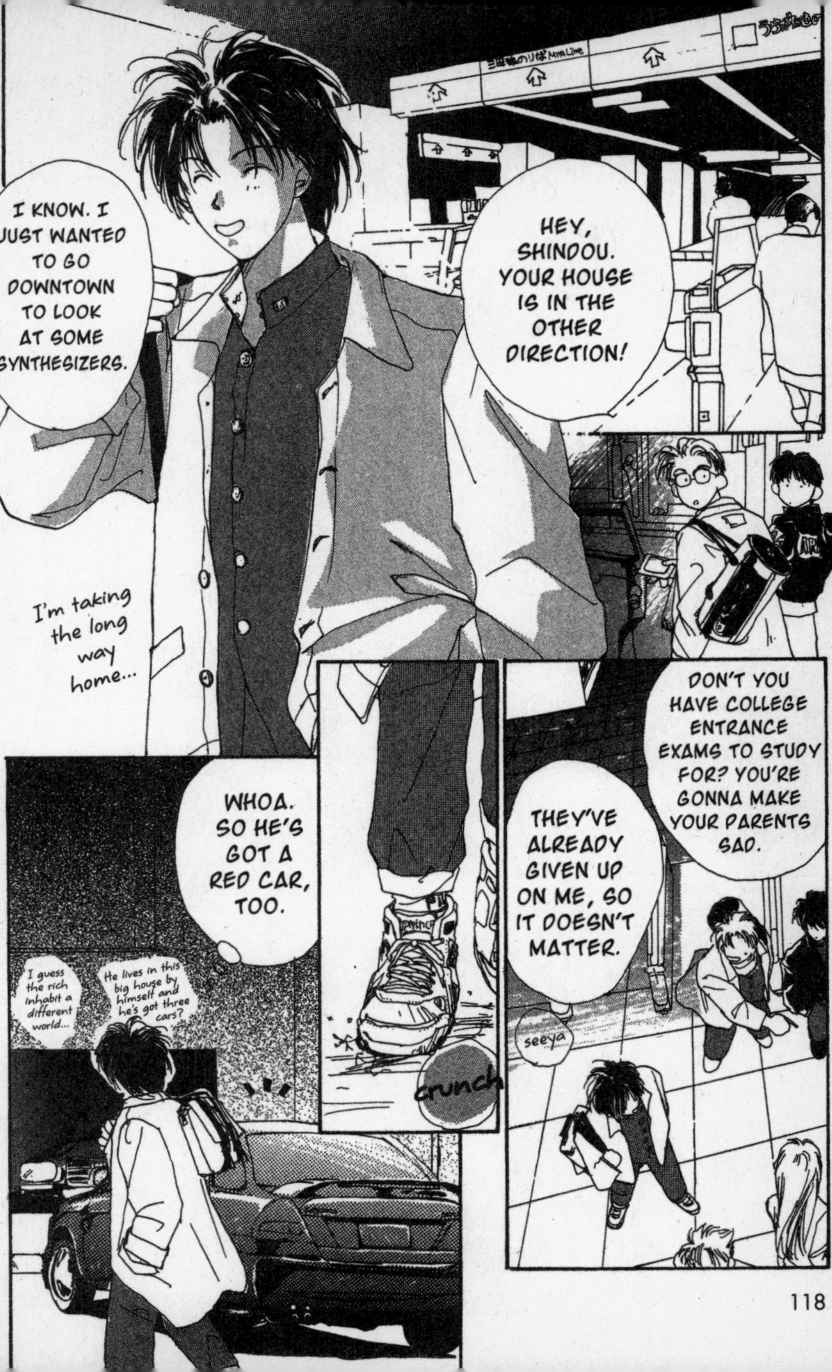
HEY, SHINDOU. YOUR HOUSE IS IN THE OTHER DIRECTION!
I KNOW. I JUST WANTED TO GO DOWNTOWN TO LOOK AT SOME SYNTHESIZERS.
I'm taking the long way home...
DON'T YOU HAVE COLLEGE ENTRANCE EXAMS TO STUDY FOR? YOU'RE GONNA MAKE YOUR PARENTS SAD.
THEY'VE ALREADY GIVEN UP ON ME, SO IT DOESN'T MATTER.
seeya
crunch
WHOA. SO HE'S GOT A RED CAR, TOO.
He lives in this big house by himself and he's got three cars?
I guess the rich inhabit a different world...

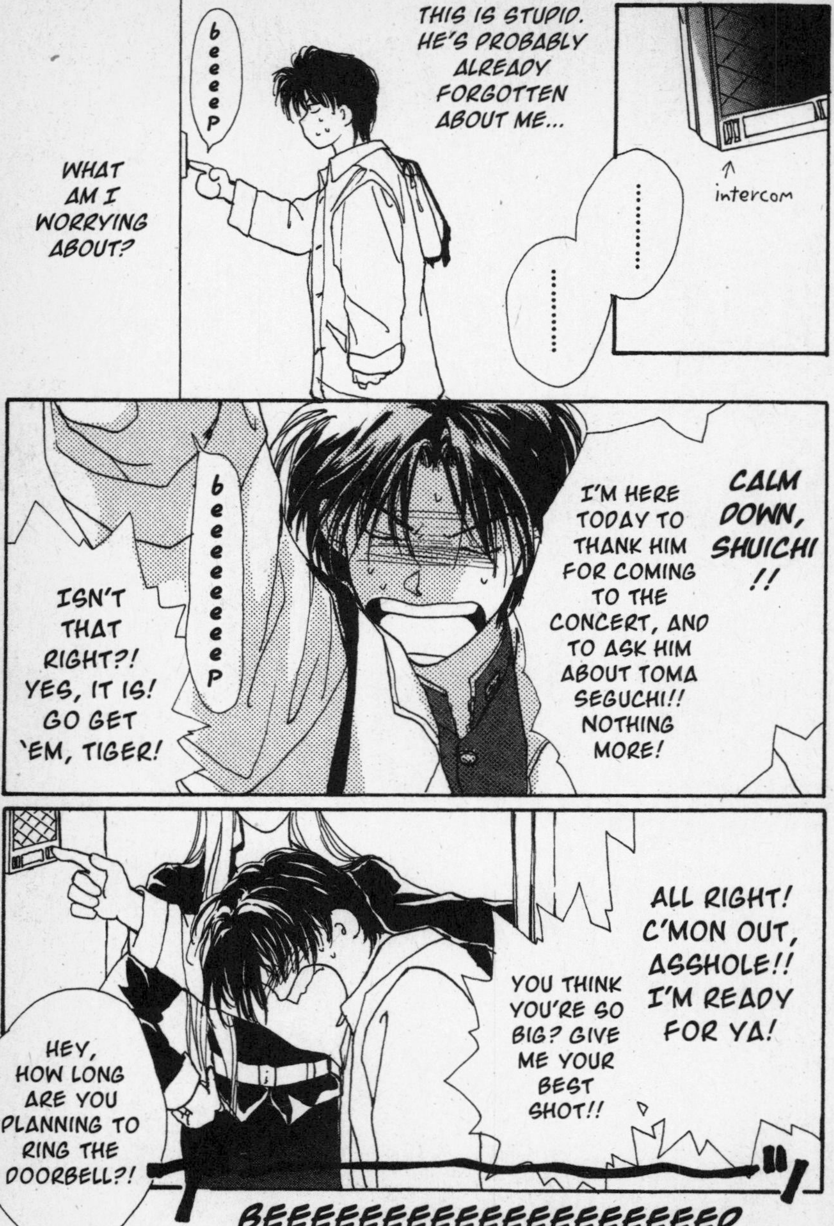
intercom
......
......
THIS IS STUPID. HE'S PROBABLY ALREADY FORGOTTEN ABOUT ME...
beeeep
WHAT AM I WORRYING ABOUT?
CALM DOWN, SHUICHI!!
I'M HERE TODAY TO THANK HIM FOR COMING TO THE CONCERT, AND TO ASK HIM ABOUT TOMA SEGUCHI!! NOTHING MORE!
beeeeeeeeep
ISN'T THAT RIGHT?! YES, IT IS! GO GET 'EM, TIGER!
ALL RIGHT! C'MON OUT, ASSHOLE!! I'M READY FOR YA!
YOU THINK YOU'RE SO BIG? GIVE ME YOUR BEST SHOT!!
HEY, HOW LONG ARE YOU PLANNING TO RING THE DOORBELL?!
BEEEEEEEEEEEEEEEEEEEEEEP

This is a tiger?

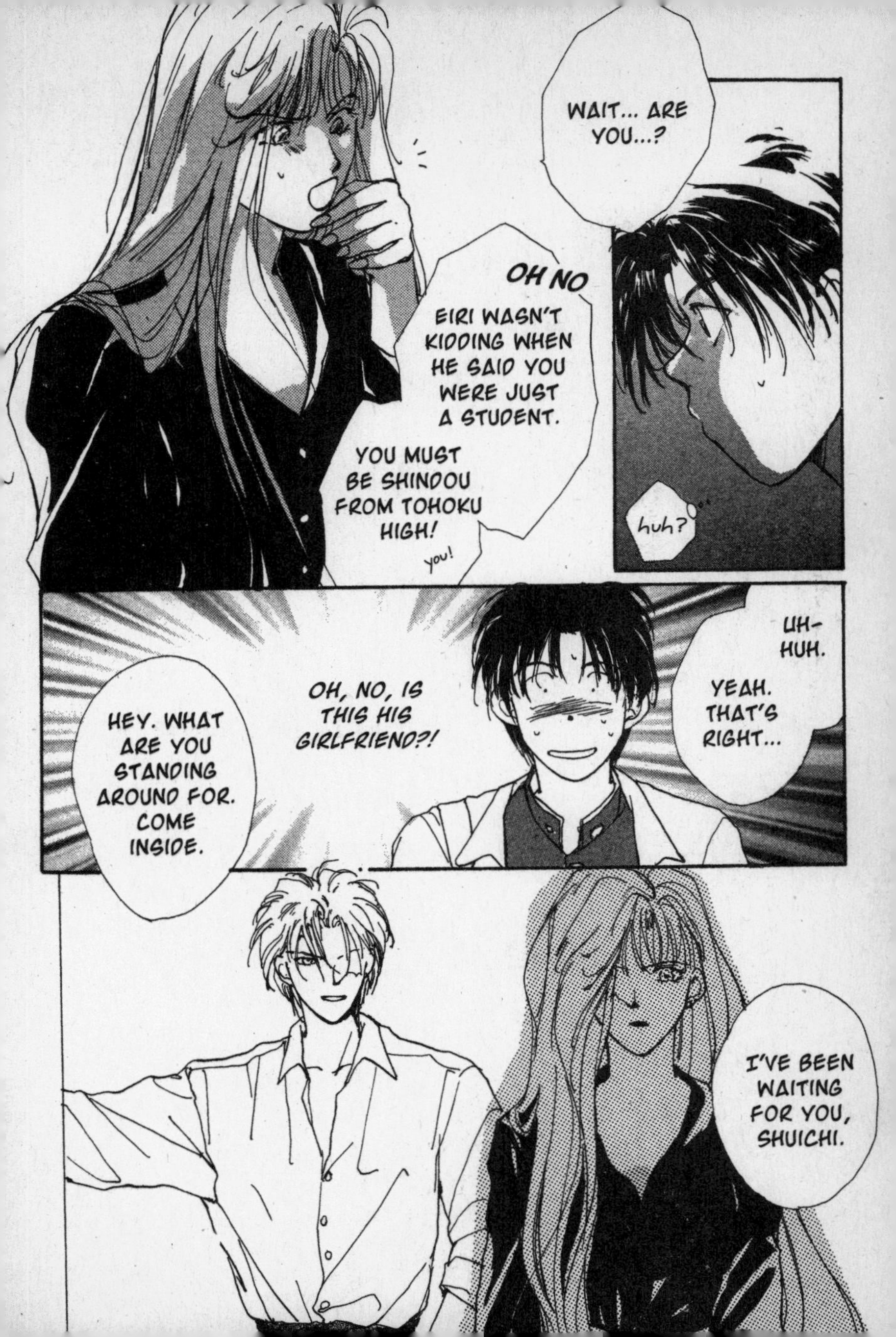
WAIT... ARE YOU...?
huh?
OH NO
EIRI WASN'T KIDDING WHEN HE SAID YOU WERE JUST A STUDENT.
YOU MUST BE SHINDOU FROM TOHOKU HIGH!
you!
UH-HUH.
YEAH. THAT'S RIGHT...
OH, NO, IS THIS HIS GIRLFRIEND?!
HEY. WHAT ARE YOU STANDING AROUND FOR. COME INSIDE.
I'VE BEEN WAITING FOR YOU, SHUICHI.

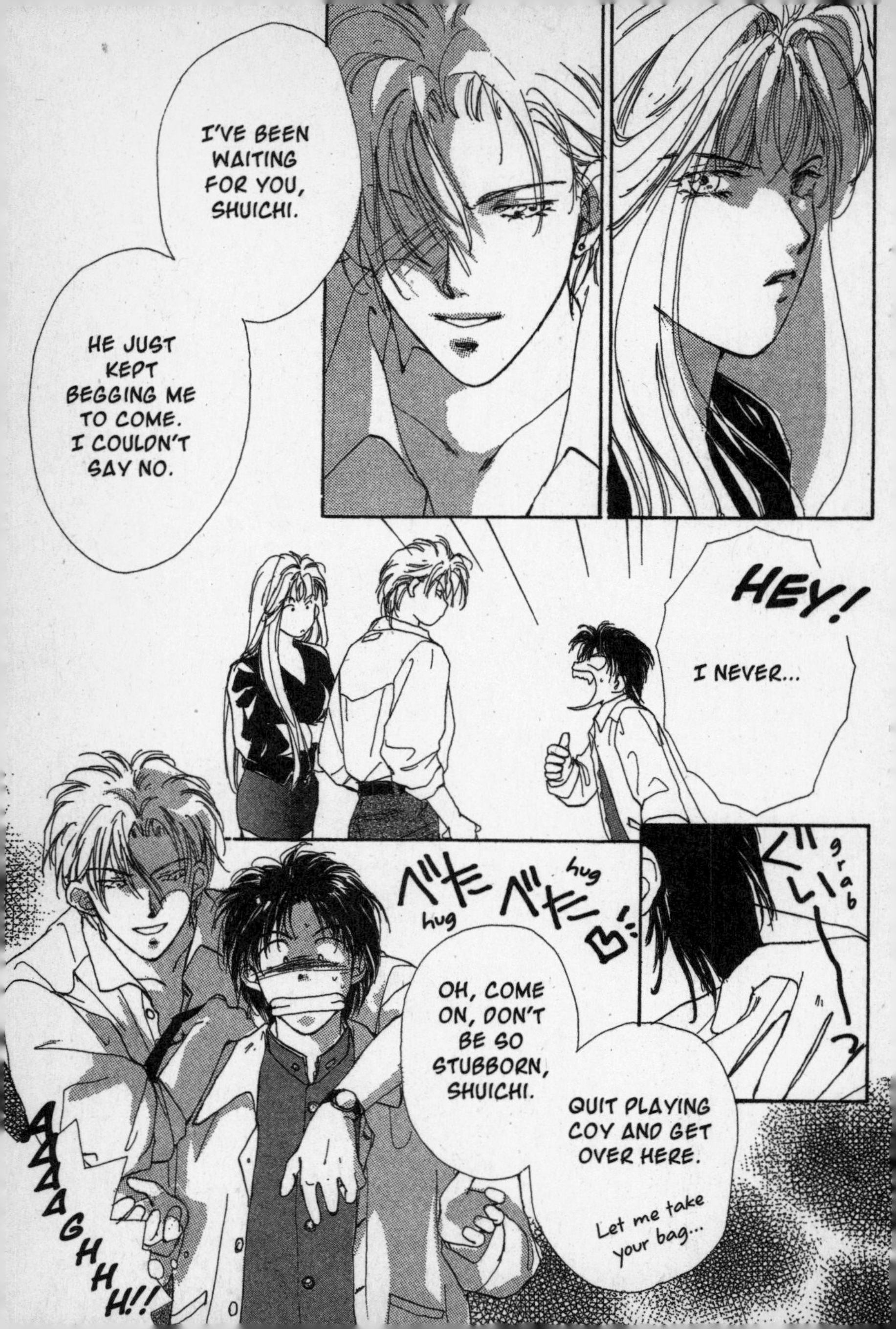
I'VE BEEN WAITING FOR YOU, SHUICHI.
HE JUST KEPT BEGGING ME TO COME. I COULDN'T SAY NO.
HEY!
I NEVER...
ぐい
grab
べた
hug
べた
hug
OH, COME ON, DON'T BE SO STUBBORN, SHUICHI.
QUIT PLAYING COY AND GET OVER HERE.
Let me take your bag...
AAAAGHHH!!

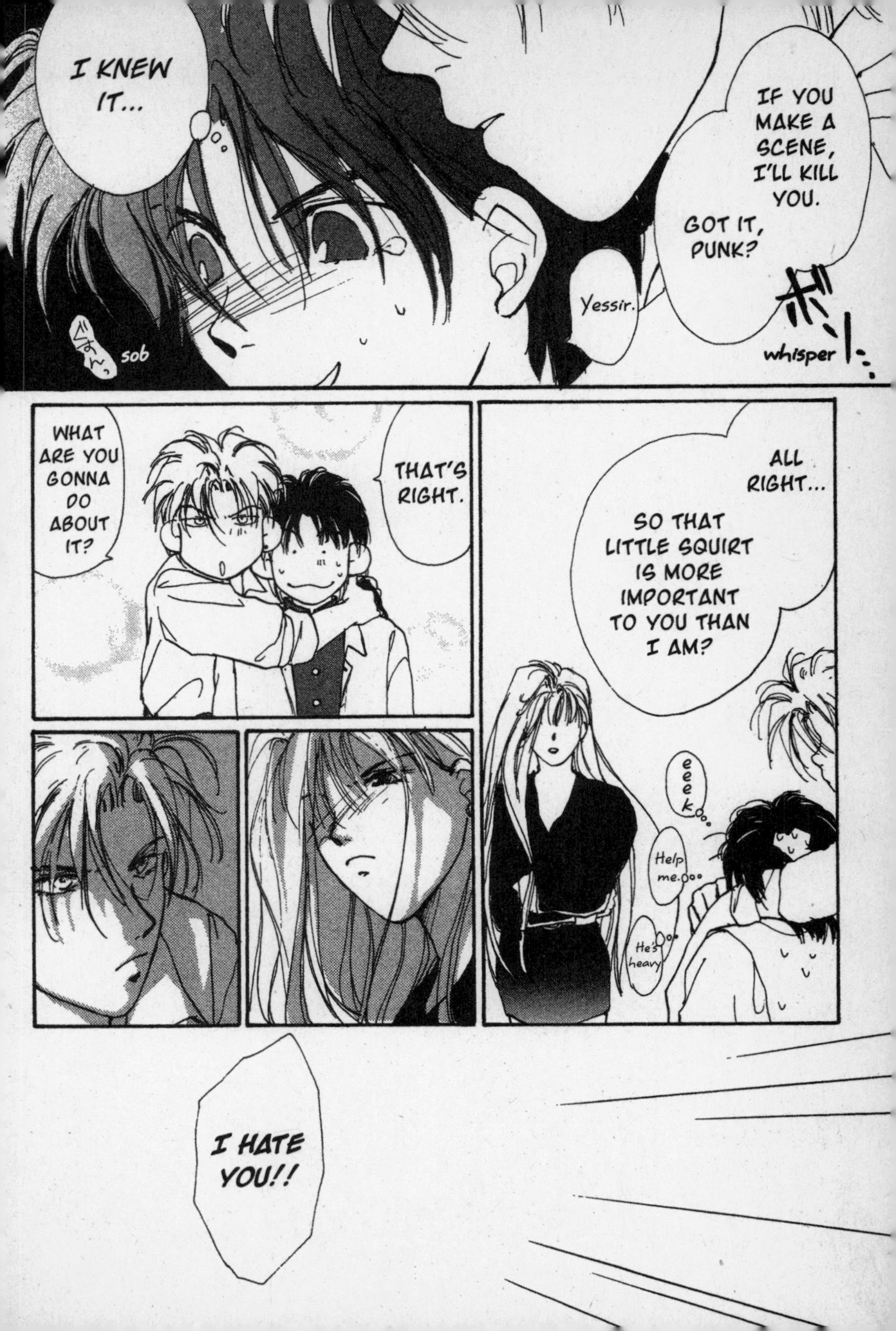
IF YOU MAKE A SCENE, I'LL KILL YOU.
GOT IT, PUNK?
whisper
Yessir.
I KNEW IT...
sob
ALL RIGHT...
SO THAT LITTLE SQUIRT IS MORE IMPORTANT TO YOU THAN I AM?
eeek
Help me.
He's heavy
THAT'S RIGHT.
WHAT ARE YOU GONNA DO ABOUT IT?
I HATE YOU!!

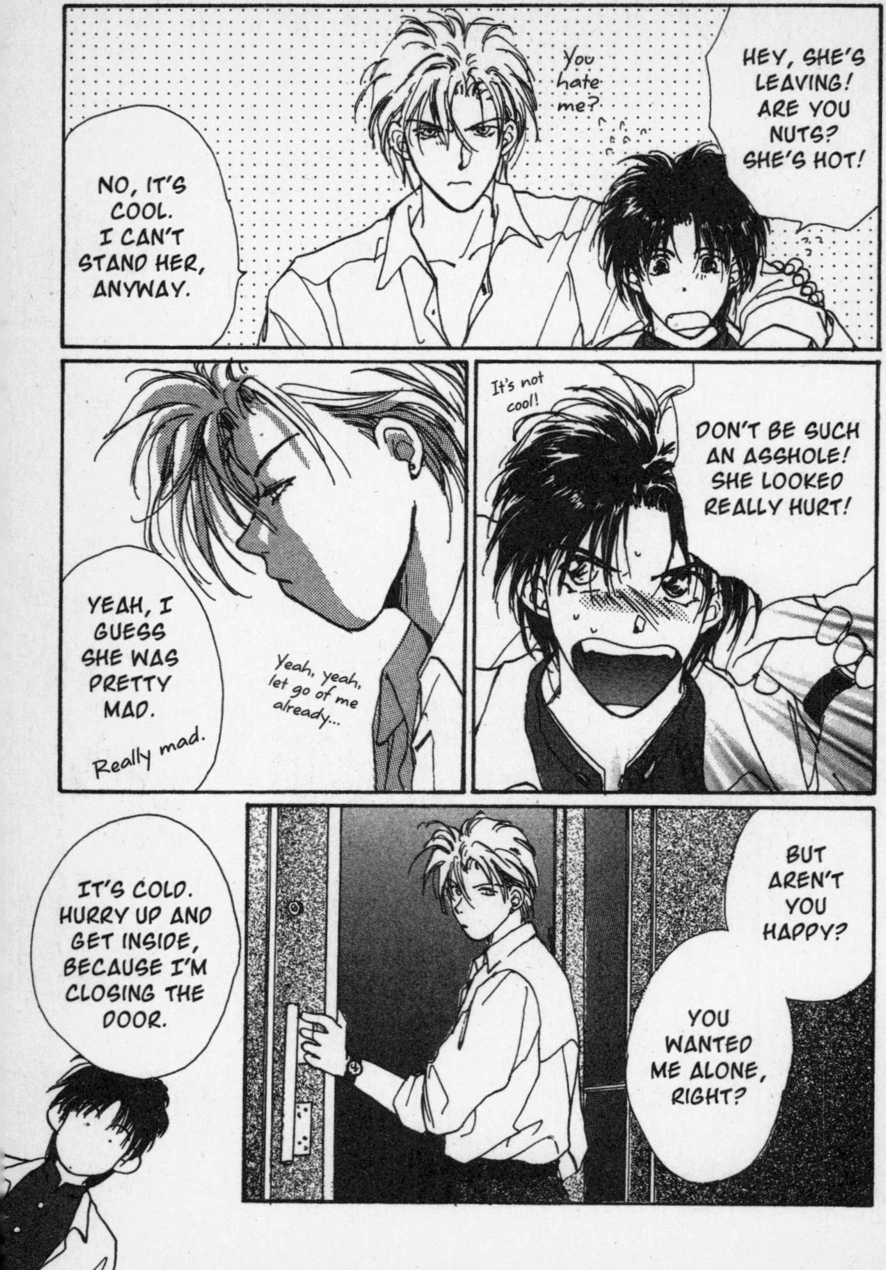
HEY, SHE'S LEAVING! ARE YOU NUTS? SHE'S HOT!
You hate me?
NO, IT'S COOL. I CAN'T STAND HER, ANYWAY.
It's not cool!
DON'T BE SUCH AN ASSHOLE! SHE LOOKED REALLY HURT!
Yeah, yeah, let go of me already...
YEAH, I GUESS SHE WAS PRETTY MAD.
Really mad.
BUT AREN'T YOU HAPPY?
YOU WANTED ME ALONE, RIGHT?
IT'S COLD. HURRY UP AND GET INSIDE, BECAUSE I'M CLOSING THE DOOR.

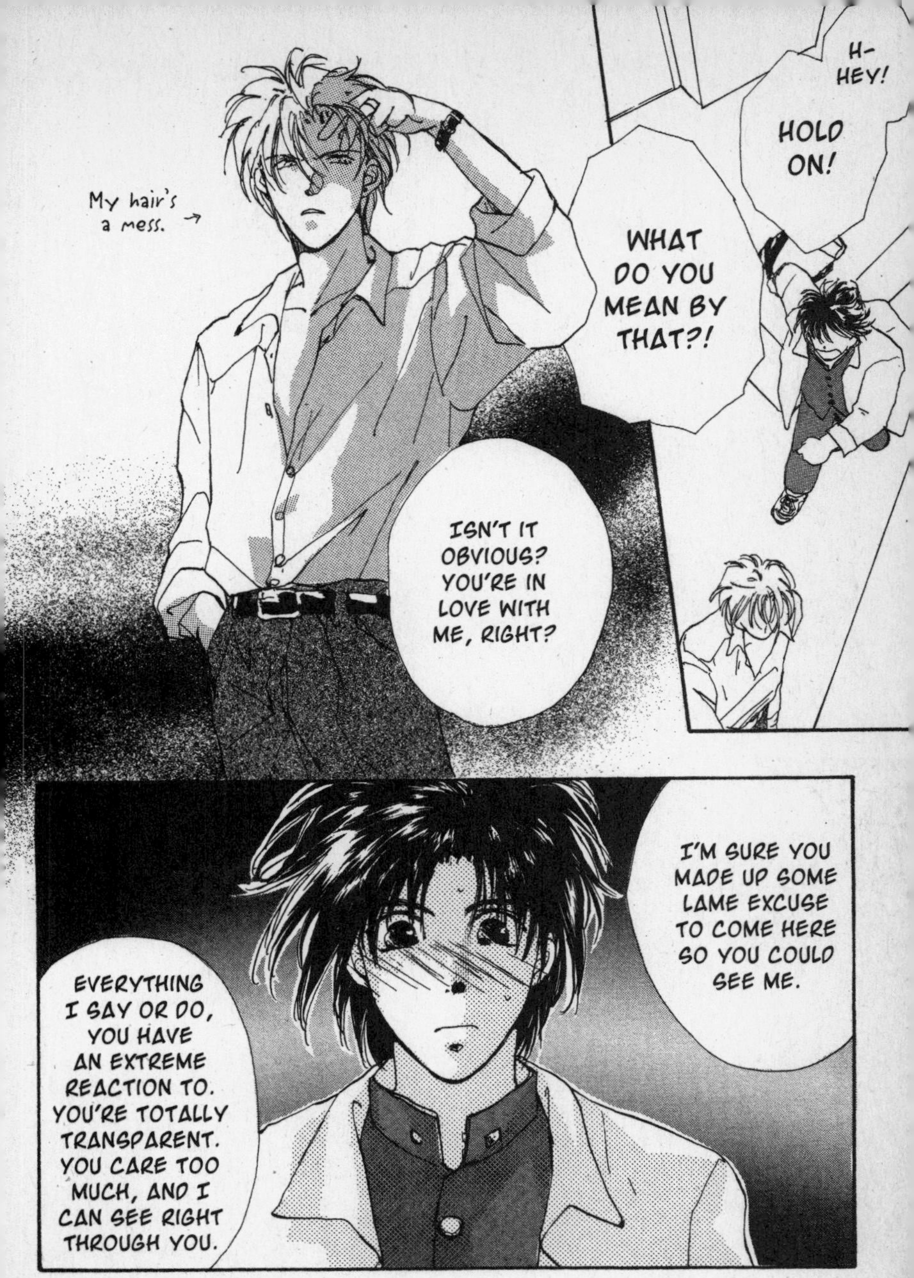
H-HEY!
HOLD ON!
WHAT DO YOU MEAN BY THAT?!
My hair's a mess.
ISN'T IT OBVIOUS? YOU'RE IN LOVE WITH ME, RIGHT?
I'M SURE YOU MADE UP SOME LAME EXCUSE TO COME HERE SO YOU COULD SEE ME.
EVERYTHING I SAY OR DO, YOU HAVE AN EXTREME REACTION TO. YOU'RE TOTALLY TRANSPARENT. YOU CARE TOO MUCH, AND I CAN SEE RIGHT THROUGH YOU.

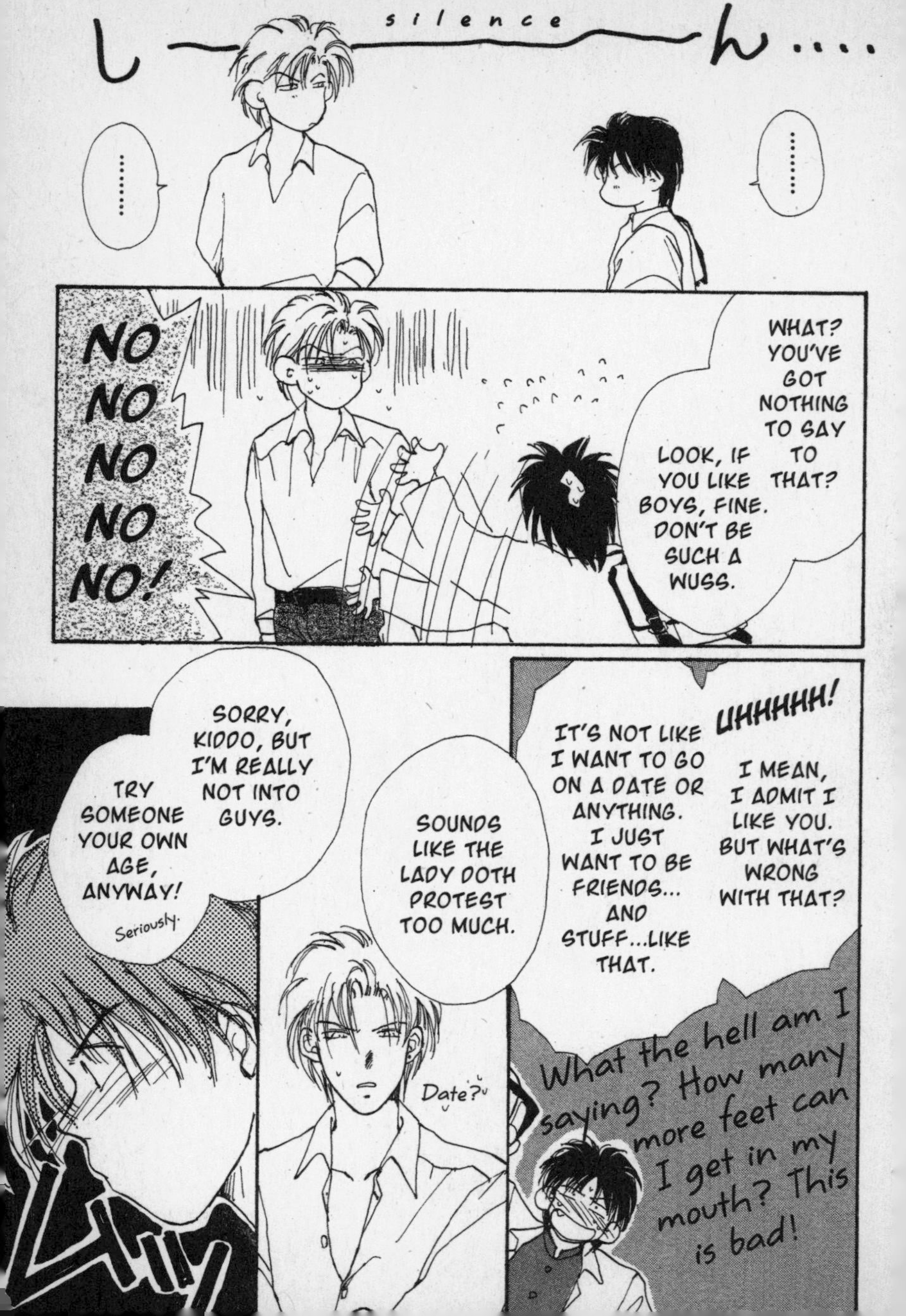
silence
……
……
WHAT? YOU'VE GOT NOTHING TO SAY TO THAT?
LOOK, IF YOU LIKE BOYS, FINE. DON'T BE SUCH A WUSS.
NO NO NO NO NO!
UHHHHH!
I MEAN, I ADMIT I LIKE YOU. BUT WHAT'S WRONG WITH THAT?
IT'S NOT LIKE I WANT TO GO ON A DATE OR ANYTHING. I JUST WANT TO BE FRIENDS... AND STUFF...LIKE THAT.
What the hell am I saying? How many more feet can I get in my mouth? This is bad!
SOUNDS LIKE THE LADY DOTH PROTEST TOO MUCH.
Date?
SORRY, KIDDO, BUT I'M REALLY NOT INTO GUYS.
TRY SOMEONE YOUR OWN AGE, ANYWAY!
Seriously.

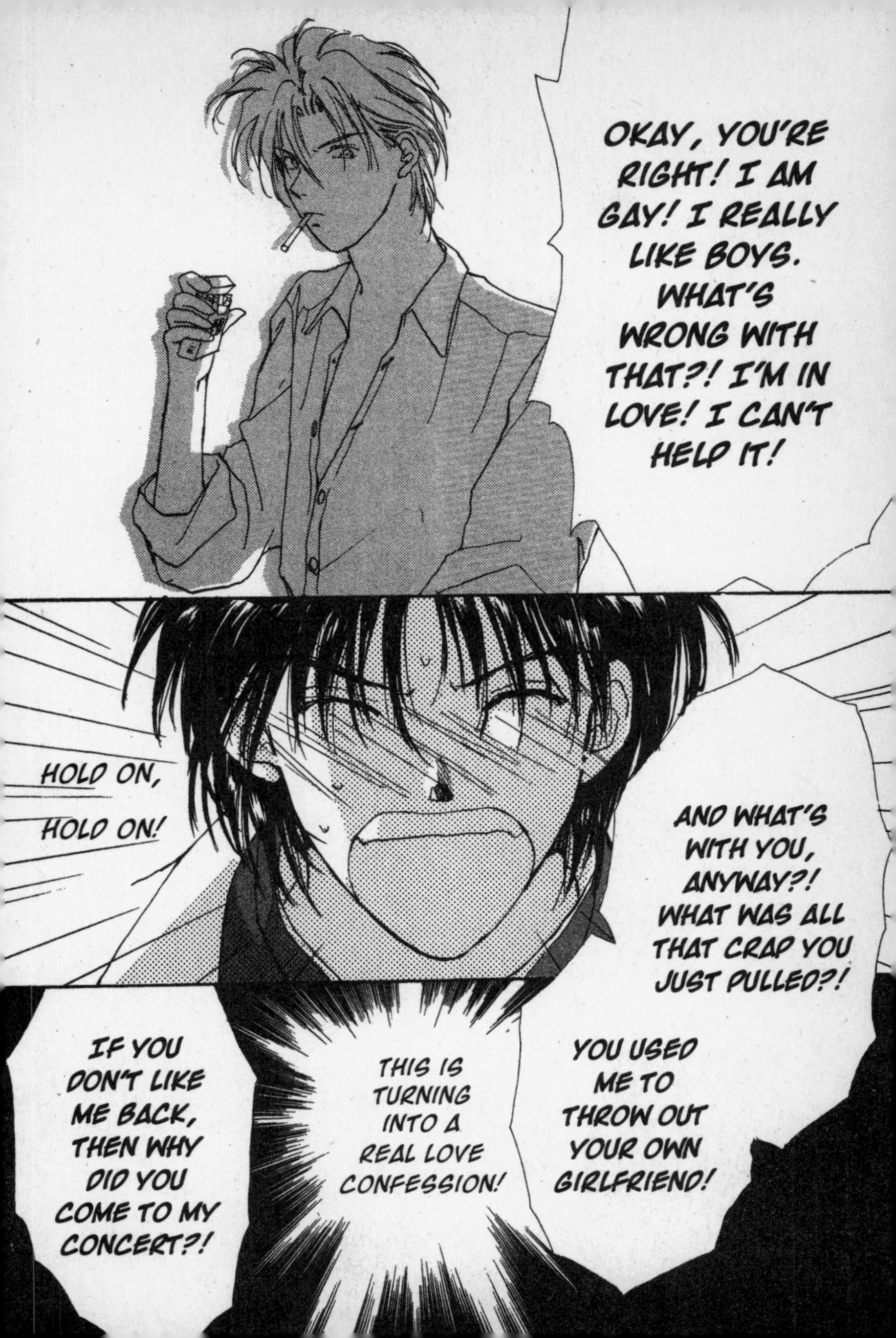
OKAY, YOU'RE RIGHT! I AM GAY! I REALLY LIKE BOYS. WHAT'S WRONG WITH THAT?! I'M IN LOVE! I CAN'T HELP IT!
HOLD ON, HOLD ON!
AND WHAT'S WITH YOU, ANYWAY?! WHAT WAS ALL THAT CRAP YOU JUST PULLED?!
YOU USED ME TO THROW OUT YOUR OWN GIRLFRIEND!
THIS IS TURNING INTO A REAL LOVE CONFESSION!
IF YOU DON'T LIKE ME BACK, THEN WHY DID YOU COME TO MY CONCERT?!

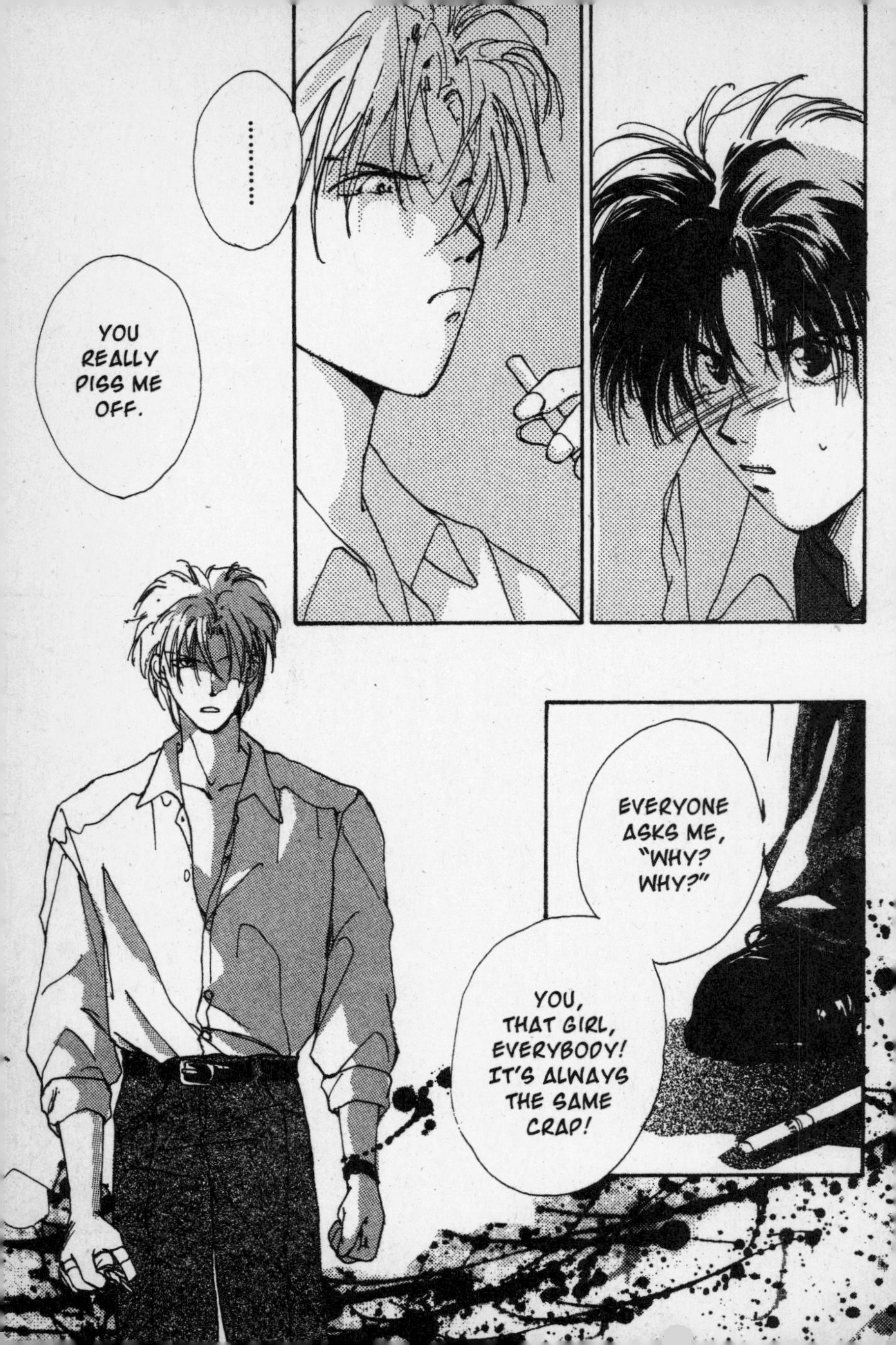
......
YOU REALLY PISS ME OFF.
EVERYONE ASKS ME, "WHY? WHY?"
YOU, THAT GIRL, EVERYBODY! IT'S ALWAYS THE SAME CRAP!

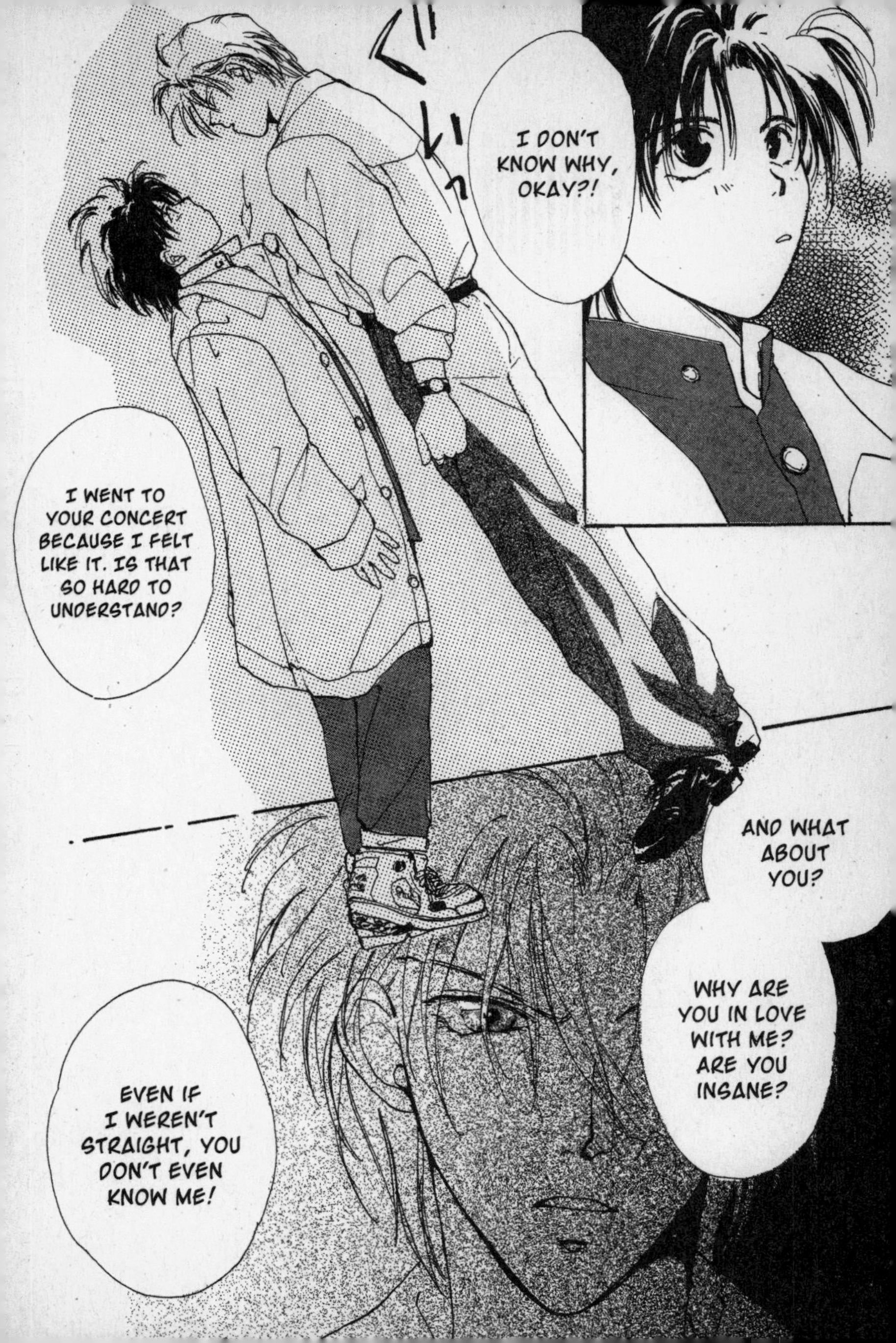
I DON'T KNOW WHY, OKAY?!
I WENT TO YOUR CONCERT BECAUSE I FELT LIKE IT. IS THAT SO HARD TO UNDERSTAND?
AND WHAT ABOUT YOU?
WHY ARE YOU IN LOVE WITH ME? ARE YOU INSANE?
EVEN IF I WEREN'T STRAIGHT, YOU DON'T EVEN KNOW ME!

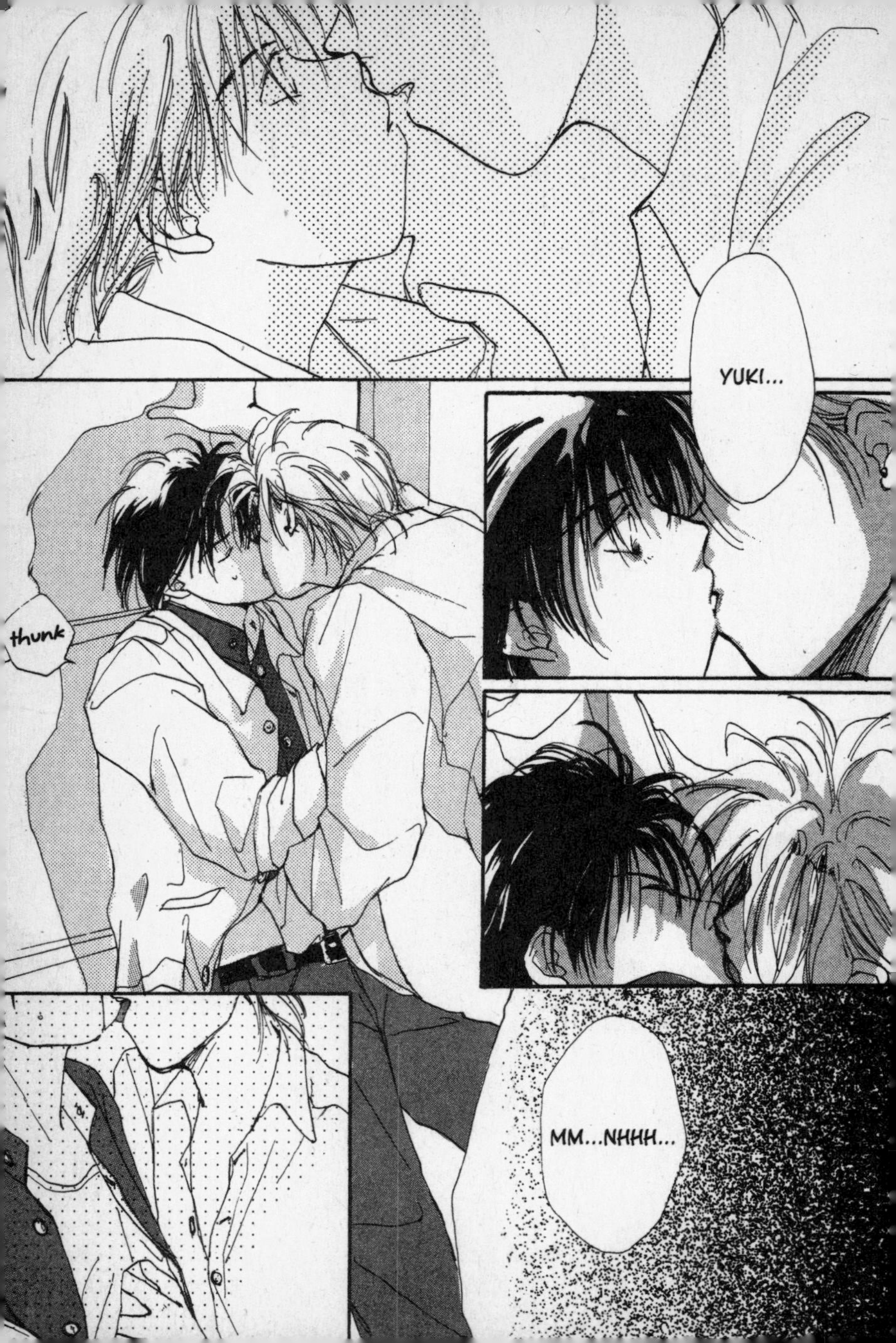
YUKI...
thunk
MM...NHHH...

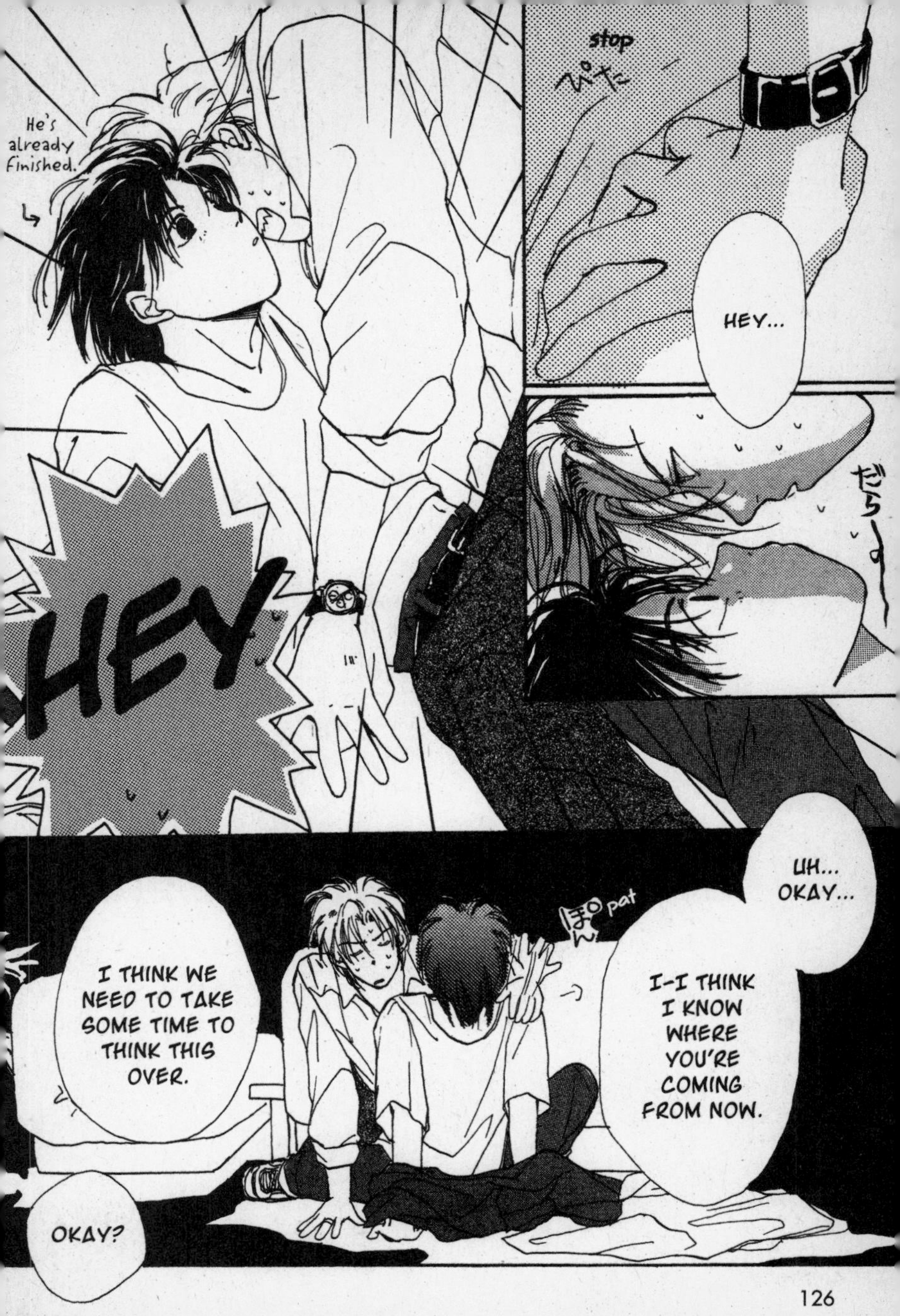
stop
ぴた
HEY...
だら〜
He's already finished.
HEY
UH... OKAY...
ぽん pat
I-I THINK I KNOW WHERE YOU'RE COMING FROM NOW.
I THINK WE NEED TO TAKE SOME TIME TO THINK THIS OVER.
OKAY?

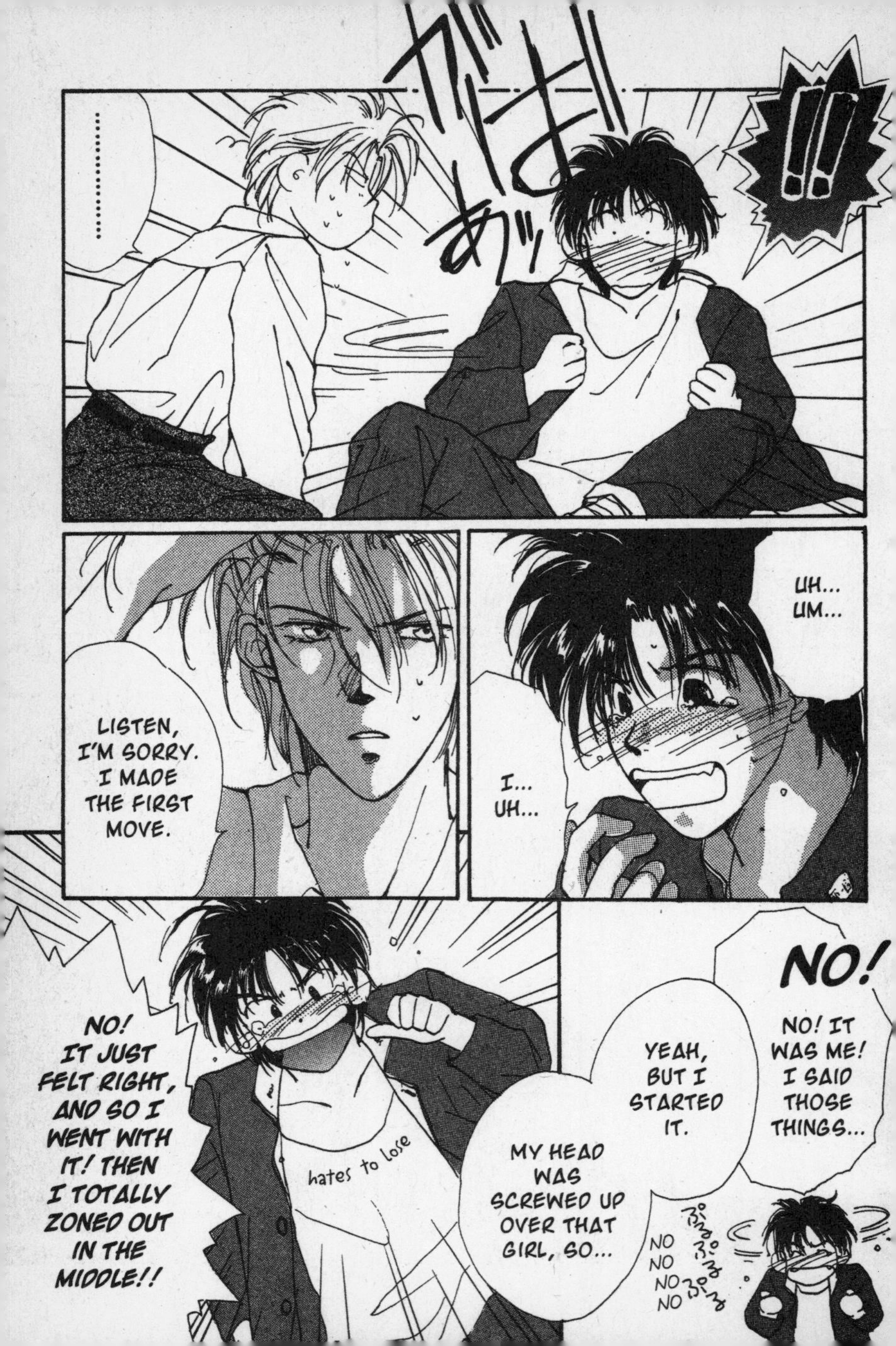
!!
......
UH... UM...
I... UH...
LISTEN, I'M SORRY. I MADE THE FIRST MOVE.
NO!
NO! IT WAS ME! I SAID THOSE THINGS...
YEAH, BUT I STARTED IT.
MY HEAD WAS SCREWED UP OVER THAT GIRL, SO...
NO NO NO NO
NO! IT JUST FELT RIGHT, AND SO I WENT WITH IT! THEN I TOTALLY ZONED OUT IN THE MIDDLE!!
hates to lose

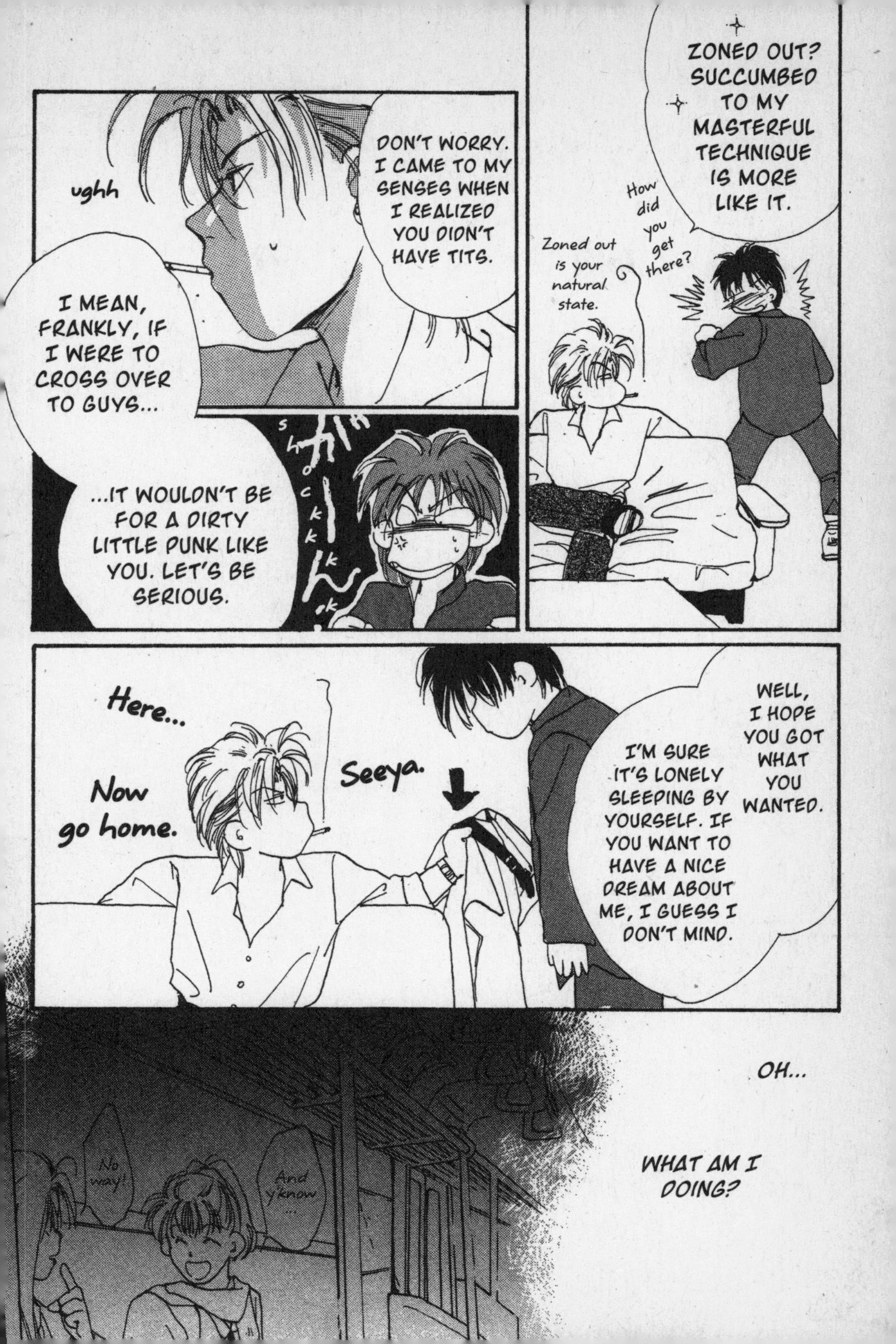
ZONED OUT? SUCCUMBED TO MY MASTERFUL TECHNIQUE IS MORE LIKE IT.
How did you get there?
Zoned out is your natural state.
DON'T WORRY. I CAME TO MY SENSES WHEN I REALIZED YOU DIDN'T HAVE TITS.
ughh
I MEAN, FRANKLY, IF I WERE TO CROSS OVER TO GUYS...
shockkk
...IT WOULDN'T BE FOR A DIRTY LITTLE PUNK LIKE YOU. LET'S BE SERIOUS.
WELL, I HOPE YOU GOT WHAT YOU WANTED.
I'M SURE IT'S LONELY SLEEPING BY YOURSELF. IF YOU WANT TO HAVE A NICE DREAM ABOUT ME, I GUESS I DON'T MIND.
Seeya.
Here...
Now go home.
OH...
WHAT AM I DOING?
And y'know...
No way!

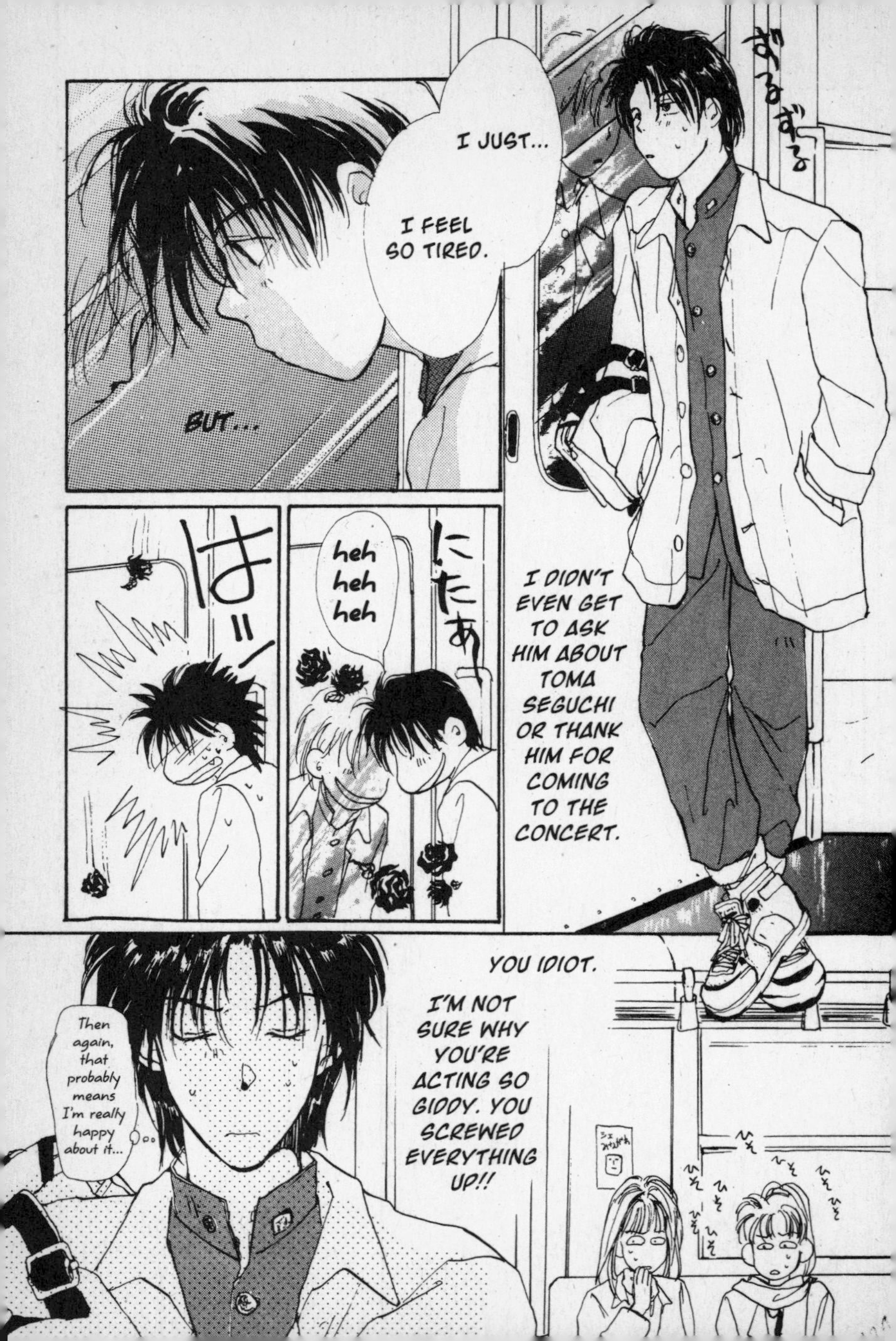
ずるずる
I DIDN'T EVEN GET TO ASK HIM ABOUT TOMA SEGUCHI OR THANK HIM FOR COMING TO THE CONCERT.
I JUST...
I FEEL SO TIRED.
BUT...
にたあ
heh heh heh
は
YOU IDIOT.
I'M NOT SURE WHY YOU'RE ACTING SO GIDDY. YOU SCREWED EVERYTHING UP!!
ひそ ひそ ひそ ひそ ひそ ひそ ひそ ひそ
Then again, that probably means I'm really happy about it...

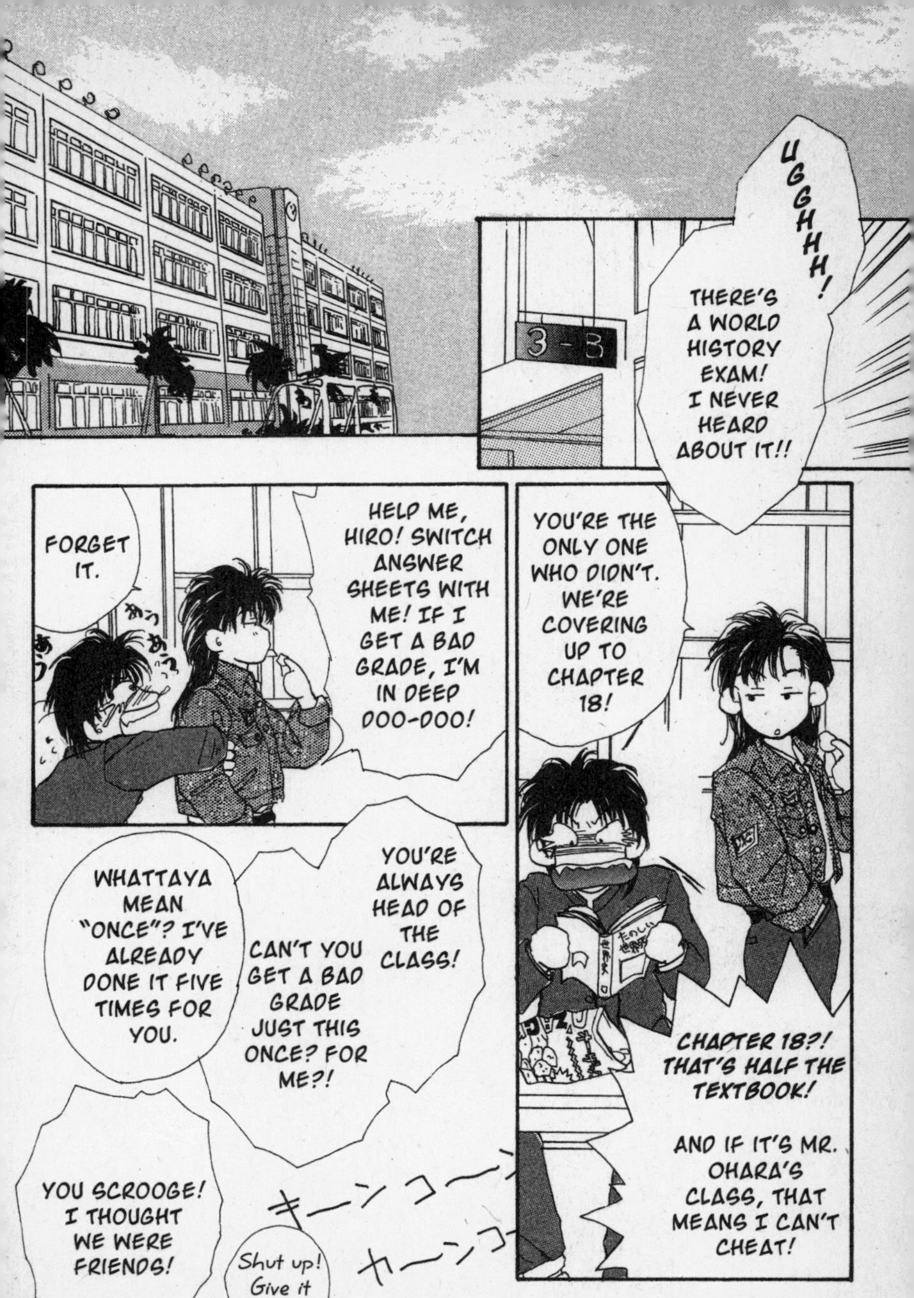
UGGHHH!
THERE'S A WORLD HISTORY EXAM! I NEVER HEARD ABOUT IT!!
YOU'RE THE ONLY ONE WHO DIDN'T. WE'RE COVERING UP TO CHAPTER 18!
CHAPTER 18?! THAT'S HALF THE TEXTBOOK!
AND IF IT'S MR. OHARA'S CLASS, THAT MEANS I CAN'T CHEAT!
HELP ME, HIRO! SWITCH ANSWER SHEETS WITH ME! IF I GET A BAD GRADE, I'M IN DEEP DOO-DOO!
FORGET IT.
YOU'RE ALWAYS HEAD OF THE CLASS!
CAN'T YOU GET A BAD GRADE JUST THIS ONCE? FOR ME?!
WHATTAYA MEAN "ONCE"? I'VE ALREADY DONE IT FIVE TIMES FOR YOU.
キーンコーン
カーンコー
YOU SCROOGE! I THOUGHT WE WERE FRIENDS!
Shut up! Give it up!

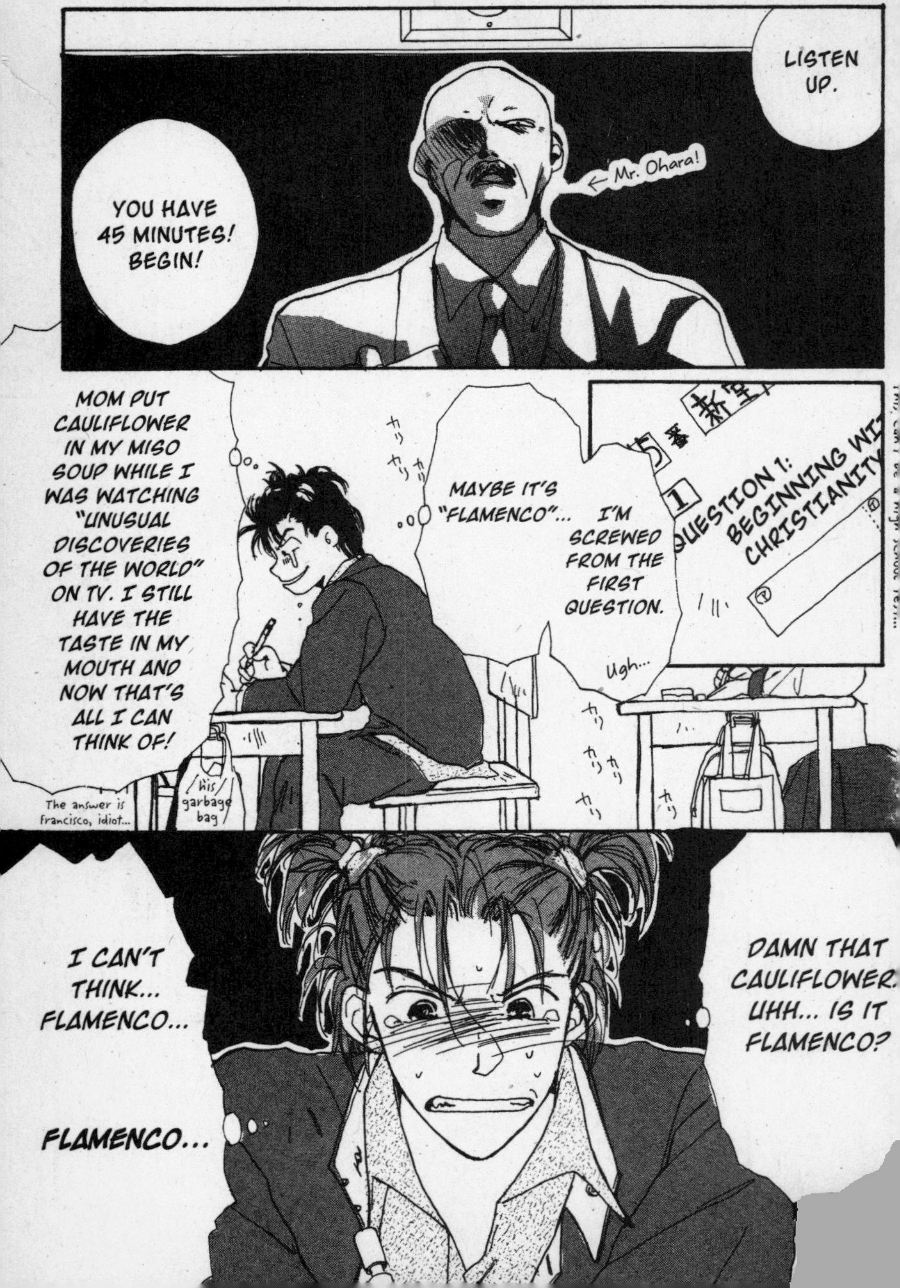
LISTEN UP.
Mr. Ohara!
YOU HAVE 45 MINUTES! BEGIN!
1 QUESTION 1: BEGINNING WI CHRISTIANITY
MAYBE IT'S "FLAMENCO"...
I'M SCREWED FROM THE FIRST QUESTION.
Ugh...
カリ カリ カリ
MOM PUT CAULIFLOWER IN MY MISO SOUP WHILE I WAS WATCHING "UNUSUAL DISCOVERIES OF THE WORLD" ON TV. I STILL HAVE THE TASTE IN MY MOUTH AND NOW THAT'S ALL I CAN THINK OF!
his garbage bag
The answer is Francisco, idiot...
DAMN THAT CAULIFLOWER. UHH... IS IT FLAMENCO?
I CAN'T THINK... FLAMENCO...
FLAMENCO...

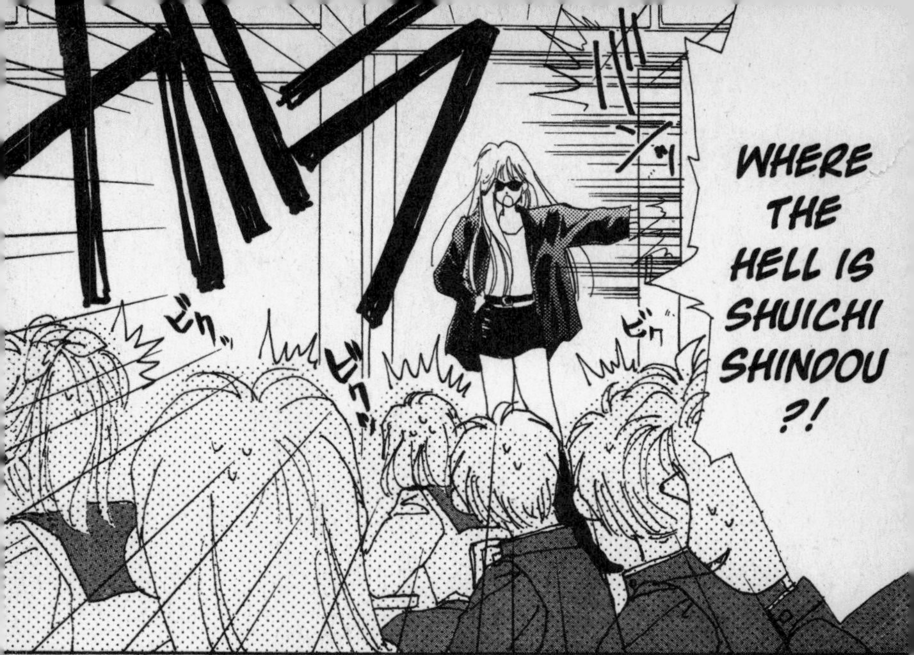
WHERE THE HELL IS SHUICHI SHINDOU ?!
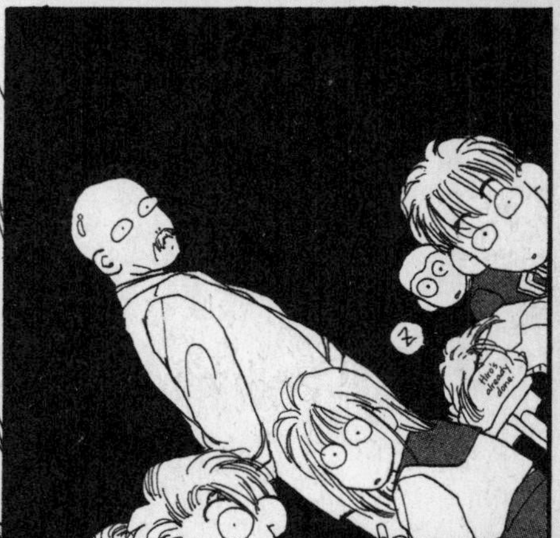
Hiro's already done.
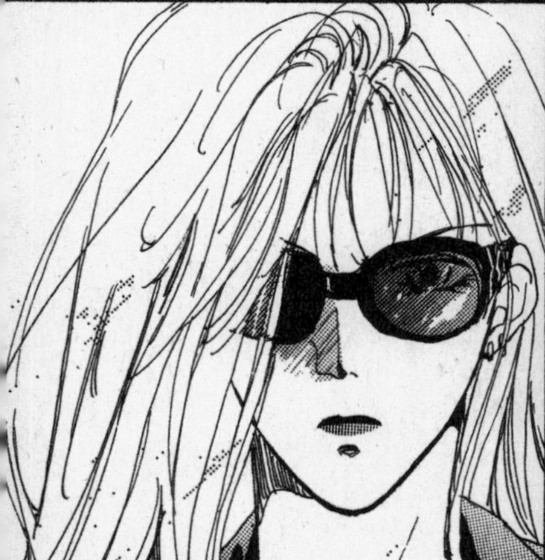

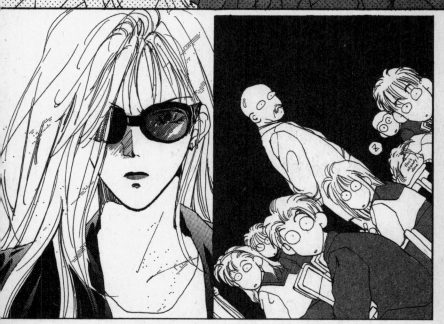

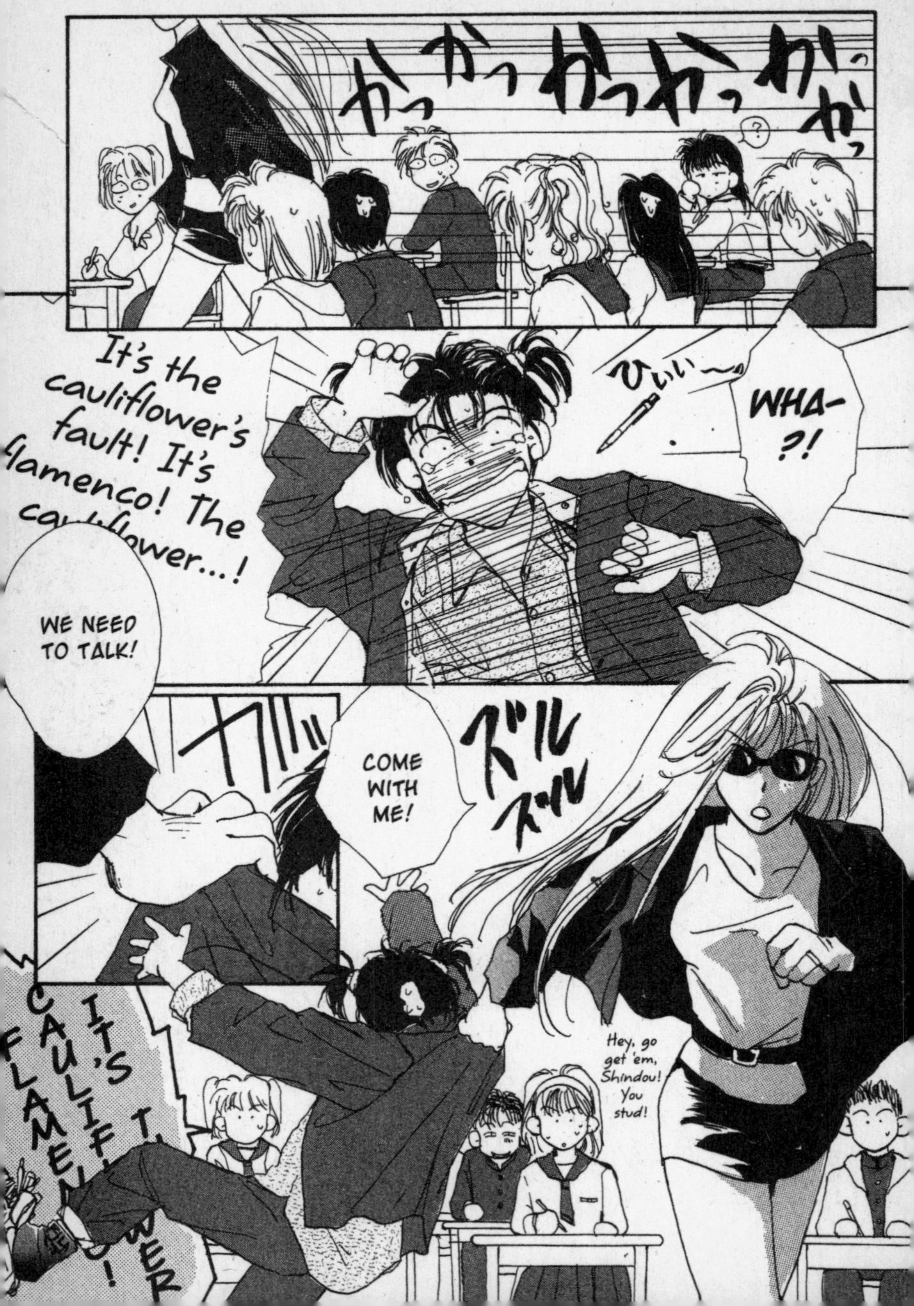
かっかっかっかっかっがっ
?
WHA-?!
ひぃぃ〜
It's the cauliflower's fault! It's flamenco! The cauliflower...!
WE NEED TO TALK!
COME WITH ME!
ズルズル
Hey, go get 'em, Shindou! You stud!
IT'S CAULIFLOWER FLAMENCO!

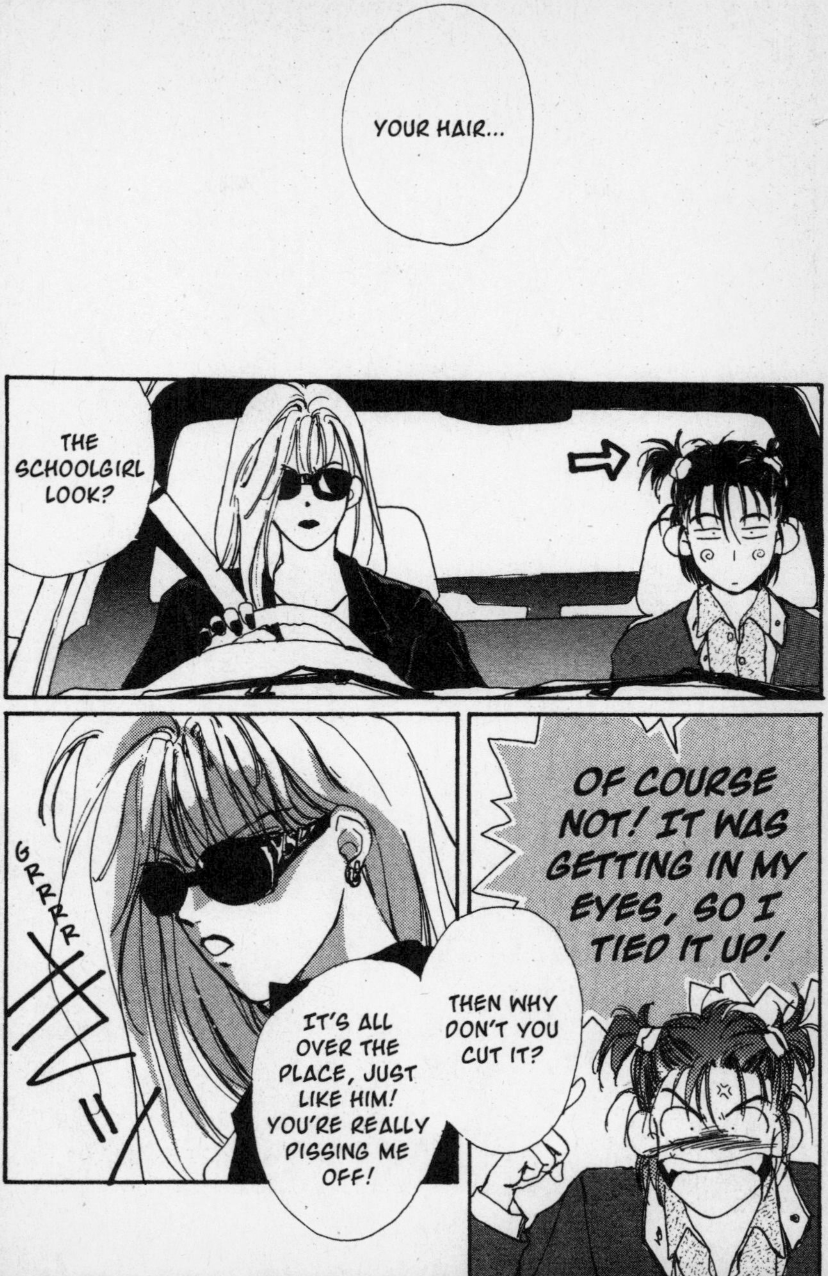
YOUR HAIR...
THE SCHOOLGIRL LOOK?
OF COURSE NOT! IT WAS GETTING IN MY EYES, SO I TIED IT UP!
THEN WHY DON'T YOU CUT IT?
IT'S ALL OVER THE PLACE, JUST LIKE HIM! YOU'RE REALLY PISSING ME OFF!
GRRRRR

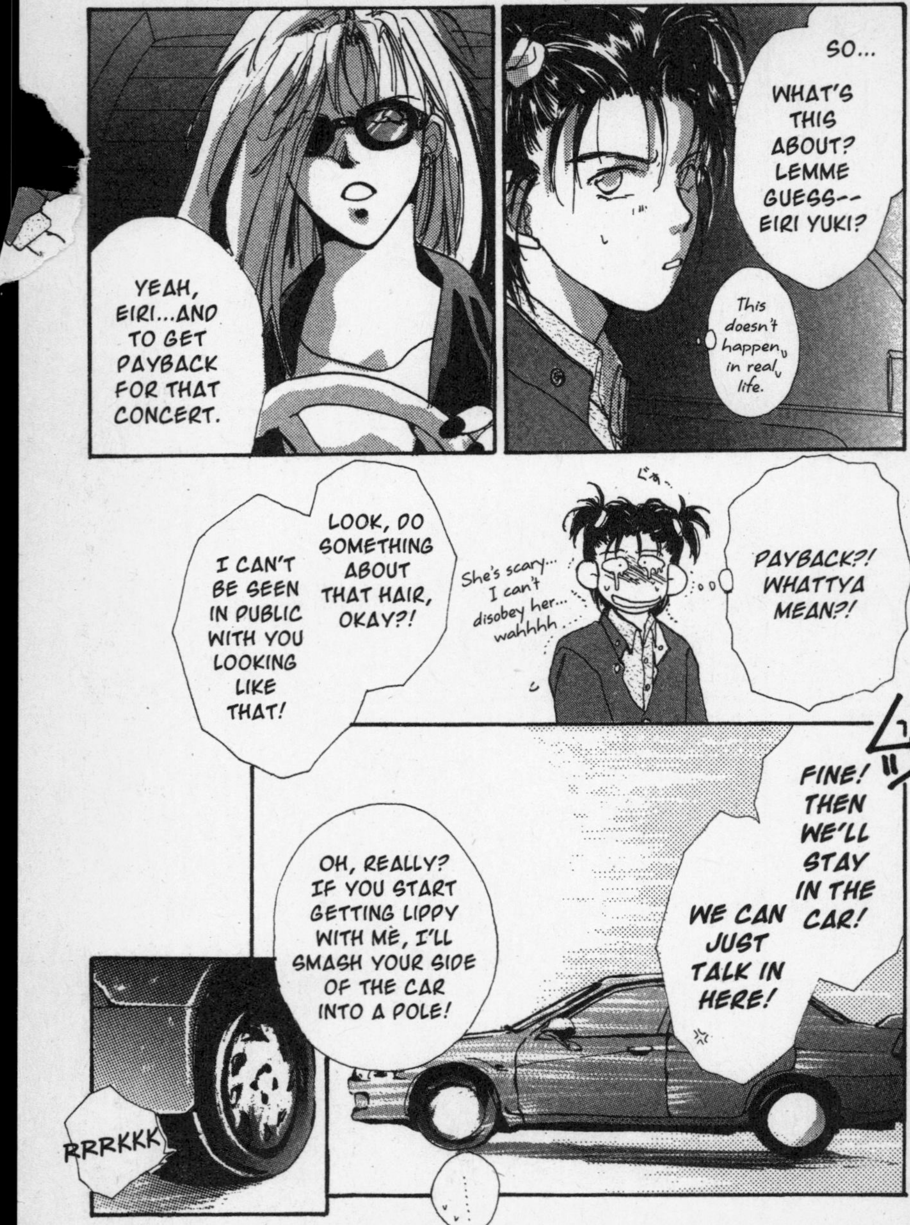
SO...
WHAT'S THIS ABOUT? LEMME GUESS-- EIRI YUKI?
This doesn't happen in real life.
YEAH, EIRI...AND TO GET PAYBACK FOR THAT CONCERT.
PAYBACK?! WHATTYA MEAN?!
She's scary... I can't disobey her... wahhhh
LOOK, DO SOMETHING ABOUT THAT HAIR, OKAY?!
I CAN'T BE SEEN IN PUBLIC WITH YOU LOOKING LIKE THAT!
FINE! THEN WE'LL STAY IN THE CAR!
WE CAN JUST TALK IN HERE!
OH, REALLY? IF YOU START GETTING LIPPY WITH ME, I'LL SMASH YOUR SIDE OF THE CAR INTO A POLE!
...
RRRKKK

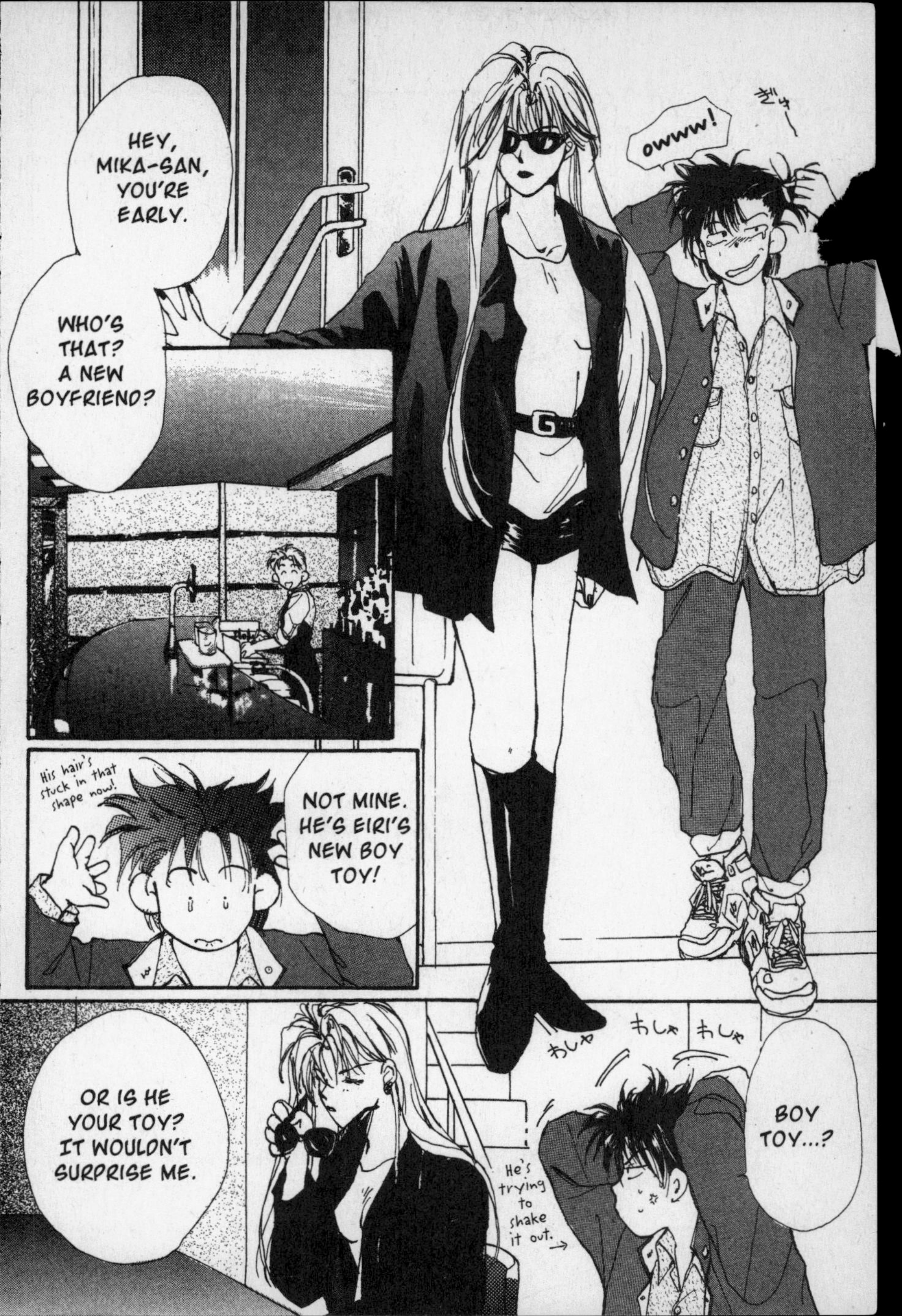
ぎゅ〜
OWWW!
HEY, MIKA-SAN, YOU'RE EARLY.
WHO'S THAT? A NEW BOYFRIEND?
NOT MINE. HE'S EIRI'S NEW BOY TOY!
His hair's stuck in that shape now!
わしゃ わしゃ わしゃ
BOY TOY...?
He's trying to shake it out.
OR IS HE YOUR TOY? IT WOULDN'T SURPRISE ME.

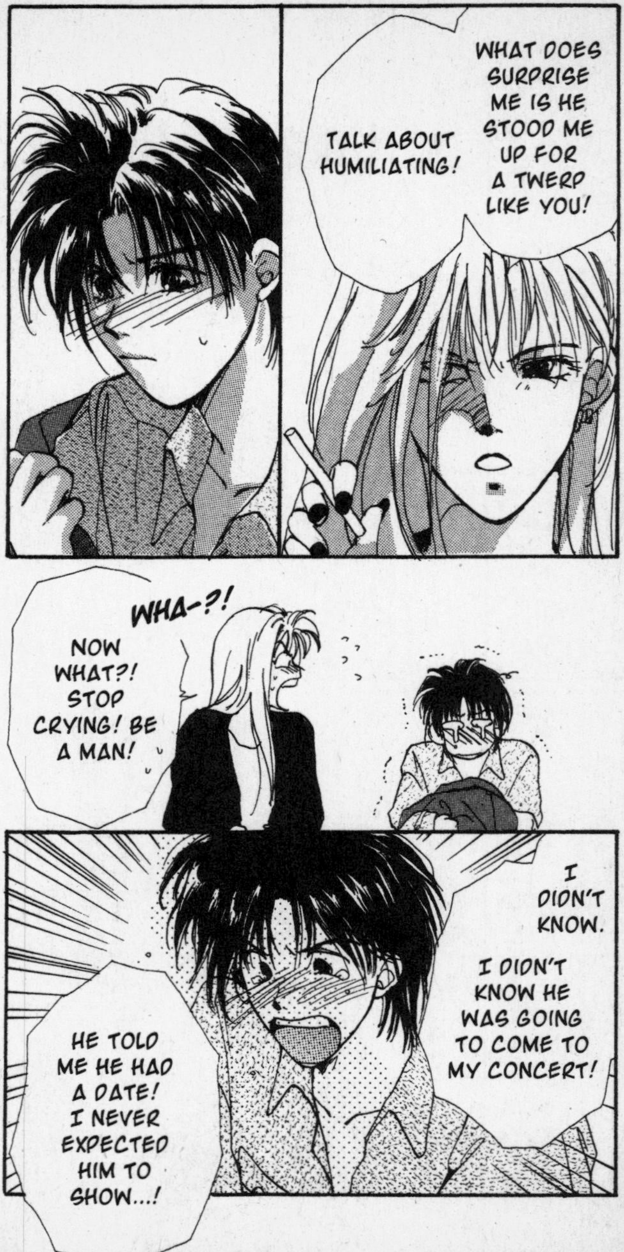
WHAT DOES SURPRISE ME IS HE STOOD ME UP FOR A TWERP LIKE YOU!
TALK ABOUT HUMILIATING!
WHA-?!
NOW WHAT?! STOP CRYING! BE A MAN!
I DIDN'T KNOW.
I DIDN'T KNOW HE WAS GOING TO COME TO MY CONCERT!
HE TOLD ME HE HAD A DATE! I NEVER EXPECTED HIM TO SHOW...!

ABOUT GRAVITATION TRACK 3

Presenting Big Sister Mika. She is one of those amazing characters that makes her own way through the story. The plot gets super complicated from here, to the point where even I start to lose track. Shuichi is quickly heading into Lolita territory. As he pushed the story in that direction, my editors fell silent. The reaction to this chapter was incredible. It was their first kiss, after all. The wall between the boys had insulated innocent readers who were wondering where this crazy Gravitation manga was headed, but now it's totally come down. I've sort of crossed a line and can't go back. It was an especially powerful kissing scene, too. I'm surprised my editors let me get away with it. I added a little more shadow tone for the Collector's edition, and I think that made it more erotic. Well, anyway, I'm not going to pull any punches. I'm going to go through with it all the way. Laugh or cry, it's my decision, 100 percent. The author is always right. So, Shuichi-kun, good luck.

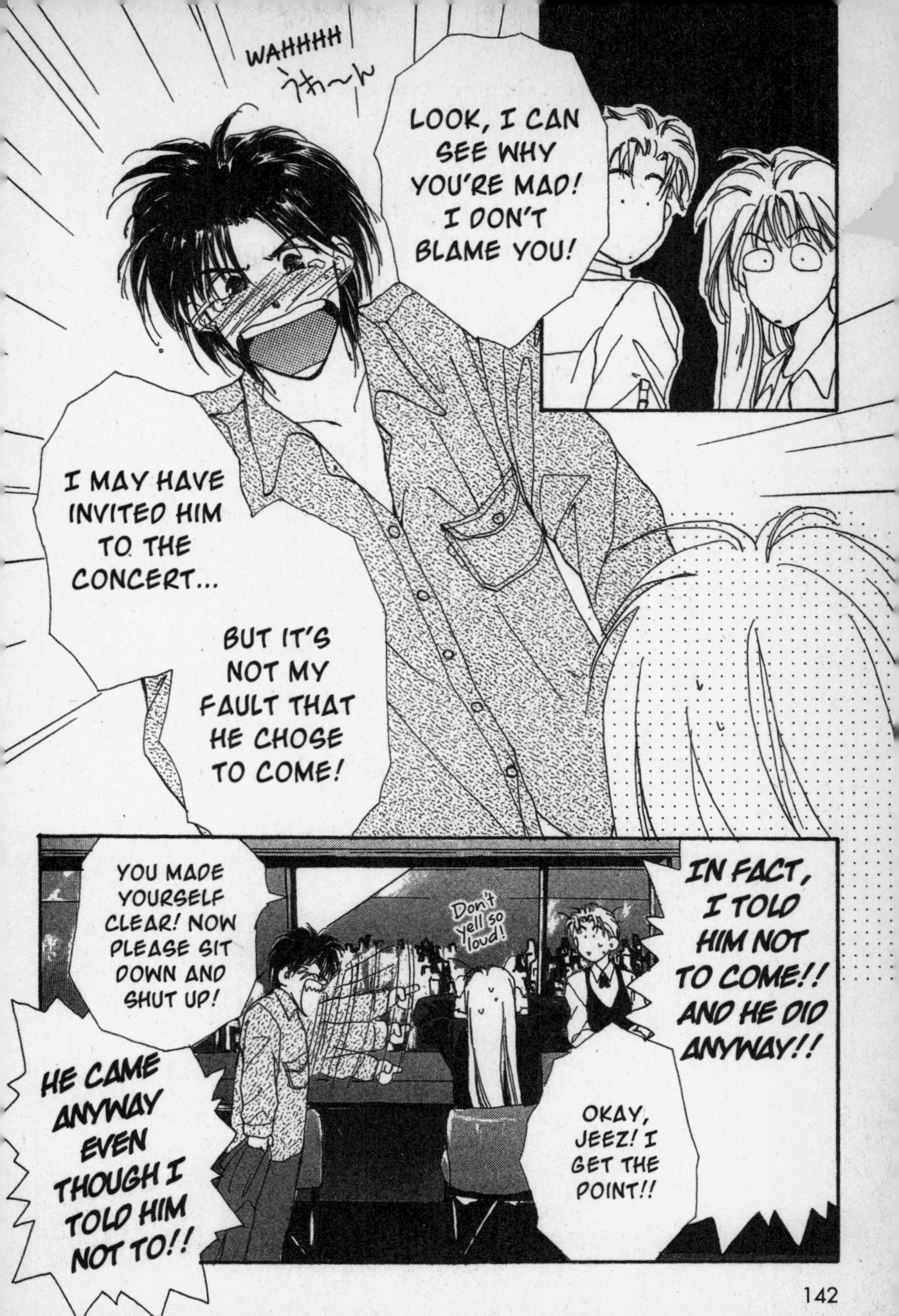

WAHHHH
うわ〜ん
LOOK, I CAN SEE WHY YOU'RE MAD! I DON'T BLAME YOU!
I MAY HAVE INVITED HIM TO THE CONCERT...
BUT IT'S NOT MY FAULT THAT HE CHOSE TO COME!
IN FACT, I TOLD HIM NOT TO COME!! AND HE DID ANYWAY!!
Don't yell so loud!
YOU MADE YOURSELF CLEAR! NOW PLEASE SIT DOWN AND SHUT UP!
OKAY, JEEZ! I GET THE POINT!!
HE CAME ANYWAY EVEN THOUGH I TOLD HIM NOT TO!!

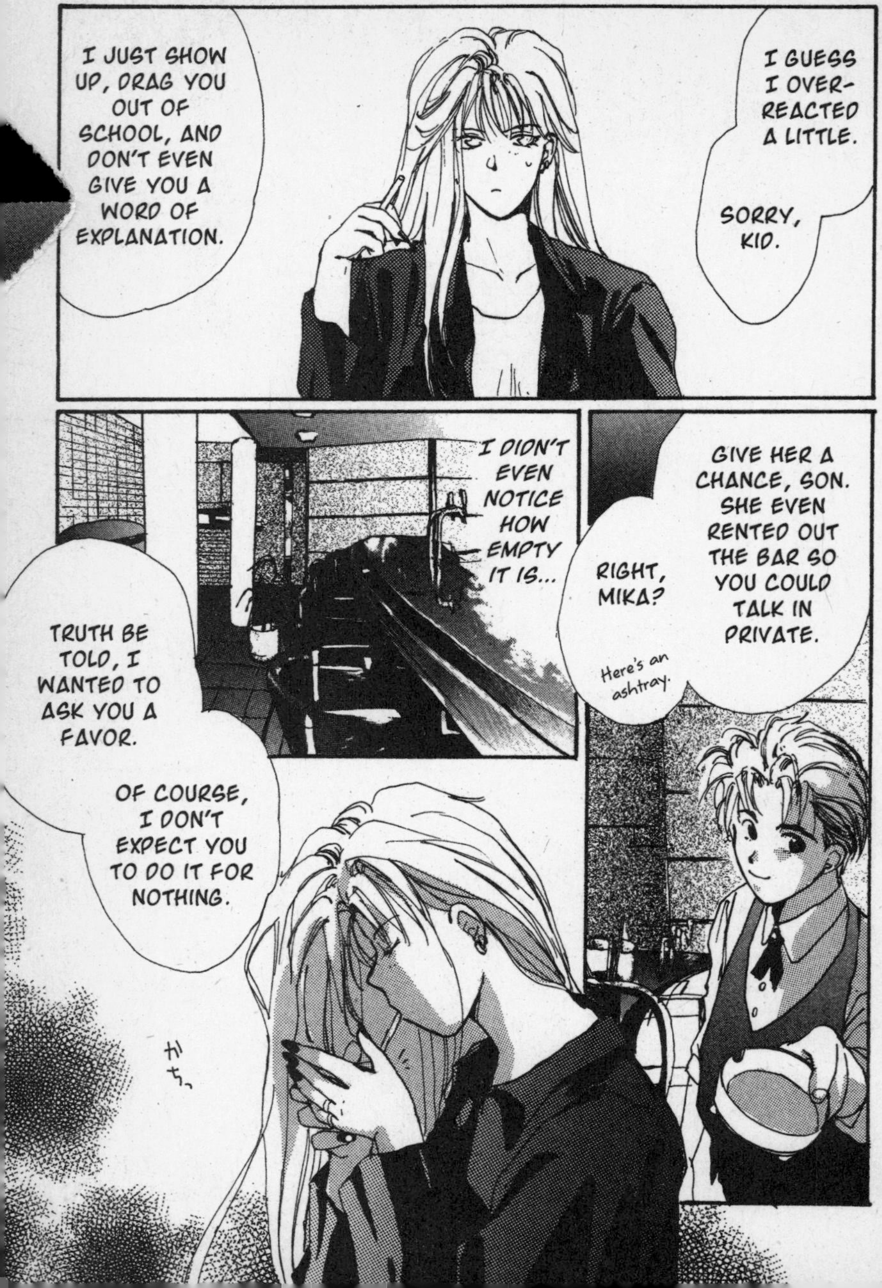
I GUESS I OVER-REACTED A LITTLE.
SORRY, KID.
I JUST SHOW UP, DRAG YOU OUT OF SCHOOL, AND DON'T EVEN GIVE YOU A WORD OF EXPLANATION.
GIVE HER A CHANCE, SON. SHE EVEN RENTED OUT THE BAR SO YOU COULD TALK IN PRIVATE.
RIGHT, MIKA?
Here's an ashtray.
I DIDN'T EVEN NOTICE HOW EMPTY IT IS...
TRUTH BE TOLD, I WANTED TO ASK YOU A FAVOR.
OF COURSE, I DON'T EXPECT YOU TO DO IT FOR NOTHING.
かち、

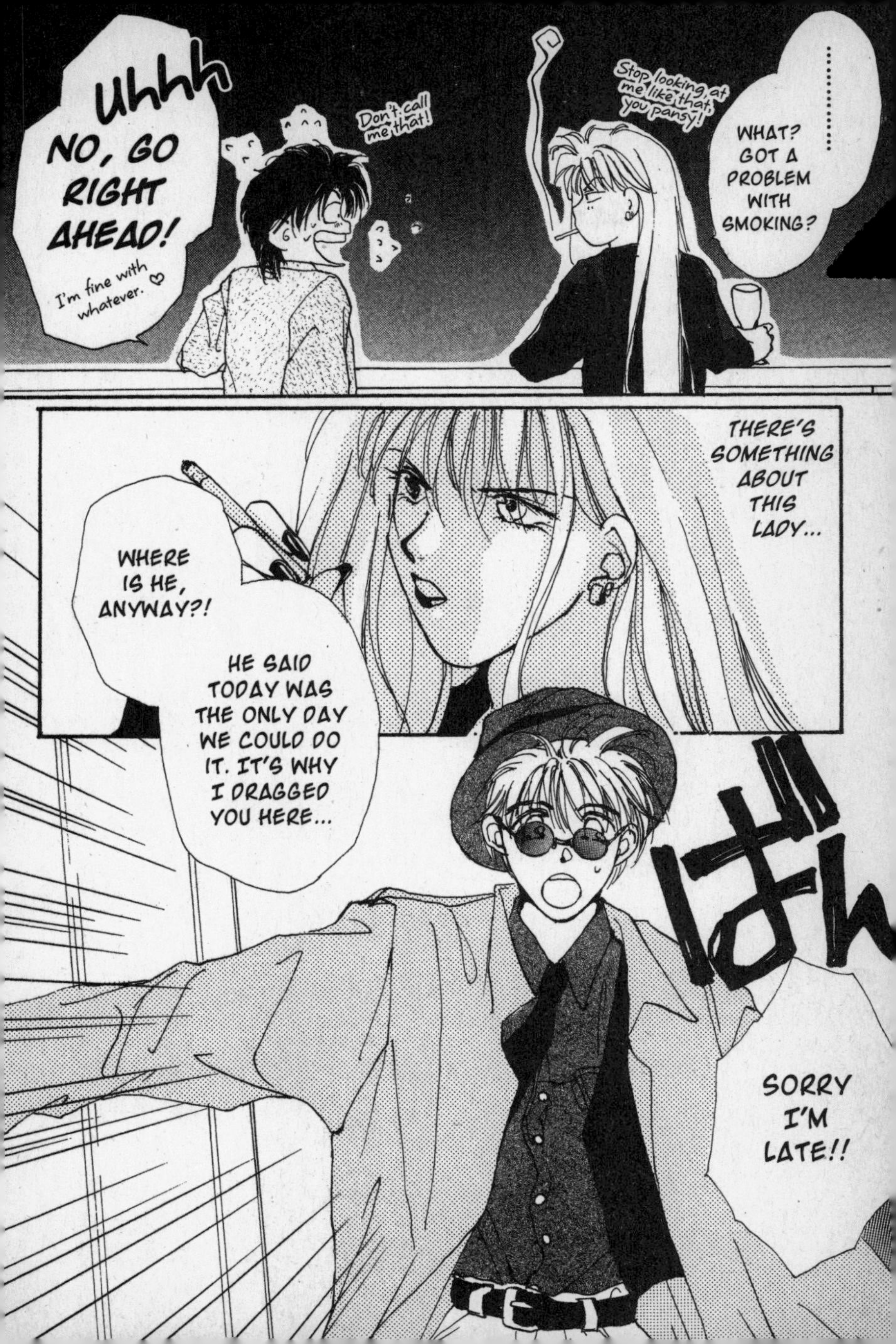
……
WHAT? GOT A PROBLEM WITH SMOKING?
Stop looking at me like that, you pansy!
Don't call me that!
Uhhh
NO, GO RIGHT AHEAD!
I'm fine with whatever. ♡
THERE'S SOMETHING ABOUT THIS LADY...
WHERE IS HE, ANYWAY?!
HE SAID TODAY WAS THE ONLY DAY WE COULD DO IT. IT'S WHY I DRAGGED YOU HERE...
ばん
SORRY I'M LATE!!

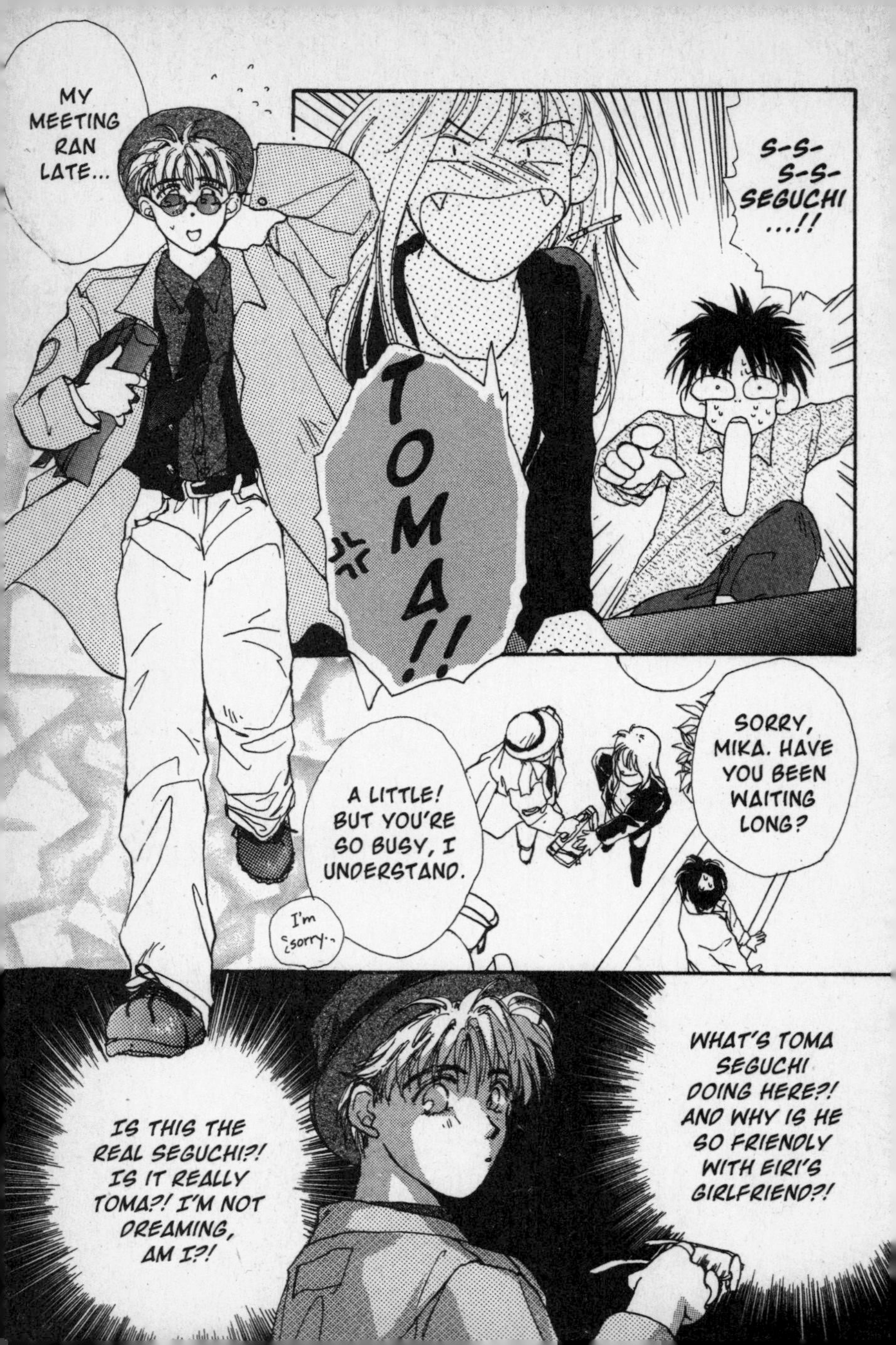
S-S-S-S-SEGUCHI...!!
TOMA!!
SORRY, MIKA. HAVE YOU BEEN WAITING LONG?
A LITTLE! BUT YOU'RE SO BUSY, I UNDERSTAND.
I'm sorry.
MY MEETING RAN LATE...
WHAT'S TOMA SEGUCHI DOING HERE?! AND WHY IS HE SO FRIENDLY WITH EIRI'S GIRLFRIEND?!
IS THIS THE REAL SEGUCHI?! IS IT REALLY TOMA?! I'M NOT DREAMING, AM I?!

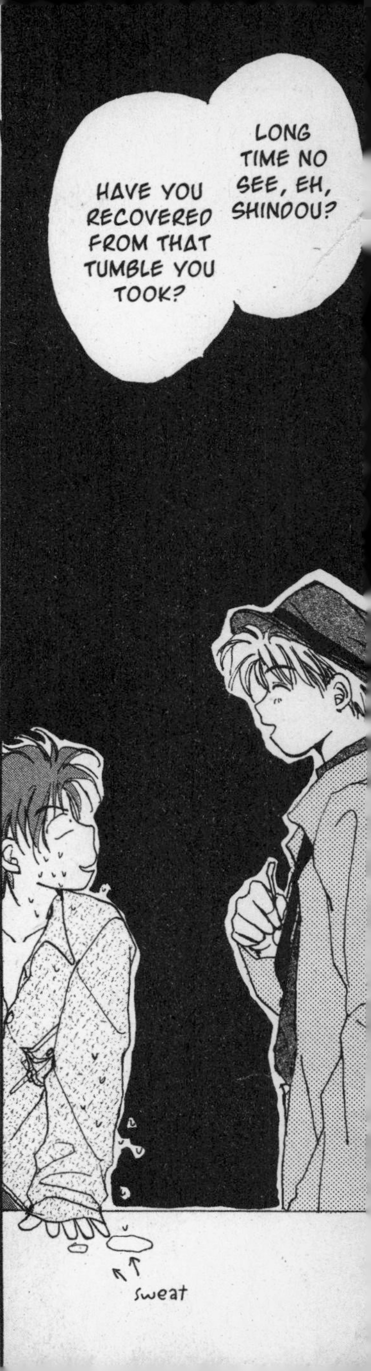
LONG TIME NO SEE, EH, SHINDOU?
HAVE YOU RECOVERED FROM THAT TUMBLE YOU TOOK?
sweat

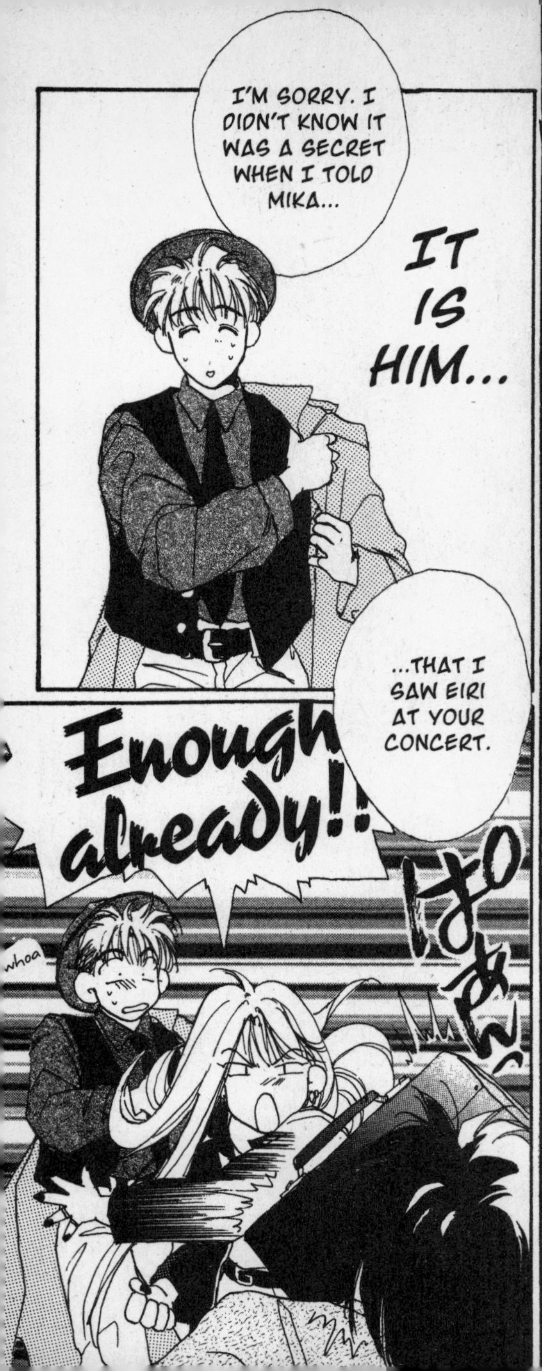
I'M SORRY. I DIDN'T KNOW IT WAS A SECRET WHEN I TOLD MIKA...
IT IS HIM...
...THAT I SAW EIRI AT YOUR CONCERT.
Enough already!!
whoa

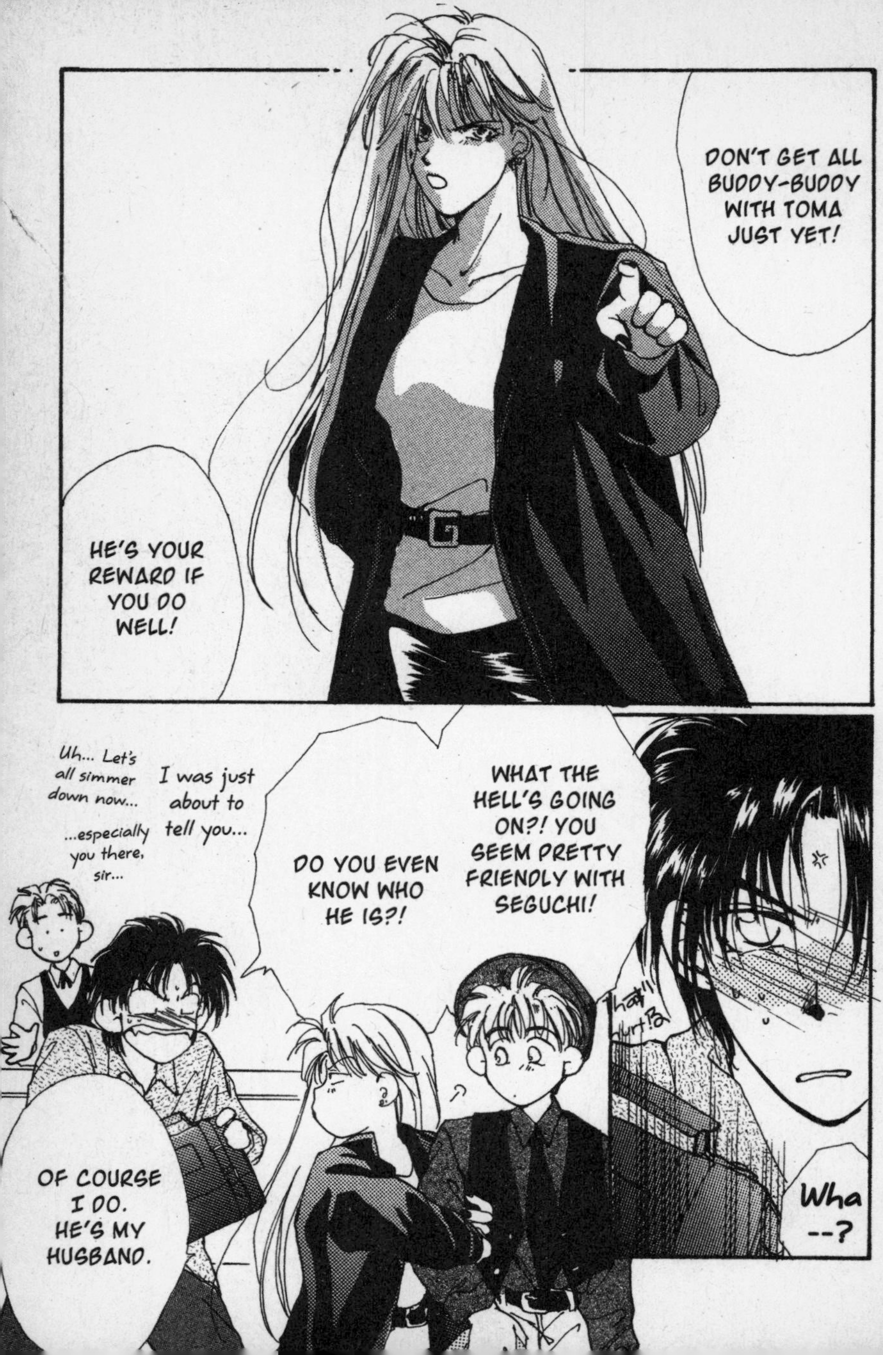
DON'T GET ALL BUDDY-BUDDY WITH TOMA JUST YET!
HE'S YOUR REWARD IF YOU DO WELL!
WHAT THE HELL'S GOING ON?! YOU SEEM PRETTY FRIENDLY WITH SEGUCHI!
DO YOU EVEN KNOW WHO HE IS?!
I was just about to tell you...
Uh... Let's all simmer down now...
...especially you there, sir...
OF COURSE I DO. HE'S MY HUSBAND.
Wha--?

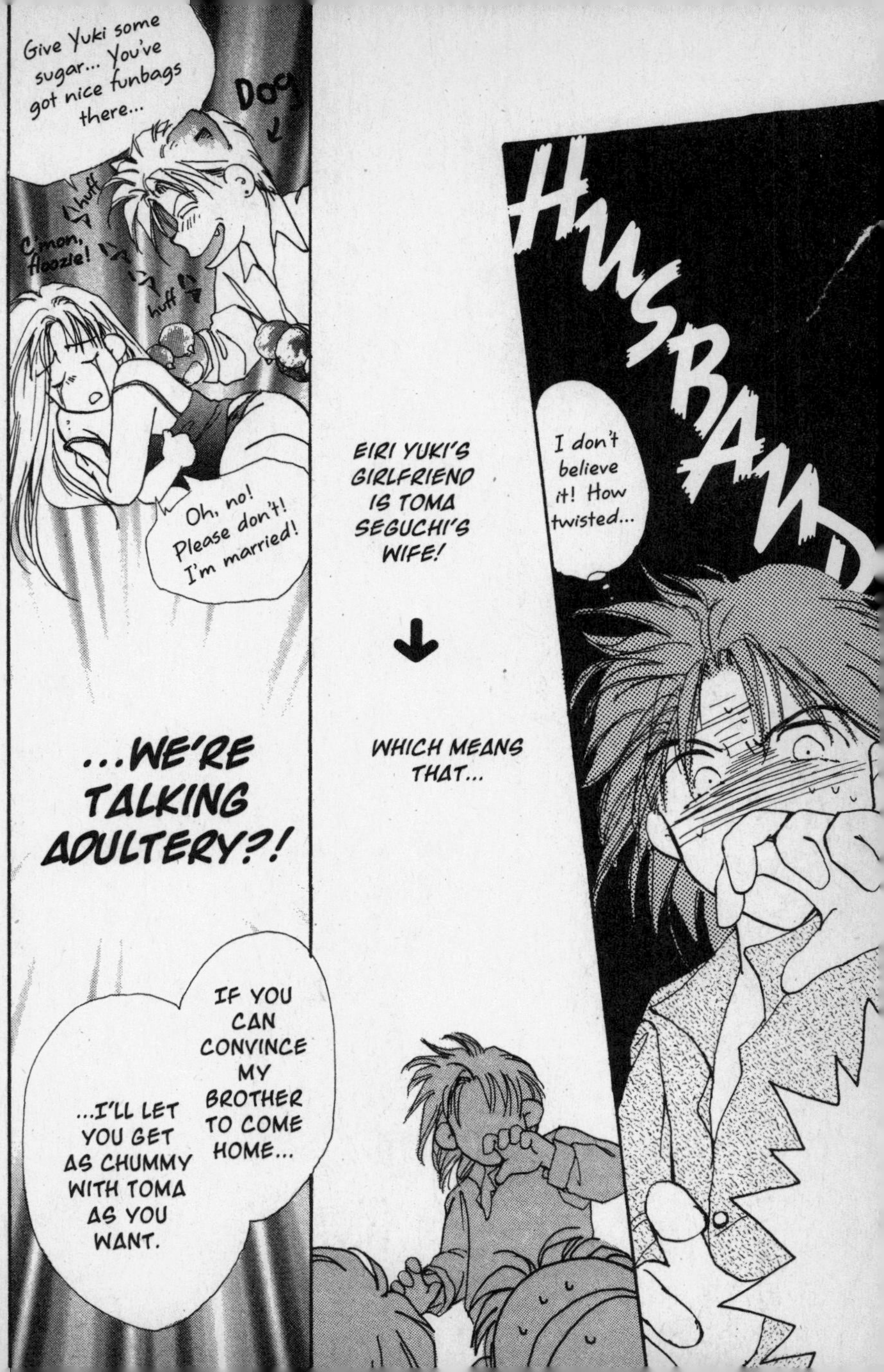
HUSBAND
I don't believe it! How twisted...
EIRI YUKI'S GIRLFRIEND IS TOMA SEGUCHI'S WIFE!
WHICH MEANS THAT...
Give Yuki some sugar... You've got nice funbags there...
Dog
huff
C'mon, floozie!
huff
Oh, no! Please don't! I'm married!
...WE'RE TALKING ADULTERY?!
IF YOU CAN CONVINCE MY BROTHER TO COME HOME...
...I'LL LET YOU GET AS CHUMMY WITH TOMA AS YOU WANT.

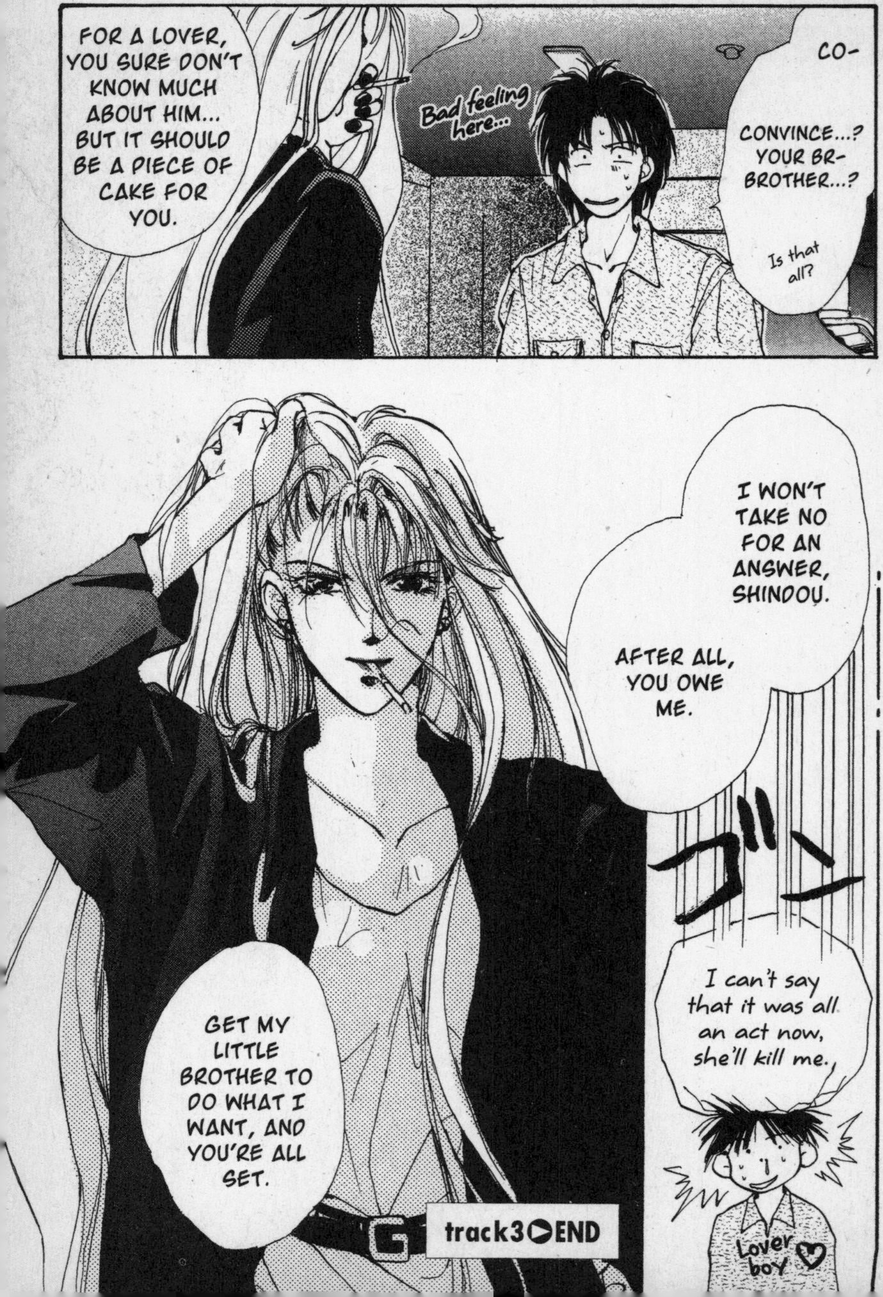
CO-
CONVINCE...? YOUR BR-BROTHER...?
Is that all?
Bad feeling here...
FOR A LOVER, YOU SURE DON'T KNOW MUCH ABOUT HIM... BUT IT SHOULD BE A PIECE OF CAKE FOR YOU.
I WON'T TAKE NO FOR AN ANSWER, SHINDOU.
AFTER ALL, YOU OWE ME.
ゴン
I can't say that it was all an act now, she'll kill me.
GET MY LITTLE BROTHER TO DO WHAT I WANT, AND YOU'RE ALL SET.
Lover boy
track3▶END

track 4

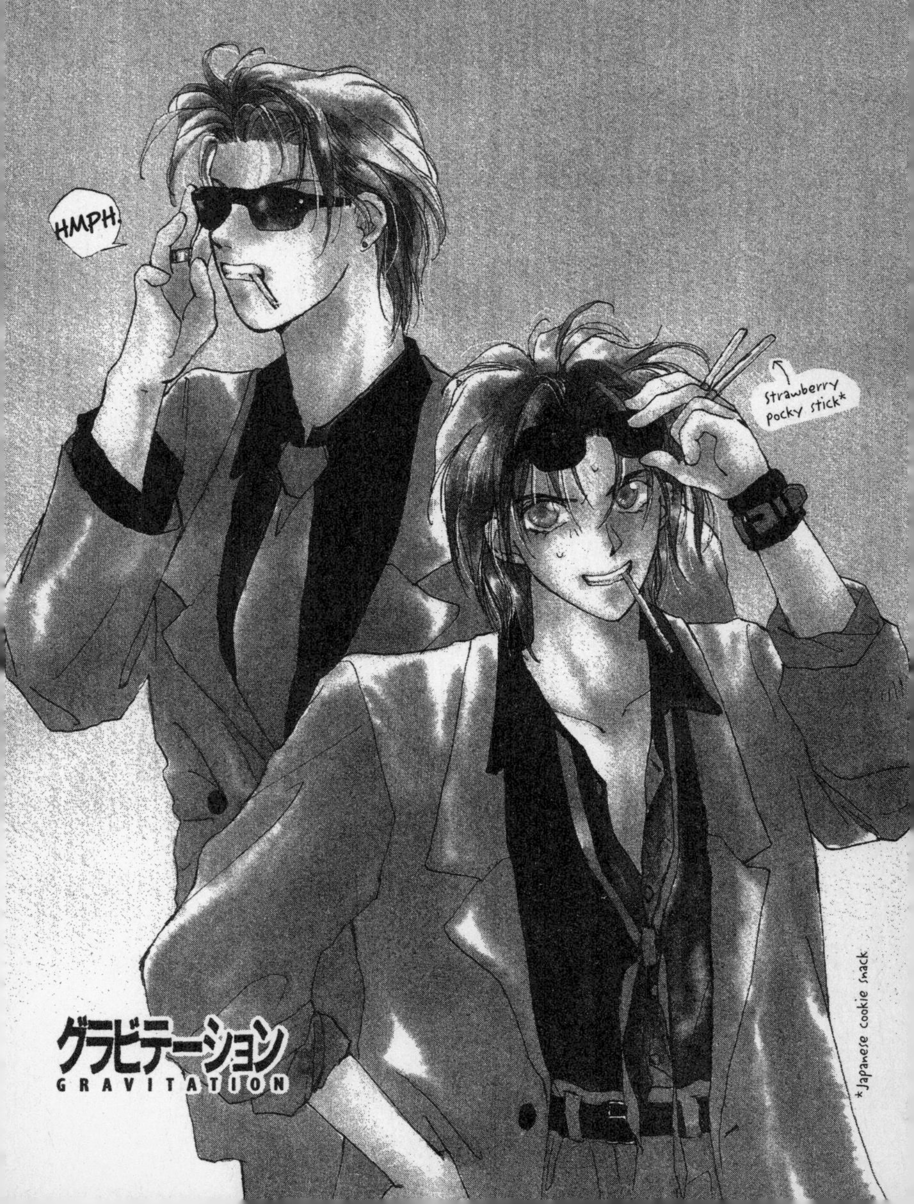
HMPH!
Strawberry pocky stick*
*Japanese cookie snack
グラビテーション
GRAVITATION

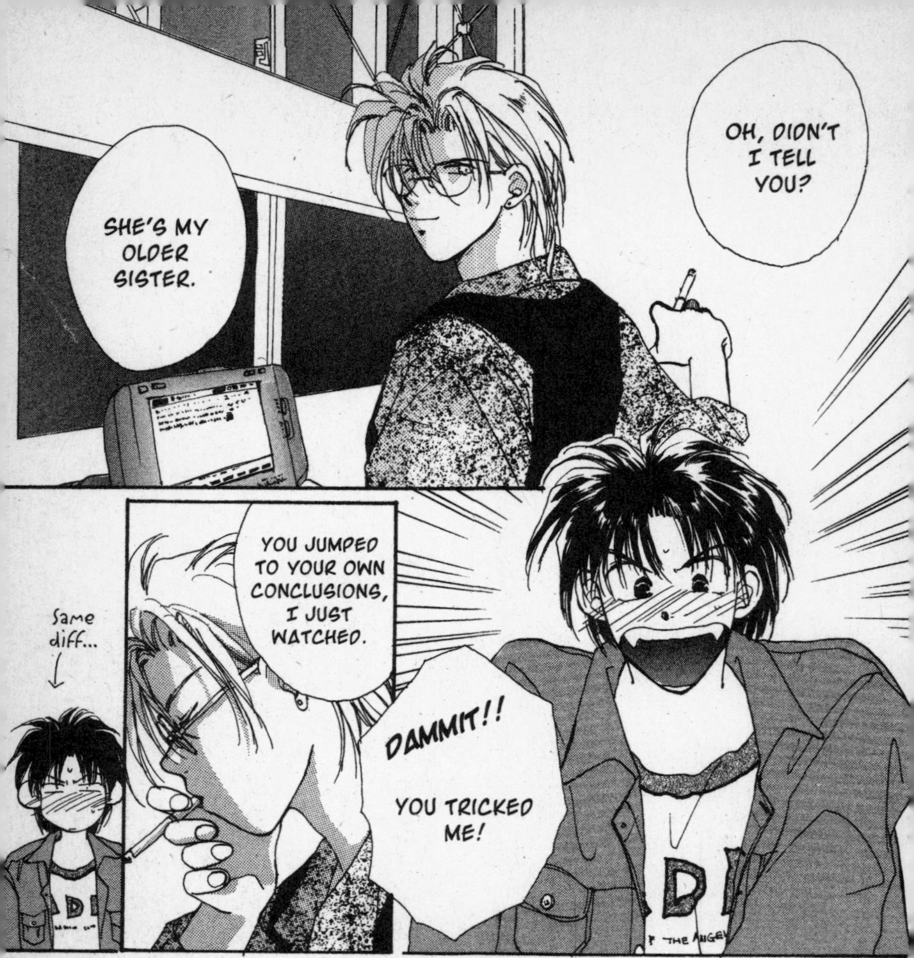
OH, DIDN'T I TELL YOU?
SHE'S MY OLDER SISTER.
DAMMIT!!
YOU TRICKED ME!
YOU JUMPED TO YOUR OWN CONCLUSIONS, I JUST WATCHED.
Same diff...

ABOUT GRAVITATION TRACK 4

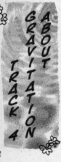

It was amazing how this episode came together. It was really tough. I had a lot of people working to lay down the shading, but the teamwork wasn't going very well. And so it turned into a big nightmare. I never want to go through that again. It was really hell. I was 90% sure we weren't going to make it. There was no time to sleep. My editors were yelling at me like monsters. I'll probably never experience a scene like that again. Somehow, I get a little sentimental when I think of it that way (who knows why?). Eiri's been giving me trouble now that he's so active and mean in the story. Just kidding! Eiri's beginning to emit some pheromone energy that affects how he's drawn. Could it be love? Sort of like Toma? I'm tantalizing you readers with everything I've got, and at the end, I leave you hanging. Outta control. To be continued.

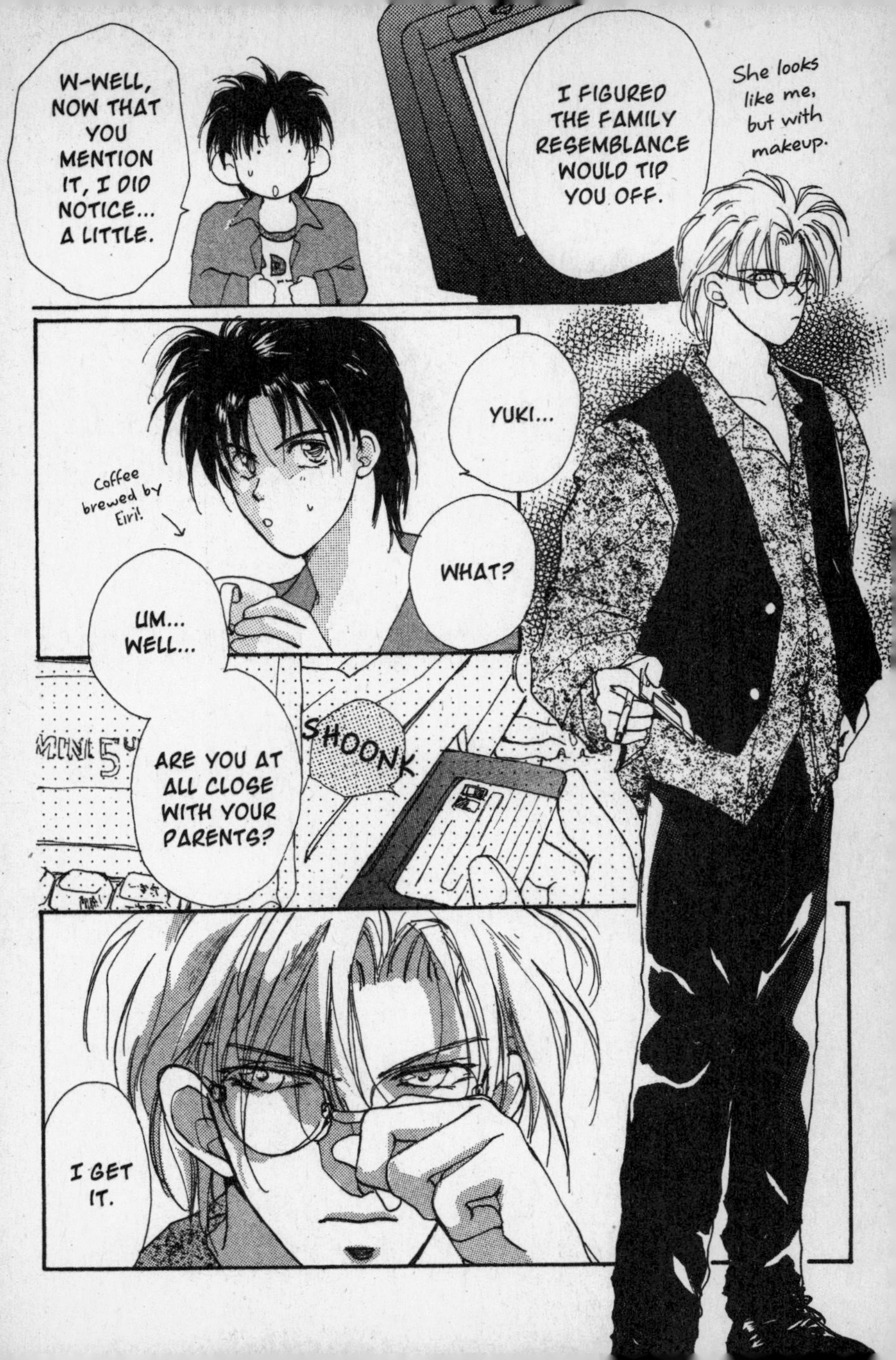
She looks like me, but with makeup.
I FIGURED THE FAMILY RESEMBLANCE WOULD TIP YOU OFF.
W-WELL, NOW THAT YOU MENTION IT, I DID NOTICE... A LITTLE.
YUKI...
WHAT?
Coffee brewed by Eiri!
UM... WELL...
SHOONK
ARE YOU AT ALL CLOSE WITH YOUR PARENTS?
I GET IT.

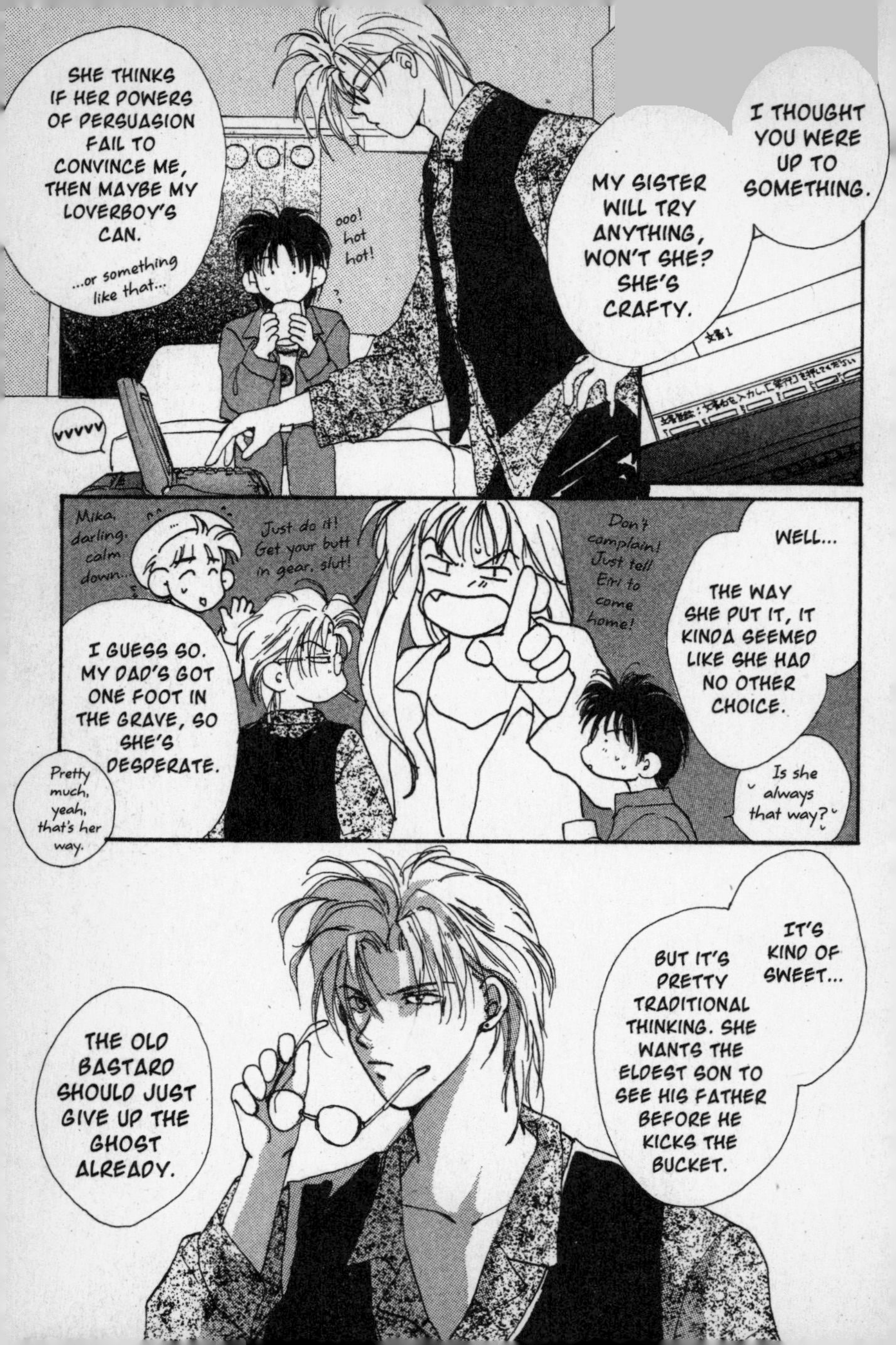
I THOUGHT YOU WERE UP TO SOMETHING.
MY SISTER WILL TRY ANYTHING, WON'T SHE? SHE'S CRAFTY.
ooo! hot hot!
SHE THINKS IF HER POWERS OF PERSUASION FAIL TO CONVINCE ME, THEN MAYBE MY LOVERBOY'S CAN.
...or something like that...
vvvvv
WELL...
THE WAY SHE PUT IT, IT KINDA SEEMED LIKE SHE HAD NO OTHER CHOICE.
Is she always that way?
Don't complain! Just tell Eiri to come home!
Just do it! Get your butt in gear, slut!
Mika, darling, calm down...
I GUESS SO. MY DAD'S GOT ONE FOOT IN THE GRAVE, SO SHE'S DESPERATE.
Pretty much, yeah, that's her way.
IT'S KIND OF SWEET...
BUT IT'S PRETTY TRADITIONAL THINKING. SHE WANTS THE ELDEST SON TO SEE HIS FATHER BEFORE HE KICKS THE BUCKET.
THE OLD BASTARD SHOULD JUST GIVE UP THE GHOST ALREADY.

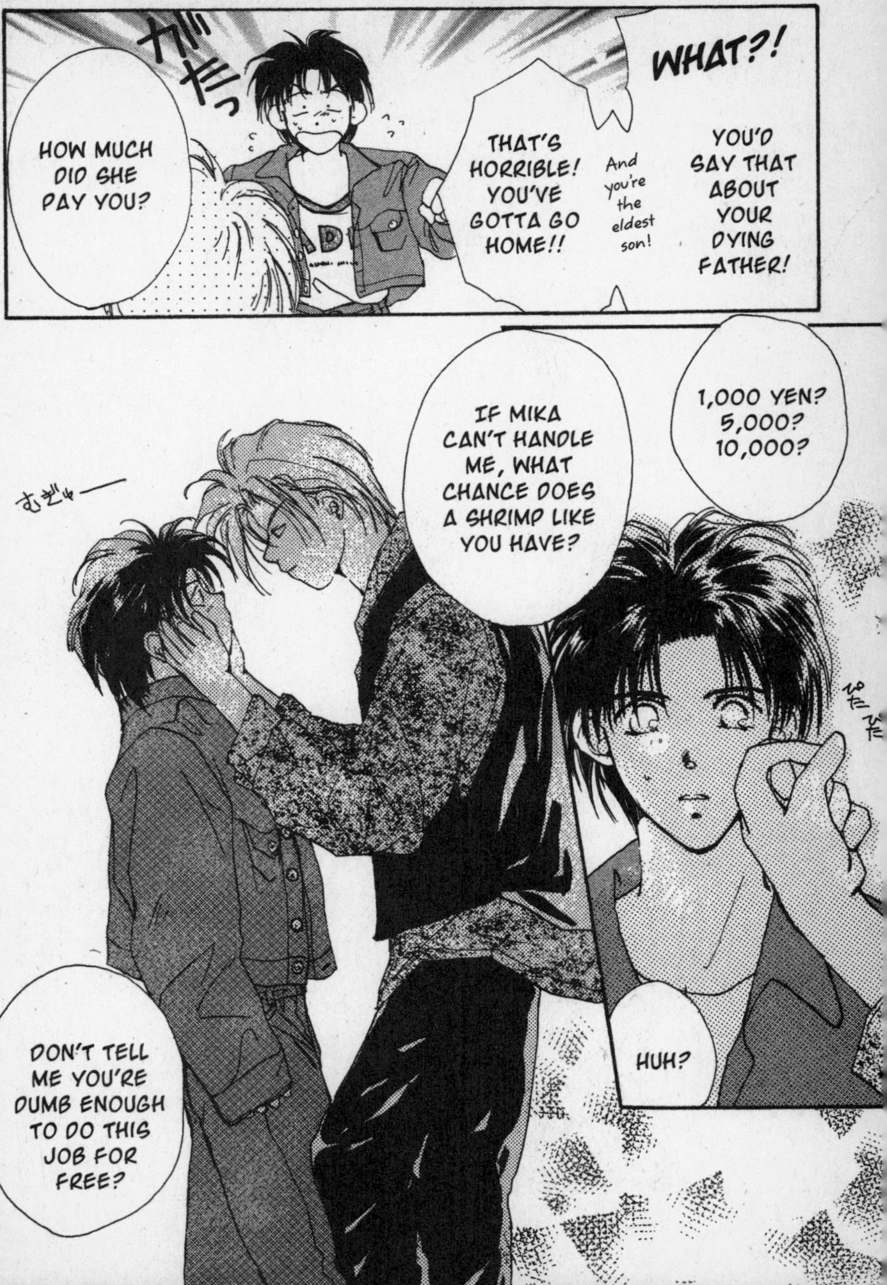
WHAT?!
YOU'D SAY THAT ABOUT YOUR DYING FATHER!
And you're the eldest son!
THAT'S HORRIBLE! YOU'VE GOTTA GO HOME!!
HOW MUCH DID SHE PAY YOU?
1,000 YEN? 5,000? 10,000?
IF MIKA CAN'T HANDLE ME, WHAT CHANCE DOES A SHRIMP LIKE YOU HAVE?
HUH?
DON'T TELL ME YOU'RE DUMB ENOUGH TO DO THIS JOB FOR FREE?

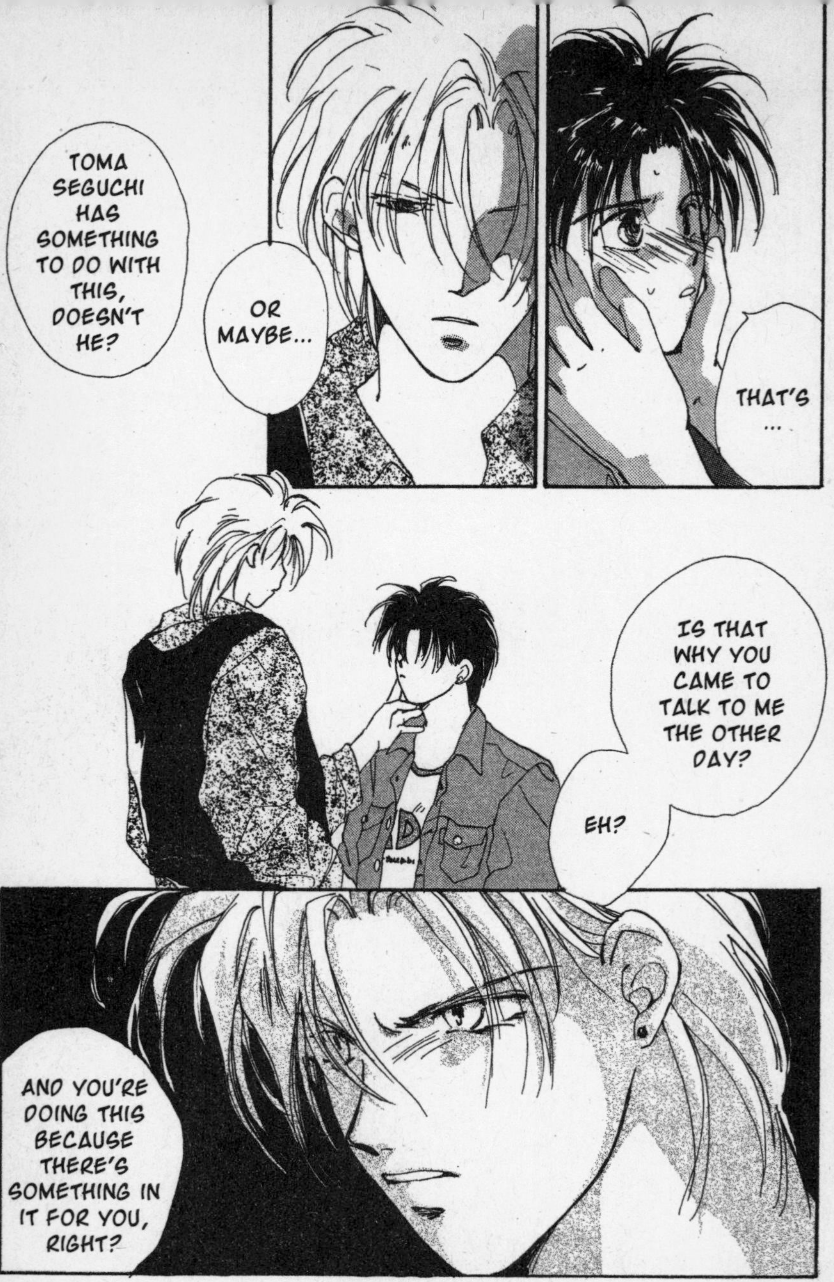
THAT'S ...
OR MAYBE...
TOMA SEGUCHI HAS SOMETHING TO DO WITH THIS, DOESN'T HE?
IS THAT WHY YOU CAME TO TALK TO ME THE OTHER DAY?
EH?
AND YOU'RE DOING THIS BECAUSE THERE'S SOMETHING IN IT FOR YOU, RIGHT?

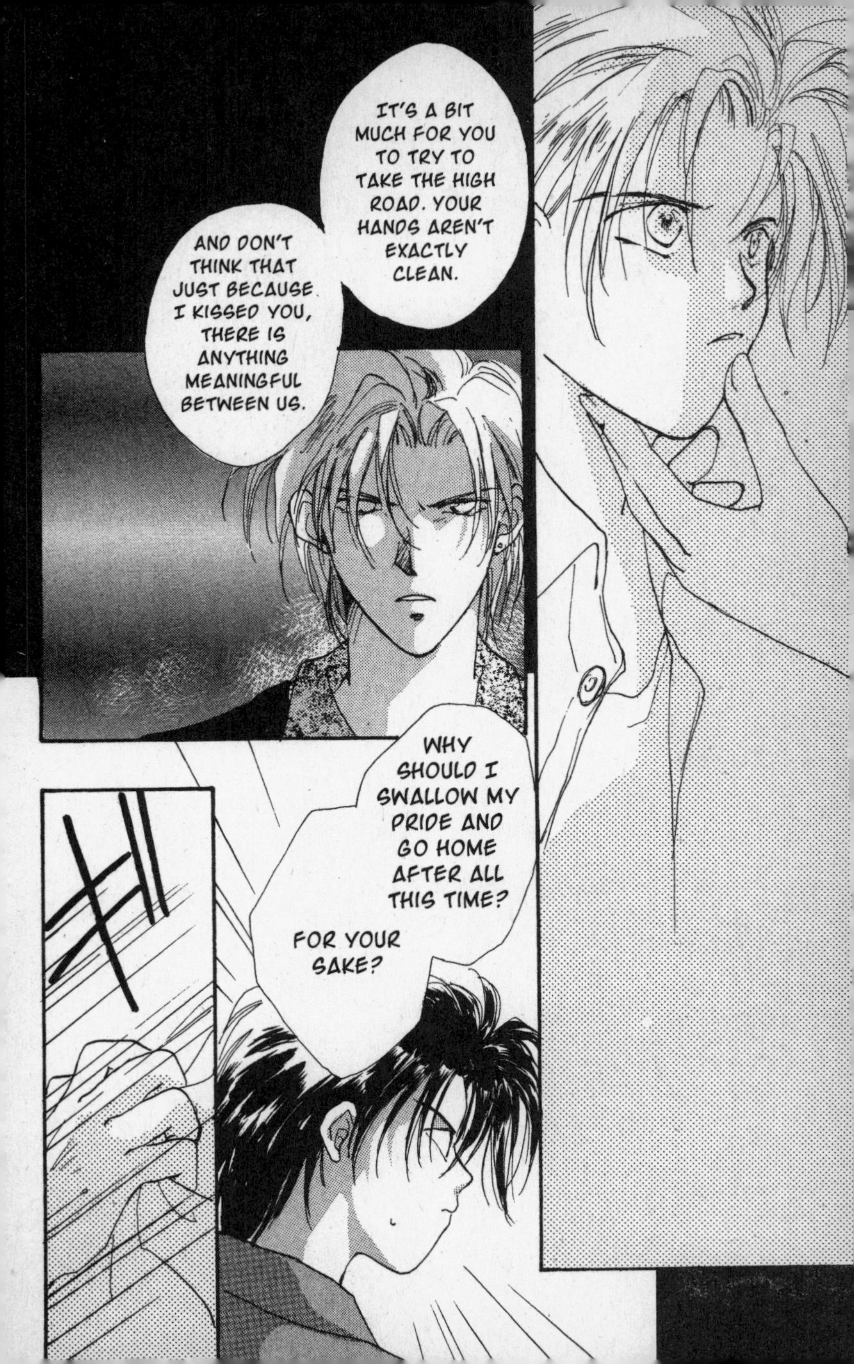
IT'S A BIT MUCH FOR YOU TO TRY TO TAKE THE HIGH ROAD. YOUR HANDS AREN'T EXACTLY CLEAN.
AND DON'T THINK THAT JUST BECAUSE I KISSED YOU, THERE IS ANYTHING MEANINGFUL BETWEEN US.
WHY SHOULD I SWALLOW MY PRIDE AND GO HOME AFTER ALL THIS TIME?
FOR YOUR SAKE?

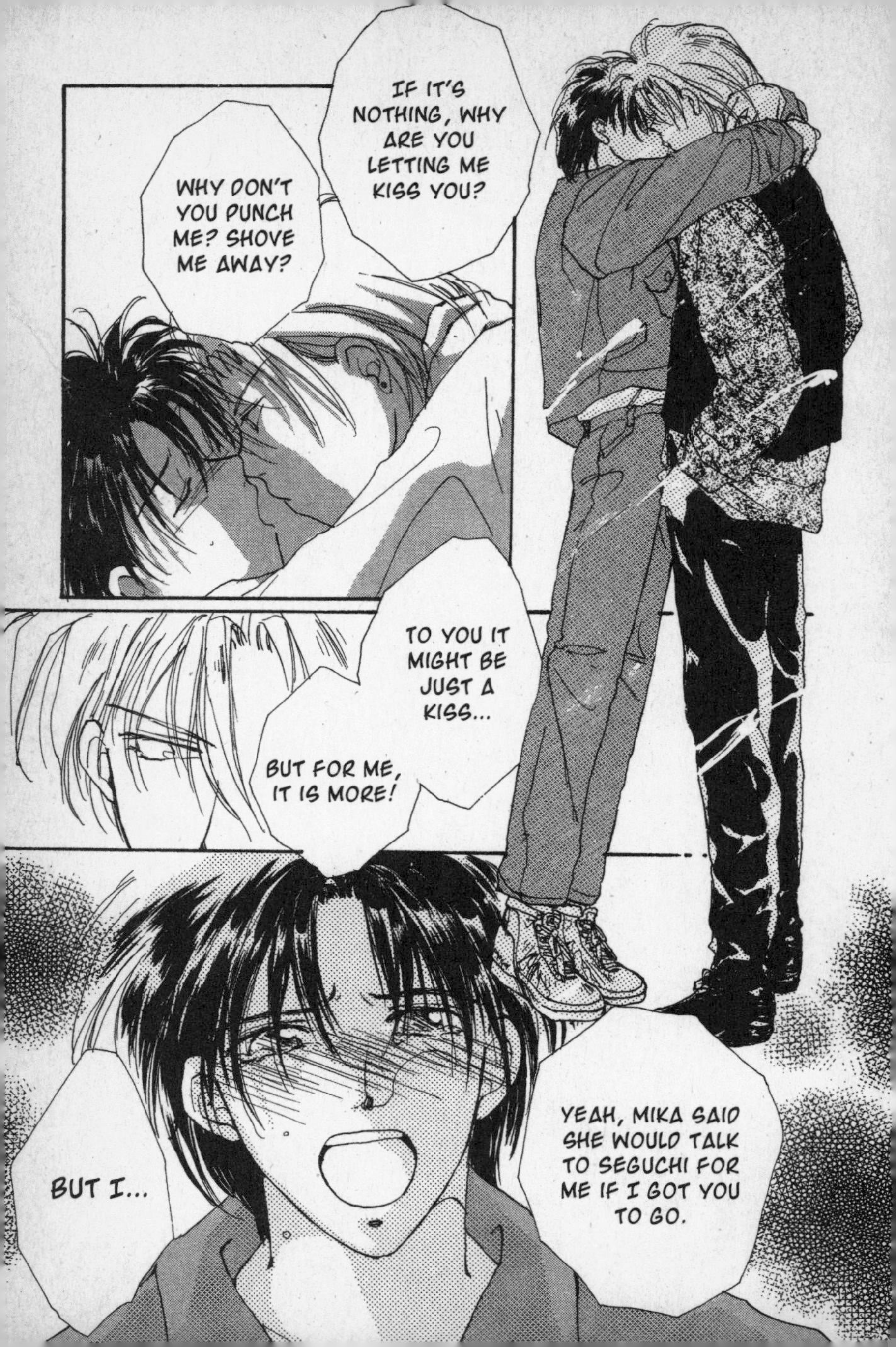
IF IT'S NOTHING, WHY ARE YOU LETTING ME KISS YOU?
WHY DON'T YOU PUNCH ME? SHOVE ME AWAY?
TO YOU IT MIGHT BE JUST A KISS...
BUT FOR ME, IT IS MORE!
YEAH, MIKA SAID SHE WOULD TALK TO SEGUCHI FOR ME IF I GOT YOU TO GO.
BUT I...

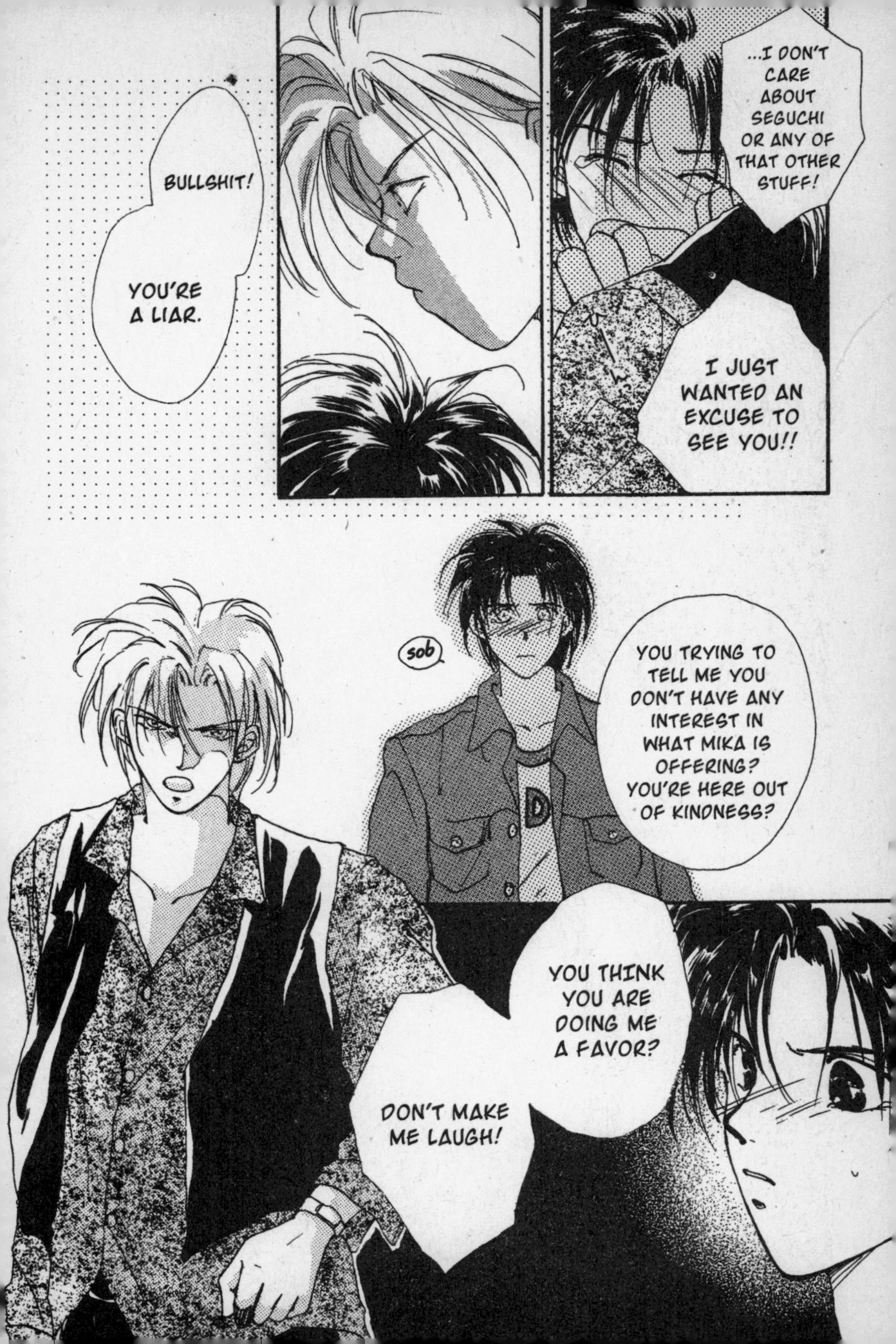
...I DON'T CARE ABOUT SEGUCHI OR ANY OF THAT OTHER STUFF!
I JUST WANTED AN EXCUSE TO SEE YOU!!
BULLSHIT!
YOU'RE A LIAR.
YOU TRYING TO TELL ME YOU DON'T HAVE ANY INTEREST IN WHAT MIKA IS OFFERING? YOU'RE HERE OUT OF KINDNESS?
sob
YOU THINK YOU ARE DOING ME A FAVOR?
DON'T MAKE ME LAUGH!

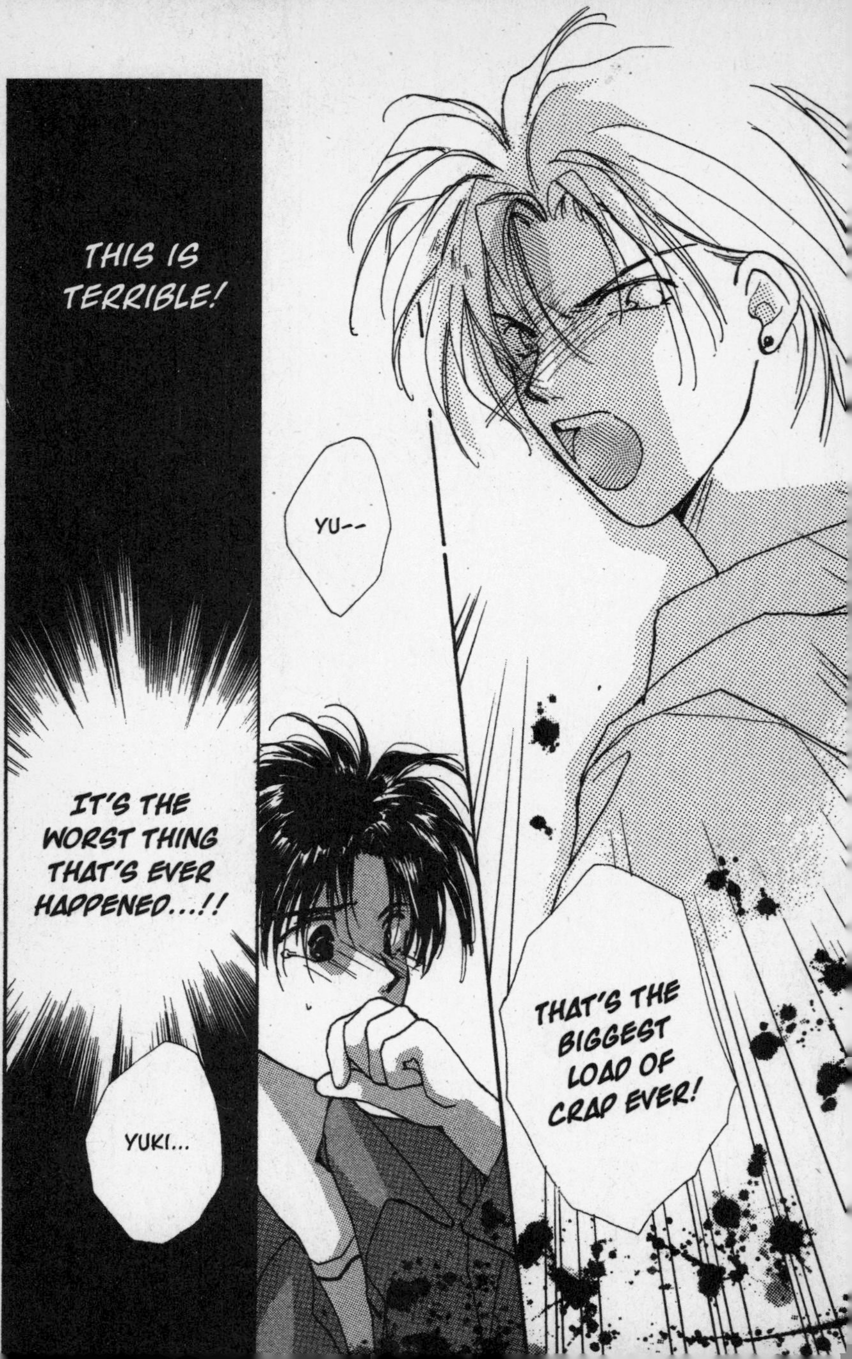
YU--
THAT'S THE BIGGEST LOAD OF CRAP EVER!
THIS IS TERRIBLE!
IT'S THE WORST THING THAT'S EVER HAPPENED...!!
YUKI...

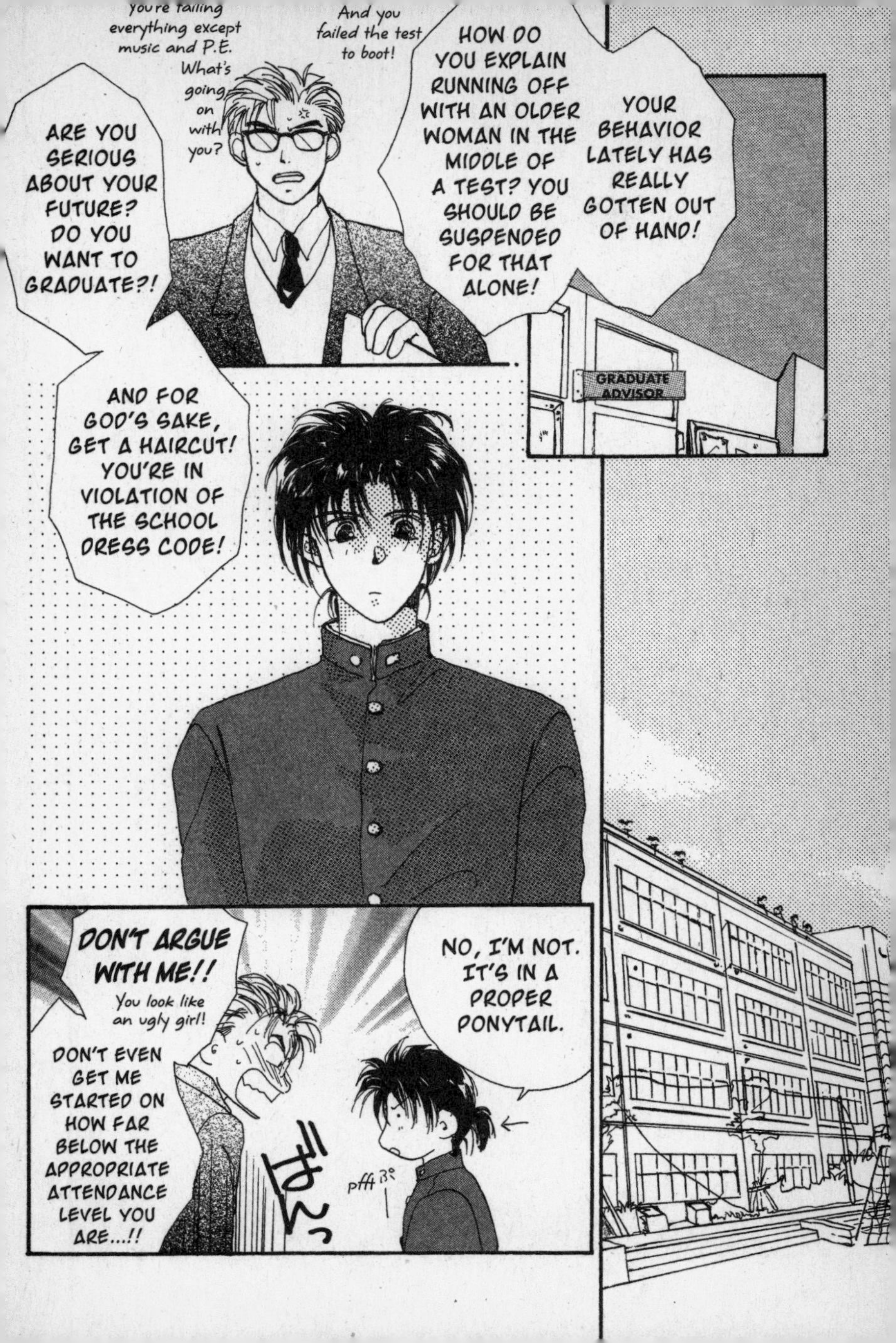
GRADUATE ADVISOR
YOUR BEHAVIOR LATELY HAS REALLY GOTTEN OUT OF HAND!
HOW DO YOU EXPLAIN RUNNING OFF WITH AN OLDER WOMAN IN THE MIDDLE OF A TEST? YOU SHOULD BE SUSPENDED FOR THAT ALONE!
And you failed the test to boot!
You're failing everything except music and P.E. What's going on with you?
ARE YOU SERIOUS ABOUT YOUR FUTURE? DO YOU WANT TO GRADUATE?!
AND FOR GOD'S SAKE, GET A HAIRCUT! YOU'RE IN VIOLATION OF THE SCHOOL DRESS CODE!
NO, I'M NOT. IT'S IN A PROPER PONYTAIL.
DON'T ARGUE WITH ME!!
You look like an ugly girl!
DON'T EVEN GET ME STARTED ON HOW FAR BELOW THE APPROPRIATE ATTENDANCE LEVEL YOU ARE...!!
pff

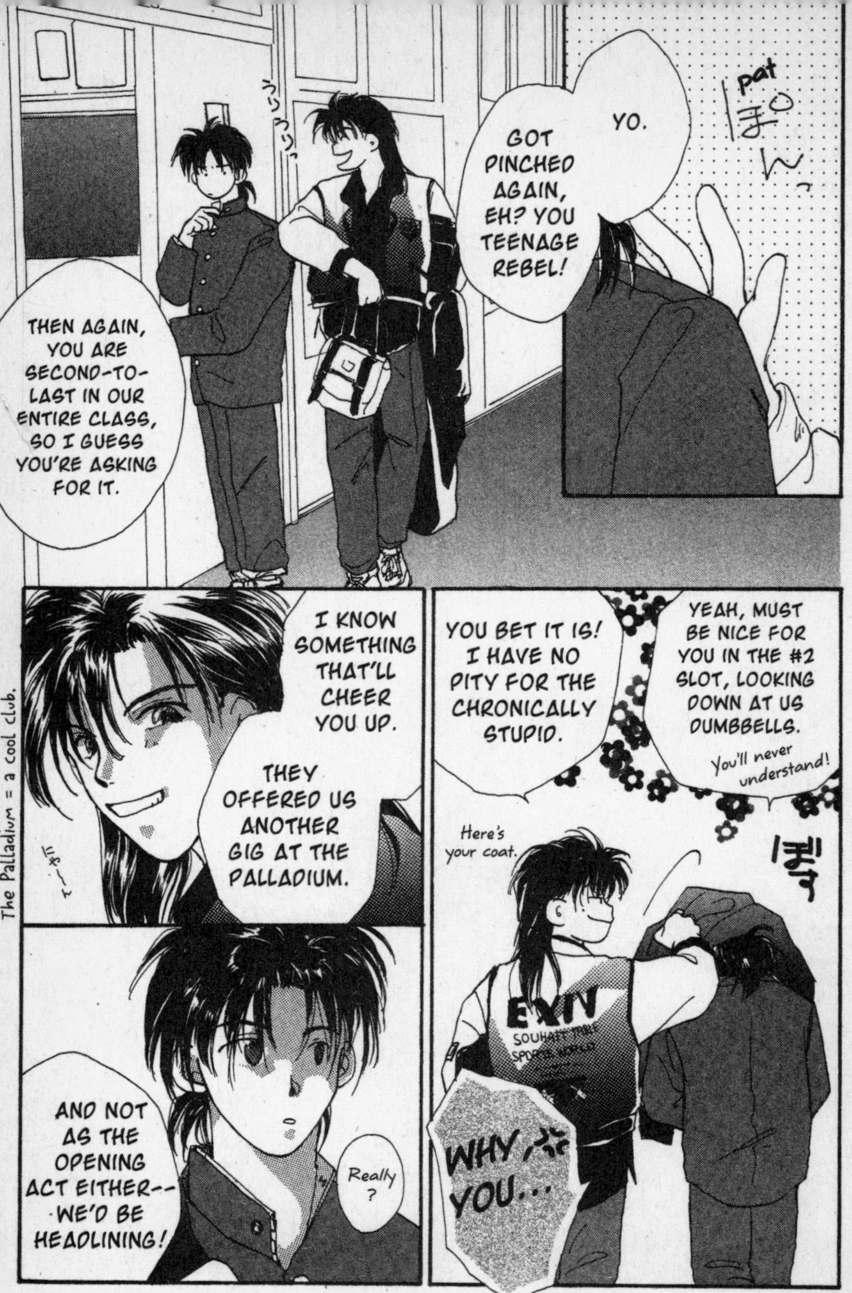
pat
YO.
GOT PINCHED AGAIN, EH? YOU TEENAGE REBEL!
THEN AGAIN, YOU ARE SECOND-TO-LAST IN OUR ENTIRE CLASS, SO I GUESS YOU'RE ASKING FOR IT.
YEAH, MUST BE NICE FOR YOU IN THE #2 SLOT, LOOKING DOWN AT US DUMBBELLS.
You'll never understand!
YOU BET IT IS! I HAVE NO PITY FOR THE CHRONICALLY STUPID.
Here's your coat.
EXIV
WHY YOU...
I KNOW SOMETHING THAT'LL CHEER YOU UP.
THEY OFFERED US ANOTHER GIG AT THE PALLADIUM.
The Palladium = a cool club.
Really?
AND NOT AS THE OPENING ACT EITHER--WE'D BE HEADLINING!

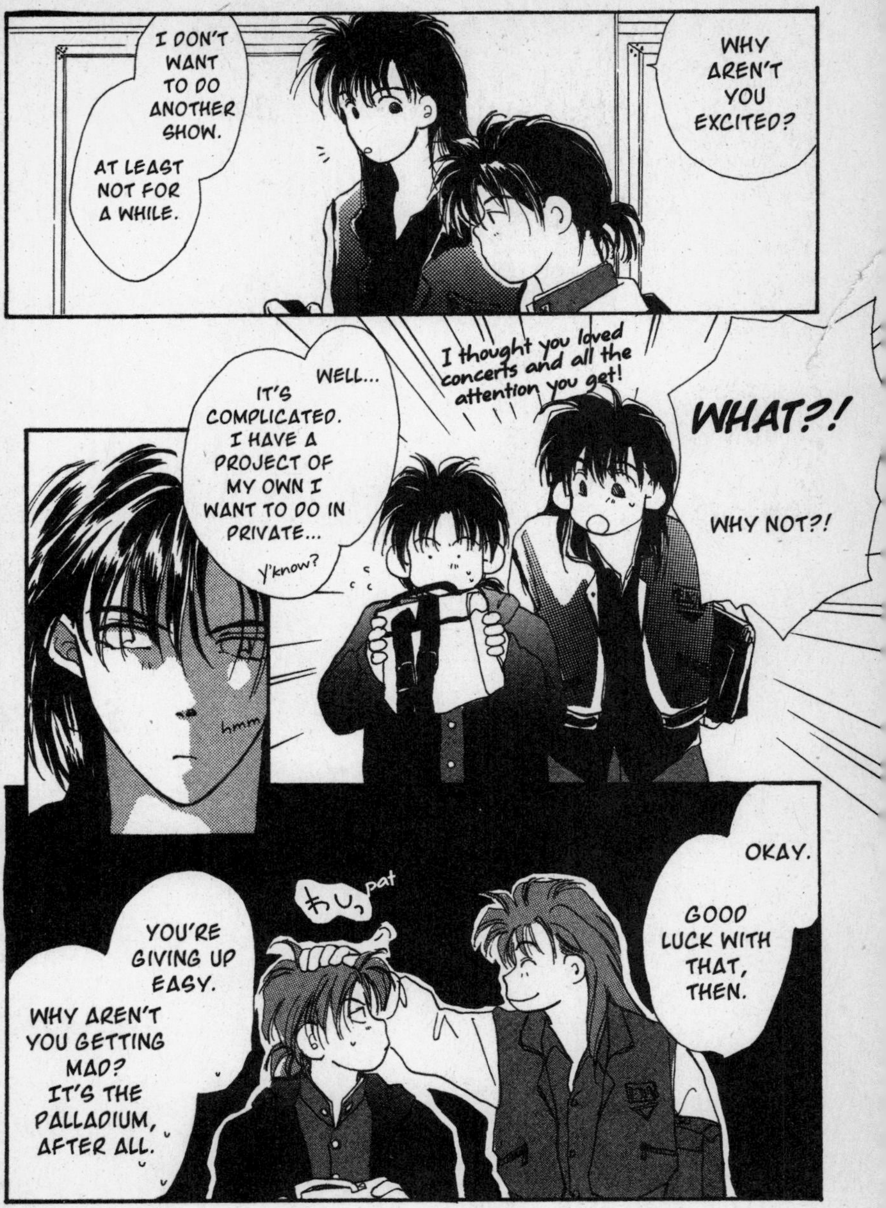
WHY AREN'T YOU EXCITED?
I DON'T WANT TO DO ANOTHER SHOW.
AT LEAST NOT FOR A WHILE.
WHAT?!
WHY NOT?!
I thought you loved concerts and all the attention you get!
WELL...
IT'S COMPLICATED. I HAVE A PROJECT OF MY OWN I WANT TO DO IN PRIVATE...
y'know?
hmm
OKAY.
GOOD LUCK WITH THAT, THEN.
わしっ
pat
YOU'RE GIVING UP EASY.
WHY AREN'T YOU GETTING MAD? IT'S THE PALLADIUM, AFTER ALL.

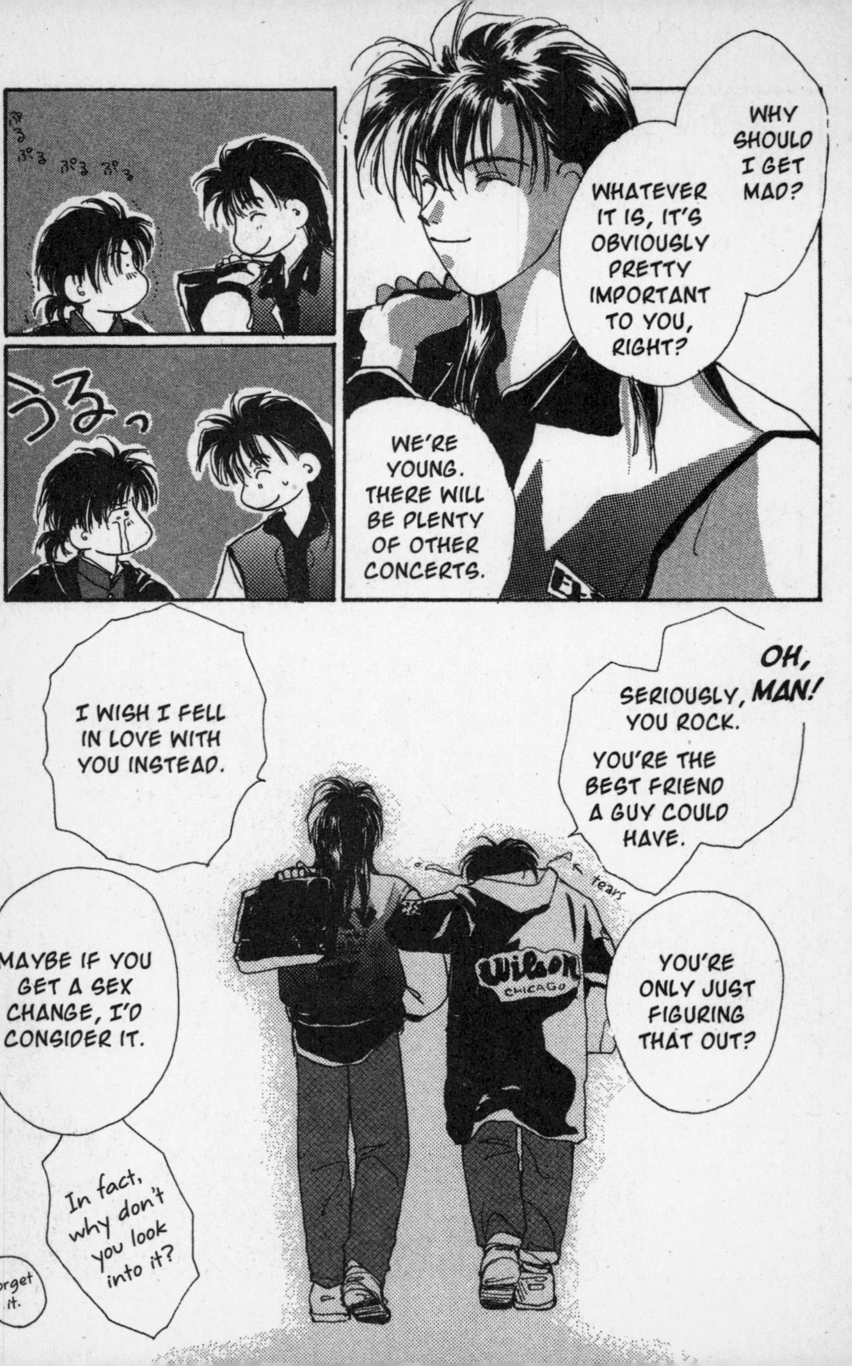
WHY SHOULD I GET MAD?
WHATEVER IT IS, IT'S OBVIOUSLY PRETTY IMPORTANT TO YOU, RIGHT?
WE'RE YOUNG. THERE WILL BE PLENTY OF OTHER CONCERTS.
ぷるぷる ぷるぷる
うるっ
OH, MAN!
SERIOUSLY, YOU ROCK.
YOU'RE THE BEST FRIEND A GUY COULD HAVE.
tears
I WISH I FELL IN LOVE WITH YOU INSTEAD.
YOU'RE ONLY JUST FIGURING THAT OUT?
MAYBE IF YOU GET A SEX CHANGE, I'D CONSIDER IT.
In fact, why don't you look into it?
Forget it.

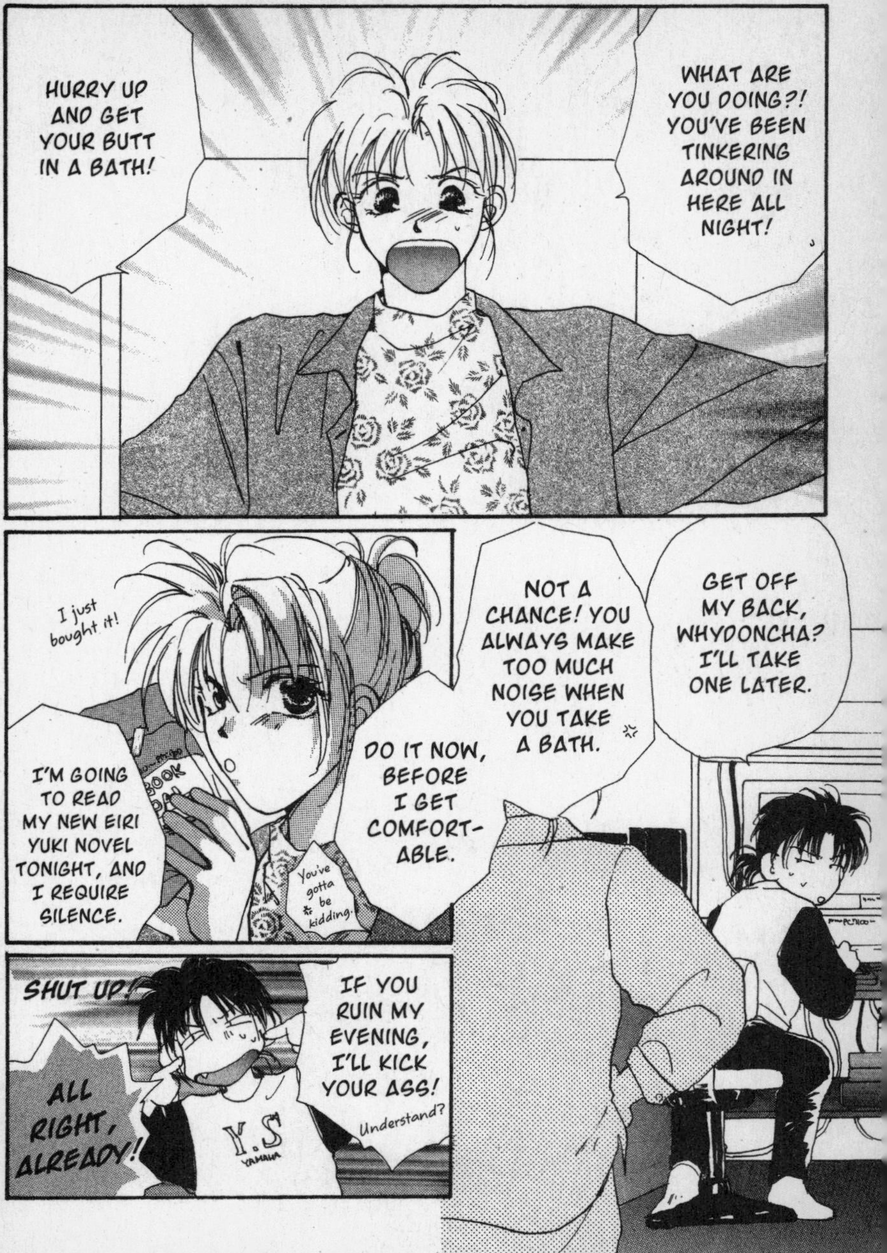
WHAT ARE YOU DOING?! YOU'VE BEEN TINKERING AROUND IN HERE ALL NIGHT!
HURRY UP AND GET YOUR BUTT IN A BATH!
GET OFF MY BACK, WHYDONCHA? I'LL TAKE ONE LATER.
NOT A CHANCE! YOU ALWAYS MAKE TOO MUCH NOISE WHEN YOU TAKE A BATH.
DO IT NOW, BEFORE I GET COMFORT-ABLE.
I'M GOING TO READ MY NEW EIRI YUKI NOVEL TONIGHT, AND I REQUIRE SILENCE.
I just bought it!
You've gotta be kidding.
IF YOU RUIN MY EVENING, I'LL KICK YOUR ASS!
Understand?
SHUT UP!
ALL RIGHT, ALREADY!

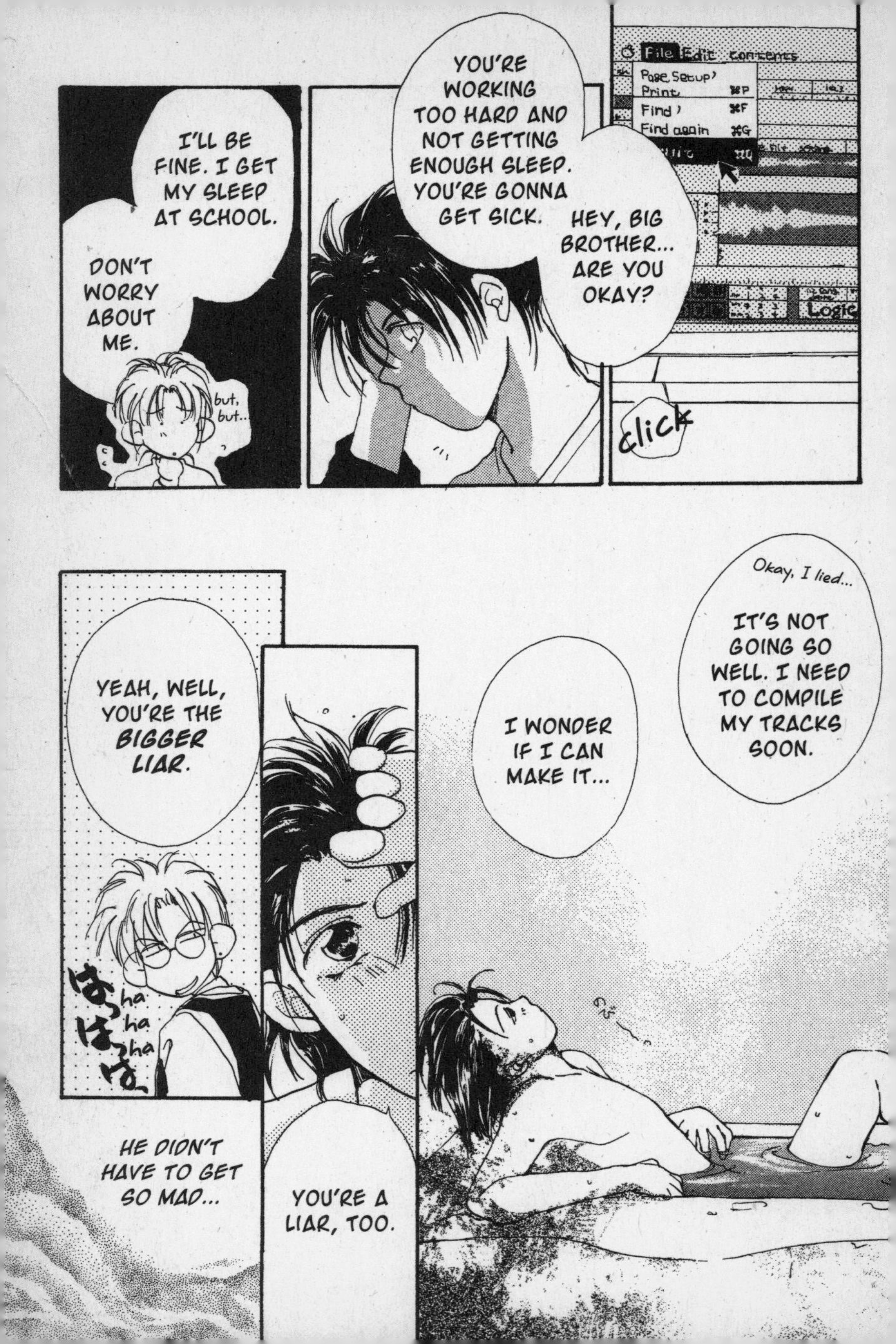
File Edit contents
Page Setup Print ⌘P Find ⌘F Find again ⌘G
Logic
click
HEY, BIG BROTHER... ARE YOU OKAY?
YOU'RE WORKING TOO HARD AND NOT GETTING ENOUGH SLEEP. YOU'RE GONNA GET SICK.
I'LL BE FINE. I GET MY SLEEP AT SCHOOL.
DON'T WORRY ABOUT ME.
but, but...
Okay, I lied...
IT'S NOT GOING SO WELL. I NEED TO COMPILE MY TRACKS SOON.
I WONDER IF I CAN MAKE IT...
YOU'RE A LIAR, TOO.
YEAH, WELL, YOU'RE THE BIGGER LIAR.
ha ha ha
HE DIDN'T HAVE TO GET SO MAD...

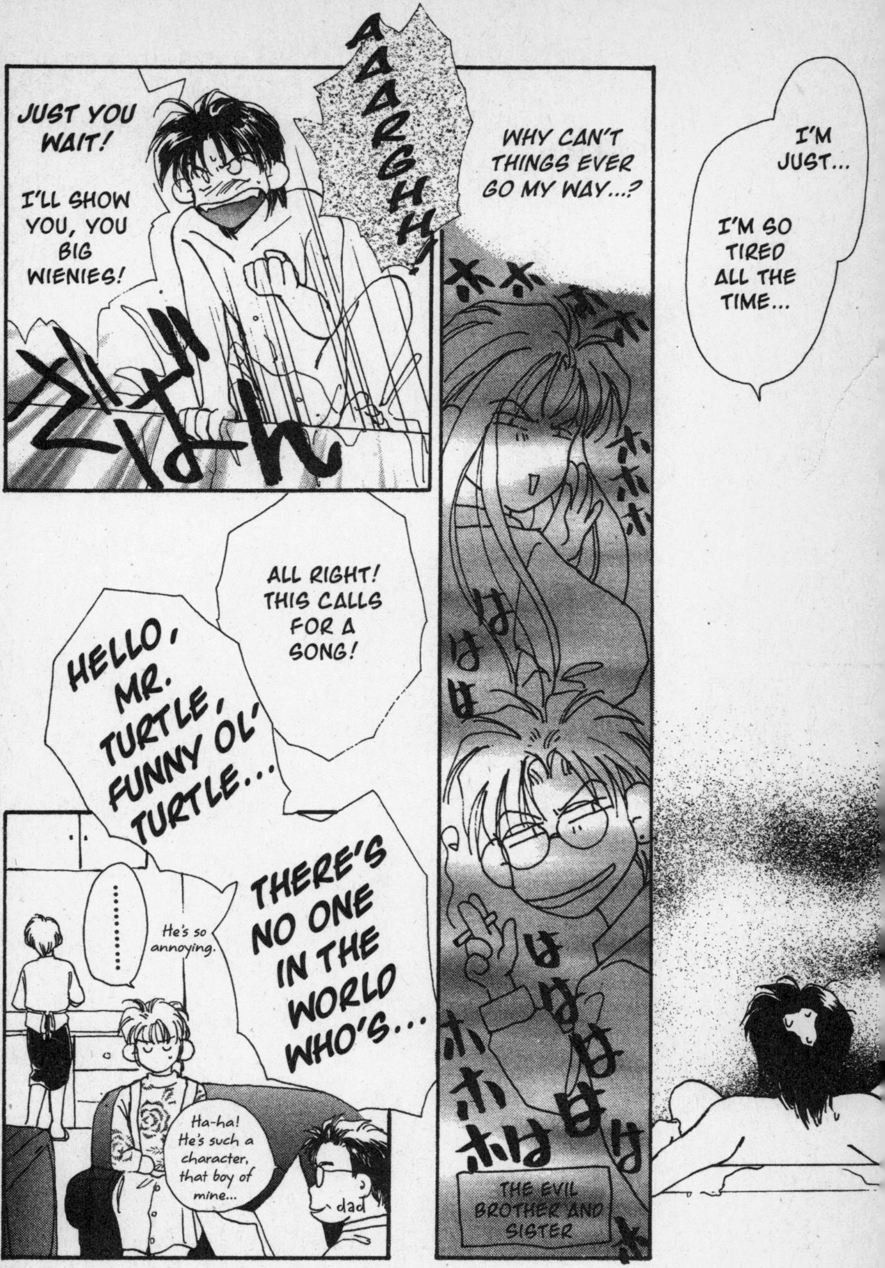
I'M JUST...
I'M SO TIRED ALL THE TIME...
WHY CAN'T THINGS EVER GO MY WAY...?
THE EVIL BROTHER AND SISTER
AAARGHH!
JUST YOU WAIT!
I'LL SHOW YOU, YOU BIG WIENIES!
ALL RIGHT! THIS CALLS FOR A SONG!
HELLO, MR. TURTLE, FUNNY OL' TURTLE...
THERE'S NO ONE IN THE WORLD WHO'S...
......
He's so annoying.
Ha-ha! He's such a character, that boy of mine...
dad

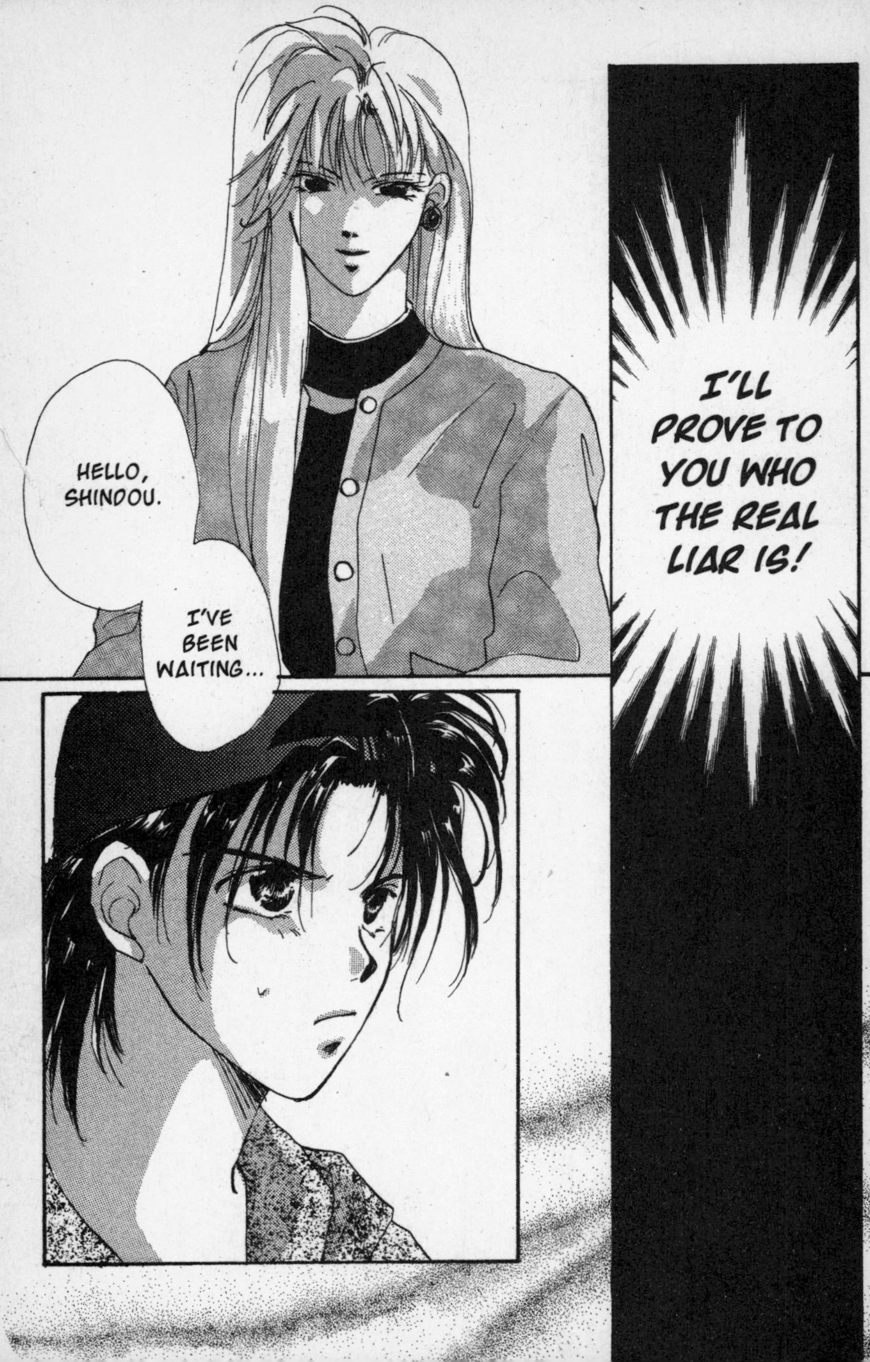
I'LL PROVE TO YOU WHO THE REAL LIAR IS!
HELLO, SHINDOU.
I'VE BEEN WAITING...

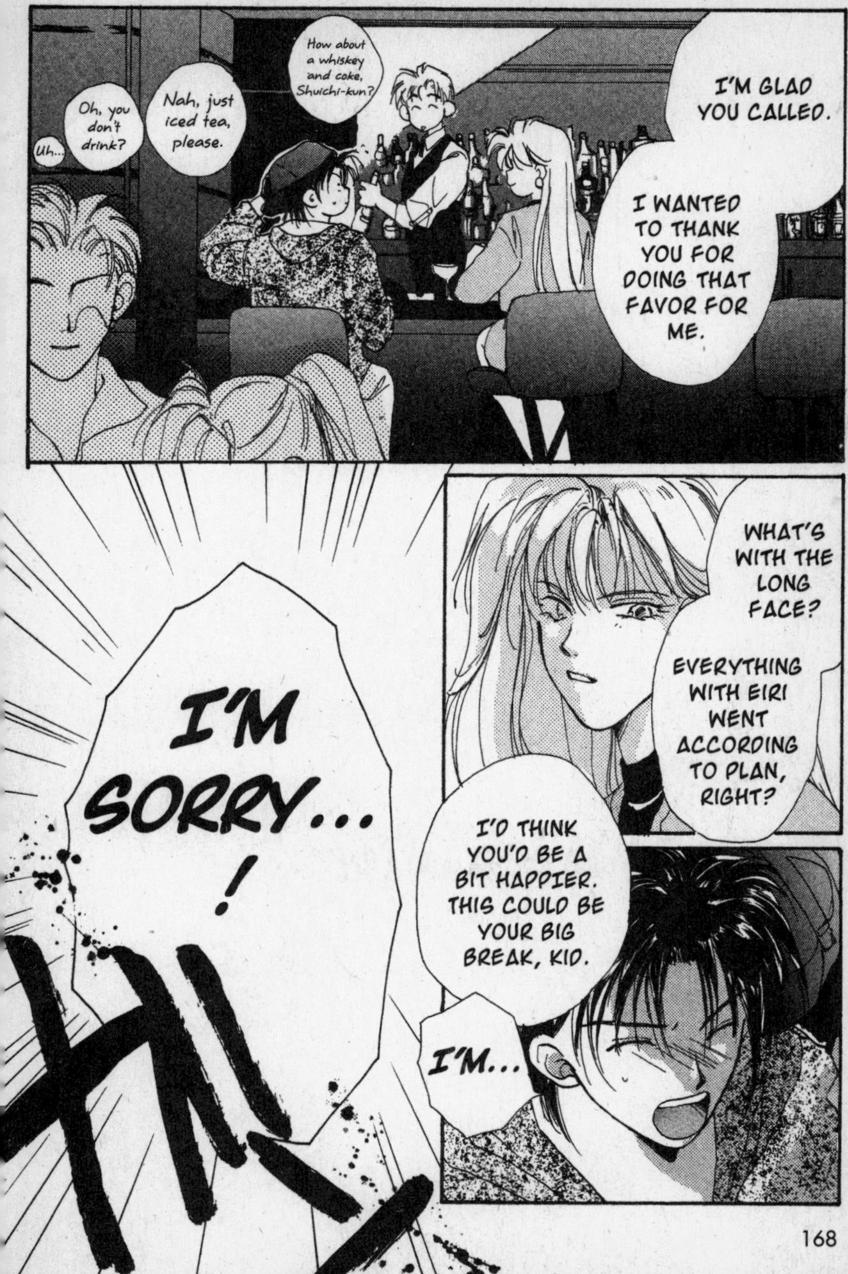
I'M GLAD YOU CALLED.
I WANTED TO THANK YOU FOR DOING THAT FAVOR FOR ME.
How about a whiskey and coke, Shuichi-kun?
Nah, just iced tea, please.
Oh, you don't drink?
Uh...
WHAT'S WITH THE LONG FACE?
EVERYTHING WITH EIRI WENT ACCORDING TO PLAN, RIGHT?
I'D THINK YOU'D BE A BIT HAPPIER. THIS COULD BE YOUR BIG BREAK, KID.
I'M...
I'M SORRY...!

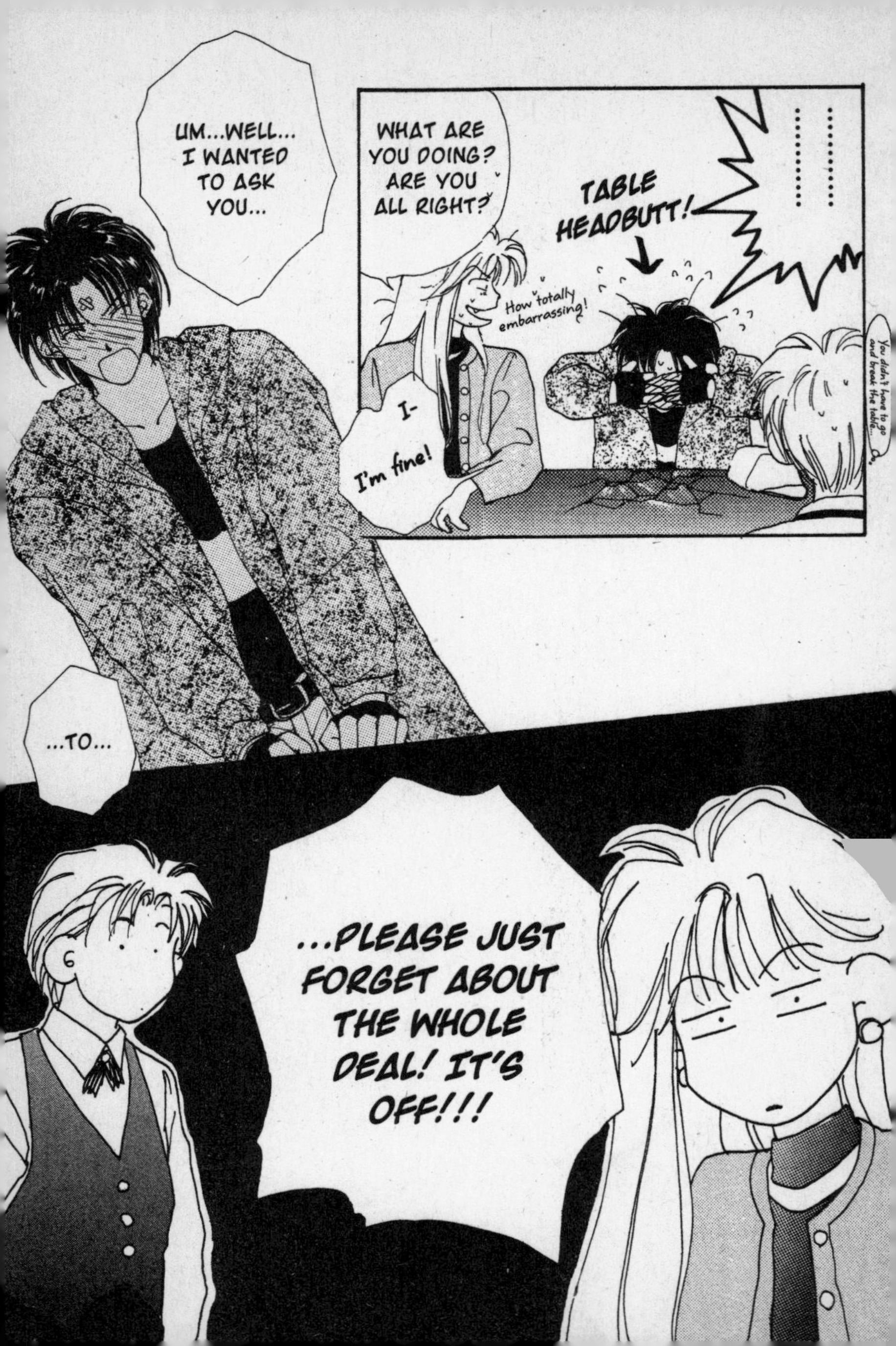

......
You didn't have to go and break the table...
TABLE HEADBUTT!
WHAT ARE YOU DOING? ARE YOU ALL RIGHT?
How totally embarrassing!
I- I'm fine!
UM...WELL... I WANTED TO ASK YOU...
...TO...
...PLEASE JUST FORGET ABOUT THE WHOLE DEAL! IT'S OFF!!!

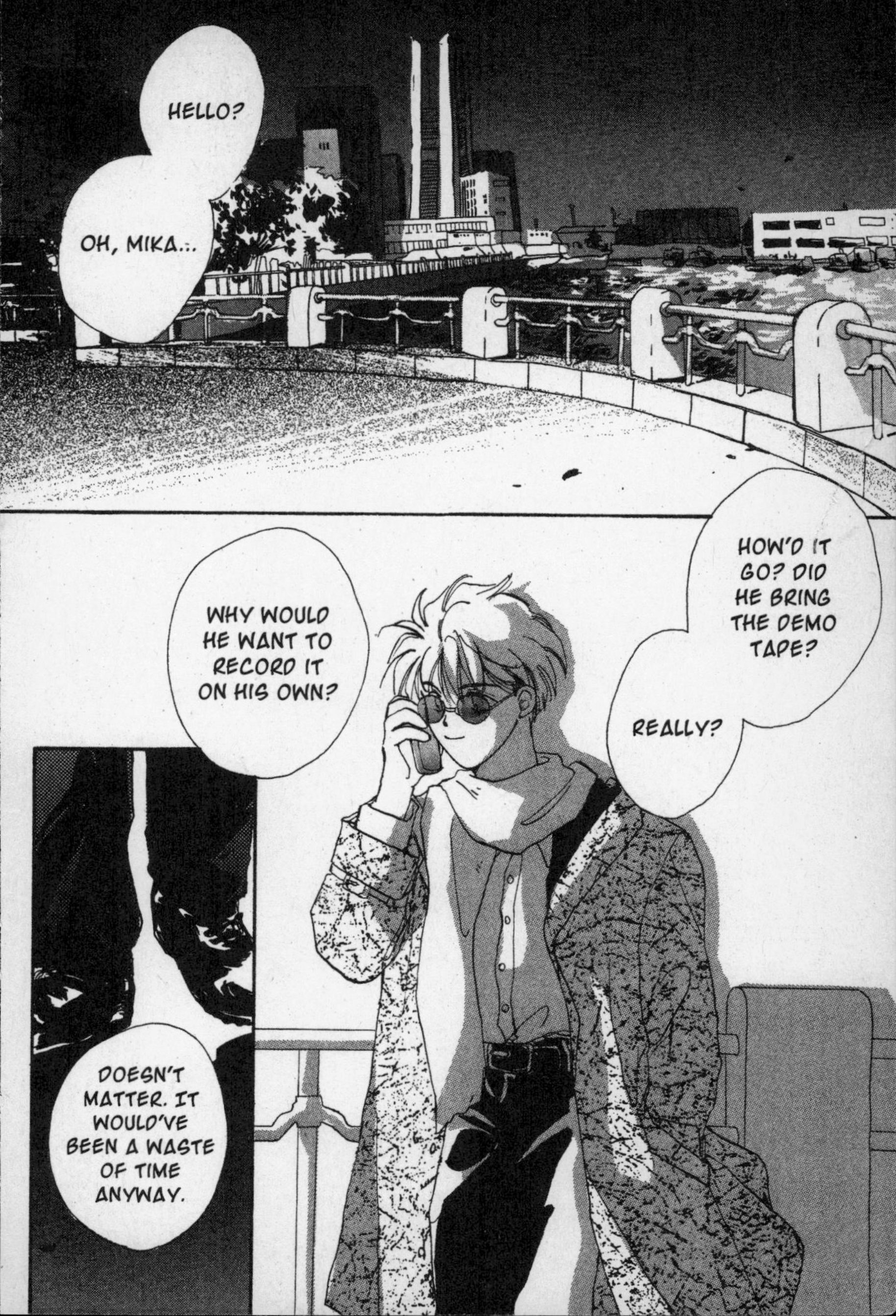
HELLO?
OH, MIKA...
HOW'D IT GO? DID HE BRING THE DEMO TAPE?
REALLY?
WHY WOULD HE WANT TO RECORD IT ON HIS OWN?
DOESN'T MATTER. IT WOULD'VE BEEN A WASTE OF TIME ANYWAY.

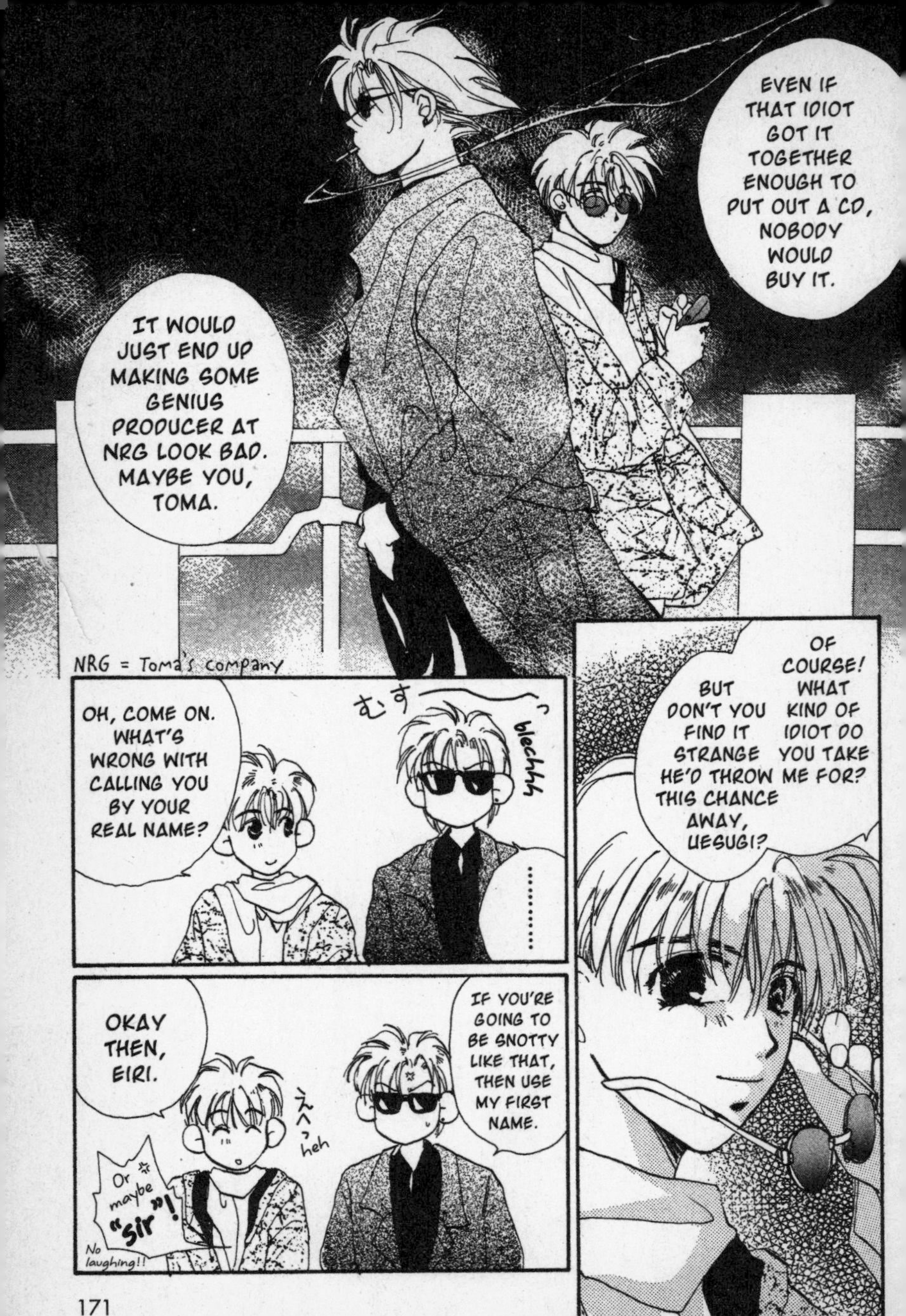
EVEN IF THAT IDIOT GOT IT TOGETHER ENOUGH TO PUT OUT A CD, NOBODY WOULD BUY IT.
IT WOULD JUST END UP MAKING SOME GENIUS PRODUCER AT NRG LOOK BAD. MAYBE YOU, TOMA.
NRG = Toma's company
OF COURSE! WHAT KIND OF IDIOT DO YOU TAKE ME FOR?
BUT DON'T YOU FIND IT STRANGE HE'D THROW THIS CHANCE AWAY, UESUGI?
むす――っ
blechhh
......
OH, COME ON. WHAT'S WRONG WITH CALLING YOU BY YOUR REAL NAME?
IF YOU'RE GOING TO BE SNOTTY LIKE THAT, THEN USE MY FIRST NAME.
えへっ
heh
OKAY THEN, EIRI.
Or maybe "Sir"!
No laughing!!

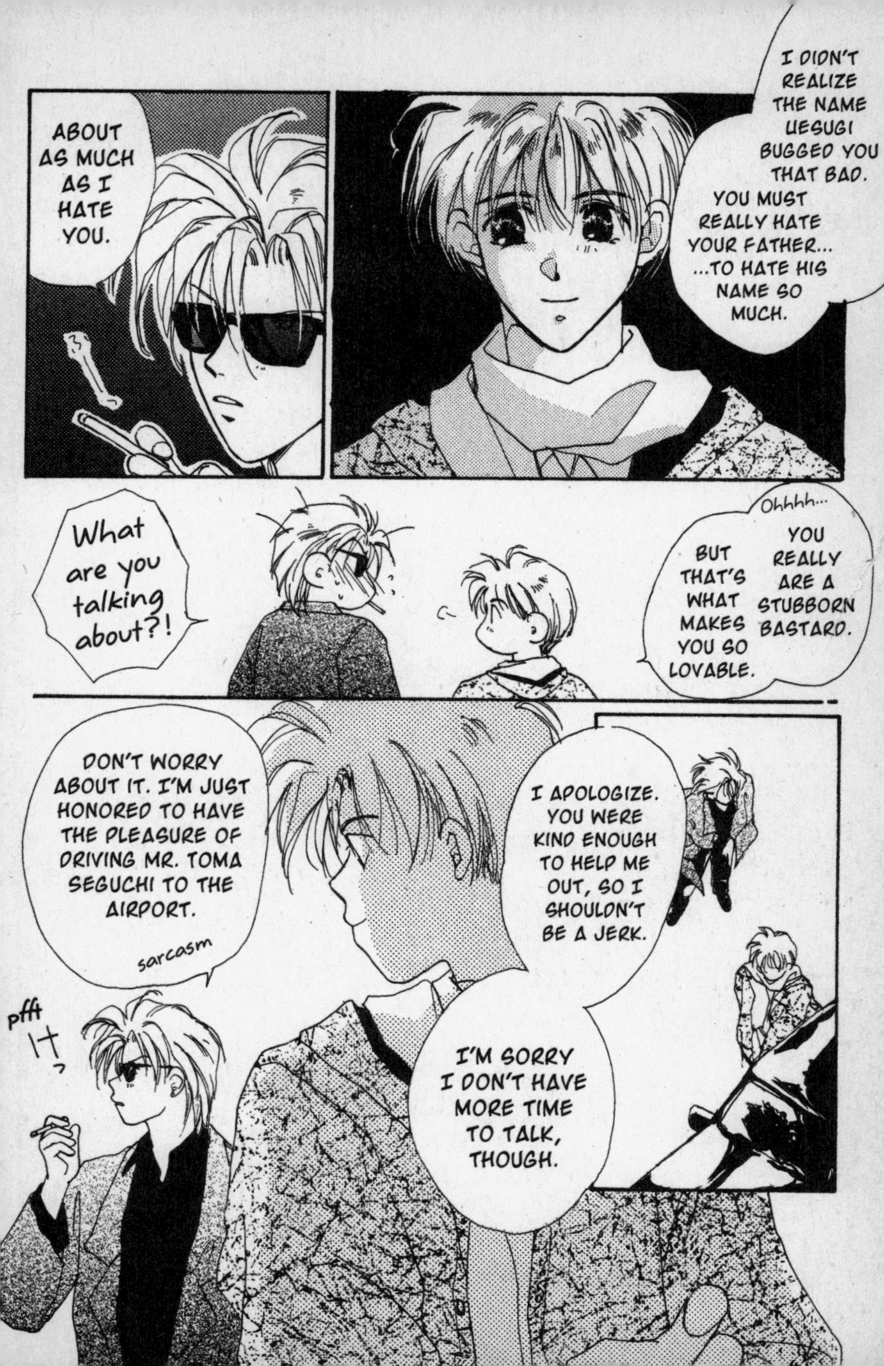
I DIDN'T REALIZE THE NAME UESUGI BUGGED YOU THAT BAD.
YOU MUST REALLY HATE YOUR FATHER... ...TO HATE HIS NAME SO MUCH.
ABOUT AS MUCH AS I HATE YOU.
Ohhhh...
YOU REALLY ARE A STUBBORN BASTARD.
BUT THAT'S WHAT MAKES YOU SO LOVABLE.
What are you talking about?!
I APOLOGIZE. YOU WERE KIND ENOUGH TO HELP ME OUT, SO I SHOULDN'T BE A JERK.
I'M SORRY I DON'T HAVE MORE TIME TO TALK, THOUGH.
DON'T WORRY ABOUT IT. I'M JUST HONORED TO HAVE THE PLEASURE OF DRIVING MR. TOMA SEGUCHI TO THE AIRPORT.
sarcasm
pfft

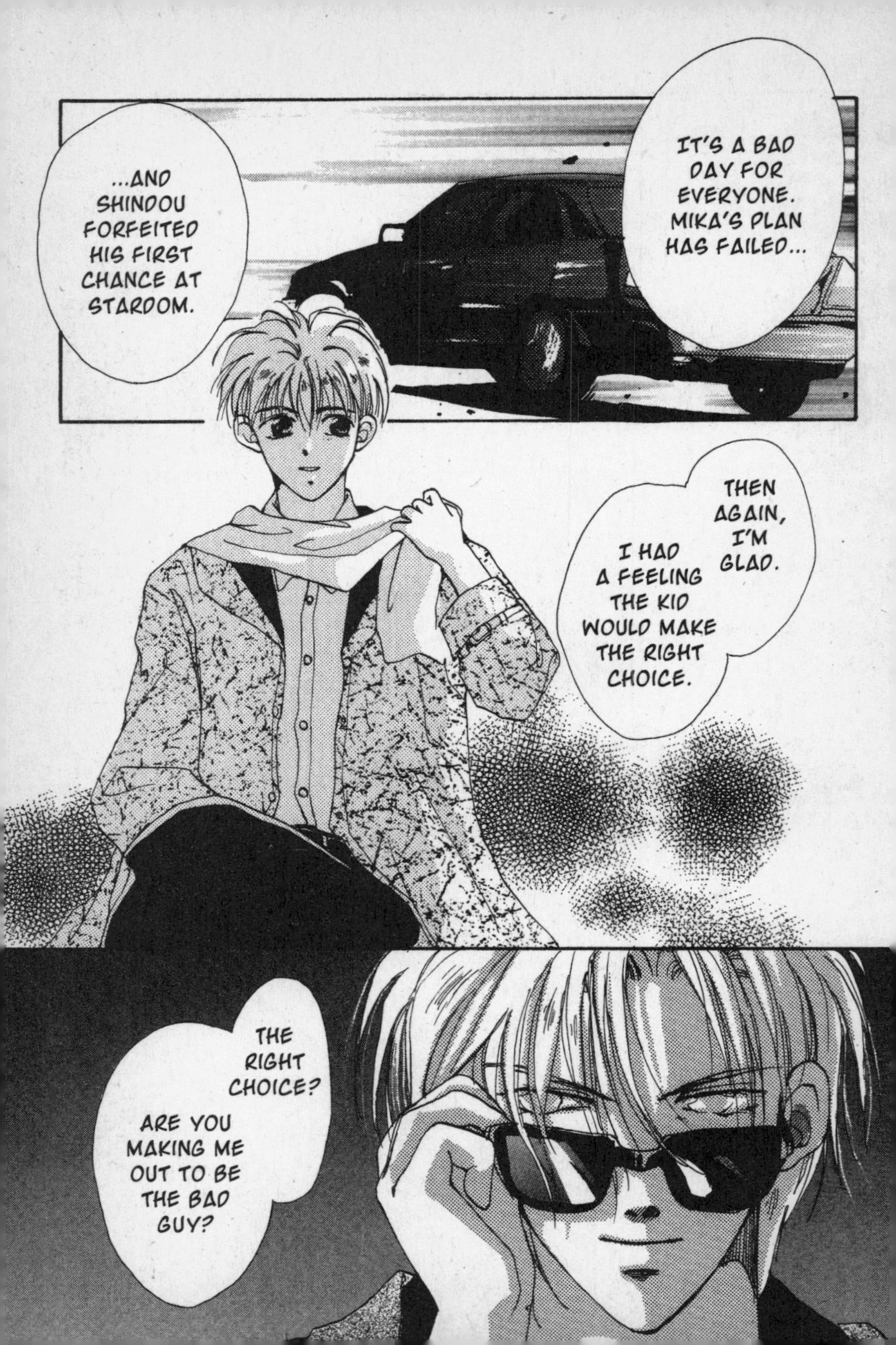
IT'S A BAD DAY FOR EVERYONE. MIKA'S PLAN HAS FAILED...
...AND SHINDOU FORFEITED HIS FIRST CHANCE AT STARDOM.
THEN AGAIN, I'M GLAD.
I HAD A FEELING THE KID WOULD MAKE THE RIGHT CHOICE.
THE RIGHT CHOICE?
ARE YOU MAKING ME OUT TO BE THE BAD GUY?

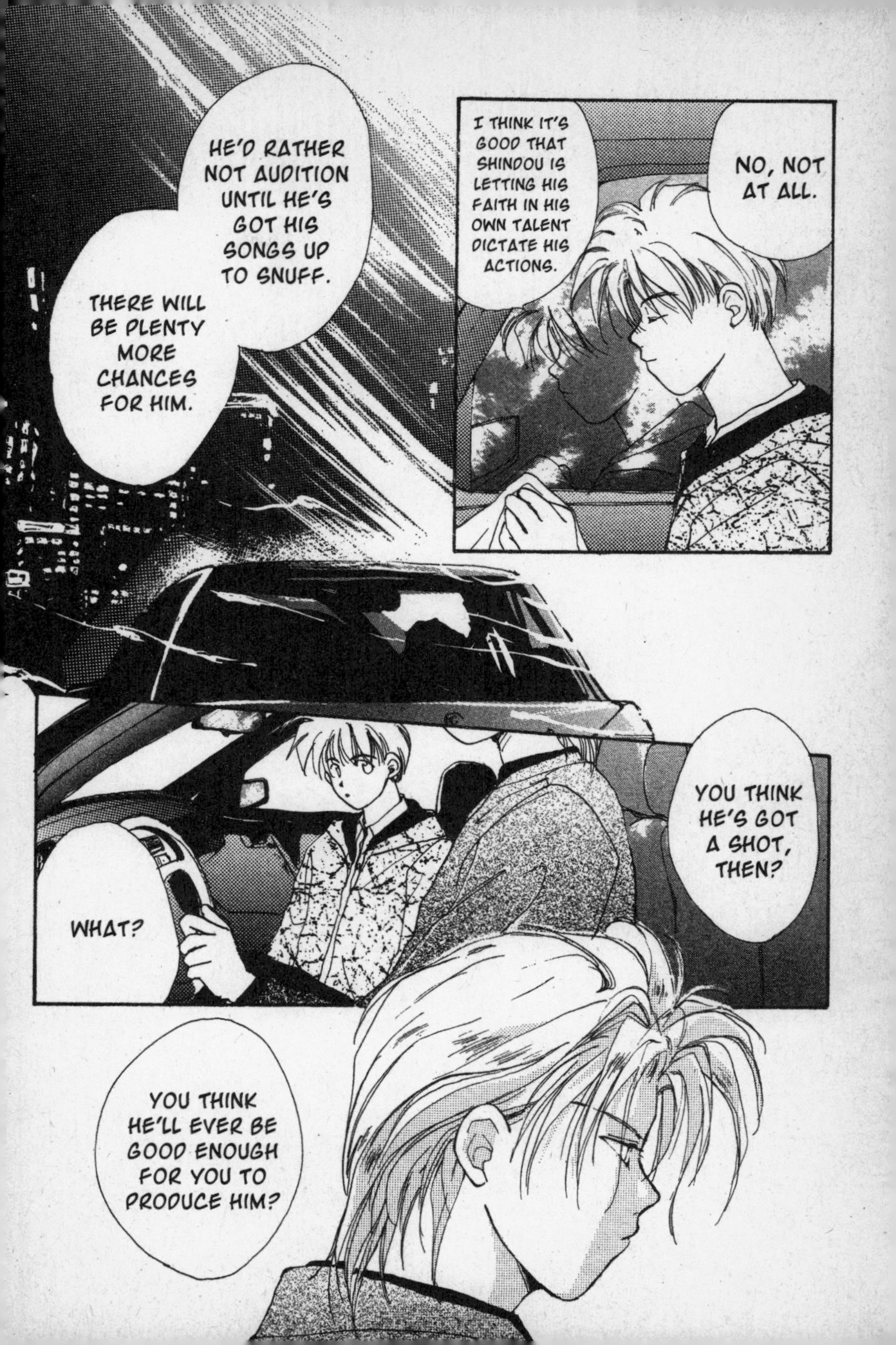
NO, NOT AT ALL.
I THINK IT'S GOOD THAT SHINDOU IS LETTING HIS FAITH IN HIS OWN TALENT DICTATE HIS ACTIONS.
HE'D RATHER NOT AUDITION UNTIL HE'S GOT HIS SONGS UP TO SNUFF.
THERE WILL BE PLENTY MORE CHANCES FOR HIM.
YOU THINK HE'S GOT A SHOT, THEN?
WHAT?
YOU THINK HE'LL EVER BE GOOD ENOUGH FOR YOU TO PRODUCE HIM?

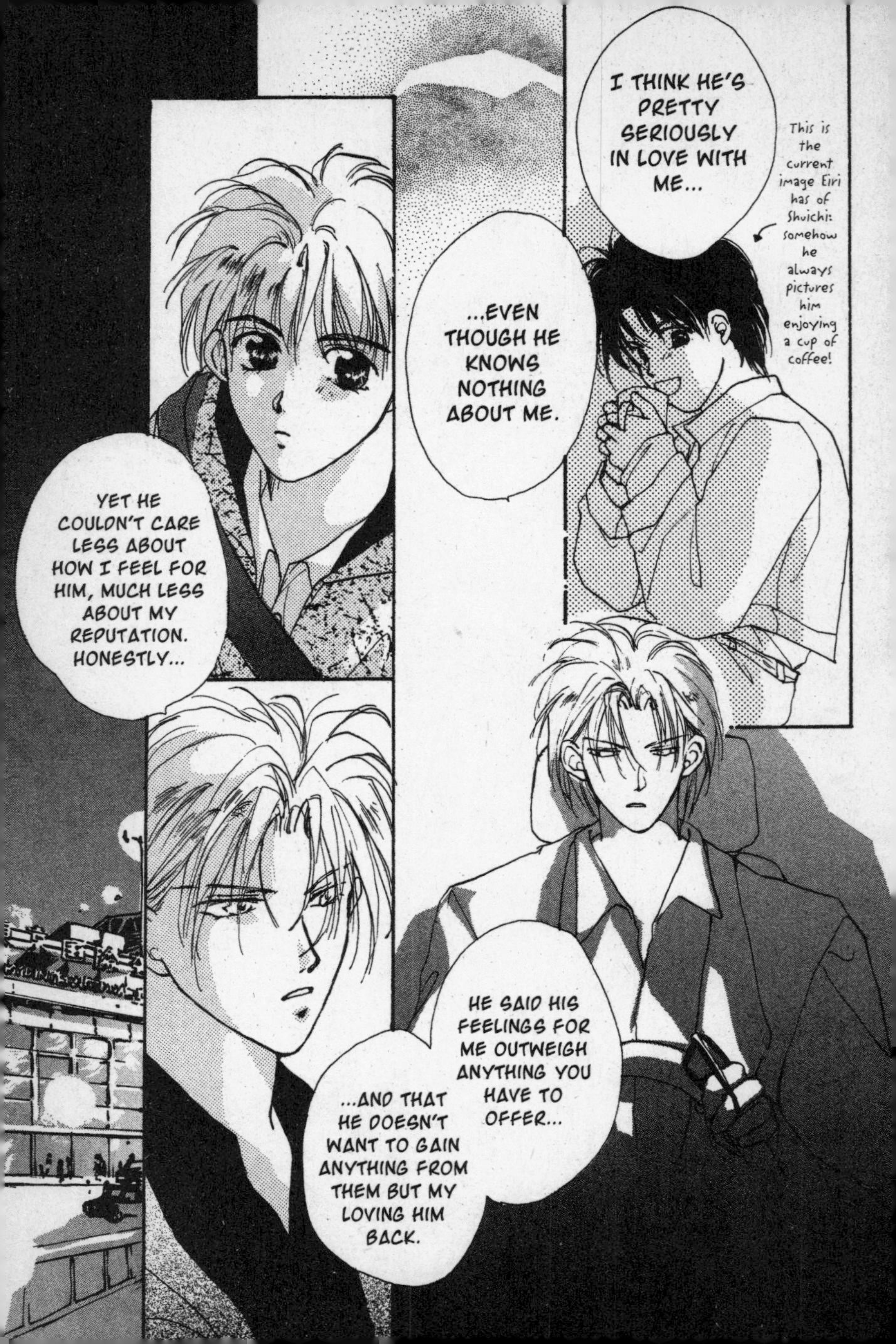
I THINK HE'S PRETTY SERIOUSLY IN LOVE WITH ME...
This is the current image Eiri has of Shuichi: somehow he always pictures him enjoying a cup of coffee!
...EVEN THOUGH HE KNOWS NOTHING ABOUT ME.
YET HE COULDN'T CARE LESS ABOUT HOW I FEEL FOR HIM, MUCH LESS ABOUT MY REPUTATION. HONESTLY...
HE SAID HIS FEELINGS FOR ME OUTWEIGH ANYTHING YOU HAVE TO OFFER...
...AND THAT HE DOESN'T WANT TO GAIN ANYTHING FROM THEM BUT MY LOVING HIM BACK.

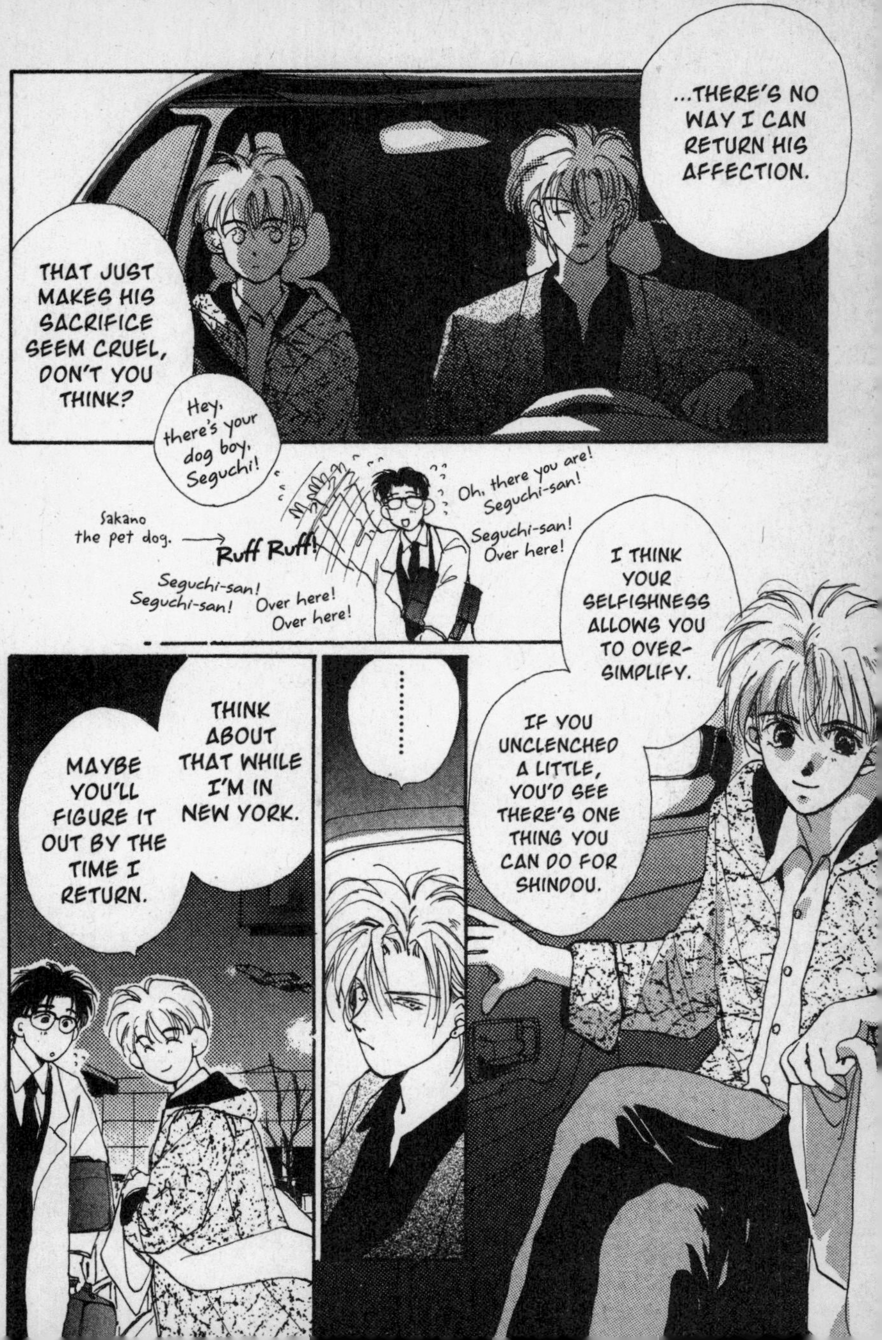

...THERE'S NO WAY I CAN RETURN HIS AFFECTION.
THAT JUST MAKES HIS SACRIFICE SEEM CRUEL, DON'T YOU THINK?
Hey, there's your dog boy, Seguchi!
Oh, there you are! Seguchi-san!
Seguchi-san! Over here!
Ruff Ruff!
Sakano the pet dog.
Seguchi-san! Seguchi-san!
Over here! Over here!
I THINK YOUR SELFISHNESS ALLOWS YOU TO OVER-SIMPLIFY.
IF YOU UNCLENCHED A LITTLE, YOU'D SEE THERE'S ONE THING YOU CAN DO FOR SHINDOU.
....
THINK ABOUT THAT WHILE I'M IN NEW YORK.
MAYBE YOU'LL FIGURE IT OUT BY THE TIME I RETURN.

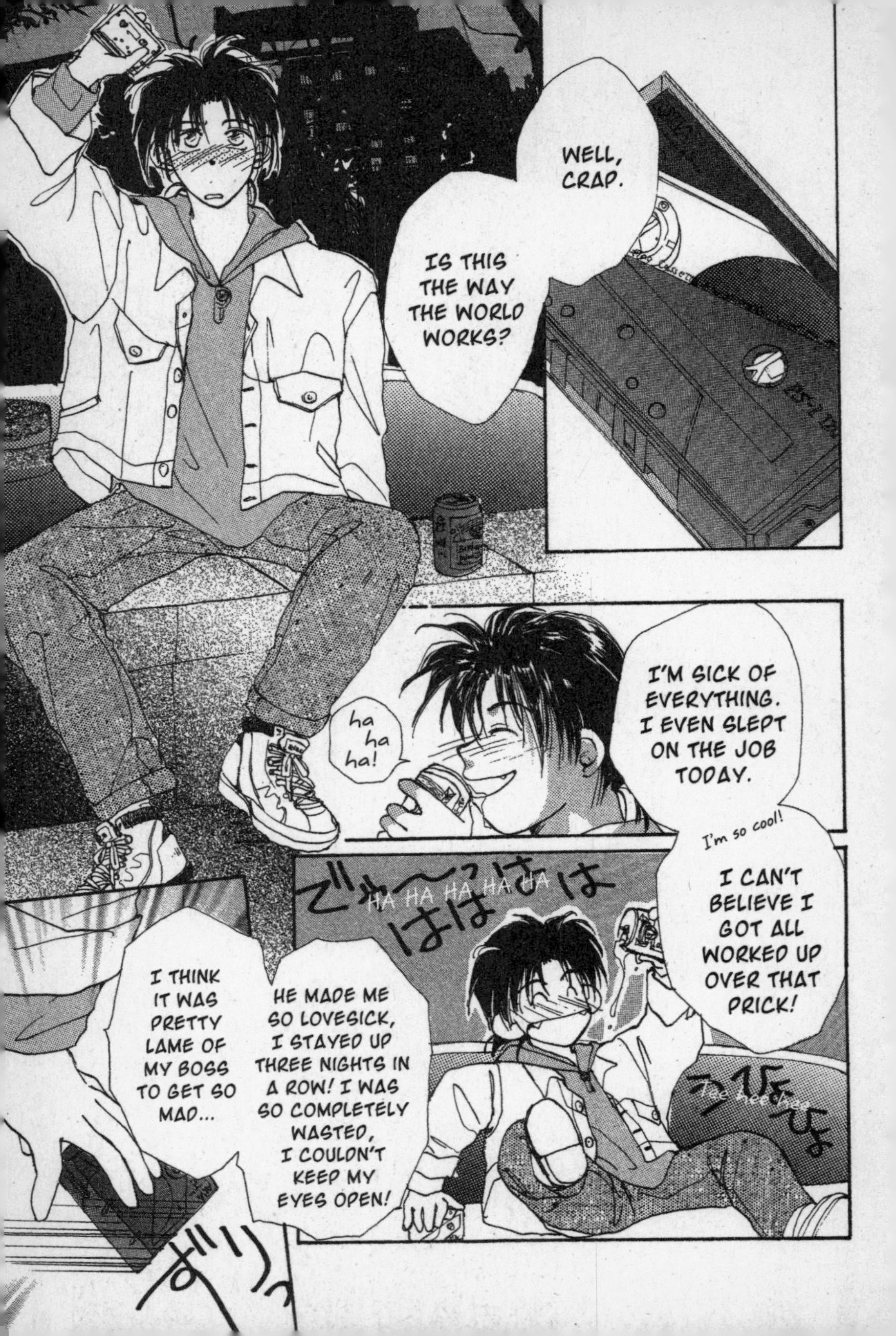
WELL, CRAP.
IS THIS THE WAY THE WORLD WORKS?
I'M SICK OF EVERYTHING. I EVEN SLEPT ON THE JOB TODAY.
ha ha ha!
HA HA HA HA HA
I'm so cool!
I CAN'T BELIEVE I GOT ALL WORKED UP OVER THAT PRICK!
Tee hee hee
HE MADE ME SO LOVESICK, I STAYED UP THREE NIGHTS IN A ROW! I WAS SO COMPLETELY WASTED, I COULDN'T KEEP MY EYES OPEN!
I THINK IT WAS PRETTY LAME OF MY BOSS TO GET SO MAD...

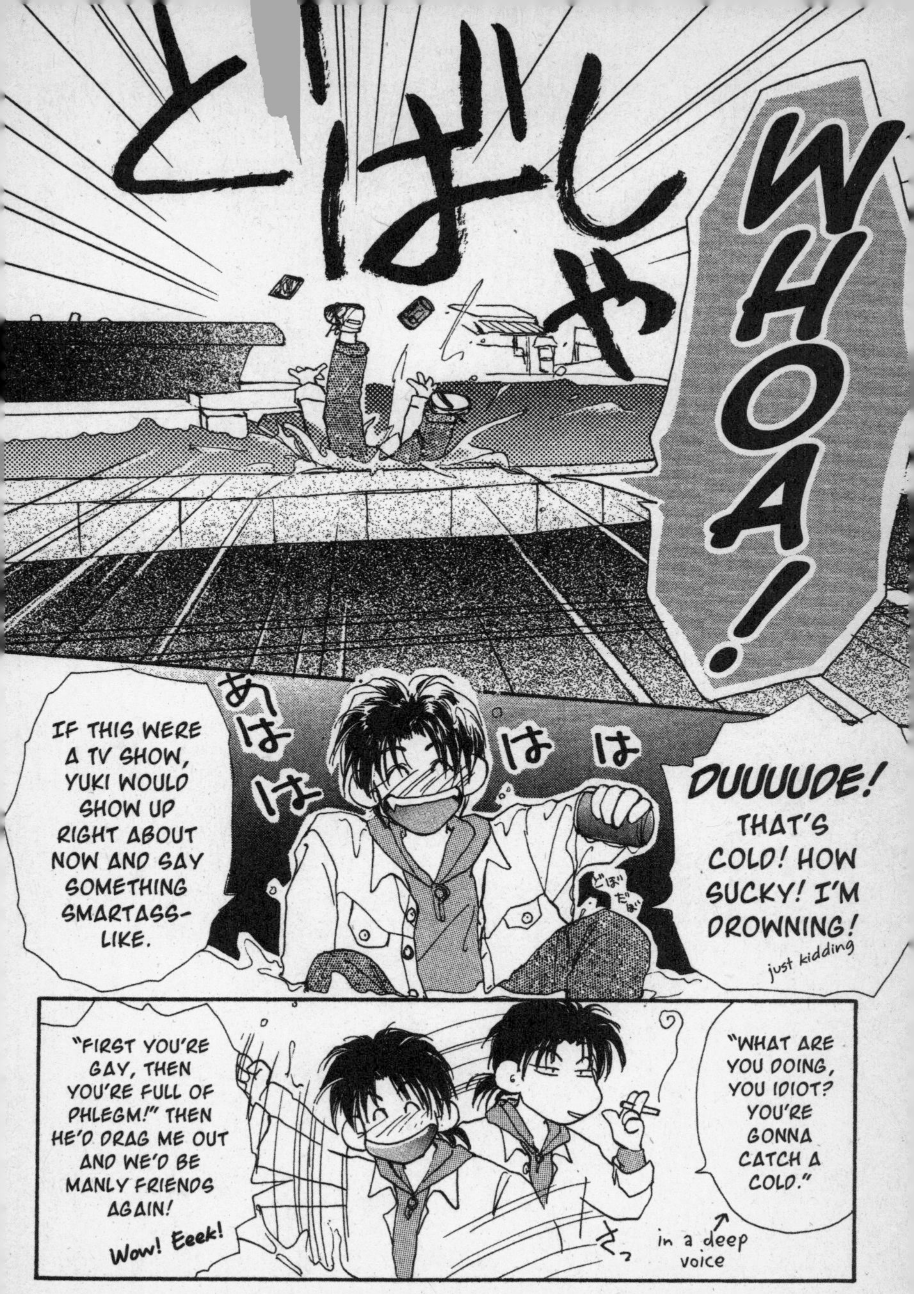
とばしゃ
WHOA!
DUUUUDE! THAT'S COLD! HOW SUCKY! I'M DROWNING!
just kidding
あはははは
IF THIS WERE A TV SHOW, YUKI WOULD SHOW UP RIGHT ABOUT NOW AND SAY SOMETHING SMARTASS-LIKE.
"WHAT ARE YOU DOING, YOU IDIOT? YOU'RE GONNA CATCH A COLD."
in a deep voice
さっ
"FIRST YOU'RE GAY, THEN YOU'RE FULL OF PHLEGM!" THEN HE'D DRAG ME OUT AND WE'D BE MANLY FRIENDS AGAIN!
Wow! Eeek!

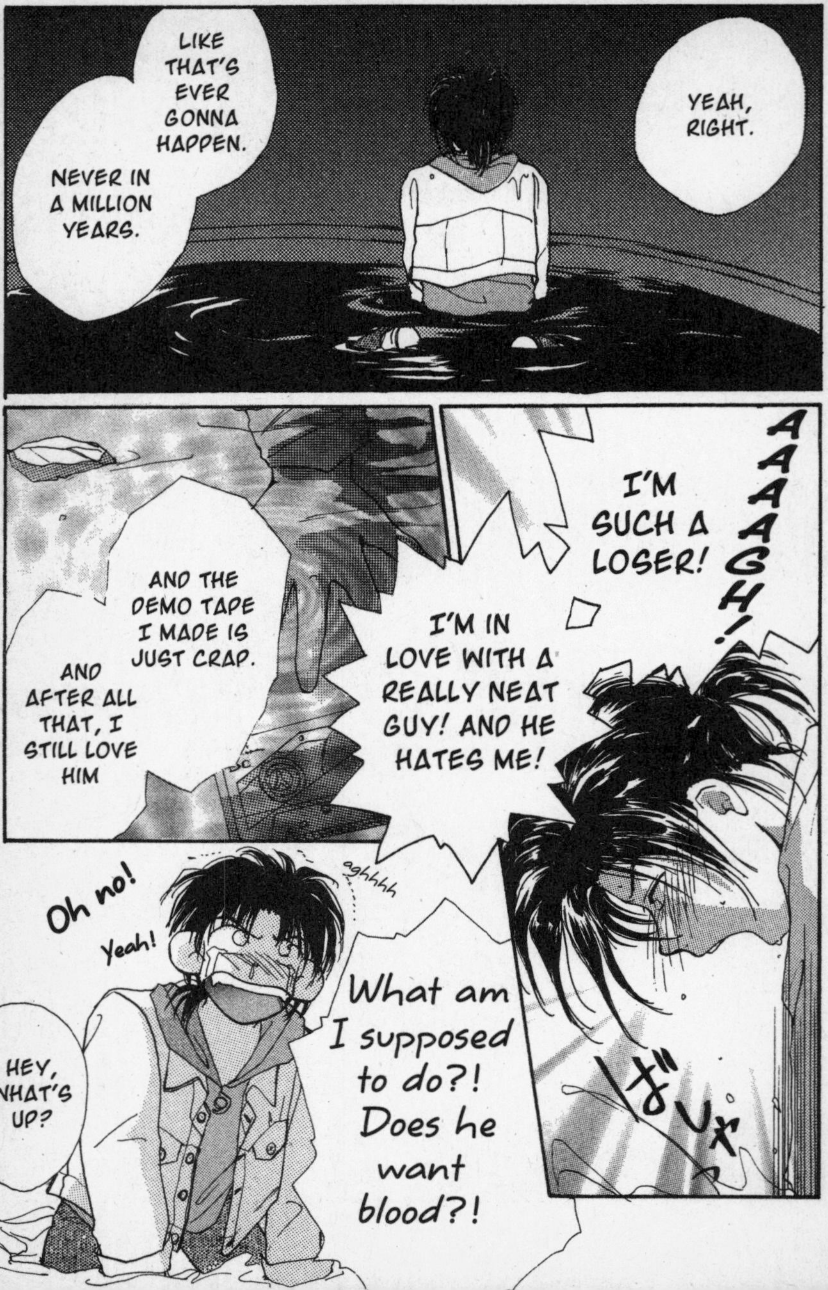
YEAH, RIGHT.
LIKE THAT'S EVER GONNA HAPPEN.
NEVER IN A MILLION YEARS.
AAAAAGH!
I'M SUCH A LOSER!
I'M IN LOVE WITH A REALLY NEAT GUY! AND HE HATES ME!
AND THE DEMO TAPE I MADE IS JUST CRAP.
AND AFTER ALL THAT, I STILL LOVE HIM
What am I supposed to do?! Does he want blood?!
aghhhh
Oh no!
Yeah!
HEY, WHAT'S UP?

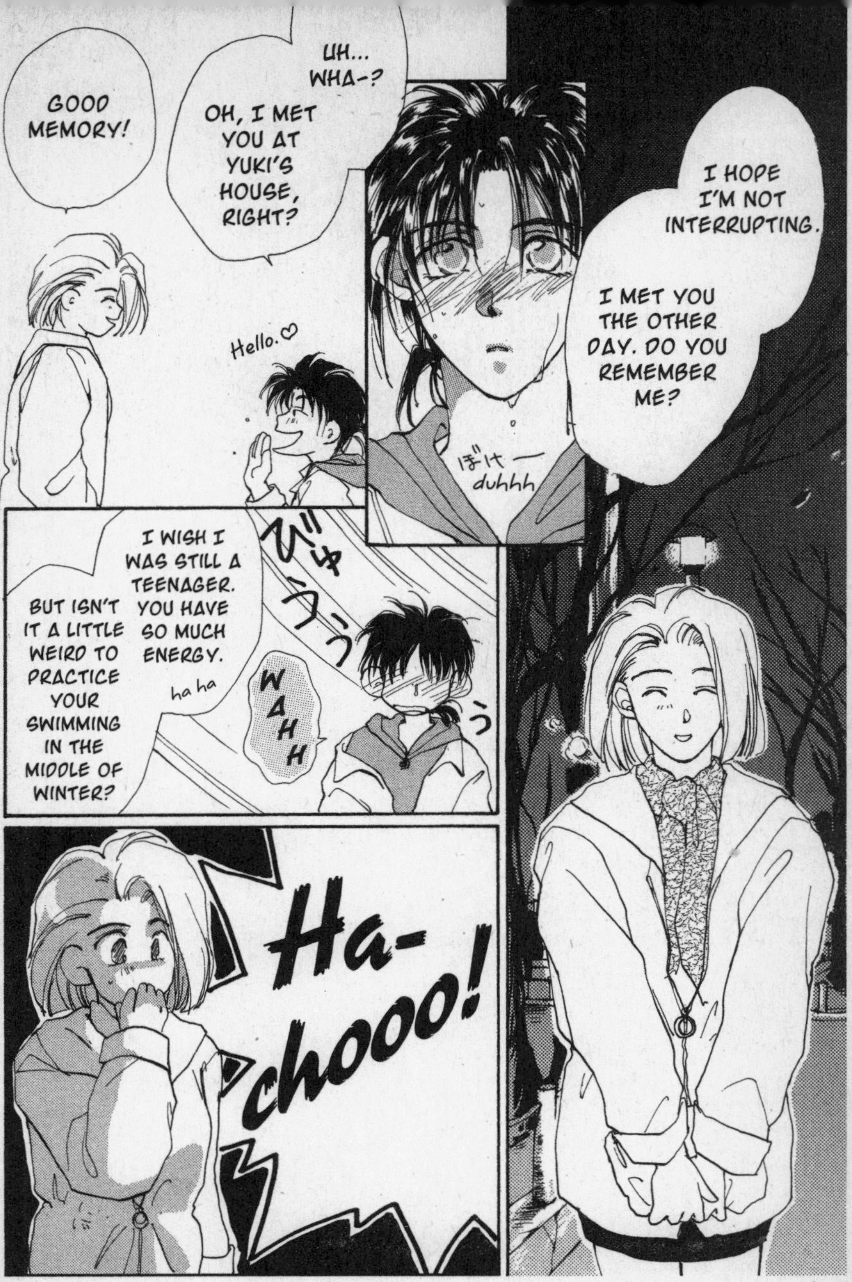
I HOPE I'M NOT INTERRUPTING.
I MET YOU THE OTHER DAY. DO YOU REMEMBER ME?
ぼけー
duhhh
UH... WHA-?
OH, I MET YOU AT YUKI'S HOUSE, RIGHT?
Hello.♡
GOOD MEMORY!
びゅうう
I WISH I WAS STILL A TEENAGER. YOU HAVE SO MUCH ENERGY.
ha ha
BUT ISN'T IT A LITTLE WEIRD TO PRACTICE YOUR SWIMMING IN THE MIDDLE OF WINTER?
you're kinda nuts, yeah?
WAHH
う
Ha-chooo!

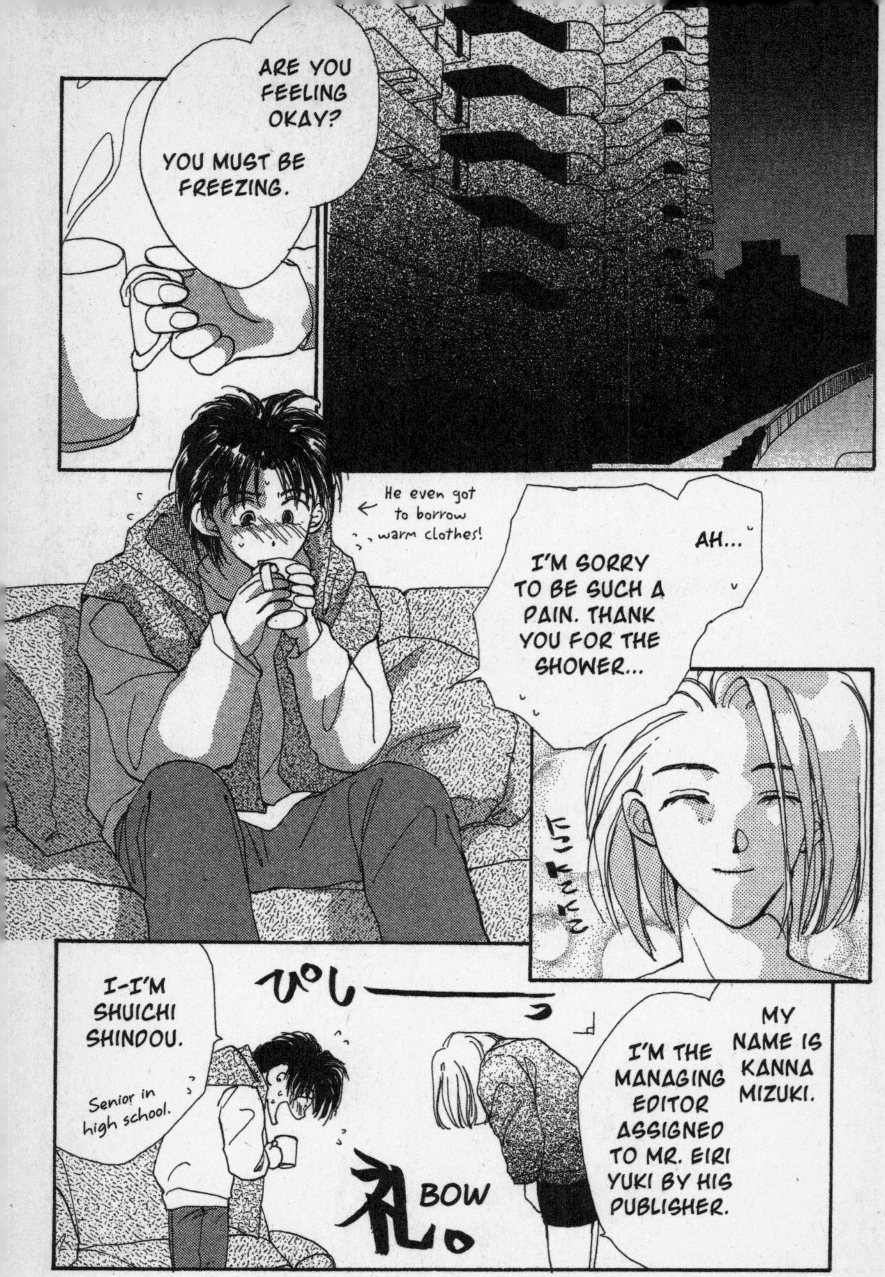
ARE YOU FEELING OKAY?
YOU MUST BE FREEZING.
AH...
I'M SORRY TO BE SUCH A PAIN. THANK YOU FOR THE SHOWER...
He even got to borrow warm clothes!
MY NAME IS KANNA MIZUKI.
I'M THE MANAGING EDITOR ASSIGNED TO MR. EIRI YUKI BY HIS PUBLISHER.
BOW
I-I'M SHUICHI SHINDOU.
Senior in high school.

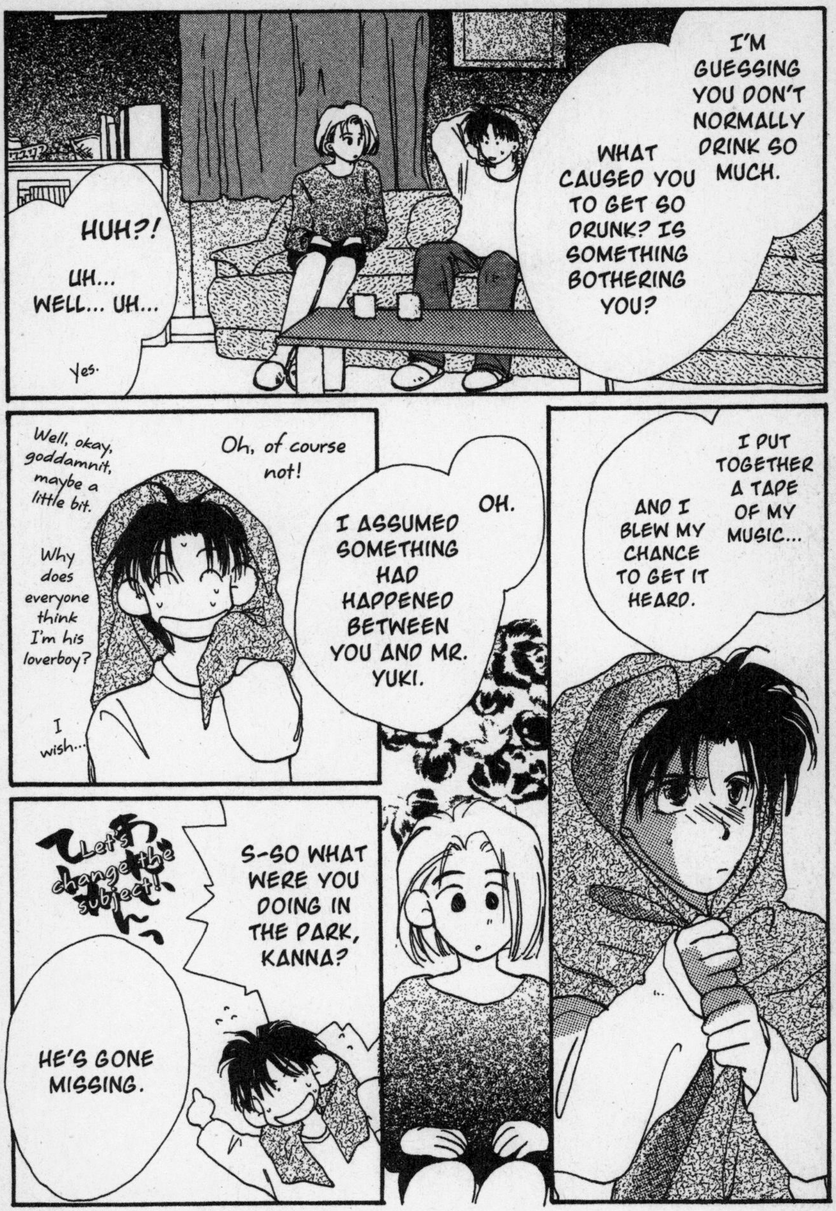
I'M GUESSING YOU DON'T NORMALLY DRINK SO MUCH.
WHAT CAUSED YOU TO GET SO DRUNK? IS SOMETHING BOTHERING YOU?
HUH?!
UH... WELL... UH...
Yes.
I PUT TOGETHER A TAPE OF MY MUSIC...
AND I BLEW MY CHANCE TO GET IT HEARD.
...
OH.
I ASSUMED SOMETHING HAD HAPPENED BETWEEN YOU AND MR. YUKI.
Oh, of course not!
Well, okay, goddamnit, maybe a little bit.
Why does everyone think I'm his loverboy?
I wish...
Let's change the subject!
S-SO WHAT WERE YOU DOING IN THE PARK, KANNA?
HE'S GONE MISSING.

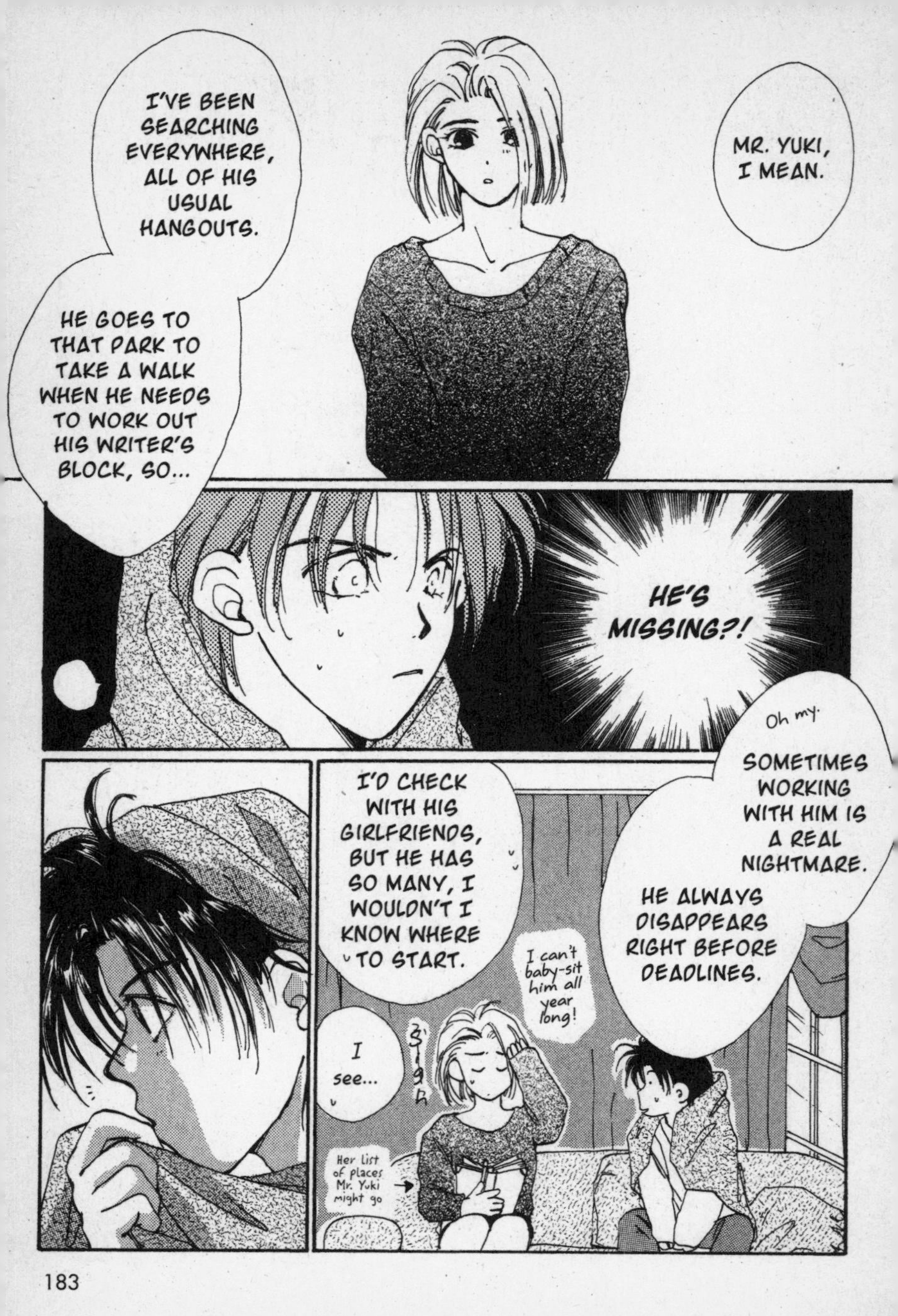

MR. YUKI, I MEAN.
I'VE BEEN SEARCHING EVERYWHERE, ALL OF HIS USUAL HANGOUTS.
HE GOES TO THAT PARK TO TAKE A WALK WHEN HE NEEDS TO WORK OUT HIS WRITER'S BLOCK, SO...
HE'S MISSING?!
Oh my.
SOMETIMES WORKING WITH HIM IS A REAL NIGHTMARE.
HE ALWAYS DISAPPEARS RIGHT BEFORE DEADLINES.
I can't baby-sit him all year long!
I'D CHECK WITH HIS GIRLFRIENDS, BUT HE HAS SO MANY, I WOULDN'T I KNOW WHERE TO START.
I see...
Her list of places Mr. Yuki might go

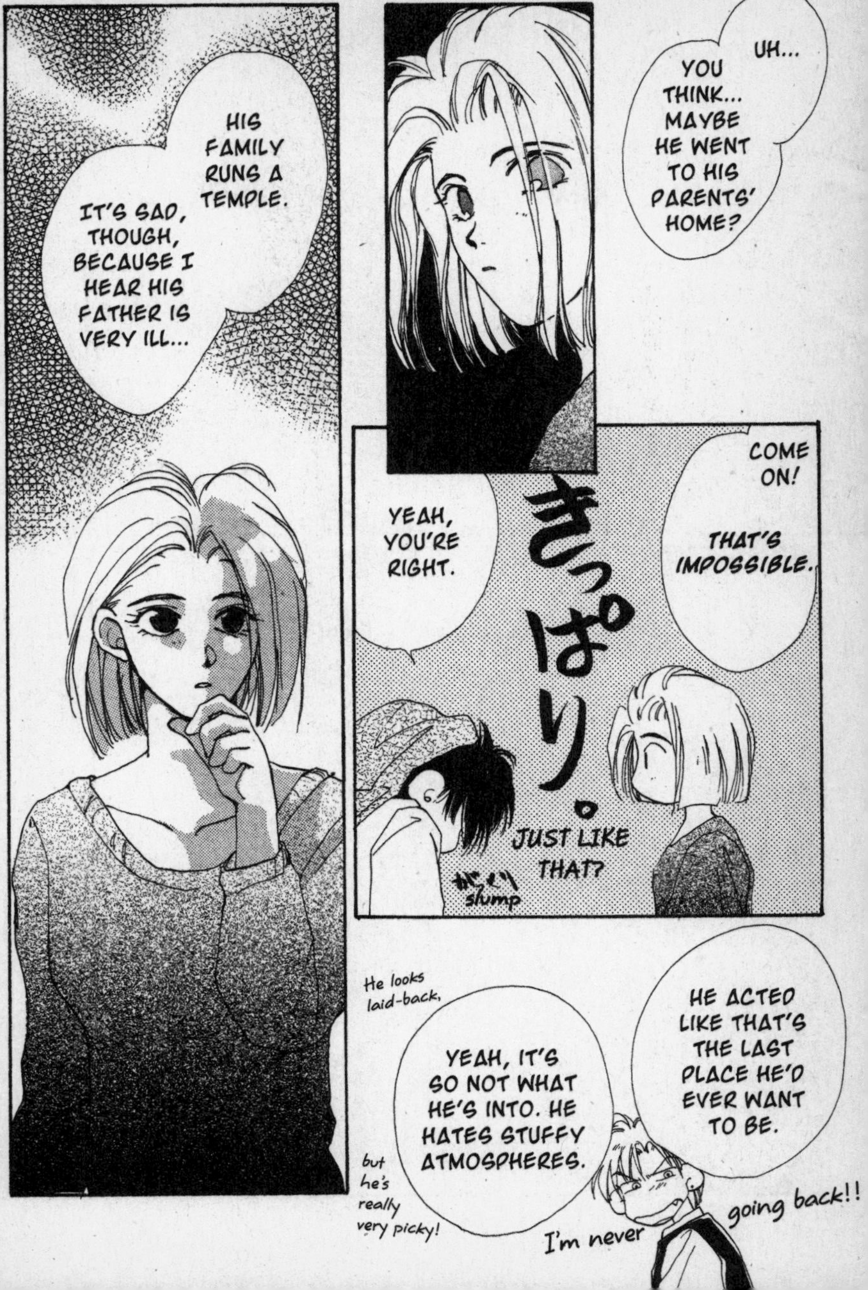

UH... YOU THINK... MAYBE HE WENT TO HIS PARENTS' HOME?
COME ON! THAT'S IMPOSSIBLE.
きっぱり。
JUST LIKE THAT?
YEAH, YOU'RE RIGHT.
slump
HE ACTED LIKE THAT'S THE LAST PLACE HE'D EVER WANT TO BE.
I'm never going back!!
YEAH, IT'S SO NOT WHAT HE'S INTO. HE HATES STUFFY ATMOSPHERES.
He looks laid-back, but he's really very picky!
HIS FAMILY RUNS A TEMPLE.
IT'S SAD, THOUGH, BECAUSE I HEAR HIS FATHER IS VERY ILL...

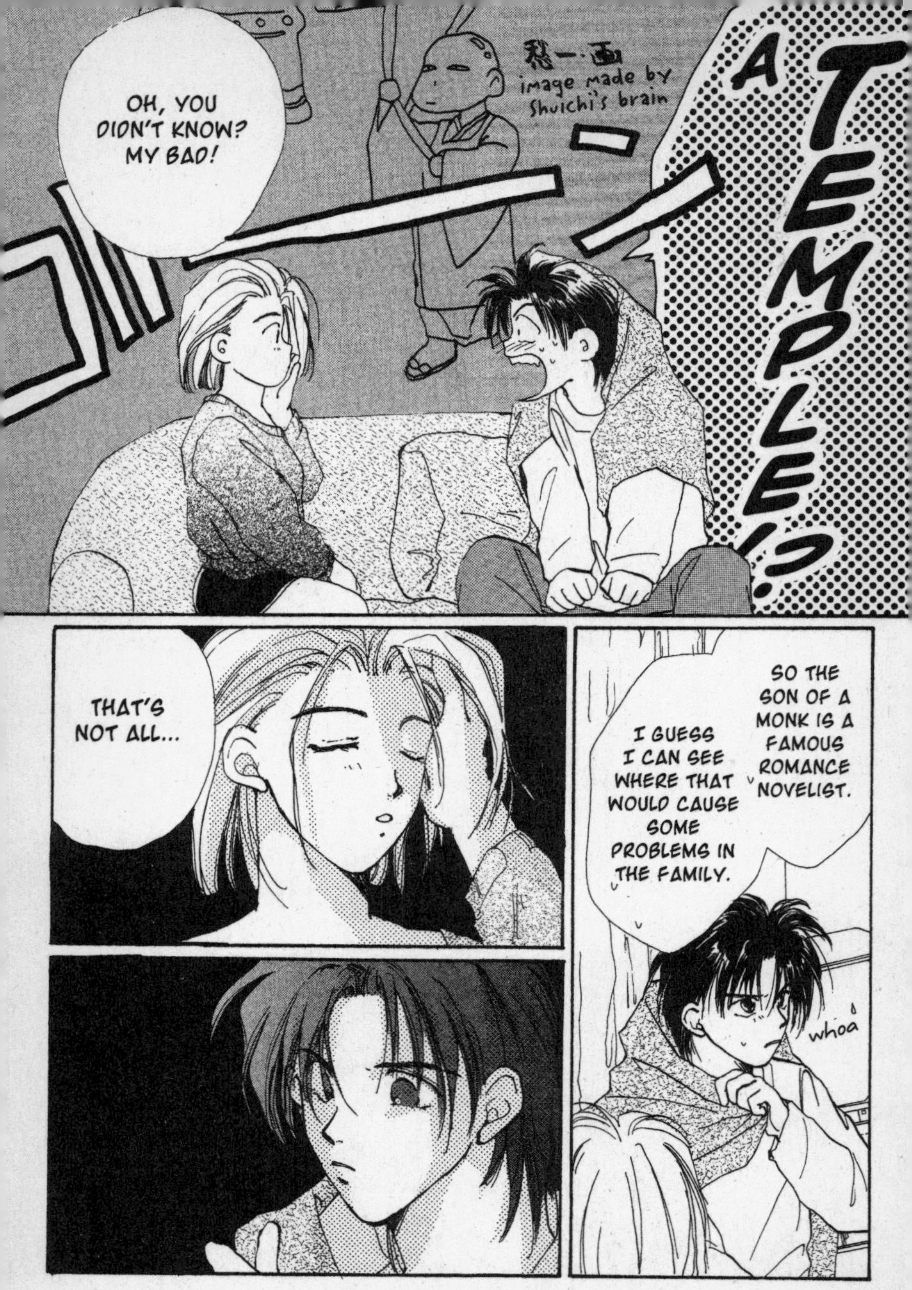

A TEMPLE!?
愁一・画
image made by Shuichi's brain
OH, YOU DIDN'T KNOW? MY BAD!
SO THE SON OF A MONK IS A FAMOUS ROMANCE NOVELIST.
I GUESS I CAN SEE WHERE THAT WOULD CAUSE SOME PROBLEMS IN THE FAMILY.
whoa
THAT'S NOT ALL...

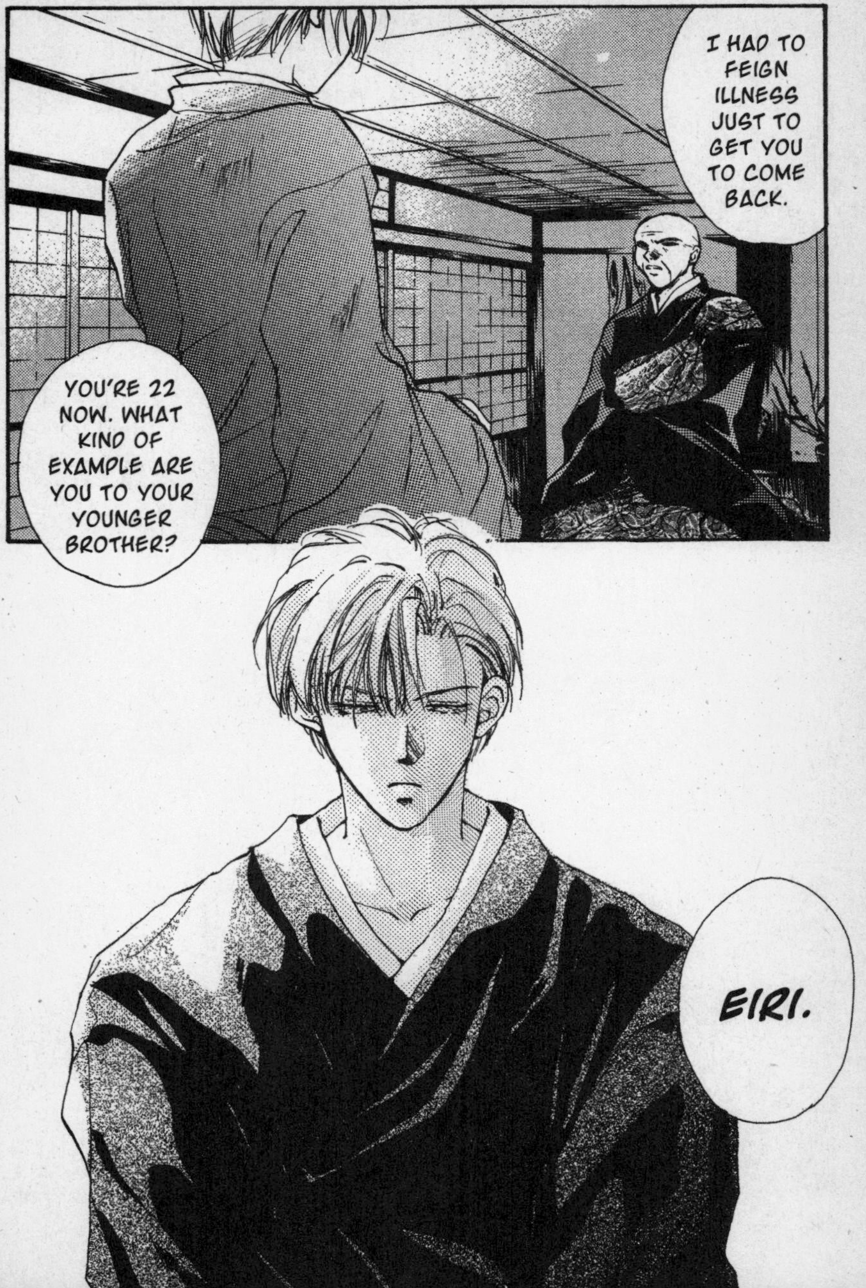
I HAD TO FEIGN ILLNESS JUST TO GET YOU TO COME BACK.
YOU'RE 22 NOW. WHAT KIND OF EXAMPLE ARE YOU TO YOUR YOUNGER BROTHER?
EIRI.

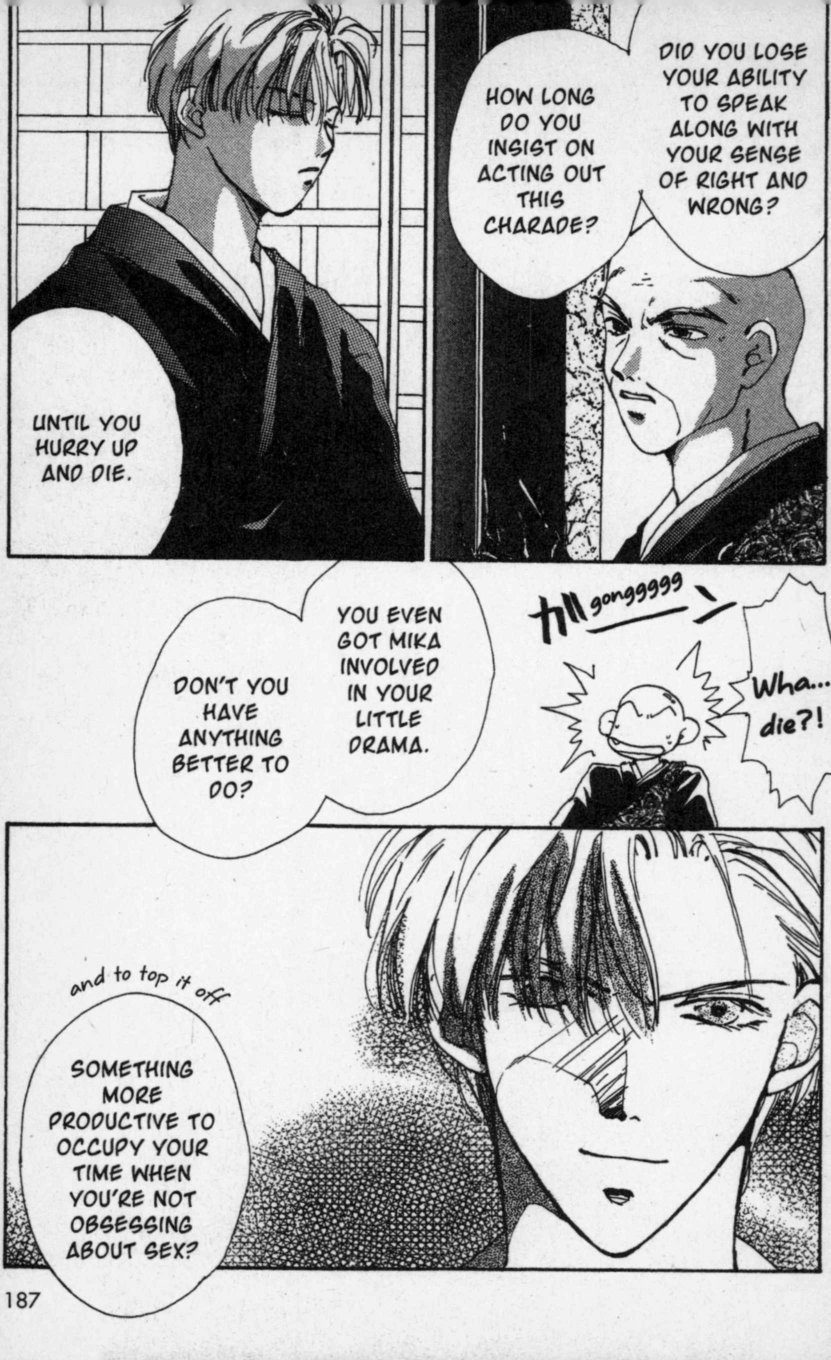
DID YOU LOSE YOUR ABILITY TO SPEAK ALONG WITH YOUR SENSE OF RIGHT AND WRONG?
HOW LONG DO YOU INSIST ON ACTING OUT THIS CHARADE?
UNTIL YOU HURRY UP AND DIE.
カ gongggggg
Wha... die?!
YOU EVEN GOT MIKA INVOLVED IN YOUR LITTLE DRAMA.
DON'T YOU HAVE ANYTHING BETTER TO DO?
and to top it off
SOMETHING MORE PRODUCTIVE TO OCCUPY YOUR TIME WHEN YOU'RE NOT OBSESSING ABOUT SEX?

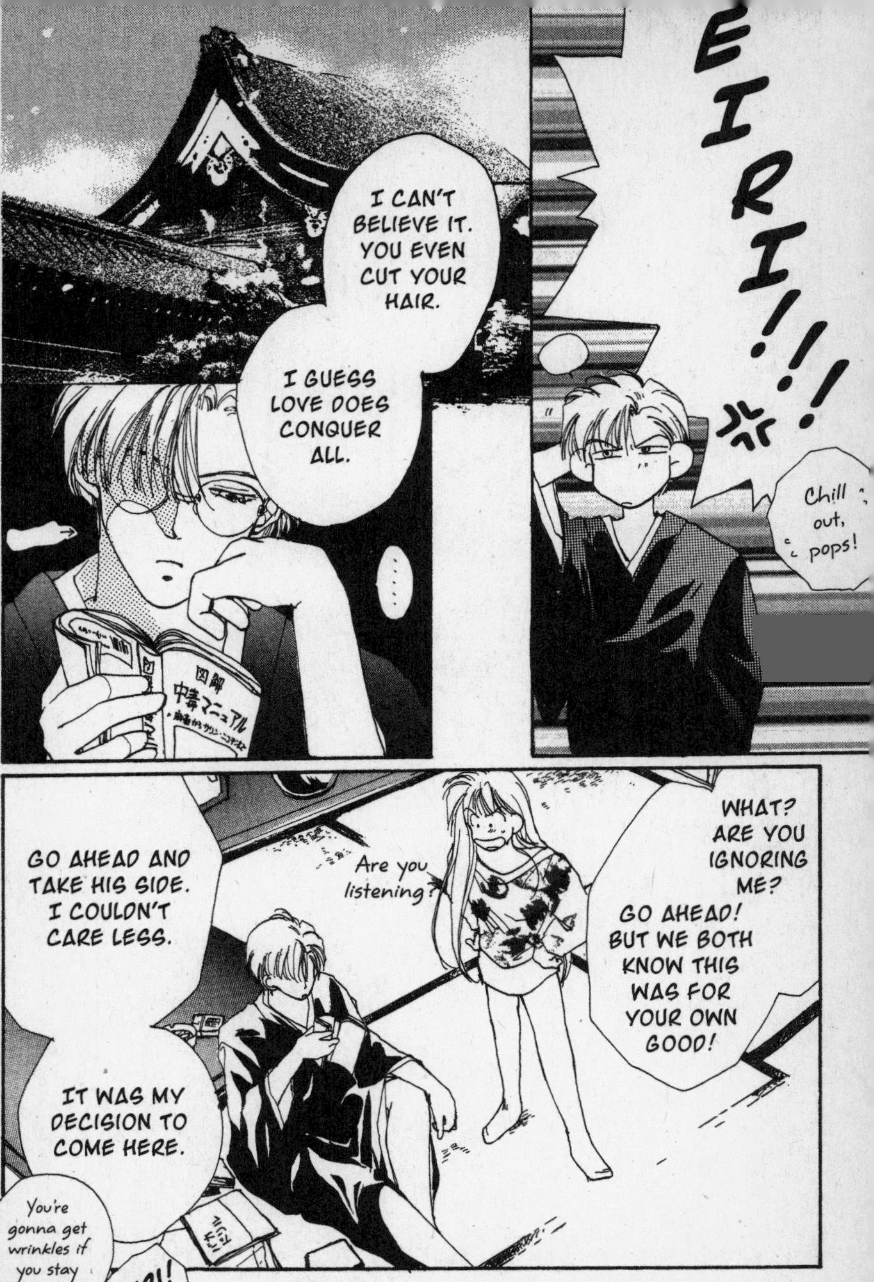

EIRI!!!!
Chill out, pops!
I CAN'T BELIEVE IT. YOU EVEN CUT YOUR HAIR.
I GUESS LOVE DOES CONQUER ALL.
......
図解 中毒マニュアル
WHAT? ARE YOU IGNORING ME?
GO AHEAD! BUT WE BOTH KNOW THIS WAS FOR YOUR OWN GOOD!
Are you listening?
GO AHEAD AND TAKE HIS SIDE. I COULDN'T CARE LESS.
IT WAS MY DECISION TO COME HERE.
You're gonna get wrinkles if you stay mad...
EIRI!

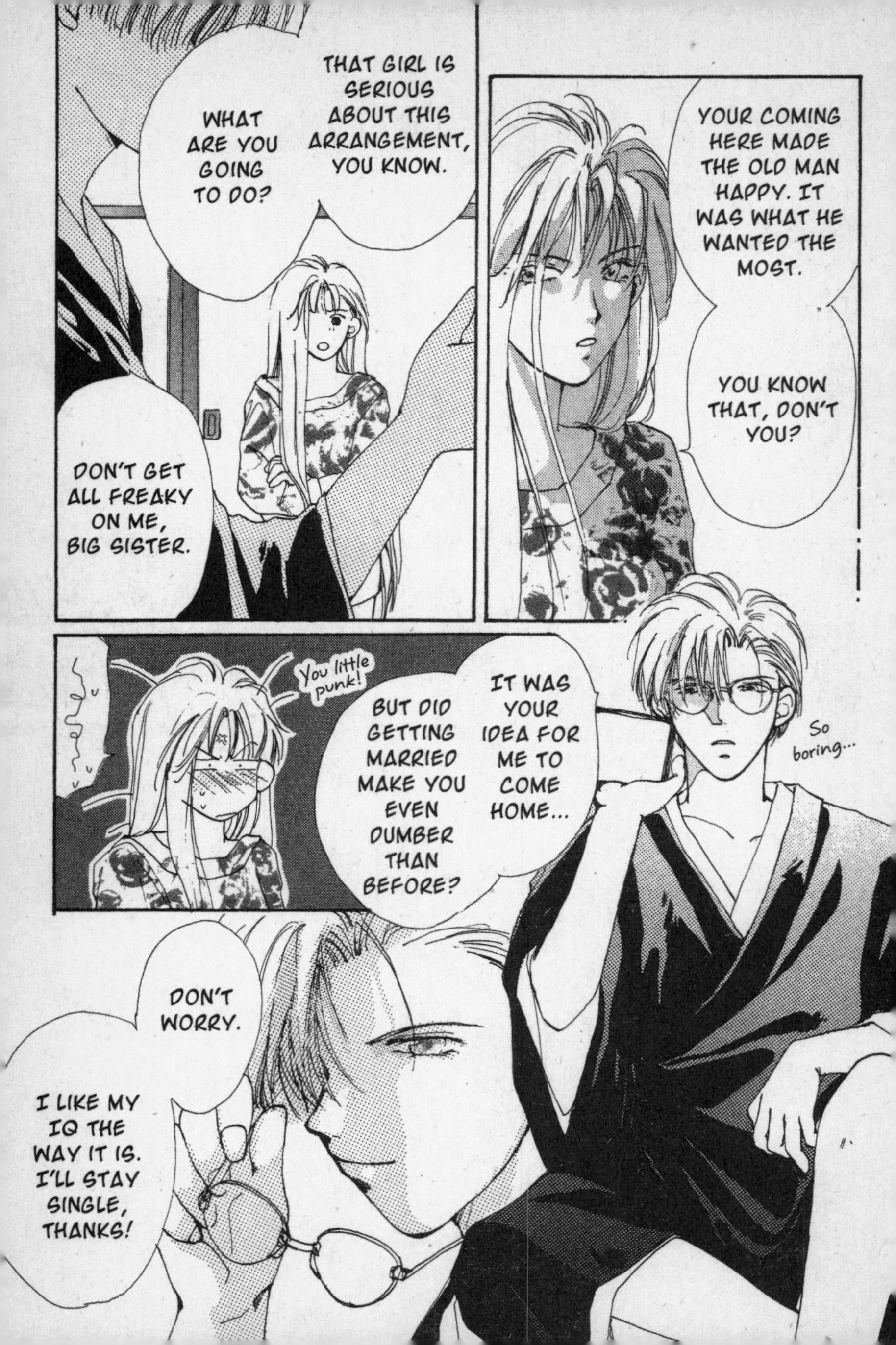
YOUR COMING HERE MADE THE OLD MAN HAPPY. IT WAS WHAT HE WANTED THE MOST.
YOU KNOW THAT, DON'T YOU?
THAT GIRL IS SERIOUS ABOUT THIS ARRANGEMENT, YOU KNOW.
WHAT ARE YOU GOING TO DO?
DON'T GET ALL FREAKY ON ME, BIG SISTER.
So boring...
IT WAS YOUR IDEA FOR ME TO COME HOME...
BUT DID GETTING MARRIED MAKE YOU EVEN DUMBER THAN BEFORE?
You little punk!
DON'T WORRY.
I LIKE MY IQ THE WAY IT IS. I'LL STAY SINGLE, THANKS!

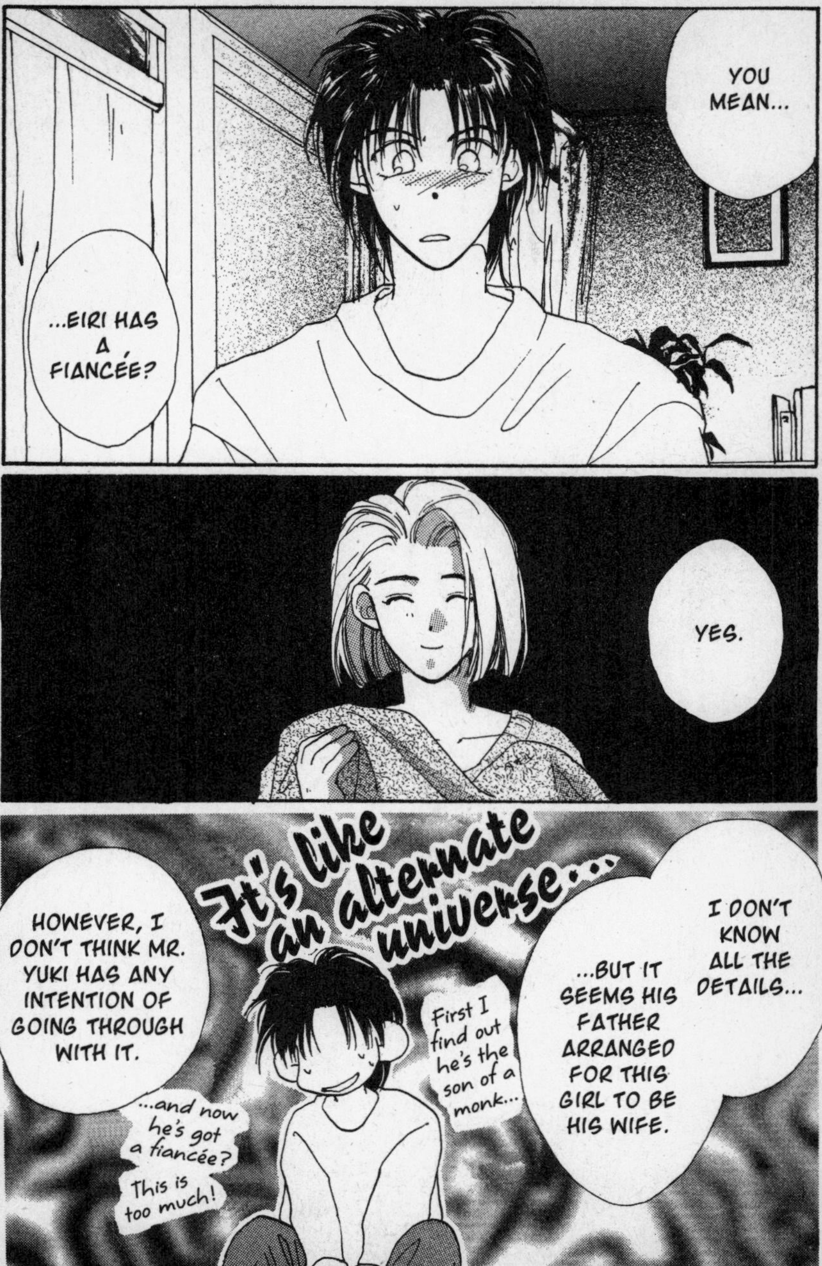
YOU MEAN...
...EIRI HAS A FIANCÉE?
YES.
I DON'T KNOW ALL THE DETAILS...
...BUT IT SEEMS HIS FATHER ARRANGED FOR THIS GIRL TO BE HIS WIFE.
It's like an alternate universe...
First I find out he's the son of a monk...
...and now he's got a fiancée?
This is too much!
HOWEVER, I DON'T THINK MR. YUKI HAS ANY INTENTION OF GOING THROUGH WITH IT.

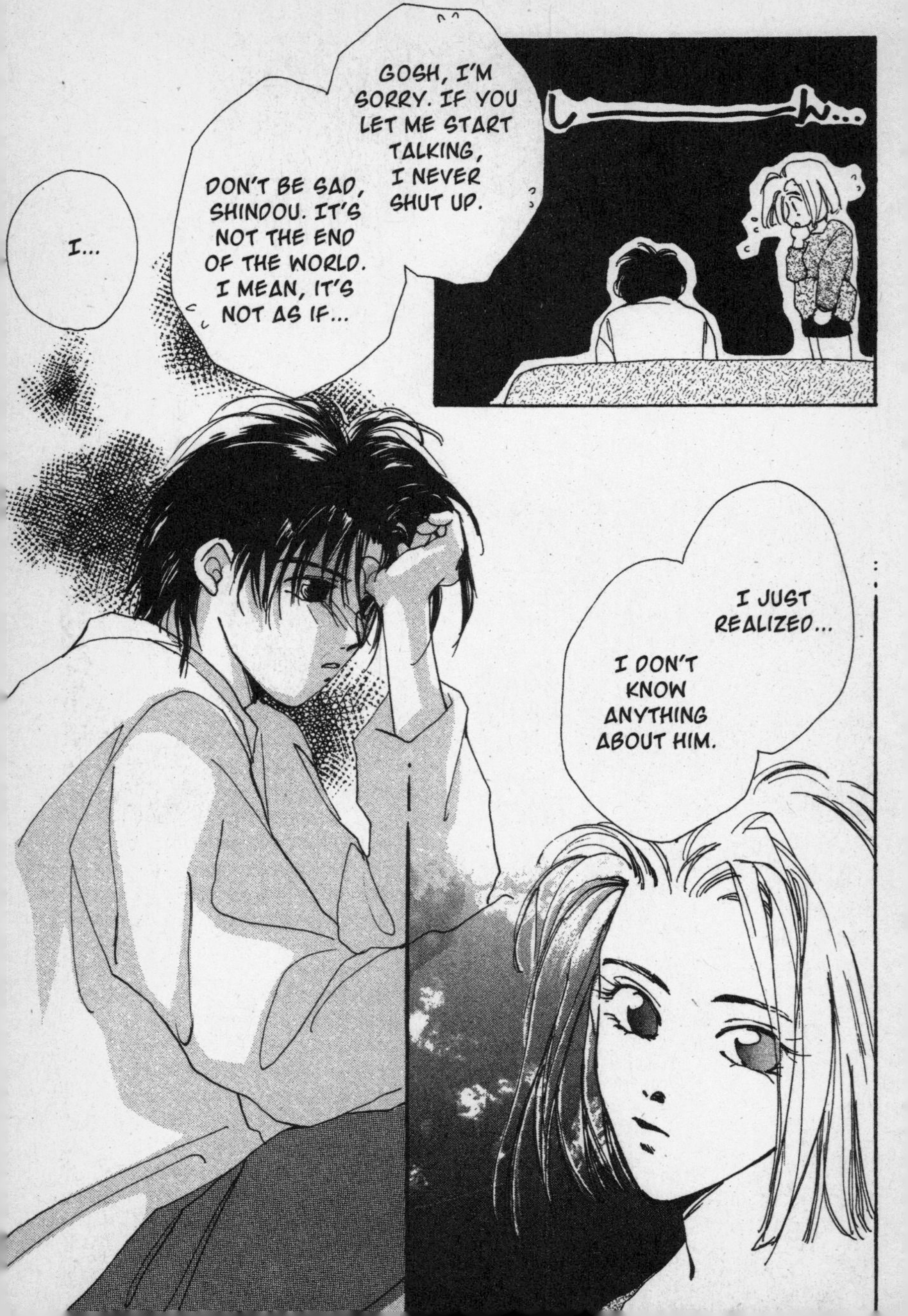
GOSH, I'M SORRY. IF YOU LET ME START TALKING, I NEVER SHUT UP.
DON'T BE SAD, SHINDOU. IT'S NOT THE END OF THE WORLD. I MEAN, IT'S NOT AS IF...
I...
I JUST REALIZED...
I DON'T KNOW ANYTHING ABOUT HIM.

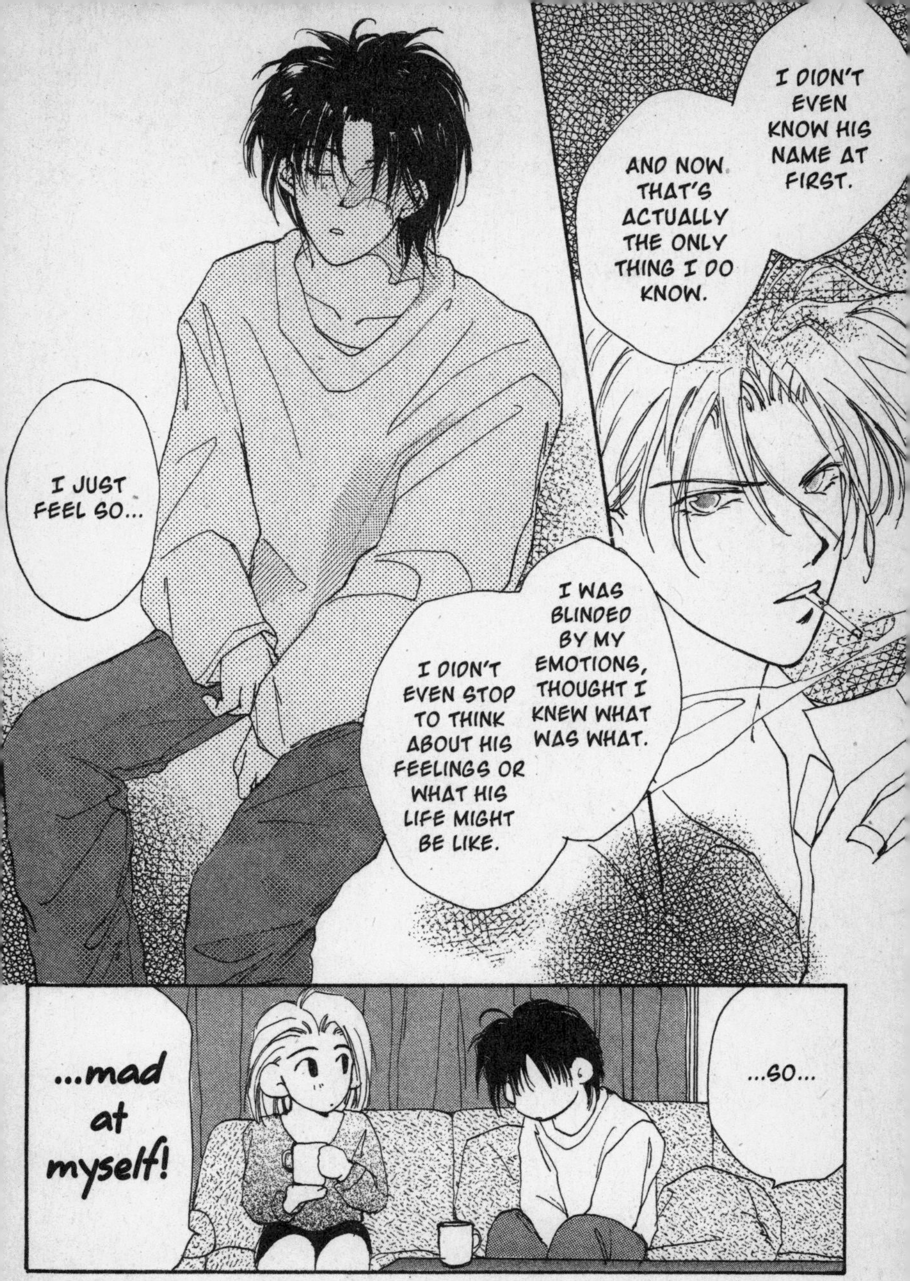
I DIDN'T EVEN KNOW HIS NAME AT FIRST.
AND NOW THAT'S ACTUALLY THE ONLY THING I DO KNOW.
I WAS BLINDED BY MY EMOTIONS, THOUGHT I KNEW WHAT WAS WHAT.
I DIDN'T EVEN STOP TO THINK ABOUT HIS FEELINGS OR WHAT HIS LIFE MIGHT BE LIKE.
I JUST FEEL SO...
...SO...
...mad at myself!

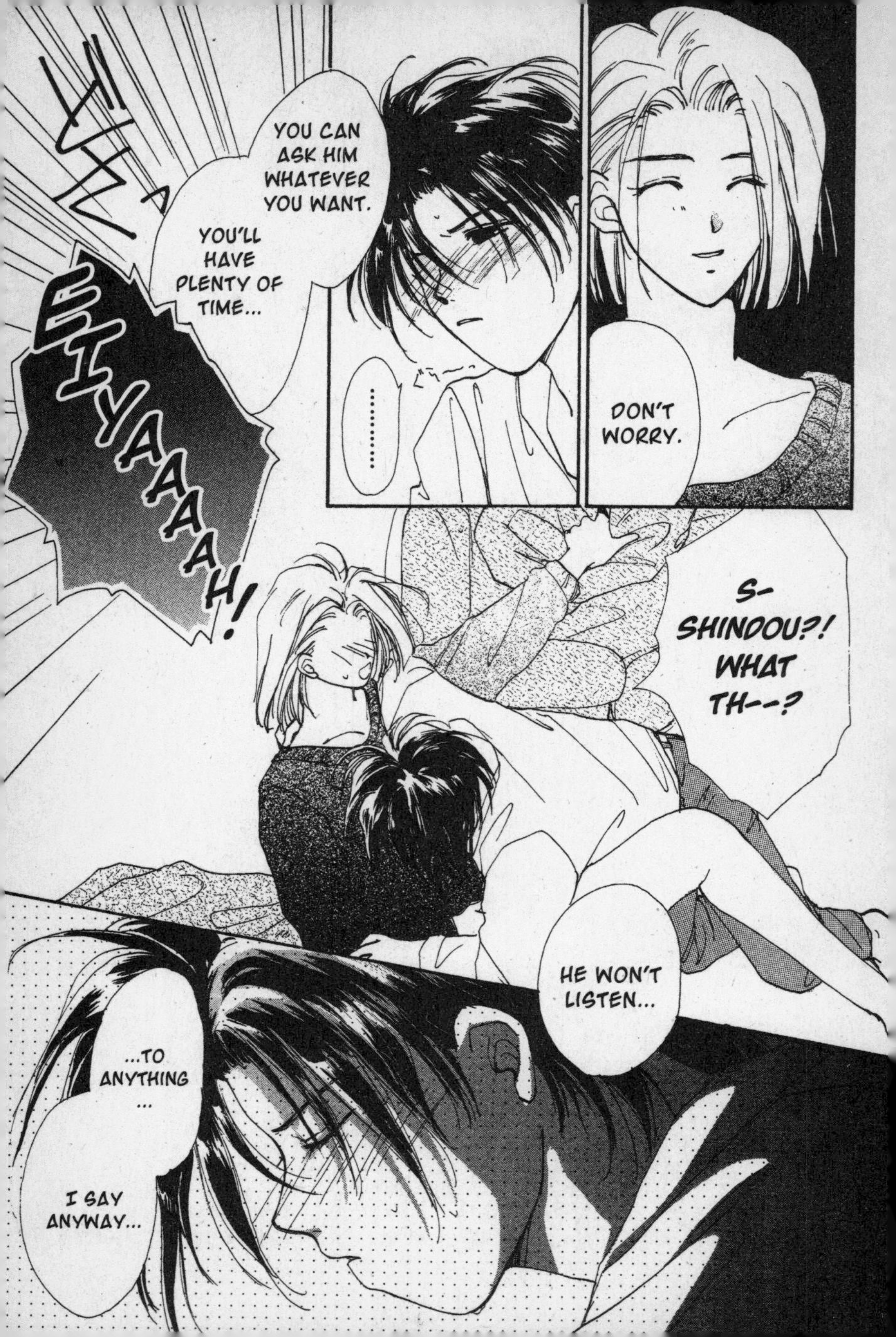
DON'T WORRY.
......
YOU CAN ASK HIM WHATEVER YOU WANT.
YOU'LL HAVE PLENTY OF TIME...
EIIYAAAAAH!
S-SHINDOU?! WHAT TH--?
HE WON'T LISTEN...
...TO ANYTHING ...
I SAY ANYWAY...

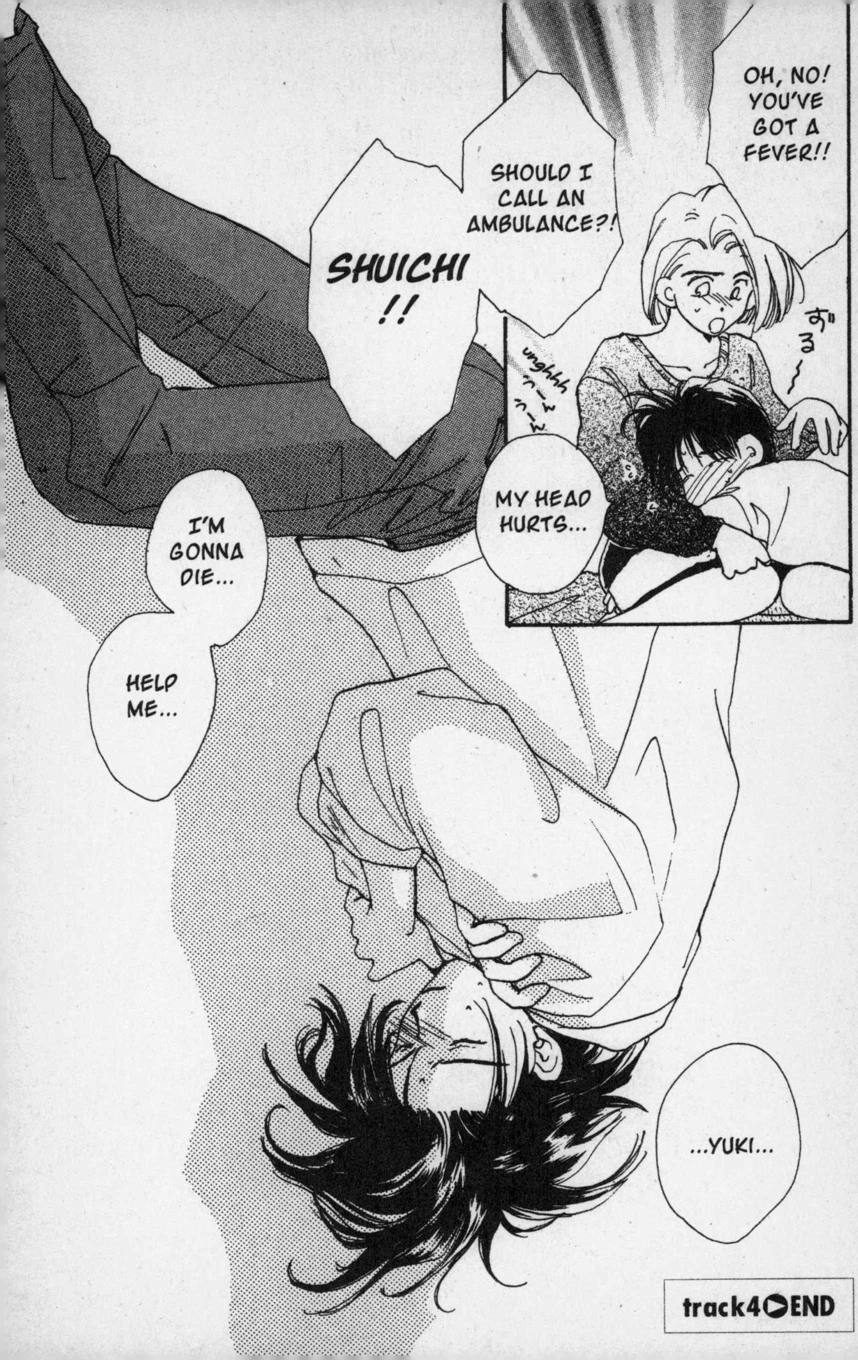
OH, NO! YOU'VE GOT A FEVER!!
SHOULD I CALL AN AMBULANCE?!
SHUICHI !!
ずる~
unghhh
MY HEAD HURTS...
I'M GONNA DIE...
HELP ME...
...YUKI...
track4 END

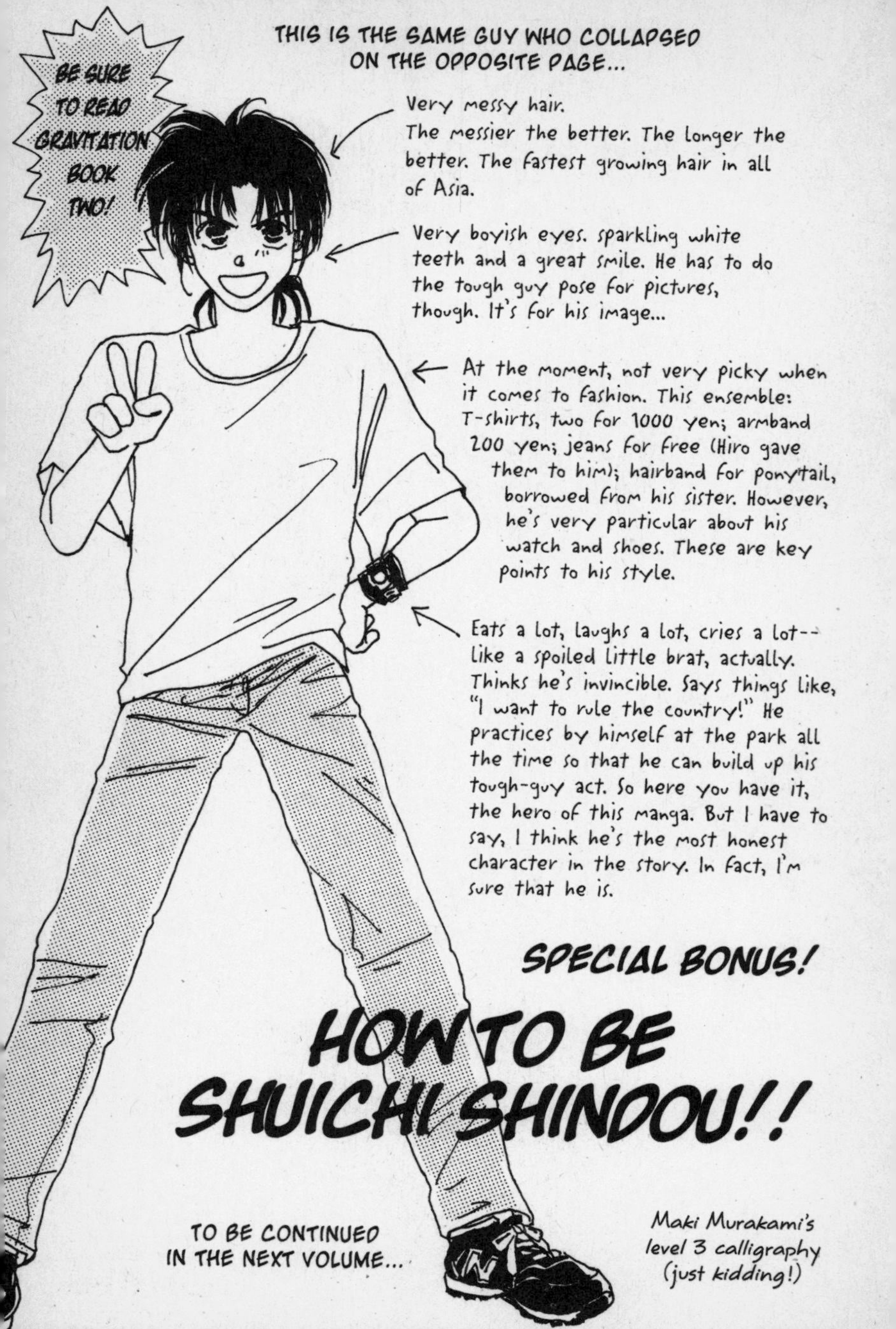
BE SURE TO READ GRAVITATION BOOK TWO!
THIS IS THE SAME GUY WHO COLLAPSED ON THE OPPOSITE PAGE...
Very messy hair. The messier the better. The longer the better. The fastest growing hair in all of Asia.
Very boyish eyes. sparkling white teeth and a great smile. He has to do the tough guy pose for pictures, though. It's for his image...
At the moment, not very picky when it comes to fashion. This ensemble: T-shirts, two for 1000 yen; armband 200 yen; jeans for free (Hiro gave them to him); hairband for ponytail, borrowed from his sister. However, he's very particular about his watch and shoes. These are key points to his style.
Eats a lot, laughs a lot, cries a lot--like a spoiled little brat, actually. Thinks he's invincible. Says things like, "I want to rule the country!" He practices by himself at the park all the time so that he can build up his tough-guy act. So here you have it, the hero of this manga. But I have to say, I think he's the most honest character in the story. In fact, I'm sure that he is.
SPECIAL BONUS!
HOW TO BE SHUICHI SHINDOU!!
TO BE CONTINUED IN THE NEXT VOLUME...
Maki Murakami's level 3 calligraphy (just kidding!)

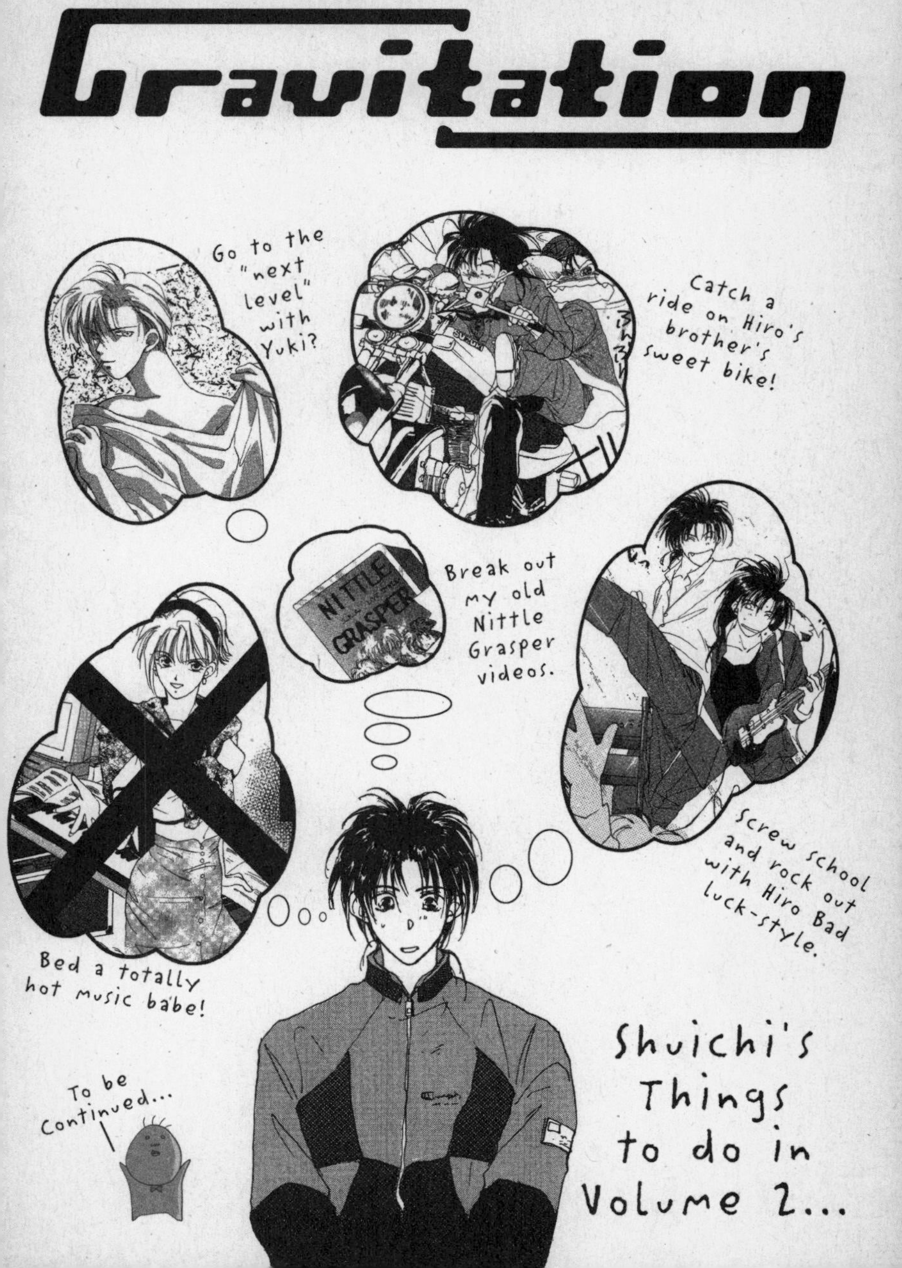
Gravitation
Catch a ride on Hiro's brother's sweet bike!
Go to the "next level" with Yuki?
Break out my old Nittle Grasper videos.
NITTLE GRASPER
Screw school and rock out with Hiro Bad luck-style.
Bed a totally hot music babe!
Shuichi's Things to do in Volume 2...
To be Continued...

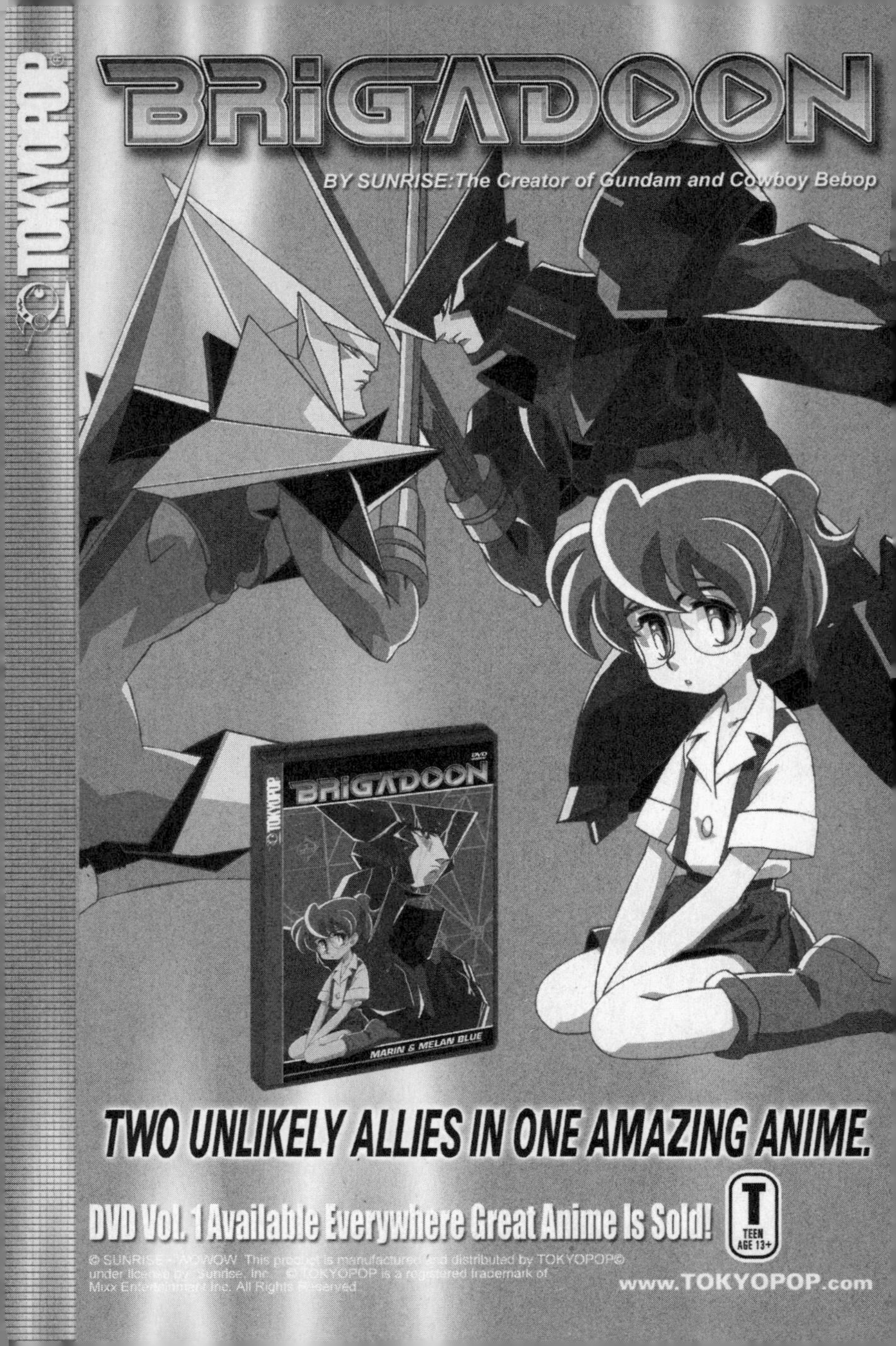
TOKYOPOP
BRIGADOON
BY SUNRISE: The Creator of Gundam and Cowboy Bebop
DVD
TOKYOPOP
BRIGADOON
MARIN & MELAN BLUE
TWO UNLIKELY ALLIES IN ONE AMAZING ANIME.
DVD Vol. 1 Available Everywhere Great Anime Is Sold!
T
TEEN
AGE 13+
© SUNRISE • WOWOW This product is manufactured and distributed by TOKYOPOP® under license by Sunrise, Inc. ® TOKYOPOP is a registered trademark of Mixx Entertainment Inc. All Rights Reserved.
www.TOKYOPOP.com

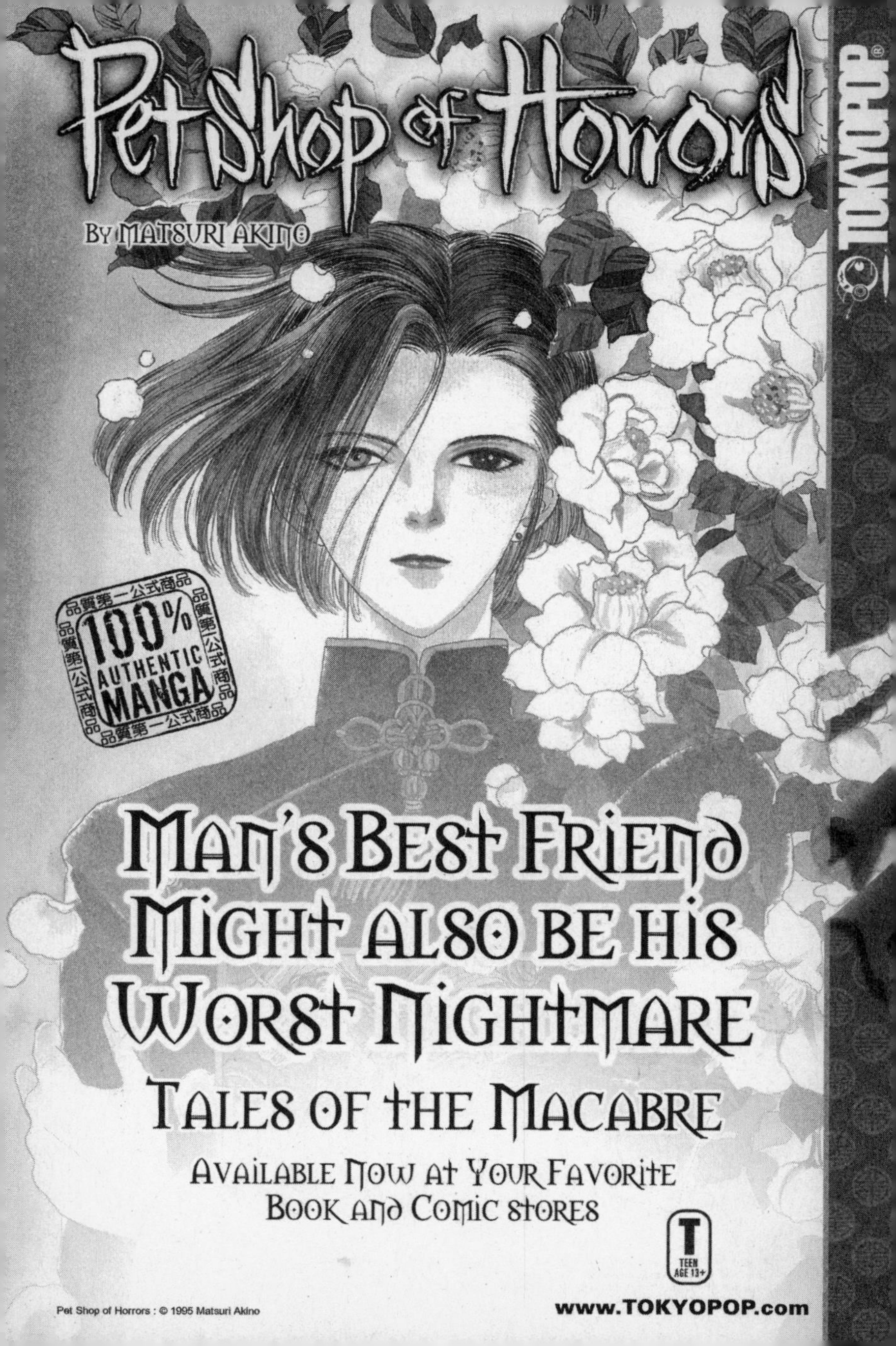

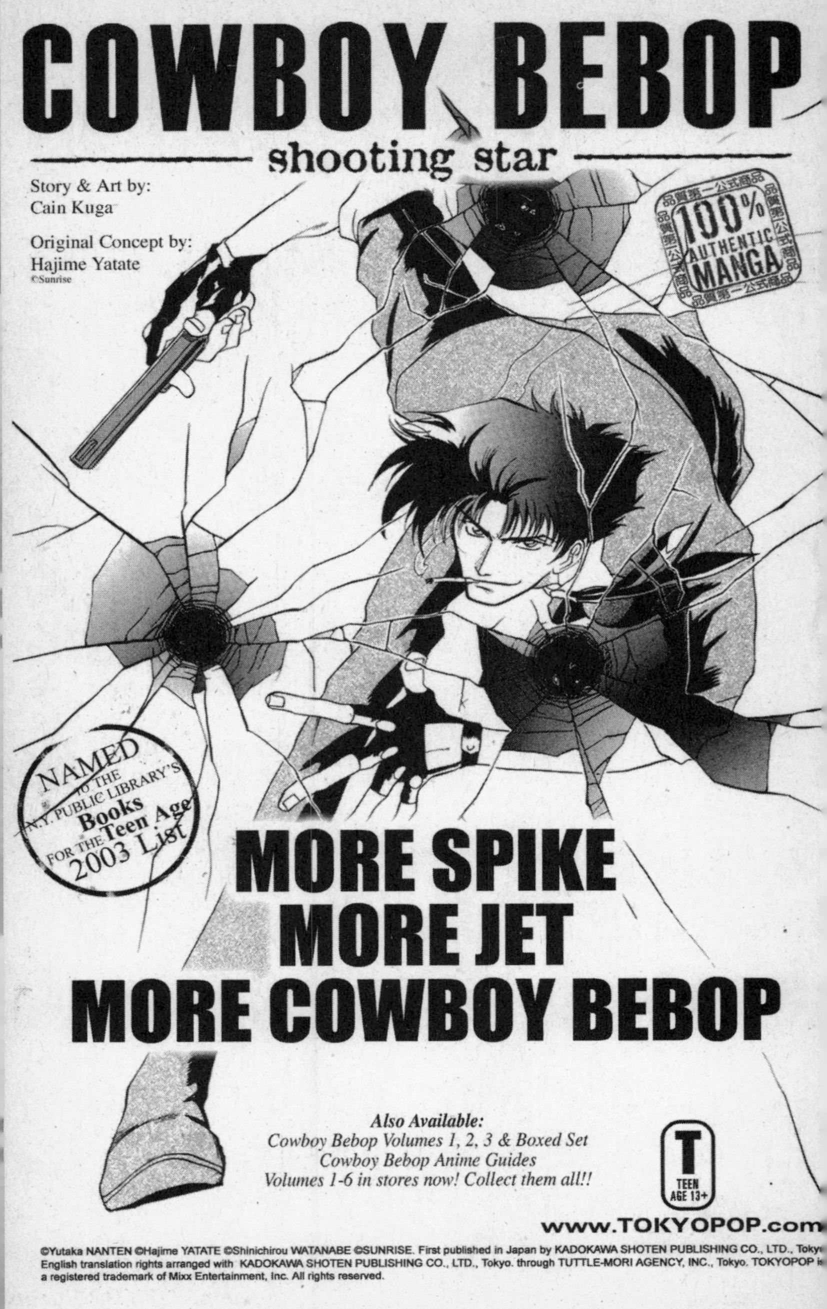
COWBOY BEBOP
shooting star
Story & Art by:
Cain Kuga
Original Concept by:
Hajime Yatate
©Sunrise
100% AUTHENTIC MANGA
NAMED TO THE N.Y. PUBLIC LIBRARY'S Books FOR THE Teen Age 2003 List
MORE SPIKE
MORE JET
MORE COWBOY BEBOP
Also Available:
Cowboy Bebop Volumes 1, 2, 3 & Boxed Set
Cowboy Bebop Anime Guides
Volumes 1-6 in stores now! Collect them all!!
T
TEEN AGE 13+
www.TOKYOPOP.com
©Yutaka NANTEN ©Hajime YATATE ©Shinichirou WATANABE ©SUNRISE. First published in Japan by KADOKAWA SHOTEN PUBLISHING CO., LTD., Tokyo. English translation rights arranged with KADOKAWA SHOTEN PUBLISHING CO., LTD., Tokyo. through TUTTLE-MORI AGENCY, INC., Tokyo. TOKYOPOP is a registered trademark of Mixx Entertainment, Inc. All rights reserved.

STOP!

This is the back of the book.
You wouldn't want to spoil a great ending!

This book is printed "manga-style," in the authentic Japanese right-to-left format. Since none of the artwork has been flipped or altered, readers get to experience the story just as the creator intended. You've been asking for it, so TOKYOPOP® delivered: authentic, hot-off-the-press, and far more fun!

DIRECTIONS

If this is your first time reading manga-style, here's a quick guide to help you understand how it works.

It's easy... just start in the top right panel and follow the numbers. Have fun, and look for more 100% authentic manga from TOKYOPOP®!

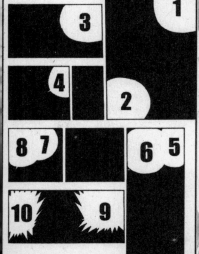